3V
;S
SH
IS
PL.

20.04.06
9. 6. 06.
11. 8. 0
4. Sept.
BV/HB HI

PH.
St James "/.
WAYSIDE
21 12
21 12
WAYSIDE

D0297221

2 1 JAN 2009   15. DEC

HS
2 5 MAR 2009   02. FEB 10.

1 9 MAY 2009   24. JUN. 10.

09 SEP 09.   MORAN
14. AUG. 10.

Brook 11.13
BARR
Prim 8/15

BLAIR, J.   328
Yesterday's Dreams

FLP

Please return/renew this item by the last date shown

worcestershire
countycouncil
Cultural Services

GA BY HA

700025023288

YESTERDAY'S DREAMS

Colette Shipley has become fascinated by the new art of photography and begins to create a record of her scenic home town of Whitby, with its tall ships and twin lighthouses. One day she encounters Arthur Newton, who shares her passion for the town's unique atmosphere. Their friendship develops but, unbeknown to Colette, Arthur is married with a young child. He has to make a difficult decision: to remain in his secure railway job, or risk the security of his family by becoming a full-time artist. A decision not made any easier by his growing attraction to Colette...

YESTERDAY'S DREAMS

YESTERDAY'S DREAMS

by

Jessica Blair

WORCESTERSHIRE COUNTY COUNCIL
CULTURAL SERVICES

Magna Large Print Books
Long Preston, North Yorkshire,
BD23 4ND, England.

British Library Cataloguing in Publication Data.

Blair, Jessica
    Yesterday's dreams.

    A catalogue record of this book is
    available from the British Library

    ISBN   0-7505-2485-5

First published in Great Britain in 2005 by Piatkus Books Ltd.

Copyright © 2005 by Jessica Blair

Cover illustration © Angelo Rinaldi/Artist Partners by arrangement with Piatkus Books Ltd.

The moral right of the author has been asserted

Published in Large Print 2006 by arrangement with
Piatkus Books Ltd.

All Rights reserved. No part of this publication may be reproduced, stored in a retrieval system, or transmitted in any form or by any means, electronic, mechanical, photocopying, recording or otherwise without the prior permission of the Copyright owner.

Magna Large Print is an imprint of Library Magna Books Ltd.

Printed and bound in Great Britain by
T.J. (International) Ltd., Cornwall, PL28 8RW

All characters in this book are fictitious and any resemblance to real persons, living or dead, is entirely coincidental.

For A, G, J and D
To say thanks for your love and support in
good times and times less so is not adequate.

Remember, yesterday's dreams do not
always become realities but they will
sustain us through them.

Acknowledgements

There are many people involved in the production of a book before it rests in the hands of a reader and I am grateful for the contribution they have made in getting this book to that final stage, not least of course my editor and all the staff at Piatkus whom I value highly.

Into that category also comes my family, ever ready with suggestion and criticism, especially Judith who has been more involved in this book. Her help with research has been meticulous and her criticism most constructive.

I thank you all as I thank my readers, many of whom show a continued interest in my work which is much appreciated.

Prologue

Arthur Newton was on a pilgrimage. There had been doubt in his mind about committing himself to it, especially on this day, 8 September 1889, but the compulsion to return to Whitby and his past overwhelmed his uncertainty. Once the train huffed out of Scarborough and settled into its regular motion, Arthur settled too. He became lost for the time being in awe of this mode of transport, so different from the horse-drawn coach he had last used on this journey twenty-three years ago in 1866 when he was thirty.

He could not help but wonder at the abilities of the men who had invented, designed, and constructed such modern wonders, and at the labourers who had built the line along this magnificent Yorkshire coast, laying the tracks at times so close to the edge of the cliffs that the train seemed to sway precariously over the sea beating on the rocks far below.

The rattle and the motion and the constantly changing perspectives reminded him that the onward movement of time always brings changes. That made him doubt if the past could ever be recaptured, but he had to try. He had begun to wonder if he should have taken a more determined course when he was last in Whitby, perhaps stood up to Rose? But that would have caused her pain and left a terrible hurt. He would

11

have suffered too, though not in the same way. He would always have had a guilty conscience, especially in relation to his daughter, Marie, who idolised him. But would this visit only heighten his desire for the life that might have been?

He pushed that thought aside and turned his gaze on the ever-changing view, seeing it with the eye of a painter, transposing composition and subtle colouring on to imaginary canvasses. He could not help but admire the magnificent sea-scapes and towering cliffs that periodically swung into view as the track twisted its way towards Whitby before turning away from the coast and then curving to bridge the River Esk.

Arthur sat upright, eyes focused on the town that clung precariously to cliffs formed over the ages around the river on its course to the sea. Houses crowded together, seeming to stand one on top of another, their red roofs glowing in the September sunshine. Ships with furled sails lay idle at quays to either side of the river; others drifted on their moorings midstream.

His heart beat faster and his body tensed at the thought of setting foot again in Whitby where so much had happened. Misgivings prompted him again. Was he right to come back? What could he realistically hope to gain by it? He could remain in the train instead and return to Scarborough, hoping the inspiration of yesterday remained with him. But that would be the coward's way out.

The train swung to the right and a glance to his left gave Arthur a view of housing developments that were new to him, an expansion on the back of Whitby's growing prosperity thanks to its lucrative maritime trade. The engine slowed, causing the carriages to jerk. Caught unawares by the motion, Arthur gripped the seat to steady himself.

The engine came to a halt with a final clatter. 'Whitby. All change!' Before he knew it Arthur was on his feet and outside the station, pausing to gaze across the nearby docks bristling with masts. Beyond lay the River Esk forming the Inner Harbour up river from the bridge that connected the East and West Sides of the town.

Arthur walked slowly in the direction of the bridge. People flowed around him, noise rang out. The buzz of conversation was overlaid by shouted greetings, mothers chiding their infants, urchins yelling in chase, hammers and saws sounding from the shipbuilding yards, ropes and timbers creaking as ships moved with the sway of the water. Overhead came the screech of seagulls, floating on air currents, ready to swoop down on a tasty morsel.

Arthur lovingly absorbed it all. He was back.

He turned up short steep Golden Lion Bank that led into Flowergate where the slope was not so testing. He had no need to rush but he did not want to delay for there was a purpose to this visit. He turned into Skinner Street, then into Well Close Square. His steps slowed as he viewed the elegant Georgian houses until he came to a halt and silently contemplated a brick house of three bays and three storeys. The doorway with its arched fanlight had a case of Doric columns. The eight tall sash windows each had twelve panes and plain lintels. These, along with the stonework running its full height at each corner of the building, relieved what would otherwise have been a severe frontage. But Arthur had never regarded it as severe; to him this house had always been welcoming, both without and within.

He tightened his lips, fighting the sadness that threatened to envelop him. He wondered who lived here now and if they loved the house as he had done? He laid his hand on the gate, tempted to push it open and engage the current occupants in conversation, but he got no further than that. There were some places best left unvisited for fear of reawakening old sadnesses. He turned away and walked slowly back to Skinner Street.

He paused at the corner and for a moment eyed the building opposite. 'Why not?' he muttered to himself, crossing the road and climbing the stairs to the tea-room above Botham's shop that sold the wonderful breads, cakes and pies that came out of their bakehouse. When he entered the tea-room his eyes immediately searched out a particular table and his heart gave a little leap of pleasure when he saw that it was empty. But when he sat down and faced the empty chair opposite he wondered if he had been right to come here. Then pleasant memories took over and for the next half-hour he enjoyed the refreshments and recollected happier times spent at this table.

Back on the street he retraced his steps along Skinner Street, Flowergate and Golden Lion Bank to the bustling riverside. He made his way slowly along St Ann's Staith, through Haggersgate to Pier Road, which he had known as the Quay, recalling past visits to the Whitby Subscription Library and to the museum housed in the same building. He kept pausing to cast his eyes over the cobles moored alongside the Quay. He watched, intrigued by a fisherman inspecting the set of his sail in one of the cobles. Across the river two more were drawn up on the beach at Collier Hope where clothes had been laid out to dry on the shingle by housewives living on Tate Hill, an area close to Henrietta Street and the bottom of the Church Stairs which led up the cliff to the old Norman church of St Mary.

All around him the life of the port went on as it must have done throughout his twenty-one years of absence. Housewives and their daughters dressed in the same fashion with scarves tied over hair neatly parted in the middle, ankle-length dresses, plain or frilled at the bottom, covered at the front by white aprons, gathered round a bearded fisherman, whose waistcoat hung loosely over his thick gansey, hoping to get a tasty meal from the fish he had just brought ashore. Arthur watched the haggling for a few minutes and then moved on towards the West Pier. So much life around him: young women sitting on the quayside, laughing at the gossip and tittle-tattle that passed between them as they knitted a shawl, scarf or jumper or idly watched a child adjust the sail on his toy boat; a man and a woman intent on mending nets did not notice Arthur pass as he moved on to the West Pier.

Across the river the East Pier ran from the foot of the cliffs towards the West Pier, both positioned so as to provide a barrier against the sea and make a safe entrance to the river. He admired the twin lighthouses rising at the piers' extremities, guides to sailors seeking refuge, welcome sights indeed to men home from the sea. Arthur felt he had stepped back in time. He moved along the West Pier. There was no need to search for the place he wanted, his steps automatically took him there as they had done on many occasions in the past. He found the place where he used to sit, made himself comfortable, admiring the panorama as he looked back at Whitby now that he could take in both sides of the river.

He sighed as an unexpected mood of contentment settled over him and pulled a small sketchbook from his pocket. He looked wistfully at it for a few moments. It was almost as good as new. It had not been taken from its hiding place in twenty-three years. Why he had slipped it into his pocket today he did not really know except that his action might have been stimulated by the same force that had insisted he come to Whitby, on this particular day.

He opened it and flicked through the pages with his right thumb. They were all in pristine condition except for one that held a head and shoulders sketch of a young woman. It was dated 8 September 1866. Arthur's eyes settled on it. The subject was sitting in a three-quarters pose facing to the right, but her head was turned so that she was looking almost directly at the artist. Her oval face had a rounded chin which made her appear resolute but gentle. Her mouth was small but perfectly bow-shaped; her nose ran straight to a high forehead, with thin brows arching over eyes in which the artist had captured a sparkle that drew the observer's attention. The

16

head was held proudly and with an air of gentle authority, which gave the impression that this young woman would follow her own mind and opinions even if they went against convention. The hair that tumbled to the nape of her neck had been draped in a flimsy tulle scarf held by a jewelled clasp to the left-hand side, close to the shoulder. It was a subtle way of framing and enhancing that enchanting face.

Arthur sat looking at the picture, now oblivious to the busy scene around him. His right forefinger traced the name written beside the date: 'Colette'. His finger paused at the end of the final stroke.

His mind drifted back to 8 September 1866, the day he had lovingly drawn the portrait of a twenty year old Colette. That drawing had imprinted her in his mind forever. A day of blissful happiness was destroyed by upheaval and loss. But it had its beginnings long before that.

Chapter One

'Arthur, hurry thissen, your pa's waiting.' Enid Newton, her voice strident with urgency, shouted up the stairs.

'Coming, Ma,' a young voice called in return but there was no sound of movement.

With a sigh of exasperation, Enid turned back to the dining-room. She caught the amused flicker of her husband's lips before he hid them with the edge of his cup. 'You can smile, Harold Newton.

17

You aren't much help in getting him off,' she chided as she came bustling over to the table.

Harold's grin broadened. He had noted that she had used his 'Sunday' name instead of the more usual Harry. She always did when she was annoyed, even just a little. She reached for the bread knife but he caught her arm before she picked it up. With a quick movement he swung her round so that she was forced to collapse on to his knees. He steadied her with his other arm around her waist and held her tight as he kissed her full on the lips. She gave a small struggle but then, enjoying the intimate closeness of their bodies, relaxed and returned the expression of his love.

'That's better,' he said when their lips parted. 'You're more nervous than he is.'

'Well, he shouldn't be late on his first day at work.'

'He won't be.'

They heard footsteps on the stairs. Enid jumped up from her husband's knee, picked up the bread knife and was halfway through cutting a slice when the door opened.

Enid's lips tightened with irritation when she still did not see Arthur. 'Celia, where's that brother of yours?' she snapped, as if her fifteen-year-old daughter could wave a magic wand and produce him.

'Still in his room, I think, Ma,' replied an unconcerned Celia as she sat down at the table.

'Oswald, go and tell him to hurry up.'

'But you've just shouted for him,' protested her younger son.

'Just go and do as you're told – now!'

As he slunk away he caught the wink his father gave him and knew there was no malice in his mother's tone.

They heard Oswald cajoling his seventeen-year-old brother to get himself downstairs. Then scuffing sounds, a pounding on the stairs and Oswald's protests at being pushed out of the way. The dining-room door burst open.

'Ready, Ma,' Arthur called breezily.

'Indeed you're not,' replied Enid indignantly. 'Just look at your tie.' She came to him, buttoned his shirt at the neck and adjusted his tie so that it sat straight in his collar. 'Your hair!'

'I combed it, Ma.'

'I can see that, but I don't know what you did after.' She used her hand to flatten it into place. 'That's better.' She glanced at Harold.

'He'll pass muster,' he confirmed, rising from his chair.

Enid's anxiety lessened; her attitude softened. She placed her hands on her son's shoulders and looked lovingly into his eyes. 'We are all proud of you, Arthur. Remember – always do what is right. Do your best and don't let the family down. Respect the people over you and those you work with. You were lucky to get this job, you think on that.'

'I will, Ma.' Arthur showed a little embarrassment at this last-minute lecture and grudgingly accepted his mother's kiss on the cheek.

Harold glanced at his other two children. 'Be good to your mother, you two.' He gave Celia a kiss on top of her head and ruffled fourteen-year-old Oswald's hair. Finally he turned to his wife, kissed her on the cheek and said. 'Have a nice day.'

'Look after him, Harry.'

'He'll have to look after himself when I leave him,' Harold reminded her, then gave her another reassuring kiss. 'Don't worry, he'll be all right.'

The look in Enid's eyes questioned that. Her lips tightened with uncertainty; a wife doubting the veracity of her husband's view; a mother doubting, yet not doubting, the capabilities of her eldest son who was about to make his first steps into the adult world.

Enid came to the front door with them and watched for a few minutes as father and son strode down the street. She was pleased that a gawky schoolboy has blossomed into a tall, confident young man. Though he couldn't be described as handsome, his well-proportioned features, set with a rugged jaw and enhanced by dark brown hair with a natural sweep, were attractive. She could not help but wonder if Arthur would cope with the big wide world in which he would find himself; an adult's world, all so new to him. It seemed as if she was saying goodbye to her 'little' boy and seeing a grown man in his place. She felt a touch of pride nevertheless. He had been a good, loving son. Oh, he had got up to all the usual boyish tricks and had thrown childish tantrums but he also showed a real appreciation of his parents, setting an example to his siblings. He was a bright boy and had done well at school, something that had stood him in good stead when he had gone for his interview at the Railway Offices. Maybe now that he had a job he would spend less time with a pencil and sketchbook; think seriously about his future and enjoy the company of new-found companions.

She turned back into the house and the sound of the door shutting seemed to mark the end of an era.

'Excited, son?'

'Yes, Pa.'

'Well, don't let it show at work. Just take things calmly. If you are over-enthusiastic you'll get put on. Be willing but not over-willing. Don't go asking for jobs, there'll be plenty come your way as office boy. Do what you are told to do and always do it with a happy smile. Keep your wits about you; note the way things are done; be willing to learn. Railway transport will be important in the future and you can grow with it, maybe achieve a highly responsible position. Leeds is expanding rapidly on the back of the railway and the other industries it is encouraging. There's a great future to be had here, lad.'

'At the interview, Mr Stokes said I wasn't the only new starter. Is that because of the expansion?'

'Aye. I know Charlie Stokes. He told me Ben Sleightholme and Giles Wainwright are starting today as well. Mr Stokes told me that Ben's a bright lad, should do well; Giles impressed him with his neat writing and sound arithmetic, just the sort of person they are looking for to train as a ledger clerk.'

Any further queries were halted when Harold turned into a shop, the bow window of which was neatly set out in such a way that the foodstuffs on display would catch the eye and tempt the customer inside.

'Good morning, Con,' called Harold breezily.

'Top o' the morning to ye, Harry.' Conan Duggan looked up from the blue sugar bag he had just filled. He was a tall man, well-built and always cheery. He had come to Leeds from Ireland when he was twenty to 'seek his fortune'. He duly married a Yorkshire lass whose father, impressed by his son-in-law's capabilities and ambition, took him on as a partner after he had gained experience elsewhere in the grocery trade. Now Conan ran the shop with his father-in-law as a sleeping partner. Through Harry calling in here most mornings, he and Conan had become friends, drawn together by a shared interest in cricket.

'First day at work for the lad?' said Con inclining his head in the direction of Arthur who had sauntered down the shop to talk to a girl of his own age busily taking apples from a barrel, rubbing them with a soft cloth and arranging them in a pyramid on a tray.

'Hello, Rose,' said Arthur. Though they had been friends since childhood he was beginning to see her in a different light. She had blossomed into a seventeen-year-old who was taking pride in her appearance.

She looked up and, seeing the mischievous look in Arthur's eyes as he reached out towards the pile of apples, glared at him and snapped, 'Don't you dare!'

He whisked one off the top. 'I only wanted that one,' he laughed.

Rose gave a little tremor of irritation. She had been caught again; reacting to Arthur's gesture when she really knew he would not upset her handiwork for fear of bruising the apples. 'You shouldn't tease me,' she retorted sharply.

He leaned closer and whispered, 'You like it.'

Rose blushed and said haughtily, 'I do not. And mind you pay for that apple.'

Arthur smiled, tossed the apple nonchalantly in the air, caught it, winked at Rose and went to join his father who was purchasing a twist of his favourite tobacco.

'See you later, Con.' Harold turned towards the door.

'Hope your day goes well, Arthur.'

'Thanks, Mr Duggan.' He followed his father, giving Rose a small wave. She blushed and turned her attention back to the apples.

Arthur fell into step beside his father, determined to match his stride. He was a man now; no more trotting to keep up. They caught the horse-drawn bus that would take them into the centre of Leeds.

They parted at the corner of Boar Lane and Bishopgate where after a brief 'Goodbye, son. Mind you do well', Harold entered a building with a semi-circular pedimented front. The lettering above the tall ground-floor windows announced that this was The Yorkshire Banking Company.

Arthur paused and looked back, feeling a sense of pride that his father worked as one of the chief cashiers in such an imposing building. He hurried on. He must not be late. But two hundred yards further on his steps faltered. Would he have time? He pondered a moment then, decision made, turned and ran through a maze of streets until, panting, he pulled up in front of a shop whose sign announced that it belonged to Ebenezer Hirst, Antiquarian Bookseller and Art Dealer. The books in the window were neatly arranged so that they could easily be seen yet did not distract from the oil painting that occupied central position.

Arthur stared at the painting, drinking in its delicate use of colours that not only depicted a pleasing landscape of a river flowing between banks of willows but also captured the mood of a misty morning. Time stood still for him as he was transported out of this street where smoke from the chimneys had blackened the dark stone. Some day he would paint as well as this... No, better! The thought startled him. He glanced at the clock above the shop doorway. He barely had time to get to work on time. If he didn't he would have blotted his copybook on his first day. Mr Stokes had warned him at the end of the interview that he took punctuality for an indication of keenness and was not one to tolerate latecomers. Arthur ran!

He took the steps into the building two at a time, ignored the people crossing the entrance in various directions and charged up the stairs to the first floor. He raced down a corridor and burst through a door into a large room with several desks, all of which were occupied. Heads were raised and knowing smiles were exchanged as Arthur half walked, half ran to the door on the left at the far end of the room. He paused in front of it, drew a deep breath to try to stop his chest from heaving and knocked on the door. Hearing the call of 'Come in', he pushed it open and, trying to bolster his confidence, entered the room.

A thin man sitting behind a desk looked over the spectacles perched on the end of a sharp nose. His black hair, thinning a little on top, had been carefully brushed into place. His gaunt cheeks gave way to a pointed chin that made him look much more of an ogre than he really was. He knew it and used that impression to control his staff, for they never knew when they might encounter an unknown side to their chief clerk.

His thin-lipped mouth grimaced as he said, 'Ah, Newton.' He glanced at the clock on the wall. The pointers showed one minute to the hour. 'I see you have made it just in time, but, from the look of your red face and the way you are trying to get your breath, it has been something of an effort. See that it is not so in the future. Young men in your present condition take some time to get down to their work.'

Arthur swallowed hard. 'Yes, sir.' He glanced at the other two young men sitting calmly to his left. They showed no such sign of exertion. No doubt they had arrived in plenty of time.

'Sit down, Newton.' Mr Stokes indicated the empty chair drawn up with theirs in front of his desk.

Arthur did as he was instructed.

Stokes cast his eyes slowly over each of them in turn. 'Very well, gentlemen.' Though they were mere boys by his reckoning, he always addressed them in the same way as he did all his staff. He believed it set the right tone for the office and established a respectful relationship between them all. He encouraged the use of surnames preceded by 'Mr' between members of his staff, though he knew out of the office, and often within it when out of his earshot, they used Christian names. 'I will start by introducing you to each other. Mr Arthur Newton is the gentleman who chose so nearly to be late on his first day and is to serve as an office boy. The gentleman at the other end of the line is Mr Ben Sleightholme. He too is to serve as an office boy. The third gentleman is Mr Giles Wainwright who is here to train as a ledger clerk.

'Now, this is an important day in your lives,' he continued solemnly. 'Your first job. You have a great opportunity here. The railway is bringing much wealth to Leeds and, as the town expands with that wealth, so too will the railway, making an important contribution not only to our locality but also the whole country. Mark my words, it will expand until every town is near a railway station. It will spread across the country like a spider's web, moving goods and people. It will enable everyone to travel and that will help other towns and districts to develop like ours. Oh, yes, we are moving into a great age, and you, I hope, will play your parts and consider yourselves lucky to be involved.' He paused, letting the vision he had conjured up impress them.

'Now, what about your work here? First I had better give you a broad idea of what goes on. All information, no matter what it concerns, comes into the outer office. It will be reviewed there by my clerks and then passed on to the various departments situated on other floors: goods traffic, passenger traffic, accounts, equipment, and so on. You two young men will be responsible for keeping the flow going from this department, the hub of the system, and seeing that it gets to the right person in the right place without delay, giving priority to matters as you are directed. You will have a table at the far end of the office on which you will sort the items for delivery. Mr Wainwright, you have been given a desk opposite Mr Chisholme the chief ledger clerk.

'You will get to know everyone else as you go along, except for the two young men to whom I will introduce Mr Sleightholme and Mr Newton. They were office boys last year and will show you what is expected of you. They have moved up to be very junior clerks. That "very" is because above them we have two junior clerks, then two senior clerks. They are all answerable to me. You will notice a door in the end wall to the left as you leave my office. This leads to the manager's office, Mr Bullock's. You only go there if called upon to do so. There is another door to his office, through his secretary's room. The secretary is called Mr Frost.'

During this speech Arthur had regained his composure but at the name Frost his lips twitched with amusement.

'Have I said something funny, Mr Newton?' queried Mr Stokes with a touch of irritation.

Arthur shook his head. 'No, sir.'

Stokes frowned and gave him a piercing look. 'I think I have, Mr Newton. If you have found something amusing I think we should all share it.' He paused, keeping his gaze on Arthur, waiting for a reply. When it did not come he snapped, 'Out with it, young man.'

Arthur was on the point of spluttering a denial, but seeing the look on the chief clerk's face knew it would be no good trying to excuse himself so he spoke out boldly. 'It was the name Frost, sir, it made me wonder if he was frosty.'

A titter came from the two new employees beside him.

Stokes frowned at them. Their amusement was nipped in the bud.

'For your information, Mr Newton, and for that of you other two gentlemen, Mr Frost is far from frosty. He's proper and punctilious, with everything done by the book. Don't ever try to take advantage of his good heart. Everything for Mr Bullock has to pass Mr Frost's scrutiny. You will be let into Mr Bullock's office by Mr Frost, and then only if it is absolutely necessary. Now, with that understood, I'll take you into the main office.' He rose from his chair, a signal for the others to do the same. As he came from behind his desk, Arthur moved smartly to the door and opened it for him.

'Thank you, Mr Newton,' said Stokes as he passed through.

He took Wainwright to Mr Chisholme and left him in his care.

'Come.' He shot a glance at Arthur and Ben who followed him as he approached the two young men sitting at desks at the far end of the room, intent on their work now that Mr Stokes was in the offing. They did not raise their heads until he spoke.

'Gentlemen.'

They looked up quickly and replied, 'Yes, sir?'

'Here are Mr Ben Sleightholme and Mr Arthur Newton. They will be doing the jobs you were doing last year. I want you to show them the ropes and the way around the building.'

'Yes, sir.' They sprang to their feet, rather pleased to leave the invoices and letters they were sorting. This was a job that, before the morning was out, they would be handing over to Arthur and Ben.

As Stokes walked away the two young men introduced themselves and shook hands with the newcomers.

'I'm Fred Carter,' said a ginger-haired youth. 'Glad to have you here so I can escape the job you'll be doing.' His voice had taken on a sympathetic tone. He was pleased to see from the expression on Arthur's face that the inflection in his voice had had some effect.

'Take no notice of him,' said the other young man. 'He's pulling your leg. It's not a bad job when you get to know it. I'm Jack Gresham.'

Arthur liked his open expression and warm greeting. 'Arthur Newton. Hope he hasn't a temper to go with that ginger mop.'

Fred widened his eyes and growled, then laughed as he said. 'I'm as quiet as a lamb.' His brown eyes were sharp and he had quickly weighed up the new employees. He liked the look of them. Ben Sleightholme was the more robust physically and had an air of wanting to get on with what was in hand whereas Arthur's bright eyes betrayed an ability to transport his mind elsewhere in the midst of what he was doing.

'Come on, let's get on with it,' said Jack who then quietly proceeded to point out the various people working in the office and explain their seniority and their jobs in a few telling words.

'Who's the other lad starting today, sitting

29

opposite Mr Chisholme?' asked Fred.

'Giles Wainwright. He's training to be a ledger clerk.' explained Arthur.

'Thought so. Chissy's always complaining he's overworked. Bit of a moaner. I reckon that comes from having a nagging wife.' He winked at Arthur. 'Make sure you don't get one.'

By eleven o'clock Arthur and Ben had been shown round the building and told what they would have to do. Fred and Jack would have taken longer over the initiation but they were aware that Charlie Stokes knew exactly how long it should take and would be checking that they were back at their desk by eleven.

Not only were the newcomers competently familiarised but they also felt comfortable with what they had to do, and in Fred and Jack felt they had met two pleasant young men with whom a friendship could develop.

Just before they returned to their desks Jack said. 'A bell will go at twelve signalling dinner break. Fred and I scoot down the street to Mrs Higgins's café and get egg and chips. Join us if you want to and bring Wainwright, but we're off sharpish at twelve.'

'Thanks,' said Arthur. 'I'll warn him.'

When he found a moment to have a word with the new trainee ledger clerk, Giles was appreciative of the offer. He had felt isolated and a trifle lonely working with men older than himself and envied Arthur's and Ben's association. On the stroke of twelve he felt glad to be drawn into their friendly companionship.

'Any of you three play cricket?' asked Fred

between mouthfuls in the café.

'I played at school, so did Ben, we were in the same team,' replied Arthur with an enthusiasm that revealed his love of the game.

'What about you, Giles?' Fred eyed the other newcomer.

'Never much good at ball games,' came the regretful answer, 'but if you are in need of a scorer I'd love to do it.' He relished the idea of producing a neat ball-by-ball account on paper.

Fred glanced at Jack. 'Looks as though we've got the new recruits we want.'

'Mebbe. Let's be knowing what they do first?' His eyes fixed on Arthur.

'Spin bowler. Bat a bit, lower order,' he replied. All eyes turned on Ben next.

'Batted number three at school.'

'Good.'

'Well? Who are we going to play for?' asked Arthur.

'I've organised a team these last two seasons to play local clubs in friendly matches,' Fred told them. 'We haven't a ground as such so we use a pitch on Chapeltown Moor for home matches. That might be rectified in the future. Mr Bullock's interested in turning it into the railway team. He's looking into the possibility of using some railway land for a cricket field.'

'Sounds promising,' enthused Ben.

'We play some evening matches but most games are on a Saturday afternoon which does present something of a problem. As you know Saturday is a working day like the rest of the week except that there is a reduced staff. So there's always someone who isn't available, though because of his own interest Mr Bullock isn't against us getting someone else in the office to do the job, provided the other person is willing and we forego our wage for that day, *and* that we don't overdo missing Saturday work. Any substitutions must be done through Charlie Stokes who will inform Frosty who'll tell Mr Bullock.'

'That's fair enough,' said Ben.

'And I look forward to recording many victories for you,' added Giles.

'Good, then here and now I pronounce you members of Carter's Cricket Club, though we are mostly known as Carter's Cricketers,' said Fred with a flourish. 'You'll be playing your first game a week on Saturday. It's a home fixture against Burmantofts. They're a fairly good team with a lot of followers so any spectators you can persuade to come and support us will be most appreciated.'

'We'll do our best,' promised Giles. 'My father's interested in cricket. He won't take much per-suading when he knows I'm involved.'

'And mine,' added Arthur. 'He's played a bit too, so I'm sure he'll come.'

'Jack's working that day so he won't be playing. If any of you three has to work, let me know and I'll fix it for you to be off. I want to see for myself what new talent I've discovered as soon as pos-sible.'

When he reached home Arthur found his father already there. His parents were pleased to see his excitement and judged that his first day's work had gone to his liking.

Though he was anxious hear what his son's day had been like, Harold held up his hand to stem the torrent of words he saw was coming. 'Sit down, son, and calm yourself.' He turned to his daughter. 'Celia, bring your brother a glass of Mrs Webster's special lemonade.'

'Yes, Father.' Accepting it as her duty to wait on her brother, she got up from her chair and left the room to go to the cook.

'Now get your breath, Arthur. Celia will only be a moment.'

When she returned and handed him the glass Arthur took a long drink.

'Good.' Harold nodded with approval. 'Now tell us all about it.'

'The work's easy enough. Everybody was friendly and helpful. I've made four special friends and been asked to play cricket a week on Saturday.'

'Oh, what's all this about then?' asked his father, a note of approval in his voice nevertheless.

Arthur explained everything to an attentive audience and finished by saying, 'Fred wants some spectators so you'll come, won't you, Father? The match will be on Chapeltown Moor.'

'Of course I'll come.' Harold hesitated a moment then said. 'No, we'll all go. It'll make a day out. We'll be able to get the horse-bus.'

Enid, who had been apprehensive about how her son would cope with his first day in the big wide world, had gradually been reassured as his story unfolded. Now she was delighted that Harry had decided they should all go to the cricket match. If the weather kept fine it would be a nice escape from the narrow confines in which she moved and there would be new people to meet. 'Maybe Con would like to come,' she suggested, knowing their friend's interest in the game.

'He'll have the shop open,' Harold pointed out.

'I know, but it would be nice for you to make the offer rather than for him to hear about it afterwards. You never know, he might get some help in.'

'I'll slip round to see him after our meal. Go and get tidied up, Arthur, and then we'll see what delights Mrs Webster has provided for a young working man.'

Arthur dashed off, delighted that today was proving such a happy one. That mood continued when he sat down and found himself presented with his favourite meal of soup, roast beef and Yorkshire pudding, followed by steamed ginger pudding.

The children were excused while Harold and Enid had coffee. As she poured it Harold left his seat at the head of the table and came to sit near his wife. 'Well, love, I told you there was no need to worry.'

She smiled. 'I know but it is a mother's prerogative.'

He patted her hand. 'Drink your coffee. He's a good son, we'll have no trouble from Arthur.'

When Harold reached the Duggans' shop just prior to closing time Conan, Moira and Rose were tidying up after the day's work so that everything would be in place for opening time tomorrow.

After greetings were exchanged, Con asked,

'How did Arthur get on today?'

'Very well it seems, made some new friends – and best of all got himself into a cricket team.'

Con was all attention. 'Good for him.'

'His first match is a week on Saturday on Chapeltown Moor against Burmantofts. All the family are going. I know it's difficult with the shop but if you can manage it we'd like you to come too, all three of you.'

Con shrugged his shoulders and spread his hands. 'Impossible, Harry, you know how it is.'

Moira, who had seen the gleam in her husband's eyes at the mention of cricket, said. 'Con, you go. I'll look after things here. We'll get Madge Hobson to come in. A young widow like her could do with the money. Take Rose with you, it will do her good to get out.'

'I don't like you working in the shop, Moira, you know that.'

'I know. You reckon we women shouldn't work, that our place is to run the home and see to our men's needs. Well, mark my word, Con Duggan, times will change and we'll all be better for it. I've had to help you before and I know the running of the shop. Besides, if I say you are to enjoy yourself aren't I seeing to your needs?'

Conan gave a little cough as if ready to contradict this reasoning but knew he didn't really want to. A cricket match involving someone he knew sounded very tempting. 'Well,' he said finally, 'if you think it would do Rose good... Would you like to go, lass?'

In the moment that he looked at his daughter, Moira and Harold exchanged knowing glances

35

and winked at each other. Harold admired her guile in manoeuvring her husband into doing exactly what he wanted to do in spite of his protests.

'Oh, I would, Father, but if you want me to stay with Mother...'

'You'll do no such thing,' put in Moira quickly. 'I'll see Madge Hobson first thing in the morning.'

'Then that is settled,' said Harold. 'We'll be able to get the horse-bus, but we'll finalise arrangements nearer the time.'

On the day of the match everyone watched the weather with anxious eyes from the moment they were awake. They hoped the early-morning mist promised a fine day. It did and there was almost no containing Arthur until the moment he left the house to meet his team-mates. They were all in good spirits when they reached the moor which was extensive enough to cater for several cricket matches without interfering with the gently exercising race horses or the people who came merely to enjoy walking in the fresh air.

After staking themselves an area to act as their pavilion, Fred went to the opposing side who had already mapped out the area they would use. Under the guise of being sociable he eyed the opposition to see who had survived from previous encounters. He returned with the news that their opening bowler who had a reputation for being very fast was playing today, curse it. There were three players he did not know and the rest he marked mainly as average with two above average, one of whom he knew had scored a hundred in a match against a team from Chapel

Allerton the previous week.

'So we'll have to be on our toes and really concentrate,' was his final advice.

'They look to have good support,' observed someone. 'And there's more coming.' He indicated a horse-bus that had just stopped. Its passengers were climbing out.

'They're ours,' called Arthur excitedly. 'My family and friends.'

'Good.' Fred nodded his appreciation.

'My father's there too,' added Giles.

'And mine,' put in Ben when he saw someone alighting from a bus that had come from the opposite direction.

'And my whole family will be along shortly,' said Fred. 'They thought they might be a little late.'

'Fred, come and meet my parents,' Arthur offered.

'All right, we have a few minutes.' He picked up a ball, threw it at the nearest player and said. 'The rest of you, a bit of catching practice.' He fell into step beside Arthur and headed for the people who had arrived on the bus. 'I'm glad you brought some support. Added to those already here, they'll outnumber the opposition.'

Introductions were made quickly and after a few niceties Fred said. 'I'm afraid Arthur and I will have to go, sir, ma'am. I should be making the toss.'

'Of course, off you go. And all the best,' replied Harold.

'We'll see you later.'

Fred and Arthur hurried away, Fred immediately seeking out the opposing captain. A few moments later he returned to his team to announce Carter's Cricketers were batting. He was glad he had won the toss, not only because he wanted his team to bat first but because he wanted to be available when his family arrived so that he could introduce them to Arthur's family, to Mr Duggan and Rose and to Mr Wainwright, for he thought that all the families would get on well.

The opening batsmen had made fifteen rather streaky runs during an uncomfortable interlude when the first man was out and Ben found himself facing the fast bowler whom he had learned had quite a reputation around Leeds.

All Fred's attention was on Ben and within a few minutes he knew he had found a gem. Ben showed no concern about the ferocity of the bowling but displayed a temperament that made him appear as if he had all the time in the world to deal with every ball, no matter how fast they came. Fred became so intent on watching him that he did not see his own family arrive until his father said, 'Hello, son.'

He sprang to his feet. 'He's a marvel, Father.' Fred's eyes were wide with excitement.

'Who is?'

'Ben Sleightholme. New recruit. Just started in the office. His timing's out of this world.'

Mr Carter watched the next three balls all of which Ben despatched to the boundary with nonchalant ease. 'I see what you mean, son. I'm going to enjoy this.'

'Come and meet his father and Arthur's family – he's our other new recruit.'

Introductions were made with expressions of conviviality and everyone was soon enjoying each other's company and the pleasure of watching Ben dominate the innings. The other batsman seemed to draw confidence from him and he too started to score runs. Soon fifty was on the board and almost before anyone realised it ninety had replaced it. Then disaster struck. The opening batsman was out and almost immediately, with forty-nine to his name, Ben followed. Three more wickets fell quickly but Fred steadied things and with support from the last two batsmen took the innings to 150.

Those who had brought refreshments shared them out and after the break, when Carter's Cricketers went out to field, Fred's sister Lizzie, who had a shock of hair as red as her brother's, suggested that she and Rose take a walk around the boundary.

Lizzie had passed a few words with Rose in the company of the others and had become curious about her. She liked what she had seen so far and wanted to know her better so had suggested this perambulation of the boundary.

'Do you want to come, Celia?' Rose felt she had to make the offer to Arthur's sister.

Celia, sitting on the grass, shook her head and said, 'Thanks, but I'll stay here.'

The two young ladies set off.

'Are you an only child, Rose?' asked Lizzie without any preamble.

She was taken aback by the directness of the question. 'Er, yes.'

'I sometimes wish I was.'

'I'm sure you don't mean it. I wish I had some brothers and sisters. It gets a bit lonely being on your own.'

'If you had you'd only be waiting on your brothers, and they'd expect it. Fred certainly does. But I tell him things will change one day. I think I've been born too soon.'

'You sound like my mother. She always says attitudes will change and then we women will be able to take on different roles in the world.'

'A wise lady. I'd like to meet her. Where is she today?' Rose explained the situation with the shop.

'Do you help there too?'

'Yes.'

'And today?'

'Mother's looking after it with some casual help. She knew Father would like to come here and said I should come with him.'

'No doubt because Arthur was playing.' Lizzie glanced at her out of the corner of her eye as she put in this remark. 'You're blushing!'

I'm not,' protested Rose, in spite of the fact that her cheeks had started to burn.

'Yes, you are,' teased Lizzie, stepping in front of Rose to face her. 'You like him, don't you?'

'I've known him practically all my life.'

'That's no answer. You do like him. Does he like you?'

'He hasn't said, but we do get on well. What about you?' Rose wanted to turn this conversation.

'Oh, I've no one in particular. Boys always shied off at the sight of my red hair. Now I'm older, young men are still a bit wary of me.'

'But you are so attractive! You have a nice heart-shaped face, that wonderful smile, and sparkling eyes that show you enjoy life whereas I...'

'Don't belittle yourself. You're attractive in a different way. Naturally pleasant, that lovely lilt to your voice.'

'Irish father.'

'Thought so. You're even-tempered too, I'll bet it takes a lot to stir you up. Your serious expression belies a touch of humour that I think is there. That should bring a mischievous sparkle to those green eyes of yours – which I would say speak of a touch of jealousy too.'

'You sound like a gypsy telling me my future,' laughed Rose. 'I'm so enjoying this conversation. I have no one that I talk to like this at home.'

'I like you too, Rose, so I propose we see more of each other.'

'I would like that.'

'Maybe you can get to more cricket matches? I think Arthur would be only too pleased to be your chaperon.' Lizzie gave a little pause and then added, 'And I'm sure you would like that too.'

Rose made no comment. Lizzie was right; she would like it.

'It looks as though my parents are getting on well with Arthur's family and your father.'

Rose glanced in the direction of the group. 'I'm so pleased. I wish Mother could have been here too.'

'That's the price of having a shop, but I'm sure there will be times when she can join us.'

'What does your father do?'

'He's private secretary to Mr Bosomworth.'

'Mr Bosomworth the mill owner?' There was a touch of surprise in Rose's query.

'None other.'

'Then he has a very good job.'

'I suppose so but he has kept his feet on the ground. He has never forgotten his humble beginnings. He worked hard, Mr Bosomworth spotted his ability and gave him a chance which Father seized. He was given more and more responsibility and with it came better pay. Father is able to see that all my grandparents are comfortable and he helped his sister through a hard time when her husband lost his job, became depressed and committed suicide. With Father's help she survived and has since met a wealthy widower who thinks the world of her.' Lizzie pulled herself up with the apology, 'Listen to me, prattling on.'

'You're not. It's nice getting to know about people. Where do you live?'

'Headingley Flats.'

'One of those new big houses?'

'It stands in its own grounds, but there are others that are bigger.'

For a moment Rose felt a touch of envy. She wondered what it would be like to live in one of the big houses in the new development on the outskirts of Leeds instead of in a house behind a shop even though it was spacious. She shook off the feeling with the remark, 'We're neglecting the cricket.'

'I've been keeping half an eye on it. Their opening batsmen are slow which shows our bowling must be good.'

At that point one of the batsmen played an injudicious stroke and sent a catch to Ben. By the time Rose and Lizzie had reached their parents another wicket had fallen.

Mrs Carter was deep in conversation with Mrs Newton but interrupted it to ask the girls if they had enjoyed their stroll.

'Father's sounding off again,' said Lizzie quietly to Rose with an inclination of her head in her father's direction. Rose made no reply when she saw that Lizzie was taking in her father's words without appearing to be listening.

'I tell you, Harry ... and you too, Con ... I admire any man who does an honest day's work, no matter what it is. There's no reason, if he works hard, applies himself and seizes opportunities, honestly and legitimately, why he shouldn't improve his lot.'

'I agree, Alec,' said Harold. 'I see it in the bank. There are those who are content to stay as they are and those who automatically look for promotion.'

'And I'll bet you are one of the latter.'

Harold nodded. 'I'll be manager of that branch one day, and then I'll look beyond that.'

'No doubt you'll do it too,' approved Con. 'Whereas I'm stuck with the shop.'

'Don't belittle yourself, Con. Since you took it over from your father-in-law, you've widened the range of your goods and increased custom threefold,' Arthur pointed out.

'There you are, Con,' said Alec. 'You must have seized your chance. And don't forget, you can go on increasing trade. Open another shop; get yourself out from behind that counter and widen your horizons. Leeds is expanding and will go on doing so. You could thrive on the back of it. Open more shops in the developing housing areas. A Duggan empire.'

'Something to think about, Con,' agreed Harold. 'The bank will finance you.'

'Aye, and Mr Bosomworth is thinking of another mill with houses for his workers close by. They'd like a good shop near them.'

Lizzie gave Rose a dig with her elbow. 'They're away, but I'll soon put a stop to it.' She indicated that there was a change taking place on the field of play.

'Fred's putting Arthur on to bowl!' she called out.

Immediately the talking stopped. Attention was concentrated on the cricket along with the hope that Arthur might stop Burmantofts' progress towards a strong position.

He bowled four balls to a batsman who treated them warily.

'Your son has a nice smooth action,' commented Alec.

It gave Harold a real sense of pride, and that soared even higher when with the next ball, Arthur's spin deceived the batsman and he was clean bowled.

No one tried to disguise their elation which mounted during Arthur's next four overs when they realised he had stemmed the flow of runs and the opposing batsmen were growing uneasy. Arthur played on their nervousness and claimed two more wickets. His effort encouraged the bowler at the other end and they both asserted their dominance to dismiss four more batsmen. But two of the lower order players made a stand and gradually the score made by Carter's Cricketers began to look more vulnerable.

All Fred's attempts to dislodge them seemed to no avail, no matter how he changed the bowling. Until he brought Arthur back on at the opposite end to which he had started bowling. Immediately they met with success. One wicket gave them the breakthrough they needed but the last two batsmen rallied to provide an exciting finish when Fred took a wonderful catch that prevented a six and gave his side victory by five runs.

There was joy among the supporters of Carter's Cricketers and, in victory, the group who had met so recently seemed to be bound in closer friendship. Alec Carter led the cheering and, with a broad smile, said, 'That win deserves a celebration. Harold, Mrs Newton and your family, please come to tea tomorrow afternoon. You too, Con, and bring Mrs Duggan and Rose. You're invited too,' he called to Chris Sleightholme and Kevin Wainwright. 'And bring your wives. We can manage that, can't we, Elsie?'

'Of course.' His wife smiled. She was used to his spur-of-the-moment benevolence and knew that their cook was always prepared for such impromptu occasions. 'We shall all get to know each other better. Come about three-thirty. We'll have tea at five-thirty, and stay for a light supper later. You'll be in time to catch the last horse-bus.'

Alec looked round everyone with a questioning look. They all gave their agreement and made their thanks.

'There you are, Rose,' said Lizzie as they walked across the moor together to wait for the horse-buses, 'Arthur's done the trick and enthused Father into making this suggestion for tomorrow afternoon after church. I'm so glad. We'll be bound to see more of each other now because there'll be return invitations all around.'

Chapter Two

The Newton and Duggan families lived near enough to the Carters' residence to walk to it. They found the iron gates open and fell silent as they approached the imposing house set at the top of a short drive. Hearing the crunch of their footsteps on the gravel, an elderly man who was weeding a flowerbed straightened up, glanced in their direction, touched the peak of his cap and resumed his task.

No one spoke; even the younger members of the family, who had been chatting gaily, fell silent. The house, on its slight rise, seemed to be inspecting them as if needing to approve any strangers who approached. The large dark stones it was built of gave it a solid look that was counteracted by the two bays of glistening windows to either side of the front door. These were matched by those on the first floor with the addition of one more in the centre of the upper storey.

The nearer they got to the house the more awestruck Moira became but she managed to whisper to Enid, 'This is a fine place. What are we coming to? Over-smart for me.'

Enid sensed her friend's unease. 'You'll be all right, Moira. You're coming to meet nice friendly people. Homely, from what I saw of them at the cricket match. They're no different from us. You'll like Elsie Carter, and I'm sure you two will get on well. And wouldn't you like a house like this one day?'

'Who wouldn't like a house like this, standing in its own grounds?' replied Moira. 'But I don't envy the Carters, I'm content where I am. Ours may not be as big as this, and at times it's a drawback being attached to the shop, but it's more than big enough for the three of us. Life isn't complicated, we're comfortable, and that's how I like it.'

Enid had no time to reply as they were almost at the house.

The drive swung round to run parallel to the house front. Grass gave way to flowerbeds. Four slabs of crafted stone led up to the front door, its oakwork pierced by two large glass panels. The new arrivals could see that they would enter a small vestibule.

The two families glanced at each other tentatively as if querying who should disturb the silence that embraced the house. The ladies were waiting for the men to take the initiative. The younger members knew they were not expected to. Harold glanced at Conan and saw that his friend was expecting him to be the one. Harold stretched out and tugged the cone-shaped iron bell-pull. They all waited in expectant unease. A few moments later they saw the house door open and a manservant, dressed in black tail-coat, black trousers and white shirt with a white cravat tied neatly at his neck, stepped over to open the door to the vestibule.

'Mr and Mrs Newton, Mr and Mrs Duggan?' he enquired politely.

'Yes, indeed,' replied Harold.

'Please do come in. You are expected.' He stood to one side while the families filed past him to find themselves in a large square hall with a wide staircase curving upwards from a point halfway along the left-hand side. Light ironwork, in the form of intertwining leaves, formed a banister. The oak floor of the hall was matched by the shoulder-high wall panelling above which hung a bright, flowered wallpaper that reflected the light streaming in through the windows.

Two maids had appeared and were taking outdoor garments from the new arrivals when Alec and Elsie Carter with Fred and Lizzie hurried out of a room to the right. Greetings and introductions were offered after which Alec announced, 'The Sleightholmes are already here,' and led the way into the drawing room.

Eric Sleightholme introduced his wife Jane, a tall, slim woman who held herself erect so as to appear even taller than she really was. Her skin was alabaster white, her manner warm and friendly. Enid and Moira knew that they had come under astute observation. Jane had quickly summed up the two friends as likeable people who, though they were close, would not hold to their friendship to the exclusion of others. Elsie,

48

who had been having a brief word of welcome with Celia and Oswald, joined the three of them. They all felt an immediate empathy with her and knew that there would be no standing on ceremony here, that she, like her husband, had not let success result in snobbery and had seen likewise it had not tainted Fred and Lizzie. This was a warm close family, one whose home would always be open to their friends. Harold and Enid, Eric and Jane, appreciated the way that their sons' success on the cricket field had brought them this friendship, and Conan and Moira were equally appreciative that, as friends of the Newtons, they had been included too. These introductions had hardly been concluded when Mr and Mrs Wainwright arrived.

At first Kevin and Beth appeared retiring but before long were engaged in lively conversation, displaying their wide knowledge, forthright opinions and jocular sense of humour.

'It is such a glorious day I thought we would take lemonade outside now and tea later, about five-thirty,' Elsie announced.

Everyone murmured their approval. They all strolled outside and, as they took a glass of lemonade from trays offered by the maids, fell into groups. The men settled down around one table, the ladies around another. At Fred's suggestion the four young men swallowed their lemonade quickly then headed down the expanse of lawn to get in a 'bit of catching practice' as he put it. Lizzie took Rose and Celia on a tour of the garden which had been laid out with a maze of paths between formal flowerbeds to either side of the lawn and circling a man-made pond in which a fountain sent water falling with a soothing rhythm. Oswald, with no one of his own age to talk to, looked around for a moment until Fred called out, 'Oswald, come and join us, maybe I'll find another cricketer in you.' Pleased to be included he ran helter-skelter across the lawn to join in.

'I'm going to stay and watch the fishes,' said Celia when the three young ladies reached the pond.

'Don't miss tea,' said Lizzie. 'When Mother announced that you were all coming today, Cook was extra busy. She'll have produced something special.'

Lizzie and Rose found a seat in a secluded part of the garden and sat down. Rose sensed that she was going to be asked something out of earshot of everyone so it came as no great surprise when Lizzie asked her if she knew anything about Ben Sleightholme.

Rose's eyes twinkled as she asked, 'Do you like him then?'

'I don't know him,' protested Lizzie weakly.

'That doesn't mean you aren't interested.'

'Well, he's so handsome.'

Rose pouted her lips as if throwing doubt on that statement.

'Don't pull a face like that, Rose Duggan! You know he is.'

'Well. I'll grant you that.'

'So, do you know anything about him?'

'No.'

'You must, he works with your Arthur,' Lizzie persisted.

'Well, Arthur likes him. They get on well. What does your brother think of him?'

'All I hear from Fred is how well Ben played yesterday, but I want to know more.'

'I can only tell you that his father is a corn merchant. From what I saw of him yesterday he seems a decent man, and from seeing my mother's attitude when she has been talking to Mrs Sleightholme, I would say that she is easy to get on with. If Ben has inherited those traits he should be easy enough to talk to.'

'Maybe we can do that at teatime,' said Lizzie, hinting that she would like Rose's help.

So the afternoon passed pleasantly, with everyone relishing their new-found friendships. With the approach of tea, Elsie decided that it was time the gentlemen and ladies mingled and, without seeming to organise them, engineered that while tea was being served.

Cups, saucers, plates, knives, spoons and serviettes had already been set on a table against the wall of the house. Now maids appeared carrying trays of white bread, whole-meal bread and soda bread, fruit scones, butter and three types of jam. Honey buns, chocolate cake, cherry cake and Shepherd's Purse tempted the most delicate of appetites, followed by enticing possets, creams and tansies. Teas and cordials were available to suit all tastes.

With food in the offing the young men had abandoned their catching. Oswald ran to join Celia, eager to know if there were any 'secret' paths around the garden, while Fred sought out Mrs Sleightholme to inform her what a difference her son would make to his batting line-up for the rest of the season.

Observing that Rose and Lizzie were on their own, Ben said quietly to Arthur. 'Let's offer those two some scones.'

'Could we?' queried Arthur, wondering if it might appear forward.

'Yes. Mrs Carter said we should help ourselves and she isn't a lady to stand on ceremony.'

They started towards the table on which the eatables had been laid out.

'Have you got your eye on one of them?' asked Arthur with a sly inference that that was the real reason for Ben's suggestion.

'Lizzie. I couldn't think about Rose. I noticed she had her eyes set firmly on you yesterday at the cricket match so I thought you and her...'

'I've known her almost all my life.'

'That's no reason not to think a lot of her.'

There was no chance for further comment. They were at the table. Ben picked up a plate of scones while Arthur carried four tea plates. They turned to the two girls who were approaching the table.

'Can we interest you in some scones?' asked Ben, confident that he would meet with acceptance.

'That is thoughtful of you.' Lizzie gave him a dazzling smile 'Shall we sit over there?' She indicated four chairs set around a circular wooden table.

Rose smiled to herself. They had not had to manoeuvre a meeting with Ben after all. He and Arthur had made the first move. Were they just being polite or was Ben interested in Lizzie? She started, disturbed by an ongoing thought. Or was Arthur interested in Lizzie? She was very pretty and in spite of her own opinion of her red hair, it was a feature that attracted male attention.

Arthur placed the plates on the table. 'I'll get some knives and jam.' He hurried away.

Ben waited until Lizzie and Rose were seated and had carefully arranged their dresses before offering them the plate of scones. Arthur returned and they all settled down to enjoy the tea during which the two young men were readily solicitous to the desires of their companions. Conversation was light-hearted but Rose perceived that Ben's attention was directed more at Lizzie than at her, though he was polite enough not to do so to her exclusion. Rose was content; she had Arthur now, and the hope that their lifelong friendship was developing into love.

'I hope you are enjoying your visit,' said Lizzie, embracing them all in her query.

They gave their unequivocal assent.

'This is a wonderful tea,' commented Ben. 'You have a talented cook.'

'Thank you.' Lizzie accepted his praise graciously. 'I'm sure you have one who is equally good.'

'Not on these types of dishes, but she is excellent with meat and fish.'

'Where do you live?'

'Not far from here, in another part of Headingley.'

'It's a wonder we haven't met.'

'We only moved here three weeks ago.'

'I'm told your father is a corn merchant.'

'Yes.'

'Doesn't he want you in the business with him?'

'Eventually, but he wants me to gain experience outside so I got this job in the railway offices. I'm very glad I did. I met Arthur and Fred and so met you.'

Lizzie blushed.

Before any more was said, Rose told Arthur, 'There is something I want to show you.' She turned to Lizzie. 'Will you excuse us?'

'Of course,' replied Lizzie, knowing that Rose was making this move so that she could be alone with Ben. Rose saw appreciation in her eyes.

'What do you want to show me?' asked Arthur as they walked away.

'Nothing in particular,' replied Rose. 'I thought those two ought to be left alone.'

Arthur smiled. 'He did express a desire to meet Lizzie so we made a point of having tea with you.'

Rose chuckled. 'Lizzie asked me what I knew about him so we aimed to get with you and Ben at tea-time.'

They both burst out laughing.

'Shall we walk?' asked Rose.

'Come with me,' said Arthur, and started off towards a path that led between some trees. She saw that they were out of everyone's view and slipped her hand into his, gratified when he did not attempt to loose her hold.

He led her to a seat let into the hedge and sat down. Opposite, the trees and hedge had been trained to give a view of the house. 'That's a lovely sight,' he said. 'The framing of the building with the trees is perfect.'

'It is,' she said. 'How did you know about it?'

'We had a break in our catching and came this way for Fred to show us where he is hoping he can persuade his father to make a practice wicket. I slipped away afterwards to make a quick drawing.' As he was speaking Arthur released her hand and drew from his pocket a sketchbook and pencil.

Rose felt her whole body tense as disappointment and annoyance welled inside her. Alone in a beautiful place, the atmosphere filled with promise, she had expected something else, not a sketchbook and pencil.

'What are you doing?' she snapped.

'I want a reference from which I can do a proper drawing later, so I'm going to add a bit more to this sketch.' Arthur flicked the book open.

'What – now?'

'I can't do it any other time,'

Rose's lips tightened. 'Must you do it now? Do you expect me just to sit here and wait?'

'Why not?'

'It's unsociable. Everyone will be wondering where we are. Besides, it's a waste of time. What can you gain by it?'

'You'll see. One day I'll be a famous artist.'

'Rubbish! People like you can't make a decent living by painting.'

'I might surprise you.'

Her hostility mellowed in response to the soft light that came into his eyes and his obvious desire to avoid confrontation. 'Will you?'

'Oh, yes, and you'll be pleased with what I achieve.'

She gave a slight hesitation before she next spoke. 'That presupposes I'll be with you.'

'Well, won't you?'

Rose's eyes widened. 'That sounds as though you expect to marry me.'

'We've known each other most of our lives and I think that is what our families expect.'

'Maybe, but so far as I'm concerned, Arthur, you've got to love me.'

'I think I do,' he replied a little tentatively.

'Think?' cried Rose in exasperation. 'You've got to know.'

He stared at her. This display of temper had added a new dimension to Rose and he saw now for the first time a young lady who, while not exceptionally pretty, was certainly attractive. She had an aura about her which from familiarity he had overlooked until this moment. Arthur did not answer her but impulsively leaned forward and kissed her lightly on the lips. He drew back and smiled at her. She saw something she had not seen before; through his embarrassment, his admiration for her was touched with something deeper.

'Now I know you are my sweetheart,' she whispered.

'We tell no one,' replied Arthur cautiously. 'It's our secret for a while.'

She realised he was serious and, so as not to upset him, agreed.

'I think we'd better be getting back,' he said eventually, and helped her to her feet. They started away from the seat.

Arthur slipped the sketchbook into his pocket, equally determined that no one, not even Rose, would prevent him from fulfilling his ambition to be an artist.

'Everyone seems to be enjoying themselves,' he observed as they walked up the lawn towards the house.

'Mother was a bit apprehensive about coming but I'm pleased to see that she and Mrs Carter are getting on well.'

'And my mother appears to have found new friends in Mrs Sleightholme and Mrs Wainwright,' added Arthur.

Just as he made that observation the three ladies joined their hostess and Rose's mother. Whatever passed between them caused laughter all round.

'In fact, I would say that they have all forged new friendships.'

'And everyone else as well.' Arthur inclined his head towards the men standing grouped in earnest conversation.

'Not forgetting Lizzie and Ben. No doubt you'll be hearing about her from him tomorrow. You'll have to tell me how they got on.'

Half an hour later Fred emerged from the house carrying, with Giles's help, a large oblong wooden box. 'Anyone for a game of croquet?' he called.

All the young folk, none of whom had played before, were eager to learn this new game from Fred and Lizzie. After a pleasant hour Elsie Carter called a halt. 'There's a nip in the air, I think we should all go inside. Lizzie, you can play the piano.'

'A talented young lady,' whispered Ben as he escorted her inside and then to the piano.

Lizzie tinkled the keys while everyone found themselves seats. Once they were settled she played a repertoire of classical music and new tunes. Everyone was captivated by her accomplished playing. When she stopped she swung round on her stool to face them and acknowledge their clapping and admiring comments, finally holding up her hands to silence them.

'Thank you. Now I am going to ask someone else to play, someone who is much more accomplished than I ... Mother.'

All eyes turned on Elsie who shook her head. 'No, no. Lizzie flatters me.'

'I do not, Mother,' Lizzie contradicted her with a loving smile.

'Come, Elsie, play my favourite piece.' Alec had risen from his seat and held out his hand to his wife. She could do no other than accept.

She settled herself on the piano stool, flexed her hands and then caressed the keys with a delicate touch. She brought magic to the air and transported her audience into another land. When she finished the silence was palpable until her audience realised she had stopped playing and they were no longer in the realm of magic. The clapping that erupted mingled with cries of appreciation.

She smiled, inclining her head in thanks. 'I'm sure someone else must play?' There was no response. 'Oh, come, please don't hide your talents.'

'I play a little,' Jane Sleightholme offered.

At the same moment Harold spoke up: 'I sing a bit. Only popular tunes.'

'Good. Then we shall hear Jane and have a sing-song with Harold.'

The evening continued in a joyous mood, and after everyone had shared a light supper they prepared to leave, making promises that before long they would all meet again. Enid, never one for leaving loose ends, suggested it should be at her house in two weeks' time, an offer that they all immediately accepted.

'I enjoyed that.' Conan Duggan leaned back in his chair and, with marked satisfaction, tapped his stomach. His breakfast plate was clean. 'A good breakfast is the best start to the day,' he added, surveying with approval the way his wife and daughter were dealing with their bacon and egg.

Moira smiled with pleasure for she knew that the cook made a special effort to have Conan's breakfast exactly as he liked it.

'We had a good day yesterday,' he went on, 'and it set me thinking during the night: would you both like to learn the piano?'

Surprised by this unexpected suggestion, both mother and daughter stared at him.

'Are you serious?' asked Moira.

'Yes. Why shouldn't you? It is a fine accomplishment for a young lady. If Rose would like to learn then you may as well do so at the same time.' He glanced at his daughter. 'Well?'

Rose was so taken aback she couldn't find words for a moment, then they poured out. 'Oh, I would. Yes, I would. Can I? Do you really mean it?'

'Of course I mean it. We should have thought of it before. Seeing the way Elsie Carter and Lizzie played made me a little envious.'

'We'll never achieve their standard,' said Moira doubtfully.

'Maybe not, but you can always try. Besides, does reaching that standard matter? If you can play reasonably well, and enjoy it, it will be an asset and you can give pleasure to yourselves and to others.'

'I must say that I too was envious, especially when Harold and Jane were able to contribute to the entertainment even though they weren't as accomplished as Elsie or Lizzie.'

'When can we start?' asked Rose enthusiastically, the remains of her breakfast forgotten.

'As soon as we get a piano and find a teacher.' Conan turned to his wife. 'Why don't you and Rose pay Elsie a visit today and ask her advice?'

Moira pondered a moment. 'Why not?' The firmness in her voice confirmed her approval of the whole matter.

Later that morning she and Rose were pleased to find Elsie at home to receive them.

'It's a pleasure to see you both again,' she greeted them warmly. She had taken to Moira and knew that her daughter Lizzie had found a friend in Rose. 'What brings you back so soon?' she asked when they were seated comfortably in the drawing-room.

'Elsie, we have come to seek your advice.' Moira went on to explain the purpose of their visit. 'We don't expect to reach the same standard as you and Lizzie, your playing was just wonderful but Conan thinks it would be an asset, especially for Rose.'

'So it will. I am a great believer that all young

ladies should learn the piano. It is a definite advantage in company; not only are you able to entertain if necessary, even if it is only for a sing-song, but it takes you into the world of music and that can make for many talking points. I am sure Conan's is a wise decision. You will not regret it.'

'We know nothing about pianos nor do we know any teachers.'

'I can help you with recommendations. But first let me ring for some chocolate.' She rose from her chair and went to the bell-pull. The maid appeared almost before Elsie had resumed her seat.

Lizzie expressed her delight that Rose was to learn the piano. 'We'll be able to play together.'

Rose laughed. 'Will I ever be that good? Your playing was a delight.'

'Practice, Rose, plenty of practice.'

Armed with the name of a piano dealer in Leeds and two teachers, Rose and her mother left in a state of euphoria.

Conan nodded with satisfaction when they told him of their progress. 'I'll get Madge Hobson to look after the shop tomorrow and we three will go into Leeds and see about a piano.'

Excitement permeated the rest of their day. When they had finished their evening meal Conan broached another thought that had occupied his mind throughout the day.

'You saw the Carters' house again today,' he said as he settled in his chair and his wife and daughter picked up their embroidery. 'Were you impressed?'

'Of course. Who wouldn't be?'

'How would you like something similar? Well,

built to your own design, of course.'

'What?' Moira stared at her husband in disbelief, her needle stopped in mid-stitch.

Rose gaped at her father. Surely she hadn't heard him correctly? She felt numb; her embroidery slipped to the floor. What was happening? A piano. Lessons. Now this suggestion of a new house. What had happened to him, her father who had always seemed so content with his lot?

'Would you like a house in its own grounds?' he repeated.

'We can't afford it,' said Moira.

'Not immediately, but I could set things up so we could in the near future.'

Elsie was mystified. 'What are you thinking?'

'I talked with Alec Carter at the cricket match, and again yesterday.'

'What has he to do with it?' demanded Moira before he had time to expand his explanation.

Conan held up his hands and said, 'Just bear with me. We have a good business here, thanks to the foundation that your father laid. As you know we have expanded and that has been in no small measure due to you, though much of your work is behind the scenes. Now I think you should benefit from all you have contributed.'

'That is most thoughtful of you, Con, but I want for nothing. I am content here and that is good enough for me. Besides, I know we couldn't afford a house in that location on our present income.'

'I know that too, but I am thinking about a scheme that will enable us to afford it.'

'Now what big ideas has Alec Carter given you?'

'He's made me think. I agree we are comfortably off, but we could better ourselves.'

'You mean, leave here. Sell the shop?'

'We wouldn't sell the shop, and we'd only leave here when the moment is right.'

'What is the point in making it a lock-up shop? We've been perfectly happy living here. What do you mean, "when the moment is right"?'

'Let me answer those questions by telling you what I have in mind. We'd open another shop, then another and another, building up a lucrative chain.'

'But that would mean using all our capital.'

'Not necessarily. We would keep some and borrow the shortfall.'

'Borrow?' Moira looked horrified.

'Why not, if we can turn it to our advantage? Handled carefully, we couldn't lose. Leeds is expanding rapidly. Housing developments will need shops close by. Alec told me unofficially that his employer has plans to build a new factory with the necessary housing for his employees. There could be an opportunity there for us.'

'And I suppose you would enlist Harold's help in raising the money?'

'Why not? What are friends for?'

'Why can't you be content with what we have? We make a comfortable living. The house and shop are ours.'

'I want better for you and Rose.'

'I am perfectly happy with the way things are, as I am sure is Rose.'

'Mother, I...'

Moira raised her hand to halt whatever it was her

63

daughter was about to say. 'This is a matter for your father and me. You cannot appreciate all the implications of this suggestion, which I think too absurd to consider, but I'll agree to sleep on it.'

Rose said nothing. Conan knew it was no good saying any more now. He had recognised the hint from his wife that she would only discuss this further in the privacy of their bedroom.

The opportunity for that did not come until ten o'clock that night

'I take it that you are opposed to my idea, Moira, but will you let me explain what else I see in the future?' Conan looked steadily at his wife who swung round on the stool in front of the dressing table when she heard him come into their bedroom.

'I admit I don't like upheaval. I don't like change. But I will listen to what you have to say.'

He brought a cane chair and sat down in front of her, taking her hands in his. 'You know I only want what is best for you and Rose and, as we have no other children, her future is in my mind. I think that you, like me, see that in all probability she and Arthur will marry one day.'

'Yes, I've long thought it would be a good match. They have known each other nearly all their lives.'

'He's a fine boy and I'm sure he would make a good steady husband. Now, just as your father took me into his business, I would seriously consider taking Arthur into ours, with your approval, of course, when the time is right. Employment in the railway offices will give him a good grounding in dealing with people and gaining commercial experience. It will be a good solid start.'

'He may like the work there and not be attracted to shop-keeping.'

'True, but this shop would give him greater independence, and if there were more than one shop he would have a real incentive to take the employment I would offer, for he would see that, through Rose, he would become part-owner of a chain of businesses.'

'It all sounds very grand, Con, but there would be risks. Our comfortable way of life could be jeopardised. There would be worry and stress for you and for me, whereas we know this shop, we know we can earn a comfortable living from it. Rose will inherit it one day. She is content with that, like me. If Arthur loves her and they marry they can follow us into this comfortable adequate lifestyle. Why seek more when that would only bring worry and uncertainty? I like this house, I don't envy the Carters theirs. Please, Con, let things rest as they are.'

He knew he was defeated. He realised that Moira's points were all sound and legitimate, whereas his did carry risks. Maybe she was right. Yes, he could still help Rose and Arthur if, as expected, they married. 'As you wish, love.' He leaned forward and kissed her.

'Thank you, Con. I hope I haven't upset you?'

He gave a slow shake of his head. 'No, you haven't. I'm a little disappointed maybe, but not upset.' He gave a dismissive wave of his hand as if he was wiping the idea from his mind. 'It was probably a wild fancy, born on the back of a throw away suggestion. Think no more of it. Concentrate on the piano we are going to get tomorrow.'

Rose lay in bed wide awake, wondering what was transpiring in her parents' bedroom. She knew her father's suggestion would be discussed and reflected on what she might have said. She was happy in the house she had known all her life. It would be nice moving to one with its own grounds but did she really want to do that? She felt secure here. Would she feel the same if they moved? They were comfortable where they were, why change it? The more she thought about it, the more she hoped that her mother would persuade her father to forget the idea of any expansion.

Chapter Three

When he had retired to his room the same evening, Arthur settled down with his sketchbook and separate sheet of drawing paper. His sketchbook he regarded as a notebook in which he could make quick depictions and pencil words to remind him of particular aspects of a scene he hoped to capture. Now he started to transfer his impressions of the Carters' house to a pristine sheet of paper, swiftly becoming lost in a task that delighted him. He thought it a magical gift that he was able to create pictures of places he had seen as well as to develop imaginary landscapes. He was thankful that he had a retentive memory: even if he hadn't his sketchbook with him he could remember the basics of anything that had attracted his attention.

He had no idea where his talent came from. Neither of his parents had either the ability or the inclination to express themselves on paper. He knew that none of his grandparents had had the ability to draw. Where he had attained this gift sometimes puzzled him, but he did not dwell on it and was only thankful that it had been given to him. He wished his parents would recognise it too. Their usual comments were 'very nice', 'very pretty', but there was never real appreciation of the artistic elements in his work. They could see no more than surface representation. He knew they thought he was wasting his time and viewed his occasional observation that one day he would be a famous artist with a certain contempt, always pointing out that artists led very precarious lives with uncertain futures. There was no outright command for him to devote his time to more useful occupations that would help to make him comfortable but he knew that was always in the back of their minds whenever he showed them a drawing which was becoming less and less often. How he wished for someone to see what he was aiming at, someone who could appreciate more in his drawings than mere surface; that there could be many underlying moods expressed there also.

Time flew by and after an hour he realised he should be getting to bed. He propped the drawing up and stood back from it. He viewed it critically then gave a little nod, a sign that he was satisfied with what he had done. He would finish it tomorrow.

He thought about it again when he lay down.

He would give it to Rose, a reminder of what had transpired between them on that bench in the Carters' garden. Sweethearts. Maybe, as a recollection of that, the drawing would focus her attention on his artistic ability more than it had been in the past, make her see that he had a real talent he wanted to develop for their good.

Three days later when Arthur left the house with his father he was carefully holding an envelope so that the picture inside it would not be creased. He was thankful that everyone else in the family was so busy no one commented on what he held. He wanted no one to see this sketch before Rose. He was highly satisfied with the drawing and hoped he had achieved something of the effect of the Carters' house through the trees as well as a reasonable rendering of the building itself.

'Are you getting settled in at the office?' his father asked as they strode towards the Duggans' shop.

'Yes, Father.'

'Enjoying it?'

'Yes,' Arthur replied. It was no lie, for he was enjoying being with his new friends, but he would rather have been settling down with pencil and paper to interpret the essence of some landscape, some person. He had felt an impulse stirring inside him to try a portrait. But who could he get to allow him to do that? His family? Rose? They all pooh-poohed his idea of being an artist. Lizzie? But she would tell Rose. Fred? Maybe dressed as a cricketer. That was a possibility. Or perhaps Ben batting. All in good time.

His thoughts were interrupted by his father. 'Don't forget what I told you on your first day.'

'I won't.'

'I'll say it again, lad, you've a good chance to progress with the railway and enjoy a comfortable life.'

'Yes, Father.'

When they entered the shop they saw that Conan had had to call for his wife to help him serve the six customers who had descended on them almost at the same moment. In spite of the bustle, Harold detected some excitement coming from Con and Moira when they saw their friends.

'Be with you in a few minutes, Harry,' Con called.

'Go through, Arthur,' said Moira. 'Rose is there.'

Arthur blessed his good fortune. Things couldn't have worked out better. He would be able to give her the drawing without anyone else being there. 'Thanks, Mrs Duggan.' He stepped to the end of the shop, raised the hinged part of the counter and went through the door that led into the house behind.

It had always intrigued him the way the shop acted as a front door, although there was also a side door that gave the building a private entrance. Stepping from the shop into the Duggans' quarters was just as if he had gone through the front door at home. He was in a similar hall with two doors off to the right, a staircase climbing from the left, and opposite the door he had just come through were two more, one of which led to the dining room with the other giving admission to the kitchen and the scullery beyond that.

He went to the first door on the right, knocked, opened it and saw he was right in his expectation of finding Rose there. 'Hello,' he said tentatively, though she was already on her feet, her face breaking into a broad welcoming smile as soon as she saw him. Her eyes lit with excitement as she came towards him.

He saw words springing to her lips but fore-stalled them by thrusting the envelope towards her and saying, 'A present for you.'

A little taken aback that she could not swiftly express the reason for her excitement, Rose muttered, 'Thank you.' She knew it was only polite to open a gift when it had been given so curbed her enthusiasm, opened the envelope and took out the drawing. She gave it a cursory glance and said 'Thank you' again before she dropped it on the table.

Disappointment gripped Arthur. He felt like a balloon that had been pricked. 'You recognise it?'

'Of course.' Her voice was almost dismissive as if he had asked a silly question.

'I thought it might remind you of something.'

'The Carters' house, I saw that.'

'I included a corner of the bench as a symbol of something that happened there.'

'Oh, yes.' He realised then she had not seen in the picture what he had meant her to see. Before he offered anything further she went on, 'Come with me, I've something to show you.' The desire to surprise him had already eliminated all thoughts of the drawing that lay on the table in testimony of her lack of interest.

Her step was brisk as she led him through the hall to the next room. She opened the door and stood to one side to let him enter. Then, with an imperious sweep of her hand, she indicated the piano.

'Very smart.' Arthur stared at the grand piano that stood across the opposite corner, placed so that light would fall across the music from the left, and give the pianist a view of the door.

'Yes, isn't it wonderful?' Rose started across the room.

He followed. Though he felt like reciprocating the dismissive way she had reacted to his drawing he was too polite to do so.

She opened the piano and idly tapped a few keys.

'You are going to learn?'

'Of course. Father wouldn't have bought it if I wasn't. I think Mother will learn too.'

'I suppose this came from hearing the Carters on Sunday?'

'Yes. It was Father's idea. I'm so excited! I'm having lessons, starting tomorrow. Oh, I'll never be as good as Lizzie or Mrs Carter, who was really wonderful, but it will be a great asset to be able to entertain our friends.'

'I hope you enjoy it.'

'Oh, I shall.'

Further conversation was halted when the door opened and Moira and Conan brought Harold into the room. His surprise was obvious but Arthur was oblivious to the general explanations, enthusiasm and euphoria. His mind was still on the disappointment he had experienced in the

71

other room.

He was only half aware of leaving the house, and of his father eulogising the Duggans' purchase. 'Maybe we should get one? It's a pity my father sold his piano, that stopped my progress. I could take it up again. You could learn.'

'Don't get one for me. I'm not interested,' said Arthur.

'Wouldn't you like to play?'

He shrugged his shoulders. 'I'm not bothered.'

Harold had detected his son's change of mood so let the matter drop.

When he'd left his father, Arthur hurried to Ebenezer Hirst's shop. He needed something to distract him from his disappointment at Rose's reaction. He might find it in a painting in the shop window.

The two different artists represented there today had used completely different techniques. Here was an opportunity to compare, to contrast, and see what varying styles could bring to his own work. They also brought home to him that he should move beyond drawing, without abandoning it altogether. He knew sound drawing technique was the basis of all good artwork but he had never had the opportunity to indulge in paints. With no encouragement from his family he had never dared ask for them, but now he was working he had money of his own. The thought jolted him. He must not be late for work! He would love to stay longer and study these pictures some more but dare not. It was only when he made to move away that he became aware of a man unlocking the shop door, but Arthur took in no details except that he wore a stiff white winged collar with a cravat of muted yellow tied at the throat.

Though he applied himself to his work with his usual ability, discussed cricket with his friends, and agreed with Ben's enthusiastic remarks about Lizzie's dexterity at the piano, Arthur's thoughts kept turning to the paintings he had seen at Ebenezer Hirst's. He must see them again, he really must. That meant on his way home in case they were no longer there tomorrow.

At five o'clock he bade his friends a quick farewell

'What's his hurry?' 'Must be a girl.' 'If it is, he's a dark horse,' were the comments he heard as he hurried away.

He brought his laboured breathing under control when he saw the paintings were still in the window. Arthur had been there a few minutes when the shop door opened and he saw that winged collar and yellow cravat once more. He glanced at a man he judged to be in his late-forties, a small man with a mop of hair that was greying at the temples, unruly in spite of the fact that a comb had been run through it. His face was thin, cheeks tending towards being hollow. His pointed nose held thin-framed narrow spectacles behind which were alert, lively eyes that would extract information and miss nothing. He wore a waistcoat that matched the colour of his cravat, a dark three-quarter-length jacket and matching trousers.

'Hello, young man.' His voice was soft, gentle, and could no doubt be persuasive, an asset in the trade he followed as a bookseller and art dealer.

'Good day, sir.'

'Ah, a polite young man.' The shopowner looked over the top of his glasses and viewed Arthur with a penetrating gaze. 'I believe I have seen you looking in my shop window many times. Probably on your way home from school.'

'Yes, sir, you will have done.'

'But now you are working.'

'You are right, sir. How did you know?'

'The change of clothes, young man. Also you came to my window one morning last week and again this morning. You never came during the morning before so I judged you must have left school. And today is the first time you have come both night and morning. Why is that? What interests you especially in my window?'

'The paintings, sir.'

'Ah! But why did you visit my present display twice in one day?' He raised his eyebrows questioningly.

'The different techniques those artists have used.'

Ebenezer was a little surprised by the answer. He had not thought that this young man would have such a discerning eye. But why not? He knew of some artists, probably little older than the person to whom he was talking, who were beginning to be noticed for their ability. Might this young man be another? The thought intrigued him.

'I think we had better introduce ourselves. I am Ebenezer Hirst.' He pointed to the name above the shop window. 'I live over the shop with my wife and three young children. You are?'

'Arthur Newton, sir.'

'And?' Ebenezer, wanting to know more, prompted him when Arthur hesitated.

'I live in Headingley with my mother and father and a younger brother and sister. I work in the railway offices.'

Ebenezer gave a nod. 'May I ask what your father does for a living?'

'He's one of the chief cashiers in the Yorkshire Bank.'

'Do you paint?'

'I draw, sir.'

'That is good. The ability to draw is important.'

'Yes, sir.'

'Do you get that from your father or your mother?'

'Neither, sir. They are not interested in art.'

Ebenezer gave a surprised grimace. 'Your grandparents?'

'No, sir. I don't know where my interest and ability come from.'

'Are you talented?'

'Sir, that is not for me to say. How do I know? But I like what I produce.'

Ebenezer nodded. This young man was honest enough. 'So you come to my window to study the paintings?'

'Yes, sir. I hope you don't mind?'

'Mind?' Ebenezer raised his arms as if he was shocked that such a question should be asked. 'It is a free country. You can look in any shop window whenever you like. I take it you don't paint because you have not got the equipment, whereas a pencil and paper are easy to obtain?'

'Yes, sir. But now I am working, I hope to be

75

able to afford brushes and paint.'

There was a note of keen anticipation in Arthur's voice. This, coupled with the fact that he came to study the paintings displayed in the window, made Ebenezer think that it might be worthwhile having a look at this young man's work.

'Would you like to show me some of your drawings?'

Arthur's eyes brightened. Mr Hirst was the first person to show any interest in them.

Ebenezer noted the surge of eagerness and therefore was surprised when he saw the light in Arthur's eyes dim and grow shaded by doubt. He realised that Arthur was frightened he would receive platitudes rather than a true assessment of his ability.

'I will give you an honest opinion. I do not believe in giving praise where it is not due, nor in holding back any criticism I think a painting or drawing deserves. To do so does the would-be artist no good. Bring me some work tomorrow, and maybe we'll discuss those two paintings in the window.'

'Thank you, sir. You are kind.'

Ebenezer gave a dismissive wave of his hand. As Arthur started to turn away, offering more thanks as he did so, the art dealer stopped him. 'Come with me for a moment.' He turned back into the shop. Arthur followed. They moved through two rooms full of books. Shelves were neatly stacked while on the floor stood several piles waiting to be sorted. Ebenezer led Arthur into a third room. He stopped in amazement. The walls were full of paintings of all sizes and subject matter. He had never seen so many, and there were as many more stacked carefully one against the other.

Ebenezer smiled at the amazed expression on Arthur's face. 'I have more through there,' he pointed to another room, 'but there are none on the walls. I keep them free to display paintings individually so that there is nothing to distract a possible buyer.'

'It's a wonderland.' Arthur's comment was made in a voice scarcely above a whisper.

'Ebenezer, tea's ready!' a shout came from somewhere upstairs.

'Ah, I will have to go, Arthur. It does no good to keep a lady waiting when a meal is ready. Come and see me tomorrow.'

'Thank you, sir. Goodbye.'

Excitement surged through Arthur as he went to catch the horse-bus to Headingley. It made his step light; he felt he was walking on air. Someone was showing an interest. But he would tell no one about Ebenezer Hirst. Well, not yet.

It took an effort to keep himself from betraying his secret. Arthur excused himself as soon as he could from the table in order to sort out what he would take for Mr Hirst to see tomorrow. He finally settled on five drawings, which he slipped into an envelope.

When this was remarked upon by his mother the next morning, as he was about to leave for work, he passed it off as some cricket information for Fred, for he realised they knew he kept cuttings from the *Yorkshire Intelligencer*.

Once he had left the horse-bus and said

goodbye to his father he hurried to Ebenezer Hirst's.

'I thought I'd drop these off before I went to work,' panted Arthur when he rushed into the shop. 'I'll call back on my way home.'

'Very well,' was all Ebenezer managed to say before Arthur was gone. He smiled to himself as the door shut. That young man must be keen! He slipped the drawings from the envelope and spread them out on the counter.

Arthur had a job to keep his mind on his work, too lost in his thoughts as they whirled round and round in his mind, in and out of euphoria at what might be and black despair at what would probably happen.

He made a couple of mistakes that Ben covered for him, but when he committed three more, after Ben had been despatched to various parts of the building, Fred sought an opportunity to have a quiet word with him while Charlie Stokes was out of the room.

'What's wrong with you, Arthur? You're making so many mistakes. I saw Ben cover for you earlier. Now you've made some more.'

Arthur looked askance at him.

Fred pointed out the errors he had made. Arthur was startled by what he had done and quickly put them right.

'If Stokes sees these you'll be in for a roasting and he'll probably make you work extra Saturdays which might prevent you from playing cricket when I want you in the team. Get your mind on the job! Is it some girl? You hurried off after work yesterday. Best stop mooning over her.'

'It's not like that. It isn't a girl. But I'll be hurrying off again after work tonight. I'll tell you about it later. I might need your help.'

Fred was prevented from extracting any more information by the return of Charlie Stokes. He kept his eye on Arthur though, and was thankful to see his friend's concentration sharpen.

When Ben, Jack and Giles remarked on Arthur's hurried exit after work had finished, Fred made no comment except to appear to agree with their speculation that he had found a girl.

Arthur was oblivious to life around him as he hurried to Mr Hirst's bookshop and gallery. His mind was on one thing: what would Mr Hirst's opinion be? Charged by anxious anticipation, his heart beat faster and a queasy feeling gripped his stomach.

Ebenezer looked up from a leather-bound book he was lovingly polishing when Arthur burst in. 'Ah, young man.' He laid the book down and stood up. 'Follow me.'

Disappointed that Ebenezer showed no enthusiasm, Arthur felt his aspirations crashing around him. Surely if Mr Hirst had thought his work any good he would have said so immediately? He followed him into the room of paintings and saw his drawings spread out across the table in the centre.

'I looked at them most carefully throughout the morning. Kept coming back to them time and time again after making a first assessment on my immediate study. My wife, whose opinion I value, has had a look at them also and this afternoon I brought an artist to see them. He is a man with a great deal of talent – Laurence Steel.'

Arthur gasped.

'You've heard of him?'

'Yes, sir. He looked at my work?'

'Yes. He and I were boyhood friends and kept in touch even when he went to London for a while. His talent developed there and he made many valuable contacts but chose to live and work from here. I think one day he may return to London, though. You admired a landscape of his in the window.' Ebenezer Hirst smiled at Arthur's amazed expression and read his thoughts accurately. 'You are right, he has no need to sell anything through me, but he has never forgotten that I made his first sale and occasionally brings me a canvas to sell, something extra among all the commissions he receives. I appreciate his thoughtfulness for his work sells readily and he allows me a generous commission.' Hirst paused.

'But I digress, you are naturally anxious to know our verdict. I made no comment about your drawings, not wanting to influence or flavour his judgement. I wished to hear if his assessment matched mine. I am pleased to say it did and was just as favourable. You have talent, young man, but it wants cultivating and guiding.'

Arthur's eyes widened with what was almost a look of disbelief. 'Really?' he gasped.

'Yes, really. Don't look so flabbergasted.'

'Mr Steel thought my work was good?' Incredulity rang in his voice.

'Yes. Just as I and Mrs Hirst did.'

'But I never thought...'

Ebenezer interrupted him with, 'The first lesson

you should learn – never underestimate yourself. The second – have confidence. The third – never hide your light under a bushel.' Ebenezer saw that Arthur was still overawed. 'Young man, you must heed these three things I have told you.' Arthur started. He had heard them but his excitement had not allowed them to make any impact. Ebenezer recognised this and immediately repeated them with a firmness that could not be denied.

'Yes, sir.'

'Never forget them. Apply them to what you do and to life in general and you will do well. I will add some more advice and then it is up to you. You have a natural talent, but if you want to develop and become a good artist you will have to work hard and not let the frustrations that are bound to come discourage you. There will be times when you will seem to be making no progress but you must develop the determination to overcome these.' He paused. He saw Arthur had taken in every word he had said. 'Well, young man, what do you say?'

'Mr Hirst, I am so grateful for what you have done. I heed you and – will do exactly what you say. I want to be an artist.' He emphasised the last word and such determination pleased Ebenezer.

He gave a nod of satisfaction. 'Good. We must make a plan. Well, that is if you want my guidance?'

'Oh, yes, please, Mr Hirst. I won't be able to do it without you.'

Ebenezer, though he made no comment, felt a surge of delight. He had always dreamed of discovering someone with artistic talent. No mean

81

draughtsman himself, he realised he lacked the spark to make him great, but he knew techniques inside out and could teach them. Here he had a young man to whom he could pass on all his knowledge, but the one thing he knew he must not do was stifle Arthur's natural talent.

'Good. We will have to make some plans but I suggest we say no more now. Go away and think about what must be done. Come back tomorrow with some ideas.'

'Yes, sir.' Arthur started to gather up his drawings.

'Don't take those. Leave them with me. I would like to look at them some more.'

'Yes, sir. And thank you for what you have already done for me.'

'It will delight me to watch your talent flower. I would like to make your first sale.'

'You shall, Mr Hirst, you shall. Not only the first but every one of my paintings and drawings that is worth selling.'

'Don't make a promise you might be tempted to break.'

'I'll never do that. Never!' Arthur held out his hand.

When Ebenezer took it he felt the warmth of friendship and thanks. Before he let go he said, 'There is one thing more, Arthur.' He paused to make more of an impact with the piece of news he had kept until last. 'Mr Steel would like to see your work from time to time. He will criticise and direct you personally.'

Arthur stared back at him wide-eyed. This could not be true. Guidance from Laurence Steel?

'Really, Mr Hirst?' Incredulity filled his voice.

'Really, Arthur Newton.' There was no mistaking that the statement was true.

Arthur felt as if he was among the clouds as he made his way home. His mind drifted this way and that, reviewing the possibilities that lay ahead, the chances that could arise, and he made a vow that at all costs he would seize them. He could not turn away from the stroke of luck that had come his way from visiting a shop window to look at some pictures. He felt he had to tell everyone, but that thought brought him up with a jolt. Could he really do that? The obvious people to share the news with would be his parents but he fought shy of that. They would not approve of his contact with Mr Hirst and what that promised. Somehow he would have to win them over but that could take time and until the right moment his first steps into the realm of art must remain a secret. But how was he going to account for his absences? It was something he would have to resolve but a solution would have to wait until he knew what course this new aspect to his life would take.

Rose? Should he tell her? He immediately decided against doing so. Hadn't she shown a distinct lack of interest in his hobby and revealed little pleasure in the sketch he had given her? What might she say if she knew that he was to pursue his interest more deeply?

This big change in his life must remain his secret for the time being.

'I've managed to arrange a match for Saturday,' Fred announced when Arthur arrived at work the next morning.

'I thought our next game wasn't until a week on Saturday,' he commented, a dissenting voice among the approval expressed by Jack, Ben and Giles.

'Sounds as though you're doubtful?' said Fred suspiciously. 'It's not that mystery girl again, is it?'

'I think you had better let us meet her,' put in Jack. 'Then we can persuade her that our cricket matches come first.'

'It's not like that,' countered Arthur. 'I'll be ready to play.'

'Good,' said Fred. 'Now, remember I told you I had got Father's permission to make a practice pitch on a piece of land? I suggest we all have a look at it after work and decide what we are going to do.'

Everyone agreed except Arthur. 'I can't, I have an appointment.'

'Oh, here we go. Girl again.'

'I've told you, there is no girl.'

They jeered at his denial.

Arthur ignored their remarks and said, 'If I had known yesterday I wouldn't have made arrangements for this meeting. Of course I'll help in the future.' He was thankful that Mr Stokes's arrival put an end to their conversation then.

But Fred's announcement about the making of a practice pitch came to his mind during the morning and he saw it as the answer to any problems that might arise later.

Arthur was quickly away from the office when it was time to leave and hastened to Mr Hirst's shop. He was serving a customer when Arthur arrived but signalled him to go through. He was studying a landscape of a valley in the Yorkshire Dales when he heard the doorbell tinkle. A few moments later Ebenezer joined him.

'Sit down, Arthur, and tell me what you have been thinking and what conclusions you have come to?' He indicated a chair and then sat down himself on the opposite side of the table after he had produced Arthur's drawings.

'Well, sir, I'm extremely grateful for the chance you have given me and hope I won't let you down.'

Ebenezer smiled. 'Good, I'm glad you have reached that decision. I believe you have great potential if you are willing to take advice on basic aspects, develop your own talent and work hard. If you do all those things I am sure you won't let me down.'

'There is one matter that gave rise to some concern.' Arthur paused, his face expressing doubt.

'What might that be?' prompted Ebenezer.

'What will it cost me? I am not earning much money.'

'Cost?' Ebenezer held up his arms in shocked protest. 'My dear boy, it will cost you nothing except for materials. I myself seek no monetary reward. That will come from the pleasure I derive from discovering a talented artist.' He gave a little pause then added, 'And Mr Steel seeks none.' He smiled at the relief he saw in Arthur's face.

85

'That is most kind of you both.'

'Say no more about it. Now we must make some plans. You will have to spend some time here. Have you told your parents?'

'No, sir.' Arthur looked sheepish.

'Why not? Don't you think you should?'

'I know they won't approve.'

'Why not?'

'They think I am wasting my time when I'm drawing.'

'Don't they take any interest?'

'They glance at my work and say "very nice".'

'And nothing more?'

'No, sir. I hardly bother to show them my sketches any more, though they know I still do some. I think they expect me to tire of it.'

Ebenezer looked thoughtful. This might prove awkward. 'I think maybe you should tell them, or let me have a word with them, or how are you going to account for your absences?'

'I've thought of that,' replied Arthur brightly as if what he had in mind would solve every difficulty. 'I have a friend who lives in a big house in Headingley, not far from us. It has extensive grounds and he is going to make a practice cricket pitch there. I and some others are going to help him. That is where my parents will think I am.'

'I am not one for deceit, Arthur,' said Ebenezer, giving him a sharp, serious look.

'It would just be for a little while,' replied Arthur in a rush, hoping to forestall any veto from his newfound friend and mentor. 'Until you thought my work good enough to convince them.'

Ebenezer pursed his lips thoughtfully then said

with a slight nod of his head, 'Very well. You know your parents, and if you think this is the best way then that is how we will do it. Won't you have to take this cricketer friend into your confidence?'

'Yes, sir. But Fred will keep my secret.'

'You won't be precluded from helping him from time to time. You play cricket as well?'

'Yes, sir.'

Ebenezer noted the enthusiasm in those two words. 'How often do you play?'

Arthur explained the situation.

'Very well, I have no objection to that. In fact I approve because I am a great believer that exercise outdoors can help in other pursuits and in work. The artist needs to study life around him in order to make observations that can be incorporated into his drawings and paintings. It may be that you'll find a niche painting cricketing scenes, or at least incorporate them into a landscape to add life to it. There's your first lesson for you, observation – the artist must always observe, make notes if you wish, anything that will be helpful when you come to do the finished picture.

'There's just one more thing I should say about your playing cricket. Sometimes you may have to forego playing. For instance, if that is an occasion when Mr Steel wants to have a word with you. We will try and avoid that whenever we can as it could lead to questions from your parents if they know there is a match in which you are expected to play.' He saw a cloud cross Arthur's face. He knew the young man had seen the possibility of future difficulty and hastened to reassure him. 'Don't worry about that now. It may never happen. Well, I think that is all for the moment. You had better get off home. Call again tomorrow at this time.'

'Yes, sir. And thank you again.'

When Arthur returned the following evening he entered the shop with a mixture of disappointment and elation. The two paintings were no longer in the window. If their absence signified a sale he would be pleased for Mr Hirst's sake but disappointed for his own because he had looked forward to examining them more closely and he wanted to ask Mr Hirst some questions about them. So his first words were an enquiry about the paintings.

'No, I haven't sold them, but have no fear, I shall. I have brought them out of the window because I want to talk to you about them.' As he was talking Ebenezer led the way through the shop to the back room where the pictures were laid side by side on the table. Ebenezer stood looking at them for a moment before he spoke again. He gave a little grunt as if he had made up his mind about something and said, 'Tell me what you see in these two pictures. Mr Steel's first.'

'Yes, sir. But first, please tell me who painted the other? I can't quite make out the signature?' He was peering at the almost indistinct writing on the second painting. 'Is that Goldsworth?' He glanced over his shoulder at Ebenezer.

'You are right, it is. Graham Goldsworth, known as GG, or occasionally as Horse in the Leeds artistic fraternity.'

'He's another Leeds man?'

'Born and bred here. Like Mr Steel he is known beyond the borders of this town though no one outside those borders would dare to refer to him as Horse. Though he may not be in the topmost class of this country's painters as yet, he is sought after and I am honoured to be allowed to sell some of his work. But now, tell me what you see.'

Arthur paused for a few moments. Ebenezer did not press him. Arthur gave a little cough to clear his throat. He did not want to make a fool of himself; he wondered what Ebenezer wanted him to say. As thought chased thought he realised that that wasn't the point. If he knew what Ebenezer wanted him to say the exercise would lose its point. He needed to convey what he saw in these pictures, not what someone else wanted him to see.

'They represent two completely different styles. Mr Steel must have made a detailed study of all aspects of nature. The work in that respect is so meticulous, so precise, yet still conveys a degree of mystery. I don't think this scene represents anywhere in particular but has been created from the imagination in order to convey to the onlooker a detailed representation of various flora and fauna, bringing them together to form a pleasant whole.

'The picture by Mr Goldsworth makes the observer immediately enquire as to the location. It may not be of anywhere in particular, it may be another picture created from the imagination, but no matter. The artist has created it in a way that is technically most accomplished but capable of infinite interpretation by the person looking at it.

It is a picture that contains atmosphere and mood in a different way from Mr Steel's.'

Ebenezer was surprised by Arthur's assurance. He had not expected the young man to deliver such an erudite appraisal. It was obvious that he must have looked at many pictures and thereby opened up, perhaps unknowingly, his own gift to be able to interpret. Ebenezer knew he was going to enjoy working with Arthur and only hoped the young man would enjoy it as well.

'That is good, Arthur, very good. Tell me, which do you personally prefer?

'Mr Steel's, sir.'

'I hope you are not just saying that because Mr Steel has offered his help?'

'No, sir, I'm not. I do prefer it.'

'Why?'

'I admire the detail in Mr Steel's work. That is something I have tried to aspire to in many of my drawings, but of course without his skill.'

Ebenezer nodded. He now knew the line that Arthur must take. 'That has only come from years of diligent work and influences he encountered in London. I will tell you a little bit about both men. They are of the same age, grew up in Leeds, became proficient enough to attract the attention of London Art dealers, and have spent a few years in London to become known and gain an audience for their work. They both decided they would return to their native Leeds while maintaining connections with London. As you see, their lives seemed to parallel each other though it was not until they returned to Leeds that they actually met.

'When Mr Steel was in London he experimented with various styles of painting and drawing, particularly after he had come under the influence of a certain group of painters and writers known as the Pre-Raphaelite Brotherhood. They admired the style of fifteenth-century Italian art that defied the authority of Raphael, master that he was. This led them to go against present-day academic painting. They prize fidelity to nature, with detailed first-hand observation of flora and fauna as evidenced by this painting of Mr Steel's. They sometimes incorporate into their work religious, medieval or literary scenes, still with the same naturalistic detail as you see here. It is a style that is attracting attention and will no doubt be a significant part of art history in the future. If you want to follow this path you will have a good teacher in Mr Steel, but remember, and I am sure he will say the same, never, ever neglect your drawing. As you can see, this Pre-Raphaelite style in particular demands that.' Ebenezer sat back, highly satisfied; he knew Arthur had been hanging on to his every word. After a moment's thought he said, 'There endeth the lesson for the day.'

'Thank you, Mr Hirst.'

'Go away and think about it. Do some drawing and we'll meet again on Monday.'

'Yes, sir.' Arthur was relieved. He had feared that Mr Hirst might want to see him on Saturday and there was a cricket match to be played.

Chapter Four

Dr Felton Griffiths straightened and looked across the bed at his friend, Peter Shipley. He gave a slight shake of his head that conveyed a diagnosis he wished he didn't have to make.

Peter felt numb, as if all sensation had been taken from him. Even though it had been expected for the past fortnight, the loss of his beloved Margot was a terrible shock. A life, vibrant for thirty-six years, had been extinguished. He had shared fourteen of them with her, twelve as man and wife. Now he would no longer hold her in his arms and share the joys of love. No longer would her happy laughter ring throughout this house overlooking the River Tees. Already he could feel the heavy pall of desolation bearing down on it.

He felt a hand on his shoulder. 'Go to your children, Peter.' Dr Griffiths' voice was filled with quiet persuasion. 'Mrs Richardson and I will take care of things.' He glanced at the nurse whom he had recommended. She had attended Margot throughout her illness and was only too willing to give her own nod of agreement. She would do anything she could to ease the burden of loss and all that it entailed.

Peter knew Felton was right. His daughters would need him, yet he hesitated. He did not want to leave Margot. Surely she would wake at any moment? Even as that thought entered his head he knew it was a delusion. His eyes filled with tears but he fought them back, remembering the promise that she had wrung from him: 'Shed no tears for me. I will be free from this terrible pain.' He felt Felton's touch again, filled with sympathy and support and reinforcing his words: Go to your children.

Peter moved to the head of the bed, leaned over and kissed his wife's cold forehead then her cheek. He took one last look, trying to burn into his mind the image of her at peace. He walked slowly from the room.

On the landing he paused and leaned on the rail that gave him a view of the hall below. He could still see Margot running down those curving stairs to fling herself into his arms when he arrived home from work. He had had the vision to establish a foundry among the furnaces on the south bank of the Tees, had foreseen great developments there, and in this year of 1853 he was being proved right. But now the wonderful future he had envisaged with Margot lay in ruins. He heard girlish chatter coming from one of the rooms below and was reminded that he had to face his daughters. How did he break the news to seven-year-old Colette and her sister Adele, a year younger? Thoughts of them revived memories of the joy Margot had felt on telling him that she was to have the first child they had both longed for but had to wait five years for. Their happiness had been complete when a sister for Colette arrived the following year. So many dreams broken now.

The thought of shattering his girls' happiness filled him with dread. He crossed the hall and opened the door to the room he and Margot had set aside for the children. They were sprawled on the floor, a board game between them. Their governess was sitting in a chair watching over them. They all looked up when he came in.

'Papa?' They scrambled to their feet.

He gave an almost imperceptible nod, which the governess caught and understood. She walked silently from the room, her own eyes filling with tears. She knew she had lost not only an employer but also a friend.

Peter crossed the room, sat down in a chair and held out his arms to his daughters. They were already coming to him, for their young minds sensed that he needed them.

As his arms came round them Colette looked up at him, her expression older than her years. 'It's Mummy, isn't it?'

'Yes, love, it is. She's gone to Jesus.'

Adele frowned as if she could not grasp the meaning behind her father's statement. 'Will she be coming back?'

'No, silly,' snapped Colette impatiently. 'She can't, she's dead.'

The word hit Peter full force then. Truth from the mouths of babes!

Adele's frown deepened and she gave a little shake of her head as if her sister's bald statement was unbelievable.

'It's true, love,' said her father. There was sadness and hurt in his voice. How he wished he could have spared his daughters.

'We'll help you, Papa,' said Colette seriously.

He hugged them both tightly and said, 'We'll

94

help each other.'

At the time those words were being spoken, Arthur Newton was running in to bowl his first ball in the match that was underway on Chapeltown Moor. He was relaxed, could enjoy his cricket in the knowledge that, at least for the present, it would not interfere with his artistic aspirations. Mr Hirst's teaching and advice would resume on Monday. His first four balls were perfect and the batsman could do nothing but block them. When he turned to bowl the fifth Arthur received a shock. His concentration vanished. The batsman took full advantage of the badly delivered ball and hit it for six. The next one received the same treatment.

A surprised and perturbed Fred said quietly as they came together to field in the slips, 'What happened to you? Those last two balls were terrible.'

'Sorry,' muttered Arthur. He glanced across the field at the figure who was strolling round the boundary. Mr Hirst! What was he doing here? He hadn't said he would come to the cricket match. Would he be here at the interval and expect to be introduced to Mother and Father? Arthur hoped not. That would really upset things.

'You're looking troubled,' remarked Fred as he handed the ball to Arthur for his next over. 'What's wrong? No more balls like those last two. Concentrate!' The words were delivered with the full authority of a captain and Arthur knew he would have to give all his attention to his bowling. It took an effort but he succeeded. But though he bowled well and kept the runs down he had no penetration and after five overs Fred used another bowler.

Arthur was relieved for his attention was caught by the sight of Mr Hirst stopping close to where his parents were sitting. A few moments later he saw them talking to each other. His heart was in his mouth. What was going on? A quarter of an hour later he saw Mr Hirst raise his hat, move away and leave the moor. Arthur's mind eased but he was still anxious. What had they been talking about? At the interval he went straight to his parents and tried to be casual when he asked, 'Who was the gentleman you were talking to?'

'Don't know,' replied his father. 'He had come for a walk on the moor, saw the match in progress and strolled over to watch for a while. He wanted to know who was playing.'

'You were bowling at the time and your father made sure he knew you were his son,' Arthur's mother put in.

'Why not?' said Harold. 'I'm proud of him. He's a good cricketer.'

Arthur nodded and, showing no more interest, wandered off to his team-mates.

With another victory, Carter's Cricketers were in a good mood as they broke up to go their various ways, having extracted a promise from Fred to arrange another match as soon as possible.

'I'm going to walk home with Fred,' Arthur called to his parents.

'Very well,' replied his mother. 'Give me your things. There's no need for you to carry them when we are going on the horse-bus.'

'Thanks, Mother,' returned Arthur, glad to be relieved of them.

'I suppose you want me to take yours and go on the bus with Mr and Mrs Newton,' said Lizzie to her brother. She had been disappointed that Rose had not been at the match but, if she dropped a hint, maybe the Duggans would bring her next time. She knew Rose wouldn't take much persuasion when Arthur was playing.

'That would be great, sis,' said Fred, handing over his boots, bat and cap before she could change her mind. 'Come on, Arthur.' The two friends set off.

'What happened to your concentration today?' Fred asked.

'Remember how you all pulled my leg about dashing off from work to see a girl?'

'Yes. You said there wasn't one. Don't tell me we were right all the time?'

'You weren't. I did say that some day I would tell you what it was about.'

'You did.'

'I need your help, Fred.'

The note of desperation in Arthur's voice was not lost on him. 'What's this about? Are you in some sort of trouble?'

'Not exactly.' Arthur went on to explain about his sketching, how he had met Mr Hirst and its result.

'Sounds as though it's a great opportunity for you.'

'It is, and because visits to Mr Hirst may clash with helping you with the practice wicket, I have to tell you that I can't help every time.'

'That's all right, Arthur. Come when you can.'

'Thanks.'

'That's not much help to ask for.'

'There's more to it than that, Fred. My parents regard drawing as a waste of time. They don't stop me but show no interest. I know how it is; they see me in a good, safe job with a comfortable life ahead of me. I see their point but I want to be an artist. I really do.'

Fred grasped the situation. 'So if anyone questions where you have been, you want me say you have been helping me?'

'Would you. Fred? Please?'

'Of course. Then some day, when you are a great painter, I'll be able to say, "he never would have been if it hadn't been for me".'

'You certainly will.' Arthur grinned and gave him a playful punch. 'Thanks.'

'What about Rose? Lizzie tells me she's sweet on you. Doesn't she approve of your sketching?'

'She's as bad as Mother and Father. But I'll show her and everyone else.'

'Good for you! But there's one thing I do ask: don't let it affect your bowling.'

Arthur laughed and explained what had happened. 'I quizzed my parents between innings. Mr Hirst hadn't said anything about me, which was a relief. I'll find out on Monday what he was doing at the match.'

Arthur's steps were quick when he left the office on Monday. His thoughts ranged over yesterday's successful occasion when their new friends had

98

visited his parents. Everyone had thoroughly enjoyed themselves and readily agreed to a suggestion from Kevin and Beth Wainwright that, if the weather were suitable, they might spend the day by the river at Kirkstall Abbey after next Sunday's morning service. Maybe he would get the opportunity to sketch the ruin, but Arthur pushed that to the back of his mind as he approached Mr Hirst's shop.

'Good day, Arthur,' Ebenezer greeted him brightly when he walked in. 'Let's go through and get started right away.'

Arthur followed him eagerly but needed to ask a question before he settled down to his first lesson. 'Sir, did you enjoy the cricket match on Saturday?'

Ebenezer gave a small, knowing smile. 'Ah, I gathered you had seen me when you bowled two terrible balls in that first over. I'm sorry if it was my fault. Was it such a shock to see me?'

'It was, sir.'

'No doubt you were wondering if I was going to say anything to your parents about our arrangement.'

'I was. And I checked between innings.'

'And discovered I hadn't.'

'Yes, sir. I was relieved.'

'And now you are wondering why I was there.'

'Yes.'

'I have a mild interest in cricket myself. Knowing you were playing, I took the opportunity to see the people with whom you were associating. I wanted to get some idea, however small, of your background and how it might affect your art. Of course I hoped your parents would be there so that I could discreetly assess their general outlook. I must say, I learned a great deal. They are good people and I imagine that you have a happy home and, apart from their lack of interest in your art, a good relationship with them. From the way they talked about you, though your artwork was never mentioned, I can see that any opposition they raise is only out of concern for you and your future. They'd like to see you in the same sort of life they have formed for themselves: sound, solid and comfortable. There is nothing wrong in that. Many people would love to have such security. My conclusion is that the best way to win them over is to produce accomplished work and make a few good sales. Let them see that you are talented and can hope to profit by your art. Now, I have talked too much. We should get on with something. I think half an hour this first time, you don't want to be too late home.'

'Sir.'

Ebenezer produced one of Arthur's unfinished sketches. 'I would like you to finish this. It doesn't matter if it isn't an exact replica of the place you were sketching but use your imagination to make it a picture that satisfies you. Try to make it come alive. I don't expect you to complete it now but I would like to watch you at work. Then take it home and finish it to your liking.'

Arthur picked up his pencil and started to sketch. Without being intrusive, Ebenezer watched him. He saw quick, decisive strokes. There was no pondering; Arthur knew what he wanted and set about accomplishing it. The pencil marks gave the outline that had been there more shape and life, and Ebenezer saw a portrait of a place take on more solidity. He also realised that Arthur was beginning to shroud it in mystery. As much as he wanted to see that development take place, he called a halt.

'I think it is time you were going home.' He saw disappointment come into Arthur's face. 'I think it is for the best. We don't want your parents asking questions.' But Ebenezer's real reason for preventing Arthur doing more was to see if the pause interrupted his ideas to the extent that he could not recapture what he had in mind when he took up his pencil again. 'Try and finish it before you call tomorrow.'

The following day Ebenezer was more than pleasantly surprised by Arthur's drawing. The interruption certainly hadn't interrupted his ideas. He had seen what Arthur was intending and now before him was the fruit of the intention, and more. The scene was alive and yet retained a slight air of mystery that beguiled the observer. Oh, there were a number weak points in the technical aspects of the drawing, and immediately Ebenezer set about pointing these out. He saw the young man concentrating on his words and absorbing the information, something that became more marked in the succeeding days. Arthur was a fast learner and willing to work hard at his drawing. It was not always easy to gain the time he wanted; he had to be cautious at home and much of his drawing was executed after he had gone to bed. When he was not going to Ebenezer's he would use his spare time sketching buildings and scenes throughout Leeds. This began to give him a knowledge of the town and a feel for its atmosphere.

The visit to Kirkstall Abbey had been such a success that the families agreed to meet there a second time. As much as his fingers had itched, on that first occasion, to hold a pencil Arthur had curbed the idea so as not to upset his parents or Rose. But he had observed well and noted it in his mind. It was an ideal subject and he was not going to miss the opportunity on the second visit.

It was a pleasant sunny day, with a breeze that did not allow the heat to become too intense. A number of families had seized the opportunity for a day on the banks of the Aire. Once the friends had established their enclave by the river, Fred and Oswald wandered off throwing a ball between them. Ben's suggestion, that they should hire a boat and go on the river, was taken up by Lizzie, Giles and Celia, but Arthur refused, saying he would rather walk along the bank. Rose's immediate disappointment vanished with the realisation that she would have him to herself.

They fell into step, and when they were out of sight of their parents she let her hand slip into his and was pleased he did not draw away.

'I think Lizzie's made a hit with Ben,' commented Arthur, glancing in the direction of the boat in which they were sitting together while Giles rowed.

'She's very attractive,' said Rose.

'She certainly is.' He spoke as if he really had feelings for her.

'You keep your eyes off her!'

'You can't stop me thinking about her.' He brought a sultry tone to his voice.

Rose turned on him but then saw the teasing twinkle in his eyes. Nevertheless she gave him a retaliatory tap on the shoulder, and scolded him for teasing her. 'Arthur!'

He laughed. 'I had you worried!'

'You did not,' she replied indignantly.

'Yes, I did. You didn't see your face.'

His laughter was infectious and she had to laugh with him. Their fingers linked even tighter.

Ten minutes later Arthur stopped walking. 'Let's sit for a while.' He indicated a fallen tree.

She made no objection for she saw that this place was rather secluded. He was most solicitous in seeing that she was comfortable before he sat down beside her. Rose took his hand again. 'Arthur, this is the first time we have been together on our own since that day at the Carters'. You did mean what you said then?'

'What? That we are sweethearts?'

'Yes.'

'Of course we are.'

'That makes me so happy.' She kissed him lightly on the cheek.

His hands came on to her shoulders. He eased her closer and met her lips with his. After a moment they would both have pulled away from shyness but something spurred them on. Their lips trembled before meeting with a passion that raced through them.

'Oh, Arthur, that was wonderful! I love you so much. I know it now,' breathed Rose after the kiss.

He gave a gentle smile but his eyes said he felt the same. He sensed he had entered a new world and left his boyhood behind forever. He had kissed girls before but not in this way. Party-game kisses had been different. This one had sent sensations through him that he had never before experienced, and he liked them. He pulled her to him again and kissed her long and hard, enjoying the feel of her, pliant to his touch. By her response he knew that she too had entered a new world.

Finally, Arthur let his hands slip from Rose's shoulders. 'That's a nice view of the abbey,' he said lightly, fishing in his pocket. He took out a sketchbook and pencil.

'Arthur Newton! None of that.'

'Why not?'

'At a time like this when you and I...' She let the unspoken words emphasise her indignation.

'But if I don't do it now...'

'There are better things to do.'

'Our future lies in that.' He held up the pencil.

'Rubbish. How can it?'

She could not miss the serious light that came to his eyes. 'One day I will make my living by my art.'

'That's what you think.' Rose gave a grunt of derision.

'I will. Maybe it will take some time but one day my paintings will be bought.'

'You really think that?' There was a contemptuous note in her voice. 'More fool you if you do.'

'Oh, Rose, if only you would take some interest in my drawing.' He was almost on the point of telling her about Mr Hirst and his opinion but drew back. Mr Hirst was right; the best time would be when he had sold some of his work. 'If only you would look at it and try to understand.'

'What is there to understand? They're only pictures.'

'They are more than that.'

'If you say so.' She looked hard at him. 'I see you are bent on this, so I'll tolerate it, but if it gets in the way of other things you'll have me to answer to.'

Arthur did not like to be threatened but curbed the retort that sprang to his lips. Rose had made a concession and he was not about to ignore that. The door had been opened a little. He did not want to slam it shut. Maybe he could widen it further. Maybe one day Rose would open it for him.

'So I can do a sketch now?' he asked tentatively.

'If you must, but don't be long. We should be getting back.'

Arthur said nothing but quickly applied his pencil to the paper.

As they neared their group who were spreading out the picnic for everyone to help themselves, he said, 'Please don't tell anyone about the sketching.'

'I said I would tolerate it, so if that's what you want...'

'It is.'

Having added a little more to his sketch that evening he was anxious to show it to Ebenezer the next day. Saying that he had to be at work half an hour earlier than usual, he arrived at Mr Hirst's before the shop was open. His knocking brought a surprised bookseller to the door.

'Sorry to disturb you, Mr Hirst,' blurted Arthur, thrusting an envelope at his friend. 'I wanted to leave that on my way to work so you could have a look at it before I call on my way home this evening.'

Ebenezer grasped the envelope and before he could say anything Arthur had gone. Ebenezer gave a little smile and a slight shake of his head in admiration of the young man's enthusiasm.

Arthur bade his friends a quick farewell after work. He took no notice of the leg-pulling about whom he might be meeting and appreciated the fact that Fred joined in. His secret was safe there.

'Have you looked at it, Mr Hirst?' asked Arthur with undisguised desire to know what the art dealer thought.

'Indeed I have. From your attitude I detect that you are more than pleased with your sketch?'

Arthur's excitement dampened. Was this a way of saying that Mr Hirst did not like it? 'I was happy with it.'

'You were actually there?'

'Yes. I did a quick sketch of the abbey and finished it off when I went to bed.'

'It was immediately recognisable. I know Kirkstall Abbey very well. You have certainly captured it, and I see that you have added a little interpretation to try to instil atmosphere and a touch of mystery.'

'Do you like it?' asked Arthur, wanting to know what Mr Hirst really thought.

'I do. You have come on by leaps and bounds. I think Mr Steel should look at this. I went to see him today. He will meet you next Saturday afternoon. Have you a cricket match? Are you working?'

'Neither, sir. I will be free to see him.' The note of excitement in Arthur's voice could not be disguised.

'Good. Be here at two o'clock and I will take you to his house.'

'Thank you, Mr Hirst. Oh, thank you so much.' Arthur was shaking with excitement. 'I can't believe this is happening.'

'We won't have any more lessons this week, but continue with your drawing and work up one or two more similar to this in style but of different subjects that we can take along with this one for Mr Steel to see.'

'Very well, sir.

'Now off you go.'

Arthur picked up the envelope and when he reached the door stopped and offered more heartfelt thanks.

Ebenezer gave a jocular laugh and waved a dismissive hand. 'Off with you – and don't be late on Saturday.'

The euphoria that surged through Arthur quickened his pace on the way home. The urge to rush in and share his good news was almost overwhelming, but he could tell no one.

The coming meeting with Mr Steel occupied his thoughts during the week and even the dullest day did not appear gloomy to him. He was one day nearer meeting the man who had assumed such importance in Arthur's mind.

After making his excuse that he was going to

help Fred with his cricket pitch, Arthur left home in good time on Saturday. He did not want to be late.

When he entered the shop a lady greeted him and he immediately thought Mr Hirst must be ill, but her warm smile put him at ease.

'You must be the young man in whose artwork my husband sets such faith.'

'Arthur Newton, ma'am.' He liked this smartly dressed lady with the motherly demeanour. Her plump figure, round rosy cheeks and sparkling eyes signified that she treated life as it came, it would never get her down. 'I'm pleased to meet you.'

'My husband talks a lot about you,' she said as she went to the door that opened on to the stairs. She opened it and shouted 'Ebenezer, Arthur is here.'

'Very well, Zilda,' came a reply. 'I'll be down in a moment, love.'

She turned back to Arthur and said, 'I'm attracted by your work, it has great promise. I hope you like Mr Steel and get on well today.'

'Thank you, ma'am.' There was a nervous tremor in his voice as he tentatively asked, 'What is he like, ma'am?'

Zilda chuckled, trying to relieve the tension that she saw in Arthur. 'I'm sure you'll like Laurence. Don't be put off by first impressions. He will appear formidable, will say what he means in no uncertain manner, but a kind heart lurks inside him.' Any further information was halted by the sound of footsteps on the stairs.

'So, are we all ready, young man?' asked

Ebenezer as he made his entrance.

'Yes, sir.'

'Then we will away. Mrs Hirst will look after the shop.

Arthur shot her an appreciative glance. 'Thank you, ma'am.'

Ebenezer gave his wife a kiss and a tight hug. 'I'll miss you.'

'Give over, Ebenezer, you're embarrassing Arthur,' she chided in a gentle tone that signified she nevertheless approved of his demonstrative departure.

'He'll be doing it himself one day,' Ebenezer chuckled.

Arthur blushed and made for the door. He had not imagined Mr Hirst in this sort of role.

As they set off down the street Ebenezer said with pride and respect. 'A good woman, Mrs Hirst, a good woman. I am indeed a fortunate man. I hope you are as fortunate in your turn.'

All Arthur could splutter was, 'Yes, sir.'

Ebenezer decided to change the subject; enough had been said and he wanted the lad to concentrate on what lay ahead. 'How many drawings have you brought?'

'Six, sir, and my sketchbook.'

'Good. You have brought the one of Kirkstall Abbey?'

'Yes, sir.'

'And some I haven't seen?'

'Four, sir, and two you have, on which I would like to hear Mr Steel's comments.'

'Ah, you want to see if his assessment matches mine?'

'No, sir. I thought he might like to see them,' muttered Arthur, caught out by Ebenezer's astuteness.

He made no further comment but said, 'Don't be afraid to speak your mind. Mr Steel will expect that. He won't want you playing up to him by trying to say what you think he wants to hear.'

'Yes, sir.'

'And don't be nervous.'

'Can't help it sir.'

'I know. Don't worry. Everything will be all right. Here's our horse-bus.'

Arthur was beginning to wonder how far they were going as they moved from the maze of streets to more pleasant surroundings at the western edge of the town.

'Woodhouse, young man! Have you been out here before.'

'No, sir.'

'A fine area.' He indicated the many trees, some of which hung their branches over the high stone walls of secluded villas.

When they had left the bus they walked another fifty yards before Ebenezer pushed open a single-width gate let into a wall beside large double gates closing off a carriage drive. A stone path ran alongside the gravel drive to the front of a large house standing in its own well-kept grounds. The lawn was immaculate and the flowerbeds all recently hoed.

Halfway to the house Ebenezer stopped. Arthur turned, his eyes querying the reason for this. The look on Mr Hirst's face prevented him from speaking. He stood absolutely still for a few moments before Ebenezer said, in a voice that was almost a whisper, as if the silence should not be broken: 'Listen, Arthur.'

He inclined his head.

'Peace! Only the joyous singing of the birds and that really adds to the silence. What a wonderful place in which to be able to paint.'

'Aye, it is, sir.' He gave a little grunt of amusement. 'But I don't live here.'

Ebenezer started off again. 'But who knows? One day you might. Develop your talent, work hard, and you could live in a house like this.'

'You really think so, Mr Hirst?'

'I do, my boy, but let's see what Mr Steel has to say.'

Though the house was no bigger than the Carters' this one made a very different impression on Arthur when he stepped inside. The Carters' house had been pleasant enough, with everything of good quality, but this one held a different atmosphere; the decorations, the furniture and the way the house was set out had all been undertaken by someone with an artistic eye. It was as if whoever was concerned was expressing themself and their whole outlook on life.

A few moments after a servant had admitted them, a man emerged in haste from a room to the right.

'Ebenezer! So glad to see you.' He held out his arms and clasped him round the shoulders.

He was slightly taller and broader than his friend but still held a well-proportioned figure. His face was thin, the pointed chin covered by a small beard. It made it hard to judge his age but

111

Arthur knew that as Mr Steel and Mr Hirst had been at school together they must be near enough the same age. Besides, his eyes contradicted the impression given by the beard; they were lively, indicating a zest for life, constantly on the move, observing, seeking new ideas. But Arthur realised how steady they could be too when a few moments later they rested on him.

'So this is the young man you have been telling me about?'

'It is, Laurence,' beamed Ebenezer. 'Arthur Newton.'

Laurence Steel held out his hand. 'I have heard a lot about you, Arthur.'

Arthur shook hands, hardly daring to believe that he was doing so with such an important artist. He swallowed hard, not really knowing what to say, and blurted out, 'And I have heard of you, sir.' Then blushed, wishing he had spoken with more composure.

Mr Steel gave a small smile and with a friendly twinkle in his eyes said, 'Well, then, we have heard of each other so we should get along famously. Come, let us all go into the drawing-room. When Maria announced you I asked her to bring some chocolate as soon as she heard Mrs Steel come downstairs.'

This room spoke even more of Mr and Mrs Steel's artistic tastes. The paintings on the walls were positioned to attract attention. Mr Steel saw that they had just done that with Arthur.

'Have you painted these, sir?' Arthur asked tentatively.

'Ah, alas, I haven't. Let me point them out to

you and then you can look at them more closely, if you wish, until Mrs Steel arrives.' He was pleased to note the way Arthur had immediately noticed them and thought it augured well for his future in art even if his own talent did not develop as hoped. 'Sit yourself down, Ebenezer.' From the centre of the room he pointed to each painting in turn. 'That one is by Holman Hunt, the next by Dante Gabriel Rossetti. The next two are by John Millais, the final two by George Stephens and James Collinson.' He cast a glance at Arthur. 'You've never heard of them?' He inclined his head and gave him a small knowing smile.

'No, sir, I haven't.'

'Well, mark my words, one day you will. They are becoming influential in the world of art. Not everyone agrees with their ideas but...' He paused. 'This is not the time to go into that. Suffice for me to say that they influenced me when I was in London. I knew them, not intimately but they influenced my own development as an artist.'

'I can see similarities to the painting that was in Mr Hirst's window.'

'Ah.' Laurence raised an eyebrow. 'That's very observant of you. Do you like this type of painting?'

'Yes, sir.'

'Well, let me say this right from the start. You should not copy it slavishly, but if you want to use that particular technique with your own ideas and feelings, interpret it in your own way and put some of yourself into the picture...'

'Yes, sir.'

Laurence went to sit down but Arthur wan-

113

dered to the picture by Rossetti. He had been there but a few moments when he heard the door open. He turned to see Mr Steel and Mr Hirst rising from their chairs and a lady entering the room. Mrs Steel? 'Rowena, my dear,' Mr Steel greeted her, and went to take her hand.

Arthur felt transported into a different world. To be affected by someone so beautiful was a new experience for him. He had physically to force himself not to stare, but as Mr Steel brought her over to introduce them, Arthur realised that she was well aware of the effect she had had. Her smile revealed that she was not offended but rather flattered by the attention she had drawn from him.

'Rowena, this is Arthur Newton, the young man in whom Ebenezer sees talent he believes should be encouraged. Arthur, this is Mrs Steel.'

'I am pleased to meet you, Mr Newton.' She held out her hand.

He took it and a tingle ran through him as he felt its soft warmth, but also the firmness of friendship. 'And I ... I you, Mrs Steel.'

Her brown hair was shot with a natural copper tint that made it glow. She had drawn it from the back of the neck and piled it high on top of her head. It took little imagination to picture it loose, cascading over her shoulders, like a peat-stained stream in spate. Her oval face was perfectly proportioned. The smile which drew people to her, revealed dazzling teeth that were matched by the sparkle in her light-blue eyes. Rowena's gaze was direct, as if she wanted to engage fully the attention of the person to whom she was speaking, knowing they would not object.

She had certainly sent Arthur's mind along tracks they had never ventured before. He wondered where Mr Steel had met such an exquisite creature? Here in Leeds? London?

'Ebenezer.' She turned to him, the delight in her voice showing her pleasure at seeing him. 'How are Zilda and the family?'

'Very well. She sends her love.'

'Return mine.'

'I will indeed.'

'You must bring her over one evening. We'll arrange that before you go.' She glanced at her husband. 'You ordered chocolate, Laurence?'

She received her answer at the very moment of asking, for the door opened and two maids came in carrying trays.

'Do sit there, opposite me.' Rowena indicated a chair to Arthur. As they all sat down one of the maids was pouring the chocolate while the other left the room.

When the maid had finished she asked. 'Will that be all, ma'am?'

'Thank you. Maria. That is splendid.'

Though her accent was not marked Arthur realised that Mrs Steel must be from the Leeds area. In the general discussion, while they had their chocolate, Rowena and Laurence guided the conversation so that they learned much about Arthur. Though they made no comment they were struck by his enthusiasm to become an accomplished artist. For his part, Arthur, did not mind telling them what he felt and about his personal circumstances. They were easy to talk to and had immediately set him at ease. Besides, he would not mind sitting here all day so that he could listen to Mrs Steel; her voice was so soft and caressing, matching the gentleness of her nature.

When Laurence saw that everyone had finished their chocolate, he said, 'I think we have been keeping Arthur in suspense long enough. What have you brought us to see?'

He picked up the large envelope. 'I've brought six drawings and my sketchbook, sir.'

'Good.' Laurence looked at his wife. 'We'll sit on the sofa, my dear, then Arthur can show us his drawings one at a time. If he stands in front of us the light will be right.'

Rowena left her chair to sit beside her husband.

Questions which he did not want to voice were rising in Arthur's mind but Ebenezer answered them as if he had heard them. 'Mrs Steel is an expert critic.'

This explanation was enlarged upon by Laurence. 'My wife knew little of art until she met me. She showed interest from the moment I told her that my ambition was to become a good artist. Through her encouragement and support I achieved what I wanted. Without her I couldn't have done it. I would always have been competent, but it was her inspiration and belief in me that made me into the artist I am. Along the way she became a good judge of artwork. Now, let us see the first one.'

Arthur took the first drawing out of the envelope and held it up.

'Half a step closer, please,' Rowena requested. 'That's better,' she added when Arthur had moved to the new position. After a few moments

116

she said, 'The next one, please.' She saw a slightly surprised look tinged with disappointment come to Arthur's face. 'We make no comment until we have seen them all,' she explained.

Relieved, he nodded and displayed the next drawing. Half an hour later he showed them the last one, the study of Kirkstall Abbey.

'Thank you, Arthur,' said Laurence. 'Most interesting! Now we will look at each one more closely. Let us use the table.' He stood up and helped his wife to her feet.

Arthur went to the table and started to spread his drawings out.

'One at a time at first, and in the order we saw them,' Rowena interrupted.

He grew a little nervous as husband and wife again viewed each drawing in turn without comment.

Once they had seen them all Laurence said, 'Now spread them out.'

Arthur did as he was told and stood to one side while Mr and Mrs Steel studied the drawings again. Finally they straightened.

'You said earlier that there is no talent for drawing in your family?' said Laurence.

'That is correct.'

'Then God has given you an amazing gift,' said Rowena.

Arthur's heart soared. Amazing gift? They must like his work.

'How old are you?' asked Laurence.

'Seventeen, sir. I will be eighteen in January.'

'I would say that those two are your earlier works.' Rowena pointed to two of the drawings.

'Yes,' admitted Arthur, surprised that it was obvious to her.

'Those two are later and these two are the latest.'

'Yes, ma'am.'

'I can see the development in your drawing. And I would say the last two have been done since you made contact with Mr Hirst?'

'Yes, ma'am.'

'He is a good teacher. Pay heed to him in the future.'

'I will, sir.' He smiled at Ebenezer and in the returned acknowledgement saw pleasure and delight that the Steels had so commented.

'What can we do for this young man?' Laurence eyed Rowena questioningly. It was obvious that he set much faith in his wife's opinion.

She did not answer him but looked directly at Arthur. 'How much do you really want to be an artist?'

'It's my burning ambition, ma'am.'

'In spite of the antipathy at home?'

'Yes, ma'am.'

'It could lead to awkward situations with your parents, and also with the girl with whom you are friendly. You say she shows no interest in your drawing?'

He nodded. 'I am determined to win them over.' There was no doubting from his tone that he meant it.

'Good,' she approved.

'It will not be easy going,' Laurence pointed out.

'I am prepared for that, sir.'

'Having assessed your drawings and your determination, I would say that if you are willing to learn, work hard and not be diverted from your aim, you could be selling some paintings in two years and be reasonably well established by the time you are twenty-two.'

Arthur could not believe what he was hearing. His eyes widened in disbelief. 'You really think so?'

'Yes. But it is up to you. We cannot do it for you, nor can Mr Hirst. Only you can earn your success. We and Mr Hirst can guide you. The rest is up to you.'

Arthur's words of thanks were stumbling. He was overwhelmed by gratitude.

Rowena smiled and held up her hands to stop him. 'Now let us have a look at your sketchbook.'

He handed it to her and after she had looked through it she passed it to her husband. His comment was, 'Good. Arthur. You must keep this going. It is vital.

'I must emphasise again that you must not slavishly copy someone else's style. If you like a particular approach and want to emulate it that is permissible but the picture must have something in it that is purely yours.'

'I have seen one of Mr Steel's paintings at Mr Hirst's shop and now I have seen these on your walls, I would like to try for a similar style,' Arthur decided.

Rowena smiled. 'I thought you might.'

'I am not just saying that because...'

'I know that,' she interrupted. 'I realised from your drawings, especially from the last two and from the later sketches in your book, that it was possibly what you wanted to do. I think that probably came about after seeing my husband's painting. You saw in it something that would likely suit your innate style.'

'Well, now it's a question of where we go from here,' said Mr Steel. 'First, you must continue to draw, Arthur. The ability to do so is paramount, as you can see from these Pre-Raphaelite works. Secondly you will have to start painting.'

'With Arthur's difficulties at home, I will ensure that he is able to do that with me,' Ebenezer offered.

'Good,' Laurence went on. 'Thirdly, listen and interpret what Mr Hirst has to tell you. Fourthly, my wife and I would like to see your work again.'

Arthur was astounded. Tears were filling his eyes as he looked round at them. 'Thank you.'

'I suggest you come back in three weeks to show us what you have been doing,' said Rowena. 'Ah, but that might not be easy for you. From what Mr Hirst and you have told us you are an enthusiastic cricketer?' Arthur nodded. 'Have you a match three weeks today?'

'Yes.' Arthur's admission was tentative as if he wished he hadn't had to make it. 'And next Saturday,' he added.

'Very well, we'll say the Saturday in between. You must not give up your cricket. Outdoor activity is good for you, it will help relax your mind. Besides, it could be awkward if your parents were going to the match and you said you weren't playing. It could cause confrontation and we must avoid that. Upset of such a nature could affect your drawing and painting adversely.'

'You will realise that for yourself as you go

through life,' put in Laurence to emphasise the point. 'Harmony, even though it is not possible all the time, will be reflected in your work. Discord will disrupt it. If that is happening, get back to a harmonious relationship as soon as possible. Sweep discord under the carpet.'

Arthur looked a trifle sad as he said. 'It may take time to win over my parents and my sweetheart Rose.'

'Don't let that worry you,' Rowena comforted him. 'I am sure we will be able to convince them. For now concentrate on the work you are going to bring us in two weeks' time.'

'Yes, ma'am. Thank you. And thank you too, sir.'

Ebenezer rose from his chair. 'We had better be going, Arthur. We have taken up too much of these good people's time.'

Rowena was escorting Arthur to the door, giving him further encouraging words about his drawing.

Laurence whispered to Ebenezer, 'He reminds me of myself at his age.'

His friend gave a knowing smile. 'And because you weren't encouraged, you are determined to help him. I thought you might be. That's why I wanted you to meet him.'

'You're a wily bird,' commented Laurence. 'But I'll tell you this, Ebenezer, I wouldn't have encouraged Arthur if I hadn't seen genuine talent there. Nurture him well.'

Chapter Five

Christmas in the house between the River Tees and the Cleveland Hills was a sad time. Peter Shipley still had not come to terms with the loss of his wife. Try as he might he failed to find a reason why God had taken this wonderful woman in the prime of life and left his daughters motherless. He listened for laughter in the house but it had gone. Though he did his best to make Christmas a happy time for Colette and Adele, he knew they sensed the effort was forced and that they too missed the joyous presence of their mother. The new year of 1854 did nothing to lighten the atmosphere that had come upon the house, and by Colette's eighth birthday in February Peter had reached a decision.

He had seen how, through the death of her mother, his eldest daughter had grown up sooner than she should have done. Adele still held on to her childhood, for she had an elder sister to shield her. Peter knew he could speak seriously to his daughters and that Adele would follow her sister's lead.

After a birthday meal, at which he had tried to be light-hearted, he sat them down on the sofa in the drawing-room and pulled up a chair so that he could face them.

'I have something I want to tell you,' he began. With hands held together on their laps, the girls looked at him with round serious eyes. They looked so innocent and endearing that his words almost choked in his throat. He had to make an effort to make them sound as normal as possible.

'I have decided to move from this house.' In that instant, seeing the shock on their faces, he wished he had put it more tactfully but the words had just come out.

'Papa, you can't! It's our home!' Adele's protest was automatic.

'Why?' Colette was trying to understand.

'It has sad memories.'

'But happy ones too,' she reasoned before he could continue his explanation.

'It has, Papa, it has,' Adele burst out, following her sister's statement.

'I know it has,' he agreed, 'but I don't like that mixture. I think we should move and make ourselves a new home where we could make a fresh and happy life.'

'Will Mummy be there?' asked Adele.

Peter saw that Colette was about to admonish her younger sister for being silly so he answered quickly, 'Your mother will always be with us wherever we are, though we will not see her. I think she would want us to move.'

Colette tightened her lips and her young brow creased into a thoughtful frown. 'Maybe you are right, Papa. If you think that it is the thing to do then we shall have to pack.'

'Can I take everything?' Adele's next question was a seal of her agreement.

Peter inwardly heaved a sigh of relief. Apart from the initial natural reaction this had been easier than he'd thought.

'Where are we going?' asked Colette.

'I think we might go to Whitby.'

Both girls stared at him in amazement, not quite grasping the significance of this.

'Do you remember Whitby? We went there for a holiday three years ago. You liked it.'

Colette gave a little nod. 'Yes, I do. It was fun.' Peter could see her mind was busy elsewhere.

'I do too,' piped in Adele, but Peter knew his youngest had not fully recalled their days in Whitby.

'But what about your work?' asked Colette. He detected a suspicion in her that they were not going to live together.

'I won't be leaving you,' he hastened to reassure them. 'I will sell most of my assets in the foundry, keeping only sufficient interest to provide us with a regular income.'

'What's income?' asked Adele.

'Money, silly!' snapped Colette. 'Go on, Papa?' She looked back at her father with a serious expression.

'It won't be for some time yet. I will have to find a new house for us to live in, and settle all my affairs here. There will be lots to see to, and there will be a brief period when it would be easier if you went to live with Uncle Roger and Aunt Pauline for a while. Would you like that?'

'Yes, yes!' cried Adele, excitement coming into her voice. This was becoming a big adventure.

Peter laughed. 'What about you, Colette?'

She smiled. 'That would be nice, but only if it is what you want us to do.'

124

'I think it would be for the best when the time comes. I'll write to your uncle and aunt. I am sure they would love to have you. You always get on so well with them and your cousins.'

It was the second week in July when Peter took his daughters by coach to Banbury, choosing to use the slower coaches that allowed for two nights of stops on the way rather than travelling on in the dark. He deemed it wisest for them all to have as good a night's sleep as the excitement of the journey and the new experiences allowed.

By the time it came to leaving the house over-looking the River Tees the girls had grown used to the idea and helped to pack the clothes and toys that they wanted in Whitby. They were looking forward also to being with their uncle and aunt. They were not strangers to them for Uncle Roger had had an interest in the foundry and he and their aunt had lived nearby until two years ago when he had sold his interest, using some of the money to buy an estate near Banbury.

When they arrived in the market town in Oxfordshire Uncle Roger was waiting for them with his brougham. His driver, standing beside the horse, came to help them with the luggage being off-loaded from the stagecoach.

'Good to see you, Peter.' The brothers greeted each other with firm handshakes. Roger turned to his nieces. 'I hope you young ladies enjoyed the ride?' He squatted in front of them and held out his arms. They came to him and gave him a hug. 'We are going to have a wonderful time, starting off with a ride in my new brougham.' He

125

indicated the four-wheeled closed carriage on top of which the driver was securing their luggage.

'A fine-looking vehicle,' Peter commented.

'I'm pleased with it.' Ever practical, Roger pointed out one of its chief assets. 'See the curved opening underneath the driver's seat? Well, that enables it to be turned in a narrow space. Come on, young ladies, inside. We shouldn't keep your aunt waiting. She'll have a fine tea ready.' He opened the door and helped them into the carriage. As Peter climbed on board and settled himself opposite his daughters, Roger called to the driver, 'All well, Jenkins?'

'Aye, it is, sir,' came the reply as the man jumped to the ground.

'Then we'll be away. Straight home with all haste.' Roger climbed into the coach. Jenkins settled himself on his seat and, collecting the reins, sent the horse away.

'First things first,' said Roger with a smile, 'how long are you staying, Peter?' He glanced at his nieces. 'I know how long you two are staying - three months. You, brother?'

'A week, if that is all right with you and Pauline?'

'Right? It's more than right. She gave me instructions to try to persuade you to stay longer.'

'I'm afraid not. There are things that need doing to the house I have bought in Whitby and I should be there to see that they are done to my liking. When it is complete you must all come and stay, and from then on we'll pay each other frequent visits. It would be good for the children to keep in touch.'

'I couldn't agree more, and I know Pauline will

approve.' Roger looked at Colette and Adele. 'I have something to show you that I'm sure will amuse you.'

'What is it, Uncle Roger?' asked Colette turning her gaze from the window to him.

'Ah, that's my secret for the moment.'

'Oh, tell us, tell us!' cried Adele, anticipating an exciting surprise.

Roger laughed. 'No, young lady, you will probably have to wait until tomorrow.'

'Oh, no!' Both girls deflated like prickled balloons.

'It will be worth waiting for.'

'Will Papa like it?'

'I'm sure he will.'

Colette looked coyly at her uncle and gave him a sweet smile. 'You're teasing us, Uncle Roger, about having to wait until tomorrow. You are longing to show us whatever it is.'

Roger laughed. 'You are a wise young lady!'

The journey continued in a joyful mood, Peter enjoying the company of the brother who was two years younger than he. They had always got on well and were good for each other. He and Pauline had given him strong support in the days following Margot's death. They were of about the same build but Roger was not as handsome as his brother, though he made up for that with his exceptional charm and ability to make friends readily.

After twenty minutes the carriage turned through iron gates with the name Welland Hall worked into them. A gravel drive ran alongside immaculately kept lawns to the front of a moderately sized manor house of tasteful design. A flagged verandah with stone balustrade ran the full width of the façade.

As the carriage came to a halt at the front of the house the door opened and Pauline appeared with her three children, Anthea, Andrew and Augusta. Eager to welcome their cousins, they came rushing past her. At seven, six and five respectively, they had been looking forward to this day from the time they had been told that Colette and Adele were coming to stay.

Pauline opened her arms to her brother-in-law and hugged him. 'Welcome, Peter, it is so good to see you. And the children.' She turned to them, squatting down to give them both a hug, 'We're going to have a splendid time while you are here.' Her own children were dashing around eager to whisk Colette and Adele off to show them their latest toys. Pauline brought order with a gentle but persuasive command. 'Children, children, quieten down! You have plenty of time to show your cousins everything. The first thing you must do is to take them to their room. Let them see where they are going to sleep.'

'Yes, yes, yes!' they all cried.

'Come on, Colette, Adele.' Andrew, as the boy, felt he should take charge.

Pauline smiled and turned to one of the two maids who had come to help with the luggage. 'Sarah, you go with them, see that they get settled.'

'Yes, ma'am.' She picked up two of the bags and went after the children who had already streamed into the house.

'They will be busy for a while.' She took her

128

brother-in-law's arm. 'Let's go inside. John and Lucy will see to the rest of the luggage. Roger and I will show you to your room and then, when you have freshened up, come to the drawing-room for some tea.'

As they went inside Peter blessed the good fortune that had brought him such an endearing sister-in-law, one who was patently devoted to her husband and children. She was pretty with an open face that could hold no malice. Her smile never seemed to leave her, and her brown eyes, ever alert, reflected a love of life. She prided herself that in spite of childbirth she had kept a slim figure that showed to best advantage in close-fitted tasteful clothes. Peter was already feeling the calming effect of her gentle serenity and ability to love on many different levels.

Once the new arrivals were settled tea was served. Pauline calmed the excitement in the children and encouraged them to do justice to the meal so that Cook would be pleased her efforts had been appreciated.

When she had finished her last morsel of cake, Colette eyed her uncle. 'Uncle Roger, you said you had something to show us?'

He turned to his own children. 'You haven't said a word?' he queried.

'No,' they chorused.

He rose from his chair, left the room and returned a few minutes later. He stood so that everyone could see the sheet of paper that he held up.

'A sheet of paper with nothing on it?' Colette

could not hide her disappointment. She had expected something terribly exciting.

'There *is* something on it.' He turned the paper over.

'A picture.' There was disgust in Adele's voice. 'Is that all?'

'It's a special picture,' said Roger. 'It is what we call a photograph. It's made in a special way.'

'It's the front of this house.' Colette was now more interested, for she could see that it was not a painting, nor a drawing.

'That's right.'

'How did you do it, Uncle Roger?'

'Well, young lady, it's very complicated but while you are here, I'll tell you all about it.' He had sensed a genuine interest in her question and was determined not to let that go. He was a great believer that if someone possessed an interest and it was grasped at the right time, a spark could well be fanned into a flame and maybe kindle a future talent.

Before they could go any further there was a knock on the door and a young lady, smartly dressed and carrying an outdoor coat and bonnet, entered the room.

'I'm sorry I wasn't here, ma'am to greet your relations. I was delayed in the village.'

'That's all right, Isabel.' Pauline made the introductions and then explained to Colette and Adele that Miss Taylor was the governess and would instruct them as well as their cousins. 'I was about to send the children up to the nursery to play,' she continued.

'I'll take them, ma'am.'

'Do you want some tea first, Isabel?'

'Thank you. I can get a tray from the kitchen and take some up.' She looked round at her charges. 'Come on, children, let us go and decide what you are going to do.'

They left the room with the children making all sorts of suggestions.

'We are fortunate in Isabel,' explained Pauline. 'She'll see that Colette and Adele are well looked after and that their education is not neglected while they are here.'

'This is most generous of you, Pauline.'

'Not at all. What are relations for?'

'Indeed. If you cannot come to your brother and sister-in-law in time of need, who can you turn to?' Roger supported his wife.

She rose from her chair, and the brothers in deference did likewise. 'I've some things to see to. Why don't you two take a stroll outside? It is still pleasant.' She headed for the door. 'I'll see you in a short while.'

The brothers strolled outside, paused on the terrace and then took to the lawn in front of the house.

'What did you think to that photograph?' asked Roger.

'Truly wonderful. I've heard of this new development but not taken any real interest in it. Hadn't the time.'

'You should. It would give you an interest when you move to Whitby. If you did it might encourage Colette and Adele to take it up too.'

'How did you become interested?'

'That photograph and some more I will show

131

you were taken by a friend who is really enthusiastic about what he calls the new art form. He considers it could be a big help to artists, though as I understand from him there are contradictory ideas about that.'

'Who is this friend?'

'Thomas Westbury. His estate borders mine to the east. Decent fellow. Rode over here just after we moved in to make himself known and offer any help and advice he could. He knows the area well, his estate has been in his family since shortly after the Civil War. His wife's a charming woman and has been a good friend to Pauline.'

'His interest in photography?' Peter prompted.

'Ah, yes. He met a fellow called Fox Talbot at Cambridge. He was a bit of an amateur artist who had used a Camera Obscura to help his landscape paintings, but was experimenting with other photographic processes. Thomas has a scientific bent and got interested. He's passed his enthusiasm on to me.'

'Good. You want something to do other than looking after your estate. So what does this photography entail?'

'It's complicated but there is so much experimentation going on that it is constantly becoming easier to take and print photographs like the one you've seen. Fox Talbot had made paper light-sensitive with the result that from the negative he produced he was able to make any number of positives by putting sensitised paper in contact with the negative and exposing it to light. Better results were obtained when waxed paper negatives were used. Now we have moved on to a process for making glass negatives and producing paper prints from those. You get better results but the processing is still a little awkward. I can see this problem being overcome one day and then processing will become easier and simpler, as well as the nature of the equipment we use to take the photograph.'

'You are confusing me somewhat, but no matter. No doubt you'll enlighten me whilst I'm here. Do you intend to invest in this pursuit?'

'I have given it some thought but have decided against. I really don't want to involve myself financially, but I will maintain an interest in it purely as a hobby.'

'I suppose there's plenty to keep you occupied on the estate from the point of view of income?'

'Yes, I run forty head of cattle beside a stable of ten mares and two stallions. The estate isn't big but it does include a village of twenty houses which means twenty paying tenants minus, of course, the cost of keeping the property in good repair. What about you? How are you going to keep yourself occupied in Whitby?'

'I don't really know. Financially I can afford to live as a man of leisure.'

Roger gave a little chuckle. 'You won't rest easy until you find something to do.'

'I haven't examined the situation in any depth yet. Maybe I could invest in a jet workshop, but I would need a good foreman who really knows and loves the trade. I know nothing about it. It would only be an investment, something to occupy my mind.'

'Is there a demand for jet?'

'I believe so from the few enquiries I've made.'

'It could be worth thinking about once you've got settled in.'

'The house should be vacated by the time I get back. Then I'm going to make some alterations so it will be best if the girls are out of the way. I'm grateful to you and Pauline for taking them.'

'It's a delight. Peter. We are only too pleased to have them and I'm sure mine are pleased to have someone else to tear around with. If things get held up in Whitby, as they often do in the building trade, don't hesitate to tell us and we'll keep them until all is ready.'

As it turned out that was exactly what happened and their stay, which should have finished in October, spilled over into December. When Pauline suggested that Peter should join them for Christmas and stay with them to see the New Year, he readily agreed, knowing that it would make for a much more enjoyable time for Colette and Adele in contrast to last Christmas.

Snow began to fall on Christmas Day and persisted well into 1855. It was not until the first week in March that travel north became possible again.

Colette and Adele were gloomy at the thought of leaving their cousins but, once goodbyes were said and invitations made for them to visit again, the excitement of seeing a new home in a new environment began to dominate their journey. Their persistent questions about it brought only the mildest of rebuffs from their father. 'I'm not going to tell you too much because I want it to be a surprise but it is in a splendid position overlooking the river with a view of the town beyond on the opposite bank. I think you'll like Whitby. Because it is an important port there is always a lot going on there.'

'Lots of ships?' queried Adele enthusiastically, the thought of the sea stirring her imagination.

'Lots,' he replied.

'They'd be good subjects for photographs,' said Colette. 'Can I have a camera to take them?'

Peter smiled. He too detected a genuine interest. 'Uncle Roger told me you had become fascinated.'

'Yes, Papa. It's magical! Uncle Roger took me to see Mr Westbury several times and he was delighted to explain everything and let me try. I know how to do it, Papa, I do. I'd love to try it myself. Please let me?'

'Now, I do not know what exactly it entails, what equipment you would need, but I'll promise you this. We'll come back to Welland Hall before very long and I'll talk to Uncle Roger and Mr Westbury then.'

Colette knew that was a firm promise and, realising she would get no further at the moment, let the matter drop, but was determined that she would not let her interest in photography wane. Apart from the magic of making pictures, she had been attracted by what she had heard when her uncle and Mr Westbury were discussing the future of photography.

They reached Whitby two days later, Peter having decided, as he had done on the journey south, to seek the comfort of a good night's rest in two well-appointed coaching inns.

They disembarked at the Angel in Whitby and Peter immediately hired a carriage to take them to his new house.

'Is it far?' Colette asked.

'No, love, it's just a short distance. We could easily walk it but we have all the luggage.'

The carriage pulled up in front of a row of brick houses known as New Buildings set back from the road.

'This is it,' said Peter, with a touch of pride, hoping his daughters would like the house. He helped them from the carriage. They stood staring at the building without moving.

The carriage driver came to see to the luggage. Observing their thunderstruck attitude he said quietly, 'Welcome home, young ladies.'

His voice jerked them out of their trance. 'Thank you,' they said politely but their enquiring expressions brought an explanation from him. 'Your father told me you were coming to a new home. I hope you'll be very happy here.' He turned to Peter. 'I'll bring the luggage in, sir. You take your daughters.'

Peter pushed open the gate, and, taking their hands, led them along a short path between flowerbeds towards the front door. A small porch was formed by pillars supporting a balcony with an ornamental iron parapet. Access from the first floor was through a glass door that matched the large sash windows to either side. Similar windows were positioned to either side of the front door and across the second floor. The woodwork had been freshly painted and glistened in the sunlight that gave the brickwork a warm glow.

'It's lovely, Papa,' said Colette.

'It is,' reiterated Adele, following her sister's example.

'Good. Let me show you the inside.'

He ushered them through the front door and there they found two women and three girls lined up ready to greet them.

One woman stepped forward, her hands held in front of her over a plain black dress that had no adornment except for a white lace collar and matching cuffs. Her black hair was drawn back in a bun. Her whole appearance was one of severity but when she spoke, not only with her voice but also with her eyes, the severe impression disappeared in an instant.

'This is Mrs Fenton, our housekeeper.' Peter made the introduction and went on to Mrs Vasey, the cook, a stout woman with round rosy cheeks, a bright smile and motherly disposition. The girls were sisters of eighteen, seventeen and sixteen, Charlotte, Hannah and Helen. Though initially wary of having to look after two motherless children their fears were soon dispelled and they realised they were going to be happy in their new job.

Colette and Adele made polite acknowledgements and then their father, anxious to show them the rest of the house, whisked them away.

Their excitement mounted as he showed them the drawing-room, dining-room, and a third room that had been set aside exclusively for them. They each had a bedroom. He would have one on the same floor and the other room on that floor was to be for the governess who would be arriving in a week's time. 'I thought I would let

137

you get used to the house first,' their father explained. To their enquiry as to what she was like he would only say, 'I think you will like her. Miss Lund is coming from Scarborough, just a few miles down the coast.'

He showed them the rooms on the second floor occupied by Mrs Fenton and Mrs Vasey, and above these in the large roof space were beds and furnishings for the three maids.

'Well, what do you think?' asked Peter as they came downstairs.

'It's lovely,' they both chorused.

'I want you to be happy here.'

'You too, Papa.'

He could almost hear their unspoken words: 'If only Mama could see it.'

He hugged them to him and with damp eyes whispered, 'If only.'

They knew he had read their unspoken thoughts and gave him a loving hug that all three held for a few minutes.

A week later, by which time everyone had settled in, a carriage pulled up outside. Colette and Adele, anticipating its arrival, were looking out of the window in Colette's bedroom. They saw a young lady step down from the carriage.

The driver handed her two valises. She stood them on the ground and surveyed the house. She saw the girls at the window, smiled with pleasure and waved. Instinctively Colette and Adele, not expecting to be seen, drew back but a moment later peered out again. The young lady was still looking at the house. She waved again. The sisters hesitated a moment then Colette waved back and

Adele followed her sister's lead. The young lady smiled then picked up her bags and started towards the front door.

Colette watched for a few moments. The lady, who could be no more than twenty-one or two, was dressed in a plain light blue dress that fell from the waist in pleats. Her short jacket of dark blue was trimmed with white fur. Her bonnet was small and revealed light brown hair. She walked with a confident step.

The newcomer was halfway to the house when Colette made a sudden dash for the door of her room. She flung it open and was running down the stairs before Adele reached the landing. 'She's here, she's here!' shouted Colette.

As she reached the bottom step, her father appeared from the drawing-room. 'Colette! That's no way for a young lady to behave. Compose yourself.'

She pulled herself up, but excitement still gripped her. 'She waved, Father, she waved.'

'All right. Calm down. You too, Adele.' He glanced at his younger daughter who had nearly tripped trying to catch up with her sister.

Peter went to the door and opened it just as the young lady was about to attract attention with the bell-pull.

'Oh!' She was taken aback that the door should be opened by the man who had interviewed her.

'Miss Lund. My daughters saw you from a window and warned me in no uncertain manner that you had arrived.' He stepped to one side, allowing her to enter the house.

'I saw them,' she said with a smile. She placed

her bags on the floor and crouched down. 'You must be Colette, and you Adele,' she said, looking at each in turn.

Adele screwed her face into a puzzled expression. 'How did you know?'

'Well, when your father interviewed me, he said his elder daughter was called Colette and she is bigger than you, you see.'

Adele pursed her lips, nodded and held out her hand. 'I'm pleased to meet you.'

'I'm Miss Lund.' She took the proffered hand.

'Don't you have a first name?'

'Yes. I am Susan.'

'But you will call her Miss Lund,' warned their father.

Susan turned to Colette. 'I am pleased to meet you too, Colette.' She shook hands and felt the desire to be friendly in the girl's touch.

'I'm sure we will get on well.' Susan Lund straightened up. She had detected a serious nature in Colette and felt she was in the presence of a girl who, though still young at heart, was older than her years in many ways. She put this down to the fact that Colette had felt the loss of her mother deeply and automatically adopted a role with more responsibility.

'Ah, here's Mrs Fenton.' Peter broke up the little cameo on seeing the housekeeper. He made the introductions and then said, 'Mrs Fenton, will you show Miss Lund to her room and then around the house and explain its running?'

'Certainly, Mr Shipley.'

'Can we go too?' asked Colette.

'Yes, please,' cried Adele.

140

Peter was about to refuse permission but Susan spoke up. 'I don't mind, Mr Shipley. It will give me an opportunity to get to know your daughters more quickly.'

'Very well,' he approved, seeing the wisdom of her statement.

Peter had become so engrossed in his newspaper that he did not realise that an hour had passed since Miss Lund's arrival until she walked into the drawing-room with his daughters. She had changed into a dress of pale yellow with a green motif of intertwining ivy. Her hair, free from its constricting bonnet, was swept loosely to the top of her head.

Peter jumped from his seat. 'Is everything to your liking, Miss Lund?'

'Delightful, Mr Shipley. I have had two very good guides in your daughters, and of course in Mrs Fenton who has acquainted me with the running of the house.'

'Oh, dear I have neglected you. Have you had some refreshment since you arrived?'

'Oh, yes, sir, Cook had a tray ready for my arrival.'

'Good, good. I hope these two haven't been in the way?'

'Not at all, Mr Shipley. They have been with me all the time. It has been a good way to get to know them. I am sure we are going to get on well.'

'Do sit down.' He indicated a chair opposite his. He noted that his daughters were about to sit on the floor at the new arrival's feet. It pleased him, and he was sorry to have to disturb them.

141

'Girls! Run along to your own room. I would like a chat with Miss Lund in private.' They pulled dissatisfied faces but did as they were told. When the door closed, he smiled. 'They did not like that. Now, as I explained at the interview, because you will have so much contact with the children I want you to feel part of the household. As you will have seen, the girls have a downstairs room of their own but they also share this one with me. You must feel free to do the same.'

'Thank you. It is a delightful room. I will use my discretion whenever you have company.'

Peter gave a wry smile. 'There is little of that at the moment, with our having just moved to Whitby.'

'I'm sure that will soon be rectified.'

He made no comment but said only, 'As I told you, you dine with us as one of the family. Occasionally I invite Mrs Fenton to dine with us, generally when there are household matters to discuss, but mostly I leave the running of the house to her. She has a property in another part of Whitby left to her by her late husband. He had just been made captain of a whaler, quite an achievement for one who was only twenty-nine. Sadly his first voyage to the Arctic ended in disaster where there was an unusually severe storm. Mrs Fenton likes to spend time at her own house and there is no reason for her not to when she has seen to everything here. She is a very conscientious person.'

'I could tell that when she was showing me round.'

'Is there anything else you wish to know?'

'I don't think so, Mr Shipley. I have been well

briefed by you all.'

'Well, if there is, don't hesitate to ask. I leave the education of my children to you. All I ask is that they become pleasant people with a good all round knowledge, able to take their place in a world that is rapidly changing. I can see attitudes to the role of women in the world altering year by year. The outstanding work of Miss Florence Nightingale in the Crimea is a case in point. I'd like my daughters to be able to be strong and independent-minded.'

'Indeed I am pleased to hear that, sir. The attitude to governesses also is changing. People like yourself who do not regard us as servants have made our role much more agreeable. There are further spheres in which I think women will begin to play important roles but in many others it will take much longer to break down the bastions of male prejudice.' Susan Lund pulled herself up short and blushed. 'Oh, dear, Mr Shipley, I'm afraid I'm sounding off.'

'Not at all, Miss Lund. It gives me an insight into your forward-looking views.'

'I am sorry if you do not approve?'

'Oh, but I do. If I had not had a tiny glimpse of them at the interview I may well not have appointed you. I too am radical in my outlook and that is why I wanted someone who would not treat my daughters as creatures who should remain subservient to the male sex. I want them to become aware of the changing world and what it might mean to them.'

'I will do my best for them. So may I ask you about Colette's interest in photography? It is unusual in one so young.'

'Ah, she has told you about that. I thought her enthusiasm might wane after our return to Whitby but it has not. In fact, if anything, it is stronger than ever. Do you know anything about it, Miss Lund?'

She gave a little shake of her head, making the light gleam on her hair. 'Not the practical side, but I have seen some exhibitions and they fascinated me. I realised from talking to people attending them that photography is going to be important in the future. It will have all sorts of uses. Not only that, but as it grows more widespread and people take it seriously I can see it is something in which women could play a role. A woman is just as capable of taking a photograph as a man after all. I would suggest that if Colette's interest continues we should encourage it. She tells me that she has asked you for some equipment.'

'She has, and I promised her that I will take the matter up when we next visit my brother, of whom, no doubt, she has also told you.'

'Yes, she did.'

'Then the next time we visit his family you must come too. If Colette is to follow this pursuit you should be there to learn something of the practical side.'

'Thank you, Mr Shipley. I really think I should go to the girls now. I have taken up too much of your time.'

'Not at all, Miss Lund. It has been a most revealing talk and I am sure the education and welfare of my daughters are in good hands.'

Susan's cheeks reddened as she rose from her

144

chair. She sensed that she would look back on 12 March 1855 as an important day in her life. 'You flatter me, sir. I hope I will not let you down. They are most delightful children.'

Chapter Six

Arthur paused in front of Mr Hirst's shop. All the joy of coming here rapidly drained from him. His watercolour of Kirkstall Abbey was no longer in the window where it had been for the past week. Feeling despondent, he pushed the door open and stepped inside.

He was met by a jubilant Ebenezer. 'I've sold it, Arthur, I've sold it!'

He stared in disbelief. 'You've...?'

'Sold it!' Ebenezer cried as he gripped the young man's arms.

The information finally hit Arthur and drove his gloom away. Why had he assumed the worst when the picture was no longer in the window?

'Wonderful, Mr Hirst! Wonderful!' His eyes were bright with joy, on his face a broad smile in which there was relief that all his determination, learning and hard work had borne this result. For him 12 March 1855 would always remain a memorable day.

During the past eighteen months it had not always been easy to fit in his art studies. His promotion to junior clerk had brought praise from his family and they had pointed out that a

145

good sound future with the railway awaited him. He had no doubt that they were right but that was not what Arthur wanted. He longed to break down their mere tolerance of his drawing and ignite a spark of enthusiasm. Maybe the sale of this painting would do that.

Maybe it would enthuse Rose, and with her backing he could well gain the approval of his mother and father. But there was doubt in his mind about this. He and Rose had become closer. Since she had taken up the piano he had escorted her to musical concerts in the town. He hoped by his doing so she would wish to reciprocate and take more interest in visiting art galleries, but she showed no such enthusiasm, only boredom, and was always eager to be away. He never protested; he liked Rose and after all they had known each other since childhood and both sensed that marriage was becoming more and more expected of them.

Most of his drawing was done in the quiet of his bedroom when he had supposedly retired for the night, but he found that whenever Rose had piano lessons he could escape to sketch outdoors or use the time to paint in the small studio that Ebenezer had set up for him behind the shop. Here he learned to develop his range and Laurence Steel would occasionally visit him to monitor his progress. Arthur's work was beginning to show Steel's influence, which in turn reflected that of the Pre-Raphaelites. And whenever he and Ebenezer had visited the Steels, Arthur had found Mrs Steel's criticism and suggestions most helpful. She was very knowledgeable of new trends in the art world.

'You are developing an attractive style, Arthur, and I am pleased to say that you are putting something of yourself and your interpretation of a particular scene into your work,' Ebenezer told him now. 'It was that which attracted this customer who readily paid two pounds for the Kirkstall Abbey study.'

'Two pounds?' Arthur's eyes widened in amazement. Someone had actually paid two pounds for something he had painted? He couldn't believe it.

'Not a princely sum, I agree, Arthur, but it is a start.' Ebenezer had misread his remark.

'No, no, Mr Hirst, I'm not disappointed but rather delighted. As you say, it's a start. I'll never forget this day, or how you and Mr Steel have helped me. I will be ever grateful to you both.'

Ebenezer gave a dismissive wave of his hand. 'I'm only too pleased to have found such talent and to help it. I know Mr and Mrs Steel feel the same.'

'Now I might get my family and Rose interested.'

'Hold on, Arthur.' Ebenezer raised his hands to caution him. 'This may not be the time.'

'But surely they'll see things differently now I have made a sale?'

'It is only one – your first.'

'You think there may not be any more?' Arthur's alarm and disappointment were obvious.

'No,' replied Ebenezer firmly, wanting to reassure him quickly, 'I believe you will sell many more but I think it would be better to make some further sales, either through this shop or by

147

exhibiting at public gatherings and society meetings, before telling your family.'

Arthur's eyes brightened as his disappointment fell away. 'If I'm exhibiting I'll not tell them but will suggest we go to the function. Seeing my paintings on display will surprise them and make them see that I am serious.'

'That's the idea, and it will be a good time for me to meet your parents and explain what has been happening and what I think the future holds for you.'

'Yes. I only hope I can keep my present excitement under control!'

Ebenezer laughed. 'I'm sure you will. Concentrate on what you are going to do next.'

'Another like the one I sold?'

'No, something different, but I am sure that you will do more of Kirkstall Abbey, interpreting it in many ways.'

'I'd like to do more of Leeds.'

'All in good time. For the immediate future, say over the next month, I would like you to return to what you were doing in our early days together – gathering stones, twigs, moss, grasses and so on, bringing them here, placing them in pleasant compositions and painting them.'

'But isn't that a backward step?' protested Arthur who had a desire to do more landscape paintings.

'Not at all. I want to see how you have progressed and to assess how much you have absorbed of the techniques Mr Steel showed you.'

Arthur said no more. He knew he owed a great deal to Ebenezer. Yes, it would be an interesting experiment to return to subjects he had first attempted shortly after meeting Mr Hirst and Mr Steel.

A month later, with Rose having a piano lesson and the cricket season not yet having started, Arthur arrived at the shop expecting to paint some leaves and fruit he had brought along with him only to find that Ebenezer had laid out some of his early work alongside that which he had completed during the last month.

'See the difference, Arthur?'

He stared at the paintings for a moment, struck by the contrast. 'I wouldn't have believed it.' He glanced at his mentor.

Ebenezer smiled. 'I thought you'd be surprised. You have been much more observant of your subjects. Your latter work carries far more detail and is the better for it. Rather than providing a general impression, which many artists are good at, your detail and the way you have executed it makes your recent work feel much more lively. I feel I could touch that leaf, that twig, which I could not in your earlier work. I expect that feather to blow away at any moment, it is so delicate. I would like to see how you can transfer the technique you have shown in these paintings to landscapes.'

'Now?' An enthusiastic note had come to Arthur's voice.

'Why not? Make up a landscape from your imagination, see how you get on.'

Ebenezer left him to it, returning now and again to see how the painting was developing but making no comment. After two hours he called a halt. 'I know you haven't finished it but there is sufficient there for me to make a judgement.'

He looked carefully at the picture, relating it to the development he had observed throughout the afternoon. Arthur had depicted a Norman church partially hidden by trees in autumn tints with ivy climbing up one wall. Gravestones, covered by moss and ivy, leaning at various angles, occupied the foreground.

'I like the detail you are putting into the natural elements; it not only brings life to the picture but also adds to the atmosphere.' He gave a little nod. 'Yes, I feel I am in the churchyard, that I have to move quietly through it. If anything, I think you have made some of your colours a little too bright but they might tone down to the eye when you have completed the stonework of the church. Execute that in the same sort of detail that you have applied to the other objects.

'I would add one word of caution that comes not only from seeing this but from what I have observed in some of this work.' He indicated the paintings of the last month.

'Don't overdo the detail. Learn what is sufficient to suit your style and subject. What I suggest is that between now and the end of the year you produce paintings of real places. Get out and about, draw, make notes, so that you can come back here and paint them. I have in mind that we might exhibit early in the New Year.'

'Arthur, do you have to draw now when everyone else is going on the river?' Rose pulled a face in exasperation that he was spending precious time sketching. 'I gave up a piano lesson because I thought you wanted to come on this picnic with our friends.'

The friends had gradually paired off. Ben and Lizzie's friendship deepened after that first meeting; then it seemed natural that Fred should show interest in Ben's sister, Grace; Giles introduced a friend, Barbara, and Jack a girl called Dorothy. Rose and Arthur made up the final pair.

Arthur said nothing. He stood up and pushed the book into his pocket, thinking, Anything for peace and quiet. But one day, Rose Duggan, you'll thank me for this book. It wasn't that he didn't enjoy himself with her, he always did; he had the ability to compartmentalise his mind, enabling him to switch from one activity to the other as if there had never been an interruption.

Arthur had become skilful at treading warily but looked forward to his first exhibition so that he could come clean with his family. It came as some relief when in October Ebenezer announced that he had secured permission for Arthur to exhibit three paintings at a bazaar in Leeds Town Hall in January. The excuses and deceit would soon be over. He would be able to pursue his art openly, but would first have to find a way to persuade his family and Rose to visit the bazaar.

He seized his chance on Boxing Day when according to tradition the Newtons spent the afternoon and evening with the Duggans. The frosty air seemed to put his mother and father in a light-hearted mood as they walked to their friends'. The ground had been thinly coated with frost, forming icy patches where damp had lingered from yesterday's light rain. It provided the young people with the opportunity to slide and they arrived at the Duggans' in high spirits. They were welcomed with Christmas bonhomie. Once everyone was settled, Conan charged glasses with wine or home-made lemonade.

'Is Arthur allowed to partake of this Spanish wine?' he asked.

'Why not?' approved Harold, noting that Conan had allowed Rose to have some. 'He's a wage-earner. For all I know he may well have supped with his friends before now.'

Arthur did not rise to the gentle question but accepted a glass graciously.

The room filled with chatter and hilarity befitting their companionship and the festive atmosphere. Everyone agreed when games were suggested. Moira Duggan produced a slipper to hide along with a reward for the one who found it; there was a great deal of teasing and laughter when they played Hot Cockles, which was followed by a more sober game of Charades. Finally Mr Duggan amused and mystified them with some card tricks he had been practising throughout the year.

The table laid out in the dining-room brought gasps of appreciation at the fare that Moira had provided from the shop. Arthur was pleased to see that it added to everyone's good humour, further heightened when Con produced crackers and everyone vied to show what theirs contained then proceeded to swap paper hats, puzzles, games, masks, fans, perfumery and other trinkets. After-wards they returned to the drawing-room where they split into groups and played cards. With those games completed there was a call for Mr Duggan to tell them some Irish stories. They had heard them all before but always revelled in Con's story-telling and knew that he was not beyond adorning them with his own embellishments. He broke off in the middle of one story to carry in the wassail bowl.

'This year we've made it in the old way, hot ale mixed with roasted and crushed apples, sugar, eggs, nutmegs, cloves and ginger,' he announced, immediately setting off everyone's desire to try it. 'Only a little for you two young ones,' he said, looking at Celia and Oswald.

Dissatisfied at not being treated like adults in the same way as Arthur and Rose, they showed their disapproval but a glance from their mother soon dispelled that attitude.

Everyone praised the mixture and Arthur was pleased that it was putting everyone in an even better mood and inspiring confidence in him to make his own suggestion.

'Two more stories,' said Conan, 'then we'll have Rose play the piano and maybe follow that with Harold playing for a sing-song.' His suggestion brought shouts of approval.

As these quietened down and Conan was about to resume his story-telling. Arthur said, 'Can I ask you all something?'

There were surprised looks at this request.

He cleared his throat. 'A lady who works in one of our offices has a stall in aid of her church at a bazaar in the Town Hall a week on Saturday. She has asked everyone employed in the railway offices to go to the bazaar and support her. Would you all come?'

There was moment's silence while everyone considered the request then Harold said buoyantly. 'Why not? Yes, we'll come, Arthur. It'll be a nice afternoon out.'

'I shan't be able to,' said Conan. 'The shop. But there is no reason why Mrs Duggan and Rose can't go.'

'Right, Arthur, we'll all go together,' agreed Moira.

He felt a surge of relief. That had been easier than he had expected. He hoped no one would change their mind and that there would be no thick snow on the day.

After work the following day he called at Mr Hirst's to tell him that his family and Rose and her mother would be coming to the bazaar.

'You haven't told them that you are exhibiting?'

'No.'

'Good. It will be a surprise – a pleasant one, I hope. I'll be there. You are happy with the three that you have chosen?'

'Yes. Are you?'

'I think that you have chosen wisely. I like that new one of Kirkstall Abbey, the one you have entitled *The Glen* is particularly attractive but I think my favourite is this one, which you have identified as *A Walk at Roundhay*. I think the composition is masterly; the way our eyes wander round the picture through the shadows of the late afternoon, to settle on the two people absorbed in their own company so that the viewer feels almost an intruder. The figures are well placed and I like

154

the way the cold stark trees help to give movement contrasted by the soft warm pink glow of the slight snowfall on the ground. The oncoming moonlight spreading its silvery tones gives the atmosphere a peaceful but slightly foreboding tone, which makes us wonder what will become of the couple. I will be surprised if it does not sell, maybe not here but at an exhibition in the Philosophical Hall where more discerning eyes will see it.'

'The Philosophical Hall?' Arthur gasped. Such a thing had never entered his mind, not at this stage. He knew it was the home of the Leeds Philosophical and Literary Society and that exhibitions were held there from time to time.

'Yes. Mr Steel and I have discussed it. He is a member of the Society and could probably get the officials to consider showing some of your work. It may not be immediately because they have such things organised for some time ahead. They hold *conversaziones* at which they sometimes ask local artists to display a work for discussion, bringing it to the attention of potential buyers. The members of the Society are influential men. Of course, any work so displayed has to be good, or should I say outstanding? I think your painting *A Walk at Roundhay* would attract them. It might be an idea to concentrate on similar pictures for a while but slip in, now and again, one that is purely a depiction of nature or with nature enhancing a landscape.'

'Mr Hirst, what can I say?'

'Nothing, my boy, just work hard and do your best. I will get these three pictures framed and hope they will arouse your parents' interest and

155

that of your young lady.'

The day of the bazaar dawned bright but the overnight frost was in no hurry to depart. Arthur kept an anxious eye on the weather, fearing the snow that had been reported in the high Pennines might come to the town. When it was time for the Newtons to depart the sky was heavy with clouds but they did not bring the threat of snow. The spirit of the festive season still hung in the air and the Newtons were in good humour as they walked to the Duggans'. They found Moira and Rose, suitably clad to combat the cold, waiting for them.

'Thinking of buying anything?' Rose asked as she and Arthur paired off.

'I might buy you something.'

She cocked a doubtful eye at him. 'You bought me a Christmas present.'

'Well, I might buy you something else.'

'Oh, flush with money now, are you?'

'By way of celebrating.'

'Celebrating? Funny thing to be celebrating, coming to a bazaar.'

'Well, we'll see.' Though it was on the tip of his tongue to reveal what they really would be celebrating, he held back, knowing it would spoil the surprise. Instead he said, 'Fred tells me that Lizzie is suggesting we all go skating next Sunday if this frost continues. What about it?'

'I'd love that. I've been hoping the flooded fields would freeze hard enough to allow skating.'

'We'll keep our fingers crossed.'

They reached the venue for the bazaar. The

room was gaily decorated with streamers and balloons. Stallholders had marked their stalls with
individual touches that left no one in any doubt as
to their reason for being there. Some were raising
money for various charities, to aid the poor and
deprived, provide toys and clothing for orphans,
add to various churches' repair funds or to aid a
variety of societies. If the stalls were occupied by
tradesmen for their own gain it was on the understanding that a percentage of their takings went
into a general fund which would be divided between various charities not represented at the
bazaar. There was the buzz of goodwill that came
from people out to enjoy their afternoon, most of
whom before they left would enjoy a cup of tea
and a scone provided by the ladies of the Parish
Church.

Arthur had a hard time keeping his excitement
under control. He was eager to see his paintings
on display but did not want to direct anyone's
attention to them. He wanted them to get a
surprise. When he entered the room where people
were moving about between stalls, his eyes swept
across the displays until they alighted on his own
three paintings. His heart started to pound. He
must get nearer; he had to see what they looked
like framed. He saw that they were being displayed at a craft stall where a variety of woodwork
was being sold: small tables, children's chairs,
serviette rings, stands for inkwells, pencil boxes,
brooches, necklaces. All were of oak as were the
frames for his pictures that had been tastefully
enhanced by off-white mounts. The oak had been
chosen carefully, not too thick, not too thin, not

too dark, not too light, just right, and he realised what a difference the correct mount and suitable frame made to a picture.

'Don't gawk, Arthur.' Rose gave him a dig in the ribs.

He started out of the reverie the sight of his pictures had generated. 'What?'

'I said, don't gawk.' Rose moved towards a stall displaying knitted garments.

He realised she hadn't noticed the paintings. But why should she? She wasn't even interested in paintings. She didn't know they were his. Disappointment welled in him. He would have to point them out to her. Or maybe his parents would see them. He looked around, trying to spot them among the mass of people. Then he saw his mother nearing the stall displaying his paintings. He kept his eye on her while edging after Rose. She reached the stall and started examining the knitwear. He stopped behind her, his eyes still on his mother.

She was examining some serviette rings. She chose five and searched in her handbag while the stallholder wrapped her purchases. They exchanged words and she paid for the goods. She started to turn away. Arthur's heart sank. She had not even looked at the paintings. He saw the stallholder say something. His mother stopped. He saw her reply and then peer at the painting of Kirkstall Abbey. She straightened, her face registering that she had seen something totally unexpected. She looked around in anxious haste. She saw her husband and quickly pushed her way through the crowd to reach him. There was a brief

158

exchange of words and from the enquiring look on his father's face Arthur realised she had not told him what she had seen. She led him back to the craft stall, directing his attention to the painting of Kirkstall Abbey. Harold peered at it just as she had done, then looked at her in amazement. They turned their attention to the other two paintings and then looked around searchingly. His father saw him, spoke briefly to his mother and then made his way over to his son.

'Your name is on three paintings, over there, Arthur. Someone's using your name!'

For a moment he was taken aback. He had never expected anyone to think that. 'It's my signature, Father.'

'What?'

'I did those paintings.'

Harold stared at his son disbelievingly then said, 'You'd better come and see your mother.' Rose had turned to see what the fuss was about. 'You'd best come too, Rose.' He started off towards his wife.

As Rose and Arthur followed she said, keeping her voice low but persistent, 'What is it, Arthur?'

'You'll see in a moment.'

They reached Mrs Newton. 'He says he did them.' Harold informed his wife.

'What?' asked a puzzled Rose.

'Those.' Arthur indicated the paintings.

Rose glanced at them. 'Yours?'

'Yes.'

'You expect to sell them?'

'I hope so.'

'But when did you do them?' asked his mother.

'You haven't any paints, unless you've secreted them away somewhere?'

'I haven't done that, Mother.'

'Well, how...?'

'I'm sorry to interrupt, ma'am, but I would like to have a word.' They turned to see who had spoken. 'Do you like your son's paintings?'

Harold gave the man with the unruly mop of hair a curious look. 'Have we met before?'

'Indeed we have, sir. Last year at a cricket match.'

'Ah, yes. I recall you now.' Harold glanced at his wife.

She gave Ebenezer a suspicious look. 'How do you know they are my son's paintings?'

'My dear lady, that is a long story, but before its telling I think Arthur should introduce us and then I will ... no, that's not right, we, Arthur and I, will explain everything over tea and scones that I shall buy.'

Arthur introduced everyone in turn to Ebenezer, and added, 'I have a younger sister and brother.'

'They'll be tearing about no doubt, trying to decide what to spend their pocket money on,' said Enid.

'When they appear they shall have a glass of lemonade.' Ebenezer turned to Rose. 'Have you no family with you?'

'My mother is...'

'I'm right here,' said Moira brightly as she approached them.

Rose introduced her to Mr Hirst.

'You must join us for the tea and scones we are about to have. I have no doubt that, as Rose's

160

mother, you will be interested in what Arthur and I have to say.'

Seeing her friend looking a little bewildered, Enid indicated the paintings and said, 'Arthur has done those. We knew nothing about them until now. Mr Hirst and he want to explain how they come to be here.'

'I think that maybe this should be a family matter,' replied Moira, a little embarrassed.

'Dear lady,' interposed Ebenezer, 'from what I have heard of the friendship between your two families, and the special friendship between Arthur and Rose, I think you should sit with us.' He glanced at Harold. 'Don't you agree, Mr Newton?' Harold nodded. Ebenezer saw them to a table around which they could all sit, and then went to place their order.

'What's been going on?' demanded Harold when Ebenezer was out of earshot. He scowled at Arthur. Neither he nor Enid had forbidden the boy to draw. If it amused him all well and good, but things had clearly gone further than that. Besides which his son had been secretive and Harold did not like that. 'Well?' he snapped when Arthur did not reply immediately.

'I would like to wait until Mr Hirst comes back,' replied Arthur quietly. He seemed composed but inwardly he was shaking. He had hated being underhand about his studies but it had been the only way. Now he could see his father's anger and that was something that had hardly ever intruded upon their relationship before. In fact, Arthur could not remember when he had seen his father in this mood before. He saw his mother place a

161

calming hand on Harold's arm, preventing the explosion she saw coming. Arthur was thankful for it. He glanced in the direction of Mr Hirst and was relieved to see that he was coming back.

'Our tea and scones will be brought in a few moments,' he informed them as he sat down. He studied the faces staring back at him. He saw anger being held back by Harold and noted that Mrs Newton's hand was on her husband's arm. Maybe he would find an ally in her. He saw bewilderment on Mrs Duggan's face and knew she was not fully conversant with Arthur's drawing. Maybe Rose had never mentioned it to her. And Rose herself? Well, she was a reasonably attractive young lady but he sensed a stubbornness in her dismissiveness of Arthur's art and, in that attitude, foresaw that she might only ever tolerate it for the sake of her own comfort and would never truly inspire Arthur. But that was personal between them, their private affair. He could not and would not interfere. He only hoped that Arthur could rise above that and devote himself to his ambition to become a great painter.

'Well, Mr Hirst, we are waiting to hear what this is all about,' said Harold. The sharp note in his voice and the touch of hostility in his eyes indicated to Ebenezer that Harold believed that his authority as a father was being usurped.

'Mr and Mrs Newton, your son has the potential to be an extremely fine artist. I am most concerned that this talent should not be lost. I think it would be a shame indeed if that were to happen.'

'How do you know this? What gives you the authority to judge my son?'

'We became friends through him looking in my shop window at paintings I display there. I am a book dealer and also have a small gallery.'

'Ah,' exclaimed Harold as if he had finally discovered the truth. 'You want to make money out of him.' He shot a triumphant glance at Enid as much as to say, I have unmasked him.

'Mr Newton,' said Ebenezer indignantly, 'if that is what you think then I will walk away from here now and never see your son again.' He rose to his feet as he was speaking.

Alarm shuddered through Arthur. This could not happen. It must not. 'Father, please, listen.' His eyes and voice were pleading. 'Mr Hirst is not like that. Let me explain what has happened.'

Refusal was springing to Harold's lips. He wanted this nonsense to finish here and now, but he felt a gentle pressure on his arm.

'Just one moment, Arthur.' His mother spoke up gently but firmly, presenting a demeanour that said, I will not be denied my say. She turned her gaze on Ebenezer. 'We know my son likes to draw and we do not deny him that pleasure if that is what he likes, but we do not want it to dominate his life to the detriment of his future. That future includes a good job in which, if he applies himself, he can move up the ladder to a responsible position that will bring him a comfortable life. That prospect is one that I believe should not be thrown away.'

'I agree with you, ma'am. I am not encouraging your son to discard such an opportunity – unless his talent and passion for art demands it.'

'And who is to be the judge of that, Mr Hirst?'

'The decision will ultimately rest with Arthur himself.'

'But he could easily be lured into a false assessment.'

'It is up to those who are concerned about his future to see that he is not.'

'And do you consider yourself to be one such person?'

'Indeed I do, ma'am. I have your son's interests strongly at heart. I would never wish to lead him up a path that would be detrimental to his future. Nor would I wish to usurp your role, nor that of your husband, nor indeed that of anyone else.' The hint behind his glance at Rose was not lost on the others.

'Arthur, we are hearing all this but still have not learned how this association with Mr Hirst came about,' interposed his father.

Arthur nervously cleared his throat and went on to explain how he used to come home via Mr Hirst's shop to look at the pictures and how they had got talking. 'When I told him I liked to draw, he said he would like to see some of my drawings.'

'I saw that he had a gift but there were deficiencies in his work so I offered to give him lessons,' explained Ebenezer.

'And those have continued,' said Arthur. 'I have enjoyed them and think I have improved,' he added modestly.

'Indeed he has, in leaps and bounds,' confirmed Ebenezer.

'He has introduced me to Mr Laurence Steel who has looked at my work and given me hints on what I should do,' said Arthur, excited to

164

reveal that he knew this important artist.

He felt deflated when his father asked, 'Who's he?'

Arthur explained quickly and had his statement confirmed by Ebenezer.

'Why did you not tell your mother and me about all this?' asked Harold. His tone was quieter but Arthur could tell he had hurt his father by his secrecy.

'I'm sorry, Father. I should have done but I was afraid you would forbid me to see Mr Hirst and have these lessons. And I did so want to have them. Please don't stop them now.' He looked anxiously at Harold. He realised that his whole future hung in the balance. He might have to make some painful decisions, depending on what his father said. Would he have to defy him or meekly submit?

Harold looked thoughtful. 'I can't deny that you have disappointed us by being underhand about this. Maybe you were right; maybe we would have refused you permission, but what has been done has been done.' He looked hard at Ebenezer. 'You really think my son has talent?'

'Definitely. How far that talent takes him is up to him, and the interest and support he receives.'

'In other words, you are saying that we have a big part to play in his development?'

'That is so.'

'But we have no interest in art; cannot pretend to see more in a picture than a pretty object.'

Ebenezer nodded and glanced at Rose. 'What about you, young lady?'

'I think Arthur is wasting his time and may even

be jeopardising a sound, comfortable future. But, like Mr and Mrs Newton, I can tolerate his whim so long as it doesn't threaten our friendship.'

Harold gave a little nod of approval. He was glad he had some backing here because he had felt a mother's natural love for her son weakening any show of support from Enid. He put in quickly before she could speak, 'You have heard what my wife has said about Arthur's future. I strongly support those words and will only approve his continued lessons if they and his painting do not impinge upon or threaten his future.'

'I accept your terms and conditions,' said Ebenezer.

'Now, practicalities. How much has my son been paying you for these lessons?'

Ebenezer raised his hands in horror. 'Mr Newton, I've charged nothing and don't intend to. I would be offended if you offered to pay me. My reward is discovering what I believe is a genuine talent, one that hopefully I will live to see blossom.'

'That is very generous of you, Mr Hirst,' Enid put in quickly, fearing that her husband was going to insist on paying and thereby offend Arthur's benefactor.

'Indeed it is,' Harold agreed then added, 'I await with interest the possible sale of one of those paintings. That would tell me a lot.'

Ebenezer did not comment but said, 'Our tea has grown cold. Let me refresh it.'

As he went to do that Arthur looked at his parents. 'Thank you,' he said quietly.

'You mind what your mother said,' replied his father.

'I will.' Arthur's mind was already dwelling on the three paintings. He hoped that one of them would be sold. It would prove something to his father.

He did not leave for home with his family but waited until the bazaar closed. Afterwards, with a heavy heart he set off home with his three paintings.

'I see you didn't sell one,' said his father when he walked in. Arthur felt as if there was an implicit 'I told you so' in his voice, but he may have been wrong.

'Well, maybe I'll sell something at the exhibition organised by the Leeds Philosophical and Literary Society in the Philosophical Hall in the autumn.'

'What?' His mother and father looked at him in amazement.

'Yes. Mr Hirst thinks he can arrange it.'

'I'll believe it when I see it,' commented his father. 'Don't you get too big for your boots.'

'You'll be putting those three pictures in?' his mother asked.

'Only the one entitled *A Walk at Roundhay*. I'll do some new ones, depending how many I'm allowed to put in. I think they will have to go before a selection committee so I'll want to have a few to choose from.'

'Remember my words, Arthur, don't become obsessed and lose your friendships, you've your whole future to consider,' his mother reminded him.

Chapter Seven

'I think you should encourage Colette's interest. Capture an enthusiasm when young and it has every chance of blossoming into something much more. Although she is only ten she is intelligent beyond her years.' Roger Shipley spoke seriously to his brother. 'She picks up things so quickly and has learned a lot from Thomas. She's always keen to see him at work.'

'I know Westbury has been good to her. I hope she hasn't been a pest?'

'Not at all. I believe that since he and Nora can't have children they enjoy Colette's company all the more.'

'Indeed, I am grateful to them for their kindness to her.'

'You think seriously about what I have said.'

Peter had brought his daughters together with their governess to his brother's in early-August and had been persuaded to stay until Peter thought they should be returning to Whitby in early-October. Although his sister-in-law, recalling how successful last year had been, tried to persuade him to stay throughout the festive time, he had decided that they should try to make a success of Christmas in their new home.

'I am sure you will,' Pauline had said when he had told her of his plans. 'You have two wonderful daughters and you have found a gem in Miss

Lund who is giving them the feminine love and attention all children deserve. She has got on well with our own Miss Taylor who tells me how fortunate you are.'

'I've thought about it and I heed your words with gratitude, Roger,' Peter told his brother now. 'I believe the governesses are taking all the children walking this afternoon. They waited to make that decision until they saw what the weather was like. And Pauline is going to arrange the church flowers, so you and I will go to see Thomas. I can seek his advice then on what to buy that will be suitable for Colette.'

'Splendid,' Roger approved. 'You will receive good advice, I'm sure.'

The brothers enjoyed the walk to the Westburys'. The sun was shining, the birds were singing and the countryside looked as if it had been swept by the hand of God. It brought a touch of sadness to Peter and the usual longing for his wife, but, knowing she would not want a melancholy mood to settle on him, he threw it off.

They were greeted effusively by the Westburys, catching Nora before she went off to help Pauline. Once she had left the house and Peter had stated the reason for his visit, Thomas took them to what he called his 'den' where he had his cameras. A desk was placed against one wall on which there was, conveniently within reach, a shelf to hold the 'part-work' by Henry Fox Talbot entitled *The Pencil of Nature*, and *Sun Pictures In Scotland*. Peter knew that the second door led to the room Thomas had made into a dark room where he processed his photographs. Thomas produced a bottle of whisky and charged three glasses. When they were all sitting comfortably, he said, 'You come seeking my advice?'

'I want to know if now is the right time to indulge Colette in her desire to take up photography or is she merely entranced by watching pictures appear on paper?' Peter explained.

Thomas paused thoughtfully, took a sip of his whisky, pursed his lips and gave a little nod. 'Many people would say she was too young, but Colette is a wise child and has intelligence beyond her years. She has a very alert brain and is a quick learner. She is sensible and knows the care that must be taken when handling photographic materials. I have let her go through the process here and she has been very competent.

'I believe that photography will take its place as one of the important art forms of the future. It will present all sorts of opportunities. I also believe that photography will offer an occupation in which a female can make her own way.' He paused, took another sip of his whisky. 'To get back to your question, I think Colette is capable but you will have to keep an eye on her. By that I mean be interested and check on what she is doing and how she is doing it. She must not try to take short-cuts or become careless.'

'But I know nothing about photography,' Peter pointed out.

'You will soon learn, and Colette will no doubt pass her knowledge on to you. If you don't want to proceed any further, the mere rudiments will be sufficient for you to keep an eye on her but don't let her see any dogmatism from you; it could destroy the real enthusiasm that I know is there,' put in Roger in support of his friend.

'Right, then we all agree that photography would be a good thing for Colette to take up, and it's not too soon at her early age?'

'Correct,' said Thomas, 'but don't think in terms of years, rather of the level of her intelligence which is many years in advance of her actual age.'

'So where do we go from here?'

'Well, she will need a camera, a tripod, the photographic plates, and a room which can be set up as a dark room where all the equipment she needs for printing can be installed. This will not come cheap.'

'I expected that,' replied Peter, 'which is one reason why I asked you if you thought Colette serious and capable enough to merit my setting her up in photography. I don't want to spend money on a whim.'

'I don't think you'll be doing that, but of course everyone can change their mind, no matter how keen they once are on doing something,' said Thomas. 'Though I don't think that will be the case with Colette.'

Peter gave a nod of satisfaction. 'Then it will be a combined Christmas and birthday present. She will be eleven when we set this up in spring next year.'

'A good idea, and a good time of the year to start, with the weather improving,' put in Roger.

'That is settled,' said Peter with satisfaction. 'I hoped that was what you would say but I was willing to take your opinion if you had spoken

171

against the idea. Thank you, Thomas.'

'My pleasure! I hope that I have been in at the start of the career of someone who will become known for her photography.'

'May I crave further advice from you, Thomas?'

He spread his hands. 'Ask away.'

'Thanks. Well, I would like a detailed list of exactly what I will have to buy and I will need a design for the dark room. If you could do that in the next couple of days before we leave, I would be...' He stopped in mid-sentence. 'No, I've a better idea, if you are willing. Why don't you and Nora come to Whitby, then you'll be on the spot to advise us? It will cost you nothing. You can charge the coach fare to me and you can stay with us and make it a holiday as well.'

'Well ... er...' Thomas gave a little laugh. 'You've caught me unawares.' He paused. 'I don't see why not, but of course I will have to see what Nora thinks.'

'Naturally. Talk to her. As I say, we are leaving in a couple of days. In that time I will talk to Colette. It is no good proceeding if she has gone off the idea.'

'I don't think she will have, but it's best to be sure.' Thomas raised his glass. 'To the future.'

When Peter and Roger returned to the house they found the governesses and children were already there. With the children fully occupied Peter took the chance to have a quiet word with Susan Lund.

'I would like to talk to you about Colette. Should we walk outside?'

She accompanied him to the lawn at the front of the house.

'What is your opinion of her? How are lessons proceeding?'

'She is a very intelligent person, sir.'

'Please dispense with the formalities, Miss Lund. You have been with us long enough and fitted into our family life so well that I wish no such ceremony between us.'

'Very well.' Susan was a little embarrassed by this but also pleased. It made her feel closer to this family she had come to love and respect. Mr Shipley was a kind and considerate man who left the education of his daughters to her, though naturally he kept an eye on their progress. She hoped she was of help to him and eased the problems associated with bringing up two girls alone. She knew how much he still missed his wife and respected the times he withdrew into himself and filled his mind with memories.

'I used the word person. I was going to say "child" but Colette is more than that. She is highly intelligent and extremely capable. Sometimes this can be a drawback, the young person can miss out on childhood things that are beneficial to the process of growing up. I am careful to maintain a balance in Colette's case. If I may say so, I think she has benefited from that. Is there anything you would rather I not do?'

He noticed the frown that momentarily marred her expression and gave a wave of dismissal as he replied, 'No, it's not that. I am thinking of allowing her to take up photography as she has expressed a desire to do.'

Susan stopped walking. He turned to her and saw her face ablaze with joy. 'Oh, that will please her so much. She often talks about it, what Mr Westbury has shown her and what he has allowed her to do. She is fascinated by the magic of it all.'

'You think she is capable of coping with it?'

'Most certainly.'

'Even though she is so young?'

'Her mind and capabilities are not as young as her years.'

'Thank you. You have confirmed what others think.'

'Good. She will be excited.'

'Say nothing. I will tell her before we leave here.' He went on to tell her what he had suggested to Thomas Westbury. 'It will be her Christmas and birthday present combined.'

'What about Adele? She might feel put out.'

'I have thought of that. I shall buy her the pony I know she wants. It was something her mother and she were planning to do when the time was right. She doesn't mention it very much because she thinks it upsets me, but now I think she should have one. Do you ride, Miss Lund?'

'I used to, but when I was suddenly left alone and everything had to be sold my pony had to go.'

'We shall put that right. You will have one too.'

Susan was so taken aback she paled. 'Mr Shipley, I couldn't.'

'You can and you shall. You will be able to accompany Adele and that will be a comfort to me.'

'If that is what you want, sir.'

He smiled. 'It is, and I said – no more formalities.'

She blushed, then returned to normality quickly by asking, 'Where shall we keep the horses?'

'I'll buy a field on the West Cliff, have some stabling erected and hire a man to look after it. Maybe it could be turned into a commercial enterprise by offering stabling to other people too.'

'Thank you for your generosity,' she said quietly, meeting his gaze head on. She thought it best to leave then. 'If that is all, I'd best be getting back to the children.'

Peter nodded. There was a brief moment when he wanted to put another question so that she would stay but all he said was, 'Yes, that is all. Thank you for your opinions.' She turned and walked away. He watched her as his lips formed one word silently to finish those he had just said: 'Susan.' Immediately he was swamped with guilt. Was seeing her as a person so wrong? Was he betraying his wife, the woman he had loved so strongly and still did? He walked slowly away from the house, disturbed by his own thoughts. He crossed the lawn not really knowing where he was walking, coming back to himself to discover he was seated on a bench that had been placed under the shelter of a yew hedge. He sat quietly and let his mind fill with memories.

Five minutes later he was disturbed by movement and, looking up, saw Colette running towards him.

'Papa, Miss Lund said you might want to see me,' she panted as she reached him and then flopped down on the seat beside him.

She looked up at him as he put one arm round her, smiled, and said, 'Yes, I do.' He kissed the top of her head. She looked at him expectantly and, with serious eyes, waited for him to continue. He explained about his present and what he proposed they do at the house in Whitby when Mr and Mrs Westbury visited them.

Hardly able to believe what she was hearing, her eyes grew wider and wider. When he had finished, Colette sprang to her feet, flung her arms round his neck and said, 'Oh, Papa, thank you, thank you! I love you so much.' There were tears of happiness in her eyes.

At about the same time Arthur was putting the final touches to the last of the paintings he had prepared for consideration by the hanging committee of the Philosophical and Literary Society. Tomorrow he would take them for Ebenezer's assessment and in two days' time they would be conveyed to the Philosophical Hall.

He laid his brush down, stood back and surveyed the painting – a country lane between low stone walls in one of which some of the stones had come loose to lie, moss-covered, among the grasses and Lady's Lace. An oak was prominent on the left-hand side, its branches overhanging the lane, its trunk scored and cracked by many winters' frost and summers' heat. The lane disappeared into a curve that led... Where? He did not know. But someone had passed this way; there were footprints in the mud, drying out after a shower, and the wheels of a wagon had left its meandering track avoiding the potholes. Arthur stood for a few moments. Reached for his brush. Maybe a dab here, a stroke there? His fingers failed to close. He could go on forever touching here, marking there, always thinking he was improving the picture when in reality he might be spoiling it. He considered it for a few moments more then nodded. He was satisfied. His six submissions were complete. This was the only one that was completely given over to nature and in it he had tried to emulate one of Mr Steel's paintings. He had concentrated more in this one on the details of nature and the fineness of his brush strokes. Not that the others were far from this technique, they were not, but here he felt he had fully achieved what he was trying to do. This one he felt sure would sell; the others perhaps because they, like *A Walk at Roundhay*, were of places in and around Leeds that would be familiar to the viewer.

He turned off the two oil lamps, placed conveniently next to his easel, leaving only the one beside his bed to give him light while he undressed and got into it. He stretched out on his back and stared at the ceiling, contented that the past eight months, since his exhibition at the bazaar, had gone so well.

Though his parents had constantly reminded him of his safe job and the need for a secure future they'd nevertheless agreed to his using part of his bedroom as a studio where he could paint in peace. He was thankful for that concession but always had the feeling that they believed they were catering to a whim which one day would disappear. They looked at his work from time to time but that was it, they looked but did not see. His paintings were no more than pictures to them and they never thought he would be any more successful than he had been at the bazaar. This fired him all the more to prove that they were wrong.

The studio in his bedroom gave him more opportunity to paint, for it meant that time was not restricted in the same way as it had been when he could only paint at Ebenezer's. The art dealer's influence was still important to Arthur and his constructive criticism essential. Mr Steel's occasional observations were also vital to his progress. It was therefore with high hopes that he approached the forthcoming exhibition.

He only wished that Rose had begun to take more interest and see his work with a greater depth of understanding, whereas if anything her interest was more superficial than that of his parents. In all other aspects of their relationship he experienced a growing closeness. He enjoyed being with her and she fitted in well with the group of friends that had grown around his workplace and cricket. Those matches were always played with enjoyment, no matter what the outcome, and that attitude swept over into their outings into the neighbouring countryside, sometimes extending via the train as far as York or Sheffield. They also enjoyed concerts, fairs and the theatre and parties in their own homes.

Rose had become competent at the piano and, though she had no aspirations to become a great player, constantly practised to maintain her standard. Arthur welcomed this for it meant there were times when, because of her practising, he could seize more time for his painting. He was always careful to show an interest in her piano-playing, though, hoping that she would one day reciprocate by giving more attention to his painting.

Life had settled down nicely. Now he approached the exhibition in the Philosophical Hall with high hopes.

The following day Arthur had to force himself to concentrate on his work and stop his mind from speculating what the hanging committee would decide about his paintings. That morning, on his way to work, he had left his final painting with Ebenezer. The other five were already with him, framed and awaiting the last. He was to go straight to Ebenezer's from work to have some tea and then they would both take the paintings to the Philosophical Hall.

Since the bazaar his painting was no longer a secret and everyone in the office wished him well when they were leaving that evening.

'Best of luck,' called Fred. 'Lizzie sends her best wishes too.'

'I'll be bringing her to see the exhibition,' Ben informed him.

'He's got his eyes on your sister.' Arthur winked at Fred, and rushed off.

'There will be five judges,' Ebenezer explained on their way to the Hall, 'so there is always one with a casting vote should that become necessary. I will help you into the building with your paintings. There will be men on duty to assist you with them and direct you to the committee room.

Then you will be on your own. You will display your paintings one at a time. The committee may ask you questions, they may not. Most likely they won't; it is the paintings they are judging not you. After they have seen them they will ask you to leave so that they can consult and then they will call you back and tell you which paintings they want to put in the exhibition. If you are to bring any away they will ring for the man who assisted you to return to help.'

Arthur's stomach tightened as they left Bond Street to enter the solid, uncompromising building. Would the gentlemen of the selection committee be as formidable? Apprehension began to charge him. His hands felt clammy. One of the pictures he was carrying started to slip. He stopped and, shuffling his hands along the frame, managed to gain a better grip. A man of middle stature dressed in black thigh-length jacket and well-pressed matching trousers came over to them.

'Good day, sirs.' He glanced at the clock on the wall, giving a slight nod as if he agreed that the time was right. 'Mr Newton?' He looked from one to the other.

'Yes.' Arthur managed to stumble over the reply that came from a dry throat.

'Tobias will show you the way and help you with your paintings.' He raised a finger, a signal to one of the three men who were standing close to the bottom of the wide staircase that divided into two as it rose towards the second floor. He turned to Ebenezer. 'You can wait in the ante-room, sir. Would you like some refreshments?'

'No, thank you.' Ebenezer thought he would be too nervous to enjoy anything. He knew how much this exhibition meant to Arthur.

One man had detached himself and came over to them. Ebenezer handed his pictures to him. The man looked at Arthur and said, 'Follow me, sir.'

His nervousness increased with every upward step. He had never been in such a palatial building but he had little time to take in any details. Reaching the top of the staircase, the man led him to a door outside which a row of chairs had been placed.

'Do sit down, sir, we have a few moments.' He leaned the pictures against the wall and did the same with those that Arthur had carried up the stairs.

Arthur sat down and rubbed his hands together in a nervous gesture.

'Your first time, sir?' In the course of his various duties over the years the porter had seen many such men and prided himself on being a good judge of character, knowing exactly how far he could go in his familiarity. He had become an expert on knowing his place. He judged that this young man would not take offence at the enquiry and that a friendly tone might help to settle his nerves.

Arthur nodded. 'Yes.'

'You'll be all right, sir.'

'I hope so, a lot depends on what they decide.' It was out before Arthur realised what he was saying. He blushed as the words faded away.

Before the porter had time to remark upon this

181

statement the door opened and a gentleman stepped out. He looked to be in his fifties, and his pinched face did not immediately endear him to Arthur. He peered over glasses perched on the end of his nose and gave Arthur a look which seemed to say, 'Oh, not another one,' even though he must have known that Arthur was expected at this time. He glanced at a notebook he held in his left hand. 'Mr Arthur Newton?'

'Yes,' replied Arthur with a slight tremor in his voice.

The man nodded as much as to convey, 'Thank goodness you are on time.' He grunted and said, 'I'm Secretary to the Committee.' He glanced at the porter standing by. 'Bring the pictures in, Tobias, you know the procedure.' Then he ushered Arthur into the room.

A long mahogany table was placed opposite the door. Behind it sat five men in matching chairs, their frames curved in such a way that should the sitter wish to rest his arms he would be comfortable. A large easel had been positioned directly in front of them at a distance that must have been worked out as presenting the ideal viewpoint since the paintings all had to comply to a specific size when framed. To the right of the easel was a vacant chair.

The Secretary led Arthur to that chair and indicated that he should be seated. Then he himself went to an unobtrusive position to one side of the room, sat down, flicked his notepad open and poised his pencil.

Arthur was aware of Tobias stacking the paintings against a chest behind the easel so that the members of the committee could not see them before each was positioned individually.

Sitting stiffly upright on the edge of his seat, he awaited his first instruction which he suddenly realised was not going to come until the porter had left the room. It gave him a few moments, which to him seemed interminable, to view the men before him. From what had appeared a sea of faces when he first entered the room he began to pick out individuals: mutton-chop whiskers, elderly with kindly eyes ... oh, they were all elderly to him, probably with no thought of modern trends in art in their minds ... horse-face who fiddled with the ends of a waxed moustache as if he wanted to draw attention to the care he lavished upon it; no-neck sitting like a toad; benevolent smiler who looked as if he might sympathise with the tension that he knew Arthur was experiencing; and finally in the centre of the group a distinguished-looking Army type whose eyes were piercing and seemed to be laying Arthur's personality bare. He concluded that this was the Chairman.

Arthur heard the door click. The porter must have left. His moment was here. Butterflies fluttered in his stomach. He heard a voice. It seemed remote, yet he answered, 'Yes.' It had begun.

'This is the first time you have submitted paintings for one of our exhibitions?' The words were clearer and he was aware now that they came from the Chairman.

Arthur gathered his wits about him. 'Yes, sir.'

'Very well. We are only here to judge your paintings to see if we think them worth displaying in our exhibition. We do not want to know any more about you ... well, not at this stage ... but we may do at some later date. We want you to place your pictures in turn on the easel in any order you like. We will not ask you to comment on the paintings. In fact, we ask you to refrain from doing so.' He glanced to left and right as he said, 'Well, gentlemen, shall we begin?' A murmur of agreement flowed along the table like a ripple on water. The Chairman fixed Arthur with his gaze. 'Your first painting, Mr Newton, please.'

Arthur hesitated for a brief moment as if he had been caught unawares and was unsure what to do. Painting on the easel! He slid from his chair, went to the paintings, fumbled. Which should he choose? He had never given an order any thought. This one? No it had better be this one. Any one. I'm keeping them waiting. He picked one out and thrust it on to the easel. He stood to one side.

'Straighten it, please, Mr Newton.'

Who said that? He did not know. Flustered, he glanced at the picture. What had possessed him to leave it like that? He put it right. You've time to gather your thoughts while they consider that one. No more panicking.

The moments passed. They moved into minutes. He saw the committee members making notes but not exchanging words. That was the procedure as he displayed each painting in turn. When they had considered the final one he was asked to wait outside.

He found Tobias waiting there. The man raised a questioning eyebrow. 'How did it go, sir?'

Arthur pulled a face. 'Don't know. I couldn't tell

what they were thinking.' He fell silent. His stomach churned. The minutes ticked away. What were they doing? Surely they must have made a judgement by now? Arthur's anxiety mounted: his nervousness increased. Then the door opened and the Secretary poked his head round the door and said, 'You are wanted back, Mr Newton.'

His heart was pounding. The men behind the table must hear it as he went, on the Chairman's indication, to the chair he had used before.

The Chairman cleared his throat, glanced along the table. 'There is nothing more, gentlemen?' There was a shaking of heads. 'Then we are all agreed?' Assent rippled from each one. The Chairman paused a moment, his eyes fixed on Arthur. 'Mr Newton, we have viewed your work with interest but I am afraid we have decided to display only one of your paintings.' Arthur's mind was going numb. He couldn't be hearing right but there was no mistaking the voice that went on to say, 'We are sorry not to be more positive about your work but we wish you well. We have your name and address and if at any time in the future we would like to consider something for a talk and discussion, which we sometimes do at our meetings and gatherings, we will contact you. And of course you are perfectly free to submit work for any future exhibition we may hold, but I would advise you that they would have to be new works.'

Arthur hardly heard the voice. His world lay shattered; his hopes deflated.

'We thank you for letting us see your work and we wish you well.'

Arthur did not stir but sat staring straight in

front of him.

'Mr Newton?'

He was startled by the sharp note in the voice.

'Sir? I'm sorry.' He pulled himself together. He had to go. He had been dismissed. He started to rise. 'Which painting have I to leave?'

'Oh, yes, sorry. I should have said. Please leave the painting, *A Walk at Roundhay.*' The Secretary was at the door now calling Tobias into the room. He gave him instructions and, as he started to gather the paintings, Arthur went to help. He left the room with a heavy heart.

'Only one, sir? I'm sorry.' Tobias offered a sympathetic word.

Arthur shrugged his shoulders and grimaced with disappointment written all over his face.

When Ebenezer emerged from the ante-room he realised the worst immediately: Arthur's distress was plain for anyone to see. Ebenezer's eyes took in the pictures. Five. 'Which one did they keep?' he asked.

'*A Walk at Roundhay.*'

'Well, that's better than none.'

Arthur's voice was a plaintive cry when he said, 'I've wasted my time!'

'You haven't!' Ebenezer put iron into his tone. He must counteract what he knew was coming.

'I have. Eight months wasted.'

'That doesn't necessarily mean they didn't like them.'

'Of course it must, and if they didn't like them who on earth is going to buy them? I've been wasting my time. I'm giving up. My family have been right all the time.'

Ebenezer gripped him by the shoulders. 'Look at me.' Arthur kept his gaze down. 'Look at me!' He slowly raised his eyes. 'You cannot expect always to succeed. Life isn't like that. When you suffer blows like this it is hard, but if you have the courage to meet them and overcome them and have faith in your own ability you will win. Don't let this divert you from your ambition. Mr Steel and I have faith in you. Don't let us down.' Arthur's lips tightened. Ebenezer pressed his shoulders. 'You hear me?'

He gave a little nod.

'Good. You must continue painting. I believe the reason only one was chosen is because your style is of the future, not in the present mode. Your natural bent lies in your love of depicting nature, not in the historical setpieces that are the rage of the Royal Academy and here among artistic patrons in Leeds. But Mr Steel's more modern style is gradually making headway and bringing the North into the modern era. You *must* be involved in that. It is the way ahead.'

Arthur nodded again.

'If you will do that we will look at other exhibitions and see if we can display your work elsewhere than in my shop. Leave these with me and I'll see what I can do.'

'As I said before, I want any sales to be made by you.' Arthur gave a grunt of derision. 'But it's unlikely there'll be any.'

'Don't talk like that, Arthur Newton. Don't! I'll handle all your sales whether they are through my shop or elsewhere. If you continue to work hard, strive always to improve, they'll sell.'

Ebenezer knew his protégé was at a low ebb and that this feeling of inadequacy might continue for some time. It was going to be hard to bolster his enthusiasm. He could only do that by encouraging and cajoling. If only Arthur had someone else to inspire him. If only Rose could give him that inspiration, but Ebenezer was afraid it might be a case of 'I told you so' when she heard what had happened today.

She was at the Newtons' when Arthur arrived home. At least she had been interested enough to await the outcome. It was obvious to all what had happened when he walked in.

'Not good?' said his mother before anyone else could comment, for she realised she would be the only one here with any true sympathy. She knew her son had set his heart on being accepted for this exhibition and had begun to appreciate the effort he was putting in, though she kept her warnings about the future to the fore. It looked as though she had been right to do so.

He shook his head. 'They have only taken one.'

His father grunted and picked up the *Leeds Mercury* as if that was the end of the matter.

Arthur's hackles rose at the implication that he had tried and failed, but he curbed his temper.

Rose had made no comment. It really wasn't her place in the Newtons' house. Now she said quietly. 'Will you walk me home, Arthur? Please.'

He nodded and escorted her from the house after she had made her goodbyes to the family.

The pale moon kept slipping behind thin cloud and then reappearing to cast a silvery sheen over the houses and gardens as they set off for Rose's home. She slipped her arm through his. 'I'm sorry,' she said quietly. 'I know how much you had set your heart on an exhibition in such a prestigious place. I'm proud that you have had one work accepted.' She stopped and, looking up at him, said pleadingly, 'But don't risk our happiness by courting such big ideas. I love you. I don't want to lose you to them.' She raised herself on her toes and kissed him on the cheek. Her lips were tantalisingly soft and lingered, sending shivers through him that drove away the cares that had hung on him since his near total rejection at the Philosophical Hall. His arms came round her waist and he drew her into a long deep kiss. When their lips parted she said, 'Kiss me again and forget the troubles that are really only of your own making.'

Arthur needed no second bidding; she had put sweet temptation into that first kiss.

He had much to think about as he walked home. Maybe Rose was right. Maybe his notions of being an artist and earning a living by it were foolish. Should he keep it as a hobby with his only desire to improve, not entertain anything beyond that? Did Mr Hirst and Mr Steel really think that he had the talent to go much further? Had they been proved wrong today? A comfortable life without any risks beckoned enticingly. He had seen in his own parents' house and in those of his friends what could be achieved without trying to take Dreamland by storm. He was still confused when he reached home. One part of him said: Accept your life as it is, while the other said, If you do, will you be true to yourself? Could he really subjugate his desire to paint, forget it altogether or even reduce it to a mere hobby without feeling the motivation to take it to the realms he had dreamed of?

He recalled Ebenezer's words. Was his painting really set for the change in public opinion that his friend had predicted? Wasn't that change already taking place as evidenced in Mr Steel's work? Or would the established Classical genre prevail since people still seemed intent on buying it? Was that where he should be directing his talents? Was that where he could prove his worth?

Chapter Eight

Ebenezer was worried. He had not seen Arthur for ten days. This was unusual. If he had no artwork to show he generally called in for a chat, to discuss some aspect of his work that might be troubling him or merely to keep in touch. But ten days? He knew Arthur would be upset after having only one painting accepted for the Philosophical and Literary Society exhibition but had judged the young man capable of rising above that, staunchly pursuing his ultimate aim of becoming an artist whose work would one day be sought after. But what reaction had there been from his parents and, probably more importantly, from Rose? Had those reactions affected his outlook, his own assessment of his future? Ebenezer was tempted to call at the Newton house but held back, thinking it might be counterproductive. The young man must come to him; surely he could not ignore their long-established friendship?

Arthur had continued to agonise over his future. Several times in the quiet of his bedroom he had picked up pencil or brush, made a tentative mark on paper or canvas and then thrown them down in disgust. He felt neither inspired nor motivated, merely a failure.

No words of sympathy or encouragement came from his family. He would come out of his present mood and then their life together would resume as normal, they believed. Rose had given him a little hope that evening he walked her home but since then had not mentioned his art. Could he rely on her tolerance in the future if he were to paint again?

He felt guilty that he had not visited Ebenezer since the day of his disappointment. He really should go. His old friend had tried to ease his depression, had tried to show him that his work still had merit and that there was a way forward. The longer he put it off, the harder it would be to erase the guilty feeling and face Ebenezer again. He'd go to see him this evening on his way home from work ... no, not this evening, maybe next week.

Fred and Arthur paused outside the railway offices, turned up the collars of their overcoats and glanced in both directions. People were not loitering but hurrying about their business to help combat the chill in the air. The sky was grey but without being threatening.

'The fields will be frozen,' commented Fred. 'Grace and I said we'd go skating. Ben and Lizzie are coming too – why don't you bring Rose? It might get you out of that mood you've been in lately?'

Arthur did not reply immediately. It would be good to go out with his friends again but did he really want to mix socially? He pulled himself up sharply. He shouldn't let his disappointment upset his relationship with them. It was Saturday afternoon and here was an opportunity to do something to help him throw off the despondency he was allowing to cloud his mind. 'Why not?' He forced the brightness into his tone.

'Good.' Fred clapped him on the back. 'We'll see you there then.' With that he headed off towards Boar Lane as if he had his mind set on some special mission and did not want Arthur along.

Arthur pulled a surprised face. Their usual route did not include Boar Lane. He gave a resigned shrug of his shoulders, stuck his hands in his pockets and headed for home, but he would call at the Duggans' on the way and hopefully find that Rose was tempted by the prospect of skating, a winter pastime she always enjoyed.

As he approached the shop he thought, 'It always seems to be open. Mr Duggan must be earning a very good living from it.' The Duggans had a fine home too where everything was of good quality and money did not seem scarce. Mr Duggan worked hard but he did reap the benefits. Rose was an only child ... would she inherit? Would she want to keep the shop whenever anything happened to her father? Arthur was startled by the direction his own mind had taken him and chided himself for entertaining such thoughts.

'Good day, Mr Duggan,' he said brightly as he entered the shop, wondering what Conan would have thought had he been able to read the questions Arthur had recently entertained. 'Is Rose in?'

'Hello, lad. Aye, she's in, you can hear her at the piano. Go through.'

'Thanks.' Arthur raised a section of the counter and passed through to the door leading to the house. He went straight to the room where Rose was playing.

She looked up when the door opened, smiled when she saw Arthur and went on playing a Chopin Valse.

Arthur leaned against the wall beside the door, which he had quietly closed, and listened. He liked Rose's playing. She was a very quick learner and had a natural ability to bring atmosphere to the piece she was playing. As that appreciation came to him his mind seized on it. Wasn't that exactly what he had been trying to do in his paintings? Maybe he hadn't done it as well as Rose had in her interpretation of music? Maybe that was why his paintings hadn't been chosen for the exhibition? His mind went to the one that would be hung. Had it more atmosphere than the others? He tried to visualise them, make comparisons. He must talk to Ebenezer about this.

The notes faded away. He came out of his reverie and went over to Rose who sat motionless on the stool as if she was still entranced by the music. He went to her side. 'That was wonderful,' he said quietly and bent to kiss her forehead as she turned with an expression of delight at seeing him.

'Thank you,' she whispered and took his hands to ease him gently on to the stool beside her. She kissed him. Not wanting to let her go, he held her by the waist.

'Come skating?' he suggested as he nuzzled her neck.

'Mmm.' She hesitated, kissed him again and then said, 'We'd better go. I've finished playing, they'll wonder what we're doing.'

They stood up and in the hall Arthur said, 'I'll slip home, get ready and be back for you shortly. Fred and Lizzie are going too.'

'Good. We'll have fun.'

By the time they reached the skating fields the clouds had thinned and the sun was making its appearance. With little wind and frosty air the conditions were ideal. Rose had put on a skirt she had had made especially for skating. It resembled one of her black day skirts shot with grey but was shorter so that the fur-trimmed skating boots she wore would not be impeded. Her thigh-length tunic fitted tightly at the waist, its only adornment the white lace at the sleeves and collar. She wore a small bonnet from which pink ribbons trailed. Arthur wore fawn trousers tucked into the top of calf-length leather boots and a waist-length jacket which was cut away to tails. A white cravat neatly tied at his throat and a low-crowned, wide-brimmed hat gave him a debonair look that had a few heads turning when they reached the skating field. Rose felt proud that he was her escort.

Swirling patterns of colour and movement were

mirrored in the glistening ice as skaters glided across the slippery surface. Laughter and gaiety filled the air. Vendors had taken their chance and around the sides of the fields had set up stalls selling steaming punch made from wine, lemon, honey, cloves and cinnamon; there were sweetmeats too with one stall specialising in comfits of varying flavours, and another in brandy balls; others offered biscuits and slices of fruit loaf.

Arthur was helping Rose with her skates when they became aware of a flurry on the ice close to them. Looking up, they saw Ben and Lizzie coming to a halt in a swirl of flakes chipped from the ice by their blades. Their cheeks were rosy from the cold and exertion.

'Hello, you two,' cried Ben. 'Glad you are here. The others are somewhere around. Come on, Lizzie, they'll catch us up.' He grabbed her hands. Laughing, she matched his movement to glide away.

A few moments later Rose was on the ice doing a few little steps to get the feel of it while Arthur made the final adjustments to his skates. Then he joined her, took her hands crossover and they glided away as if they had been in perfect step all their lives. Their smooth movement fell into a leisurely pace and they were soon exchanging greetings on the ice with Fred and Grace. By the time they had been round the field three times they had seen Giles and Barbara and Jack and Dorothy. The laughing, teasing group's enjoyment was heightened by showing off their skating abilities, the tumbles they took, and by the physical closeness of their skating companion.

Fred and Lizzie came alongside Arthur and Rose. 'Will you take Lizzie to the stall selling punch – that one over there?' Fred indicated one that was set a little apart from the others. With that he pushed himself off across the ice, leaving Arthur and Rose wondering what this request was all about.

They skated around the field to the stall he had indicated. A few moments later, Giles and Barbara arrived and then Jack and Dorothy appeared with Fred.

'Punch for all,' he said to the man behind the stall and made some remark that made the man chuckle.

They were all grateful for his generosity and as each received a steaming glass of sweet-smelling liquid they moved into a happily chattering group. When they had all been served and he had got his own glass Fred joined them. The clouds had cleared from the sky but the light was fading. 'Specially constructed poles, mounted with faggots, were being lit around the edge of the field so that skating could be enjoyed throughout the evening.

'It's going to look lovely when their light glistens on the ice and mingles with the moonlight,' commented Barbara dreamily.

'And very fitting,' said Fred. There was something in his voice that drew everyone's attention. He glanced round at them all. 'I have something important to say.' He paused for effect. Everyone, wondering what was so important on a carefree occasion such as this, hung on his every word. 'I have asked Grace to marry me and she has said yes.'

For a moment there was a shocked silence and then excited chatter broke out. Congratulations flowed, well-wishes were called, joyous laughter filled the air, particularly when Fred produced a tiny box and gave it to Grace who opened it to reveal a ring set with diamonds.

'This calls for another punch!' called Arthur, and immediately ordered more from the man behind the stall who was soon caught up in the general euphoria.

Fred stood with his arm round Grace whose eyes were damp with joy and announced, 'Maybe her father won't approve. I've him to ask yet.'

Grace laughed. 'He will! I can twine him round my little finger.'

'She can that,' called her brother. Ben looked at Lizzie, 'I hope you can do that with yours?'

'That sounds like a proposal,' she said, not afraid of being forthright.

'It is,' said Ben.

Lizzie let out a whoop of unabashed delight and flung her arms round his neck to kiss him, whereupon everyone else let out teasing shouts. Another round was called for and the stall-holder was hoping the other couples would become betrothed here and now.

They skated and chatted well into the evening. With the moonlight sending a silvery sheen across the ice and suffusing the atmosphere with romance no one wanted the evening to end. But end it did finally and they all went their separate ways, knowing that they could never repeat such an enchanted time but that to recall it would always be sweet.

As he and Rose walked home arm in arm, Arthur with their skates dangling from his other hand, the world seemed to hold no troubles. It was theirs and theirs alone. No one else could share these moments when they'd just enjoyed being with each other. Arthur thought he might never feel like this again. This afternoon and evening had been wonderful; what he had thought would be merely a skating outing had turned into so much more. There had been joy and laughter and whole futures had been mapped out. There was so much to life; so much to be shared. He stopped beneath some trees, the moonlight trellising the ground with their leafless branches, and turned Rose to him. 'Marry me?' he whispered.

She looked up into his eyes. 'Yes.'

He kissed her hard and long and the world stood still for them.

'Arthur, you have made me so happy. I think I have loved you ever since our families became friends,' said Rose as they walked slowly on. She squeezed his arm.

'That seems a long time.'

'You?' she asked.

He waited a moment. 'I don't really know. Girls were girls.'

'I know, and we got in the way.'

'I was well aware of you, but I think you really set my heart aflutter that day I started work. I felt I was an adult then and you seemed to be too.'

'I remember that wink you gave me as you tossed an apple in the air. It made you seem so grown up and made me think you fancied me.

You'd never done that before.'

'Well, now, Rose Duggan, I'll wink at you whenever you like.'

She laughed and then became serious. 'When are we going to tell everyone?'

'There's no time like the present. I will ask your father when we reach your house.'

'Is that wise?' It seemed a half-hearted query.

'Why not? What is the point in delaying? He's going to say yes or no, no matter when I ask him, we may as well know sooner than later.'

'He won't say no.'

'So you are another one who thinks they can twine their father round their little finger?'

She laughed. 'I know it. What an evening – three engagements! Do you think the others will have a double wedding?'

'I hadn't thought of that. I suppose it's more than likely. We could make it a triple celebration.' He chuckled at the thought.

Rose gave him a playful punch. 'Not likely! I want that day to myself.'

'And you shall have it.'

'You must have enjoyed yourselves, you've been so long,' observed Mrs Duggan when they walked in.

'It was wonderful. So many people there, all our friends. The weather got better, the sky cleared to give a wonderful moonlit night. The skating field was lit by burning faggots placed all round the edge of the field. It was so pretty.'

'It would be nice to go skating again,' commented Conan wistfully.

'I remember when you used to take us when we

199

were children, until you had that nasty fall.' Arthur was trying to pluck up courage to say what he really wanted to.

'Damaged my ankle badly. I'm so glad you were able to take Rose. There'll be more opportunities if this cold weather lasts.'

Mrs Duggan had gone to the kitchen to make some chocolate. Rose glanced at Arthur and went to help her mother.

He cleared his throat. 'Sir,' he began nervously, 'may I ask you something?'

Conan eyed the young man. It was something serious when Arthur used the word 'sir'. 'Certainly.'

'Well, sir, I have...' Arthur coughed. 'I want to know if ... well, it's like this, sir. I have been...' He hesitated, bit his lip and was about to go on when Conan spoke up.

'The answer's yes, you can marry her.'

'Well, sir, I was thinking...' Conan's words hit him then. Arthur stopped talking stared at Mr Duggan and gasped, 'You knew what I was going to say!'

'Seeing you as nervous as you were, spluttering like you did, not knowing exactly what to say next, meant only one thing to me: you were going to ask me if you could marry Rose.' Conan pushed himself up from his chair and held out his hand which Arthur took with great relief. 'I should be delighted for you to marry her. We've known you a long time. You've grown into a fine young man and have good prospects in your job. I'm sure what you learn there will stand you in good stead should other opportunities come along in our expanding town.'

Arthur was a little bemused. To what was Mr Duggan referring? Why would he want to leave his job unless it was to paint? And, after his failure, did he really want that?

'I presume you have asked Rose and she has said yes, otherwise there was no point in asking me?' Mr Duggan broke into his thoughts.

'Yes, sir, I did and she accepted.'

'Well, let's get the ladies in. I presume Rose was keeping her mother in the kitchen while you asked me.' He went to the door and called for them.

Moira was smiling as she came in. 'I suppose you've approved, Conan?'

'Would you have had me do otherwise?'

'No, I am delighted.' She came to Arthur and hugged him before kissing him on the cheek. 'I am so pleased. I know you will look after her and make her happy.'

'Of course I will, Mrs Duggan.'

Con had enfolded his daughter in his arms. 'Thank you, Papa,' she whispered.

'Be happy,' he returned.

'I will.'

Con went to the sideboard and brought out a bottle of champagne. He glanced at Arthur. 'I've been saving this for a special occasion and I think this is it. What if we go to break the news to your parents and then we can all celebrate together?'

'Yes, sir.' Arthur was pleased; this seemed to set the seal of approval on the forthcoming marriage. He was sure his parents would feel the same.

The party arrived at the Newtons' flushed with

excitement. Arthur ushered them into the house.

Wondering who was coming and what all the jollity was about, Enid and Harold came from the drawing-room wearing curious expressions. They showed delight at seeing their friends but looked askance at them also.

'Mother, Father ... Rose and I have just got engaged,' announced Arthur.

For one split moment they did not take in the statement. Then, when it had made its impact, congratulations flowed. Hugs and kisses were exchanged. Hands were shaken, backs were slapped, tears of joy ran down cheeks, and more excitement was created when Celia and Oswald appeared to learn that they were to have a sister-in-law.

Glasses were brought to the drawing-room, another bottle was added to the one Con produced, and the couple's health was drunk.

The Newtons saw that their son would be settled in a stable marriage in comfortable circumstances, able to lead a life of reasonable comfort and maybe even more so if he continued to apply himself to his work as he had done up to now.

When the excited conversation had died down a little, Enid ventured to make the enquiry that Moira had not been bold enough for. 'Have you decided on a date for the wedding?'

'Mother,' laughed Arthur, 'we've only just got engaged! But there's talk of the Queen coming to open the new Town Hall in 1858. It would be a memorable year for us to marry. That is, if Rose approves?'

'I think it is a splendid idea,' she agreed, 'and it

gives us plenty of time to get everything ready.'

'And find a suitable place to live. By that time I should have gained another promotion so we would be able to afford a nicer place than we could now.'

'That's very sensible thinking,' approved Conan. He was about to make another proposal that would also affect the lives of the young couple but held back in the belief that this was not the right time. That should come after they were married and settled in their own home.

Arthur lay in bed staring at the ceiling. He had drawn the curtains back to allow the moon to lend his room its silvery, peaceful atmosphere. Had it cast its magic earlier and prompted his proposal to Rose? Had the romantic atmosphere of the skating fields induced his friends to seal their love for each other? Had it contributed to his own declaration to Rose? The excitement of the day had faded and now, alone, he wondered about the future, his job, his painting, his ambitions, desires and this new responsibility he had brought upon himself. What would Ebenezer say to it? Arthur could no longer postpone seeing him face to face.

When they left church the following morning, Rose readily agreed that they should go to the Carters' to break the news to their friends rather than let them hear it second hand. They were pleased to find that Grace and Ben were there. When they broke their news there were more celebrations. As they walked home Arthur's mind turned once more to Ebenezer. He hoped his friend would be just as enthusiastic as everyone else.

Butterflies fluttered in his stomach as he approached the shop on his way home from work the next day.

When the door opened Ebenezer looked up from the pile of books he was sorting. His eyes met Arthur's. Their hurt expression was swiftly banished by one of pleasure, but Arthur had caught the underlying feeling and felt guilty.

'Arthur! My dear fellow.' Ebenezer came with outstretched hands from behind the counter.

Arthur took them and, finding no condemnation in their touch, embraced his friend, saying, 'I am sorry I haven't been to see you before now.' True guilt and regret were evident in his tone.

'That's all right, Arthur. Don't upset yourself. I was wondering how you were, that's all, and if you would be bringing any more work for me to see.'

Arthur grimaced and gave a slight shake of his head. 'I'm afraid I haven't.'

'No matter.'

'I tried to start several times but found I couldn't even draw a line.'

'You've let the disappointment get to you. Come through and sit down.' Ebenezer led the way into the next room, wanting Arthur to be among pictures rather than books. 'It's understandable when you had worked hard and set your sights on having all your paintings accepted. But, Arthur, we all have our disappointments. You'll have many more. They will be a test of your character and determination. You have got to rise above rejection, learn from it. I think you have the temperament to do so, and if you are successful your art will only benefit. You can't allow one setback like this to affect your whole future. You must continue to produce work, strive for improvement. I know you can.' Ebenezer stopped. He had got carried away, and as he was speaking had begun to sense that Arthur had something else on his mind. 'There's something else, Arthur, isn't there? What is it?'

'I got engaged on Saturday,' he replied a little sheepishly.

Surprise and shock showed on Ebenezer's face but he quickly assumed an expression of pleasure. 'Arthur! Congratulations. I hope you will be very happy. Rose, I presume?'

'Yes.'

'I'm sure she will make you a good wife.' And Ebenezer did believe that. He could see that she would make a good home, have pride in it, and as long as she was comfortably off would support her husband and be a good mother to his children. But he did wonder if this would have an effect on Arthur's art. He did not express any such doubt. That would be fatal. Instead he might use this to better advantage. 'Now you have something else to work for and your art can bring you in an additional income which I am sure will be useful.'

'If I sell.' There was doubt in Arthur's voice.

'Of course you'll sell, but you can only do that if you paint. We should make a plan. Let us consider the paintings the committee rejected. I have them here and have kept looking at them since. As I told you before, I believe the principal reason for refusing them was that they were not

205

in the present historical style, but they are no worse for that. That committee was looking for the merely conventional. They're stuffy, don't really see eye to eye with Mr Steel, but one day even they will realise that art does not stand still. Now let's look at your pictures again.

'You have handled your subject matter competently, particularly in these three scenes of Leeds. You have observed well. Perhaps less so in the two rural landscapes which tend to be a bit flat. The spatial handling is shallow but that is something you can overcome. I think the overall thing that is lacking is atmosphere. It is present in the one canvas they have kept but less so in the others. I know you attempted it by doing those scenes of Leeds by night but I feel that there you were relying chiefly on the darkness to create atmosphere whereas you should have been imbuing the darkness itself with atmosphere. You can achieve this by using a variety of colours to bring the darkness alive and create an exhilarating atmosphere too. Do you understand what I am getting at?'

'Yes. But I thought too much colour would detract from the night-time effect.'

'It could, you have to be careful how you use it. Think of moonlight. Most people would say it was white but you as an artist can see many more colours in it and in the way it affects those colours in the objects and scenes you observe. It is only by creating these subtle differences, and occasionally exaggerating them, that you will get the atmosphere you seek. But it is going to take a lot of practice. Are you going to be able to do that now?'

Arthur knew Ebenezer was referring to his betrothal.

'If you think I am worth persevering with, I will make the time.'

Ebenezer eyed him seriously. 'Haven't I always declared my faith in your work? I would not waste my time pretending you could be a very good artist if I did not really think so. But, as I have said before, I can't do it for you. The exhibition has given you a platform from which you can go forward. It is up to you now. If you are bound upon this course it will need a lot of hard work; you will need to paint as much as you can, and I would ask you to cover a variety of subjects – landscapes, still life, portraits, buildings, from real life and from the imagination, and make use of a wide variety of colour. I have not unveiled a rosy prospect, good work does not come easily, but I think you are capable of producing it if you are willing to devote time to painting and are not easily distracted. If you think you will be, you had better give up here and now. Only you know how much the desire burns within you.' He paused but Arthur did not respond.

'I think it would be best if you went away and considered what I have said. Weigh up your expectations and desires against the demands life will exert on you now. Then come back to me with your decision.'

Chapter Nine

'Colette, put your book down for a moment.'

She and her father were enjoying the May sunshine while sitting on an iron seat, resplendent with colourful cushions, in the garden to the front of the house. Birds sang in the trees, the may was beginning to blossom in the hedgerows, bringing the promise of new life. Susan Lund had taken Adele to see the horse and pony that had arrived last week and had been comfortably housed in a large field and new stable on the West Cliff.

Colette laid down *The History of the Fairchild Family* by Mrs Mary Martha Sherwood. She was sorry to abandon such an engrossing story but her father wanted to talk. She looked up at him, wondering what was coming.

'As you know Mr and Mrs Westbury answered my letter and are due here on the twenty-fifth for four weeks.'

'Yes, Papa, I know,' Colette said in that precise way she had of talking whenever the atmosphere became serious. She placed her hands together on her lap.

'Well, you also know that one of the reasons they are coming is to advise me on your interest in photography and what it entails.'

'Yes, I know,' she confirmed, feeling a little irritated. She knew all this and wanted to get back to her book; she had left it at an exciting part.

'I don't want to waste Mr Westbury's time. You are only eleven, are you sure you want to take up photography?'

'Papa, we have been through this before and the answer has always been yes. My mind hasn't changed since you last asked me.'

'You know it will be expensive, but I don't mind that if it is something you really want to do and won't tire of very soon.'

'I do want to do it and won't easily tire of it,' she replied convincingly.

'Very well! We shall look forward to the Westburys' visit.'

'May I get back to my book now, please?'

Peter smiled. 'Of course.'

'I'm sorry I couldn't make the weather better for your arrival in Whitby.' Peter hurried Thomas and Nora Westbury into the shelter of the Angel Inn when they alighted from the coach that had brought them from York. Driven by a wind from the sea, rain lashed Whitby, bouncing off cobbles, filling the gutters, and turning roadways into quagmires.

'I have a carriage waiting to take us home, I'll see to your luggage.' Two youths had been unloading it from the coach into the entrance of the inn. Thomas quickly identified his five cases. Peter tossed a coin to another youth and told him to see them safely stowed in the carriage. When all was ready he helped his friends scurry across the soaked ground to the vehicle. Within a short time he was ushering them into his house and out of the wind and rain, which seemed bent on making their first impression of Whitby miserable.

Servants were waiting to take their wet clothes, see to their luggage and, along with Peter, show the visitors to their rooms. Colette and Adele had been waiting eagerly to greet them, excited at having them to stay. Miss Lund renewed their acquaintance also and they were introduced to the housekeeper and the rest of the staff so that they felt at home.

Once they had refreshed themselves and had taken tea, Peter suggested that he show them the rest of the house which would also afford Thomas the opportunity to make an initial assessment of the rooms and choose one suitable for Peter to adapt for Colette's photography.

'Miss Lund, I suggest it might be wise for you to accompany us and also to be there when Mr Westbury is teaching Colette. I think you and I should understand the rudiments of the procedures as a safeguard. If your own interest becomes deeper then so be it for it will be a decided advantage.'

Susan was in total agreement, in fact she welcomed the chance to learn something new, something in which there could well be a future. Besides she wanted to help Colette as much as she could.

By the time they had toured the house Thomas had noted the very room he thought would be suitable. It was to the back of the house with access to the outside and had only one window. At the moment the room was only used for the storage of a few garden implements. When Thomas voiced his opinion about the suitability of this room, Peter remarked, 'I was wondering what to do with it but this is clearly the answer. I'll have it cleared out and refurbished as you see fit.'

'Let me do some measuring. I'll draw up plans and, if you wish, you will be able to start the work after the weekend.'

'How about that, Colette?' Peter smiled and winked at his daughter whom he was well aware had been eagerly taking in everything Mr West-bury had been saying.

She grinned, too overwhelmed to say anything. A dream she had held since first seeing those photographs at Uncle Roger's was coming true.

'I'll start measuring up tomorrow, if that's all right?' Thomas glanced at Peter.

'Perfectly. Have the run of the house.'

'We'll try not to intrude too much.'

'You won't be. You are our guests. And when you have decided what is to be done, you must get to know Whitby on a better day than this.'

'You are most kind.'

'No more than you for what you are doing for Colette.'

Thomas gave a dismissive wave of his hands and said, 'Let us go to the drawing-room, I have something to show you. I think there will be time before our evening meal. Seven, I think you said?'

'That's right,' affirmed Peter, and ushered everyone to the drawing-room.

Colette was so busy talking to Miss Lund that she did not notice Thomas leave them. As she sat down, the girl frowned. Her glance took in every-body. 'Where's Mr Westbury? I thought he had something to show us?'

Nora smiled. 'He'll be back in a minute. And,

211

Colette ... you too, Adele ... I suggest that Mr and Mrs Westbury is too formal. Why not call us Aunt and Uncle?'

The two girls glanced at their father, seeking his approval.

'I think that is a good idea,' he confirmed.

Colette and Adele relaxed. They had been hoping he would say that. At that moment the door opened and Thomas appeared carrying two boxes.

'These are presents from your father who asked me to buy them for you,' he said, smiling and handing one box to Colette and the other to Adele. 'He wanted them to be a surprise.'

With an excited rush Adele was into hers first. 'Ooh!' Her eyes opened wide as she peered into the box. She brought out a riding jacket and matching hat. She looked at Thomas. 'Oh, thank you.' She jumped up then and rushed to her father. There were tears of delight visible in her eyes as she hugged him. 'Thank you! Thank you. It is so lovely.'

Colette, who had paused when her sister had revealed what was in her box, now continued to open hers. She stopped and stared in disbelief. She gulped. Her eyes were damp and she almost choked as she expressed her thanks to her father. Then she very carefully took out a wooden, rectangular box, lovingly dovetailed and polished. The neatly milled brass fitting on one side gave away its purpose. 'A camera! Oh, it's wonderful. Thank you, Papa. Thank you again and again and again.'

Everyone smiled at her delight. 'I hope you get much pleasure from it,' said her father. 'I expect to see wonderful things.'

The two gentlemen lost no time over the refurbishments the next day, and before noon Thomas had decided what should be done. He put his proposals to Peter who accepted them without question as coming from someone with experience. He hired the necessary labour and, overseen by a conscientious foreman, alterations were made to the chosen room, and sinks, cupboards, shelves and racks built in. Because chemicals would be used, Thomas insisted that a large ventilator be placed in one of the outside walls and be so constructed that light could not infiltrate it. A glass-house studio, the door glazed with yellow glass, was attached to the outside. The same sort of glass was used over the gas burners to give a safelight in the room.

The construction work was completed in two weeks, during which time Colette had to curb her impatience. However she was kept fully occupied with Thomas's lessons, which he also extended to her father and her governess. He was pleased with the way that Susan quickly picked up the procedures, for, as careful and capable as he knew Colette to be, it was better that someone else knew what she was doing and could help if necessary.

'I know that the procedure sounds complicated and fussy but, once you have got used to it, the process of taking photographs and making prints will become easier. Master the present techniques and future developments in photography will come more easily to you,' he explained. 'People are experimenting all the time, trying to make things easier for the photographer. They realise that cameras will have to be smaller and easier to handle. New ways of developing and printing will also have to come, particularly as photography becomes more popular.'

'Do you think it will ever become that popular?' asked Susan.

'Certainly. People will realise its many uses. If we consider portraits, for instance, only the well-off can afford to have one painted – previously the poor could not record themselves. But as photography becomes more readily available and cheaper, everyone will be able to have a photograph instead. And think of all the other images that can be made, records of places and whole ways of life. What I have seen of Whitby, so far, has made me realise what a wonderful place it will be to record through photography: the narrow streets climbing the cliffs, the piers and lighthouses, the bridge, the quays, the old church, the ruined abbey ... then all the activities, the ships coming and going, the rope-making and sail-making, the fishing, the jet workers, the sailors, the housewives, the urchins...'

'Wouldn't that apply to anywhere?' queried Susan.

'Oh, yes,' agreed Thomas, 'but some places exude more atmosphere than others and Whitby is one of those. I think a unique photographic record could be made here.'

Colette, lying in bed that night, her mind fired by what she had heard, resolved to document Whitby life and capture its special atmosphere.

A week after his engagement Arthur lay in bed casting his mind back over the last few days. The night he had walked home with Rose, and the following talk with Ebenezer, had become turning points in his life. He had considered Ebenezer's views; he had also thought about Rose's attitude to his painting; one was enthusiastic seeing a promising future, the other lukewarm, seeing it only as a hobby that shouldn't be allowed to impinge on a comfortable life. But what of himself? What did he really want?

He turned on to his side, reaching out to turn down the oil lamp. He paused, turning back the bed-clothes and swinging his legs out of bed. He stood up, hesitated a moment then carried the lamp to his desk where he picked up a pencil. He held it poised above the paper and then made a mark. His pencil flowed, line following line, each vibrant, meaningful, yet economical. His mind was sharply focused, each detail as clear as if the subject of his drawing was there before him. He did not have to think. He was inspired. Twenty minutes later he laid down his pencil and propped up the picture so that the light fell across it. He sat looking at it for five minutes, assessing what he had done, analysing his thoughts. Satisfied, he gave a little nod as if he was setting a seal on what he had done and on the decision he had made. He laid the drawing down. He picked up his pencil and, in neat copperplate writing, wrote one word beneath the picture: Rose.

Arthur stirred. Daylight was streaming through his window. He became wide awake, remembering what he had done before he slept last night. He jumped from the bed and went to his desk. Rose looked out at him from the sheet of paper, his lines bringing her vividly to life. He marvelled that he had created such a good likeness from memory; maybe she had inspired him. Whatever it was, the likeness could not be denied, it was a masterpiece of craftsmanship and amply repaid all the hours he had spent drawing people from memory. Drawings he had never shown Ebenezer. It pleased Arthur greatly, but more than that he was delighted to see that he had captured Rose's character. There was tranquillity here, a hint that she valued a peaceful life, but he had also brought out the underlying steel without marring the touch of humour revealed by her smile. This portrait had made him draw again and he silently thanked Rose for that. But could he see something else in her expression? Was she telling him she should be the most important thing in his life, that she would not tolerate a serious rival in his art?

It was a thoughtful Arthur who finally dressed to go to work. His pencil work had shown him he had finally got over his disappointment at having most of his work rejected by the Literary and Philosophical Society, and yet this drawing seemed to carry a warning from Rose too.

His mind was still troubled as he walked to work but by the time he reached his desk he thought he had a solution.

A fortnight later Arthur walked into Ebenezer's shop and waited patiently while his friend served a customer. The wait set his heart racing a little

216

faster than it had been. How would Ebenezer view the painting he had brought with him? During the last two weeks he had not mentioned to his friend what he was doing, only that he was bearing in mind what Ebenezer had told him and would bring the new work to show him once it was finished. He had completed it last night, viewed it again this morning and, satisfied, had brought it for Ebenezer to see and hopefully sell. Start selling and Rose might be converted.

'This is going to be most interesting,' said Ebenezer as he led the way to the next room. 'You have had me eagerly anticipating how my advice has affected your work. I know it can't change quickly, it will be a gradual development, but at least I hope to see that you have understood what I was getting at.'

Arthur said nothing but laid the picture down and carefully removed the paper with which he had protected it. He stood back to let Ebenezer view it.

The silence that came into the room then was filled with shock and disbelief. Finally it was broken.

'What on earth is this?' Ebenezer's words were charged with critical contempt. This was far from what he had expected.

'A painting I hope you'll be able to sell.'

'What?' Ebenezer's face clouded with anger. 'I wouldn't disgrace my window with it.'

'But you told me the paintings that are selling are traditional, mostly depicting historical scenes. I've done just that with this painting of people going to church.'

'I can see what it is, but it is nowhere near a standard that would make it saleable. You have abandoned all that you have learned except for the rudiments of drawing. There is no atmosphere here. You've lost that by forsaking detail. The touches of it that you had started putting into your paintings was bringing them to life. This picture is wooden because it is not in the personal style that you had developed. Did you really think you could just turn away from it like that and succeed? I can see you have looked at the traditional artists and thought you could emulate them, but take your figures ... they are not alive! Let me tell you that painters in the Grand Style follow certain rules and worked hard to improve their natural talent and get where they are. I directed your natural talent into the direction I thought would be best for your future, and we were getting somewhere.'

'The Philosophical and Literary Society didn't think so,' countered Arthur.

'Old fogeys with their heads in the sand!'

'I thought if I did something in the style and subject matter that sells it would be easier to succeed and so impress Rose and win her over.'

'You certainly won't do it with that picture! You are not being true to yourself with something like that and it shows. No, Arthur, I won't damage your reputation...'

'I haven't got one,' he cut in roughly.

'And never will with work like that. Your other work was shaping up promisingly. Once the Pre-Raphaelite style becomes more widely known your work will come to prominence on the back of it. You will benefit because that style of painting will become sought after. You will be there almost at the start. It is already catching on in London. That interest will spread, and when it reaches Leeds you will have paintings ready to sell.'

'But that's going to take time,' protested Arthur.

'You've got to be patient. You've got to work hard. Keep painting and you will improve. That can only result in paintings that will sell. Now take that out of here ... or better still, let me throw it away. Focus your mind on what you were doing so well.'

Arthur knew it was no use trying to argue. Being eager to sell, had he rebelled this way as a protest? He knew Ebenezer had his best interests at heart. Why had he thought he knew better?

'I'm sorry.'

'Who are you apologising to? I don't need it. It is yourself to whom you should be apologising for drifting away from the path you were taking.'

'The correct path?' Arthur nodded.

'Yes.' Ebenezer's word was sharp, decisive in its confirmation.

'What do you suggest I do now?'

'Concentrate on local places, but in the style you were previously developing. Get more natural detail into them and really make the atmosphere come alive. Use those scenes of Leeds I'm sure you have in your sketchbook. Develop them.'

Arthur left for home in a much more contented frame of mind. He realised his soul had not been in the painting he had taken to Ebenezer. He should never have let himself be swayed by

219

seeking instant sales. By the time he reached home he knew what he really wanted and how he was going to set about achieving it.

Life settled into a pattern. Arthur did most of his painting in the evening but did not let it impinge on time spent with Rose and his friends. Rose fortunately became more immersed in her music and that afforded him the painting time he wanted. His work progressed well, it was as if he had found a new wellspring of talent. Ebenezer was delighted, especially by the way that Arthur had adapted his suggestions. The only setback was that the painting exhibited in the Philosophical Hall was returned unsold. But Arthur had steeled himself for the worst and soon pushed this disappointment to the back of his mind. He saw how, since that submission, his work had improved and that gave an added impetus to his new output.

At work he gained the promotion he had hoped for. It made things easier for the impending marriage and enabled him and Rose to find a house rather than move in with her parents. Everything was falling into place. The only thing that Arthur wished was that his fiancée would take more interest in his painting. She tolerated it, made kind remarks about it, and that was that. But he was determined not to let her indifference divert him from his ultimate aim.

The year moved on with excitement mounting in Leeds amidst preparations for the visit of the Queen to open the new Town Hall on her way from Osborne House on the Isle of Wight to

Balmoral in September.

At first Lizzie and Ben and Grace and Fred planned to have their double wedding the day before the Queen's visit but they soon changed their minds when Arthur and Rose informed them that they had chosen July as their wedding month so that they would be settled before the Queen's visit and would be able to enjoy all the excitement of that as well as their own special day.

Arthur and Rose attended their friends' weddings two weeks before their own. Fred and Grace, Ben and Lizzie, were back from honeymoon and present in the parish church to see Rose and Arthur married in their turn. It was a simple ceremony attended by the families and their immediate friends, the Carters, Sleightholmes, Wainwrights and Hirsts. Rose wore a simple dress of grey corded silk and wool with a motif of embroidered intertwining leaves and roses. The bodice came tight to the waist with pleats running from the shoulder to a central point at the waist; the fitted sleeves came to the wrist. The lace bonnet was small and tied under her chin with a large pink bow.

When she walked down the aisle on her father's arm, Arthur's heart thumped. 'Beautiful,' he whispered to himself, and wondered how she would view the presentation he was to make her later at the reception.

Although they had not the same large garden as the Carters for a reception, Moira Duggan excelled with providing tempting fare in her own home. The whole proceedings went happily with everyone enjoying each other's company. As the time neared for Arthur and Rose to leave, she slipped away to change into her going-away clothes. His admiration surged again when she entered the room. He stepped forward.

'I have a little present for you, love,' he said.

'Another?' Rose showed her surprise as she took the package from him. 'Do I have time to open it now?'

'Yes, the carriage to take us to the station hasn't arrived yet.'

She unfolded the paper wrapping and stood speechless for a moment as she stood staring at her own portrait. Silence filled the room as everyone waited to know what held her attention.

'Me,' she whispered almost to herself, and looked up at Arthur with her eyes damp. 'Oh, Arthur, it's beautiful. When did you do this?'

'In the evenings, in my room. It's from memory, so you see how you have impressed me?'

'Thank you.' She kissed him on the cheek, and passed the drawing for everyone to see.

Admiring comments came from everyone present. Arthur was principally anxious to know what Ebenezer thought and managed to get his friend's opinion as everyone was saying goodbye when the carriage arrived.

'That portrait is good, Arthur. It gives you another medium to exploit but don't neglect what you are trying to achieve in oils.'

'I am hoping that Rose will be so impressed she will come round to accepting and understanding my ambitions.'

Ebenezer nodded. He made no comment but sincerely hoped the same. He knew what a difference the understanding and encouragement of a wife could mean.

After all the excitement of the wedding, the carriage felt very quiet as they settled down for the drive to the station. Rose took her husband's hand in hers. 'Thank you for the drawing, Arthur. It is so nice to know you were thinking of me. It will hang where we will see it continually and be reminded of this wonderful day.'

He smiled and kissed her.

Arriving in Scarborough they hired an open carriage among the many that had assembled at the station for the arrival of the train. Amidst the bustle and buzz the cabbie stowed their luggage safely and enquired their destination.

'Mrs Symonds' lodging house on St Nicholas Cliff,' Arthur informed him.

'A wise choice, sir, the best in town,' said the driver as he saw them comfortably settled before climbing on to his seat and taking up the reins.

Rose raised an eyebrow appreciatively at her husband. He had made all the arrangements. She had not interfered, knowing that he wanted their final destination to be a surprise after they had agreed to honeymoon in what had grown into a fashionable resort because of its reputation for remedial waters, and expanded even more with the coming of the railway in 1845.

The drive was not far, passing along the main thoroughfare and two minor streets before turning into St Nicholas Cliff, an open area with imposing buildings, positioned to give them views across the South Bay. A railed promenade garden occupied the space between them and some smaller dwellings nearer the edge of the cliff. The neat flowerbeds were colourful with roses, lavender, pansies and cinquefoil. People strolled around the paths within the garden or around its perimeter, the ladies in the latest fashions and colours, the men in their thigh-length coats or short jackets with tails, their top hats set at jaunty angles. Rose drank in the scene with silent excitement.

'This is the life,' whispered Arthur as the carriage drew up outside a three-storey brick building with large sash windows and a heavy oak central door set within an attractive pediment. He was pleased by the exterior and hoped the inside of the building and their rooms matched the attractive outside. He had saved especially for this after making enquiries where to stay in Scarborough. He had hesitated about the price initially but had foregone purchasing some art materials; he would manage with what he had until he had saved up again after the honeymoon.

The cabbie carried their luggage inside where they were warmly welcomed by Mrs Symonds in person. She had an amiable air which not only extended to her visitors but also to her staff whose appreciation was shown in their eagerness to respond to her commands.

'Because you indicated this was a special time, sir, I have reserved you a bedroom with a small adjoining sitting room and, of course, all the latest private facilities,' she explained. 'I hope you will be very comfortable and enjoy your visit. If there is anything you require, ask any of the staff.'

They were shown to their rooms where, without appearing to show undue haste, Rose went to the window to see the view. She heard the door click and knew they were alone. She turned round to see a smiling Arthur watching her. 'Oh, it's all so wonderful!' she cried, and rushed to him with outstretched arms, hugging him as his arms came around her waist. 'Thank you so much. I never expected this luxury.'

'We only get one honeymoon,' he whispered.

Their lips met and expressed much of what was to come.

During their ten days in Scarborough they made love, gentle and passionate, lost in a world of their own, making precious memories that would fill a lifetime, ever remembered, ever treasured.

They enjoyed relaxing in their rooms and taking leisurely meals, chatting with other guests. They marvelled at the views across the South Bay, watched the ships in the harbour: fishing vessels leaving and returning with their catch, some of which was sold immediately on the quayside to housewives and traders, some to suppliers of inland towns; colliers bringing coal from the Tyne or merely seeking a berth for the night before proceeding to London. They explored the castle on the headland from where there were stunning views of the coastline to north and south. Rose enjoyed the shops in the newer part of the town but did not take to the old town as did Arthur who saw its potential as a subject for atmospheric paintings.

He was even more enamoured of such a subject when they made a day visit to Whitby. He was highly taken by the town, especially on the east side of the River Esk, feeling the enormous power of its atmosphere, and promised himself that one day he would return to paint it. But Rose was not attracted, much preferring the elegance of Scarborough where one could escape from the bustle and everyday life of the harbour and its nearby narrow streets with their accompanying squalor. In Whitby it semed to her that there was no such escape. The riverside with its quays and shipyards was always present, exerting its influence, turning its surrounding in some parts to dirt and poverty within the narrow confines of the streets.

She was only too pleased when their day in Whitby was over and they were back in Scarborough where she could enjoy promenading in the gardens or sauntering among the fashionably dressed visitors who, mixing with Scarborough's wealthy middle class, walked out on the South Cliff, especially on a Sunday. Most certainly the Newtons would come back here for a holiday.

When they reached Leeds they went straight to their new home and Rose gave a squeak of delight when she walked into the drawing-room and saw that her piano had been brought to the house while they were away. Arthur was pleased too, for he realised it gave him the excuse to establish a studio in the small adjoining room, giving him the opportunity to paint while she was at the piano. After such a wonderful honeymoon and the fact that Arthur had welcomed her instrument, Rose could do nothing but agree to his suggestion.

'But, Arthur,' she said running her hands up over his shoulders, 'you won't spend all your time in there, will you?'

'Of course not, my love,' he said as he enfolded her in his arms. 'but let me pursue my interest just as you are following yours.'

'Very well. Only don't get carried away with your big ideas.'

Ebenezer was delighted to see his friend. 'You had a wonderful time?' He laughed. 'That's a silly question. Of course you did. Did you do any sketching?' He gave another laugh. 'And that's a silly question too. Of course you didn't. You hadn't time.'

'You're right, Ebenezer, I hadn't. But I noted that Scarborough has wonderful subjects that I could turn into paintings which might sell to the visitors now frequenting the resort.'

'That's good to hear. Will you try some?'

'Yes. But I saw what I consider even better subjects with more atmosphere in Whitby. *That's* a place I would really like to paint.'

Ebenezer detected a real enthusiasm for Whitby. 'I know neither place. Maybe it would be a good idea for me to pay them both a visit now it is easy to get to Scarborough by train? I could see what has attracted you, decide whether there is a market there and possibly make contact with art dealers in both places.'

'Would you?' asked Arthur, excitement at the prospect showing in his eyes.

'Of course. It could benefit us both. In the meantime I'd like you to develop your studies of Leeds. Oh, but have you a place in which to paint?'

'Yes. I can set up a small studio at home.'

227

A fortnight later when Arthur walked into Ebenezer's shop he carried two paintings. Ebenezer's eyes lit up. He had been wondering how his protégé was getting on and if he had been following the suggestion of developing his Leeds sketches. Arthur unwrapped the first picture and stood it on an easel so that Ebenezer had a good view of it by the light coming from a left-hand window.

Neither spoke. As much as he wanted his friend's opinion, Arthur did not want to interrupt Ebenezer's concentration. He glanced at him but could read nothing in his impassive expression.

Five minutes that seemed like an eternity passed then Ebenezer said sharply, 'The other.'

Arthur placed it on the easel after taking the first one off. Silence filled the room again. Another five minutes passed. Arthur thought he could stand it no longer. He had to say something. A question was forming in his mind when Ebenezer moved. He brought a second easel and placed it next to the other, indicating to Arthur to put the first painting on it. He studied them for a few moments.

'You have used the same technique as you did in the *A Walk at Roundhay* painting, but it is much better in these. Do you like doing evening scenes?'

'At the moment, yes. I like the idea of exploring the atmosphere of the approaching night especially in the context of buildings and people. Lamplight enables me to do this.'

'You have executed lamplight very well in this picture *Late Afternoon, Park Row, Leeds*. The atmosphere is set by the glow of lights in the buildings and the people returning from their daily activities. I like the lack of detail here in contrast to that of the well-observed figure of the man lighting the gas lamps, making us think of the warm homes that the people are returning to. I love the colour of the gas light reflections on the wet cobbled Street. Much of the same applies to *End of the Day, Boar Lane, Leeds,* where of course you have more light coming in from shop windows. You have handled this well especially by adding a soft moonlight that descends upon the figures, which are less detailed than the rest of the picture. This gives movement and we see that even with oncoming night this is a busy street. I would like to show these to Mr Steel and his wife. I will try and arrange for them to come here but we may have to go to them.'

'Whatever you decide.'

'Very well! I'll see what I can do. Call in on your way home tomorrow.'

'Sorry to disappoint you,' said Ebenezer when Arthur walked in the next day. 'Mr and Mrs Steel are away until the fifth of September.'

'The day before the Queen is due in Leeds?'

'Yes. They must be coming back for the event. That means we won't be able to see them until the eighth at the earliest. I think we should give them a day or two to settle in, but I'll leave word suggesting that we call on them on the tenth.'

'That's going to mean an anxious wait,' replied a disappointed Arthur.

'The time will soon pass. Besides, I'm sure you'll

get swept up in all the excitement of the Queen's visit too. I hear there are lots of preparations being made, and it will present some opportunities for sketches to record a unique occasion. Meanwhile, why not do another painting that we can take along with these two?'

'I may as well.'

'Then let me make a suggestion that could widen the scope of your painting and eventually lead to commissions of a different kind.' He paused and looked hard at Arthur, trying to interpret his reaction.

Arthur smiled. 'You won't know what I think until you tell me.'

Ebenezer's eyes twinkled with amusement. He had been caught out. 'Perspicacious!'

'Now we're on to big words,' teased Arthur.

With the mood lightened, Ebenezer moved on to his suggestion. 'Try an indoor scene. Say a smartly dressed lady looking out of a window. Maybe she is about to go for a walk and is wondering if it is going to rain, or else looking out for a visitor.'

'But I've just developed a detailed style in my outdoor scenes!'

'But think of the detail you can exploit in the type of scene I'm suggesting; on her dress, the pictures on the wall, the furnishings, the doorway ... and through that what we can see of the next room, maybe a chest of drawers, some plants, a chair. Get the idea?'

Arthur nodded. His imagination had been fired. 'So household items take the place of buildings, grasses, stones, and so on?'

230

'Exactly. Your technique is being transferred to an everyday scene about the house as well as to the person. And if that person is recognisable so much the better because this type of portrait, the sitter among their personal property, could definitely lead to commissions.'

Arthur nodded thoughtfully. 'I'll see what I can do.' An idea was already forming as he walked home.

He worked hard on it for he wanted to have it finished the week before Queen Victoria's arrival.

When Fred and Lizzie suggested that, together with Arthur and Rose, and Ben and Grace, they should make that week one of celebration the answer was, 'Why not? We may as well make this visit one to remember.' They planned parties at each other's houses, and when they invited Giles and Barbara and Jack and Dorothy to join them it extended their partying to five nights, leaving a day to view the decorations and decide on a place from which to view the parade to the Town Hall.

Preparations in the town had been going on for months. They had all glimpsed some of them but now, in good spirits and with much laughter, they toured the streets enjoying the conviviality of the crowds who, like themselves, wanted to be included in this special occasion, the like of which they would never see again. They admired the skill of those who had erected the magnificent decorations on shops and factories along the route. Householders had played their part too in decorating the outside of their homes in colourful ways to welcome the Queen to their town. Flags

231

flew in every street; banners proclaimed the people's sentiment: God Save The Queen, or respectfully referred to Victoria, and Albert, Prince of Wales. Poles had been erected to support garlands and streamers, while elaborately decorated triumphal arches formed entrances to some of the streets along the route.

Arthur suggested that they should be early in order to get as near as they could to the station to see the Queen arrive at quarter past six on the Monday evening, the station platform and the wooden stands opposite the entrance only being available to ticket holders. His suggestion paid off for although they were some distance away, and would not be able to see the Queen step out from the station, they were able to catch glimpses of the troops on horseback drawn up to escort the royal carriage.

The buzz of excited anticipation that emanated from the good-humoured crowds subsided when they heard the military band strike up with the National Anthem. 'She's here! She's here!' Their charged exclamations that sent the news sweeping back along the streets were lost when artillery fired a salute.

Fred was the first to detect movement in front of the station and deduce that the Queen must be getting into the Royal carriage. A few moments later the escort started forward, their plumed helmets and colourful uniforms adding to the kaleidoscope of colour. With impeccable precision, horses under control, they rode in front of and behind the Royal Party of the Queen, Prince Albert and the Princesses Helena and Alice. Once the Royal carriage was seen a great cheer went up and swept ahead of the procession, resounding along the route and through the side streets, displaying the public's affection in a swelling tribute to Her Majesty and her family.

Once the carriage had passed them, Arthur grabbed Rose's hand and called to the others, 'Come on.' He led the way, pushing and weaving through the milling mass of people until he turned into a quieter side street. Everyone was too excited to ask where they were going but automatically followed him. He knew that the Queen was staying at Woodsley House, the Mayor's residence, so led his party there to be caught up in the crowds awaiting the arrival of the Royal Family. Security was tight around the house but they got a good view of the arrival of the Royal Party. Determined not to let the evening wane, once the Queen had gone inside the ten friends made their way through the town, enjoying the illuminations and the jovial atmosphere.

The following day they met again and continued with their celebrations, following, as well as they could, the Royal procession after it had left Woodhouse Moor where thousands of Sunday School children had given the Queen a rapturous welcome. Arthur and Ben manoeuvred their party along Briggate, West Street, Queen Street, Park Place and East Parade to the Town Hall. The crowds were thick but Arthur did not worry.

'Where are we going?' Rose asked when he deviated from the route she expected.

All the others posed the same question, concerned that they would miss the Queen's arrival at the Town Hall, but the only answer they got was, 'You'll see.'

He hurried them along a side street and turned into another where he stopped and rapped on a door. It was opened a few moments later by Ebenezer.

'You said to come if we could manage it,' said Arthur.

'I did, my boy, I did. And I'm glad you are here. Follow me.' He hurried up the stairs, paused on the landing, opened a door and called out, 'They're here.'

Immediately a young man, his wife and two children appeared, together with Mrs Hirst and her family. Introductions were quickly made and Arthur thanked Dorian and Freya Hirst for their hospitality, explaining to his friends that Ebenezer had passed on a suggestion from his nephew and his wife that they would be pleased to have them view the arrival of the Queen at the Town Hall from their home.

'You are all welcome,' said Dorian. 'Use this room and the next as you will.'

Charged with excitement, the ten friends expressed their thanks and delight again when they saw that from these first-floor windows they had an unobstructed view of the front of the Town Hall. Its imposing entrance of a flight of bow-shaped steps leading to a line of towering Corinthian columns with three pairs of double doors, beautifully carved, was only bettered by the dominant clock tower where similar columns supported the housing for the clock and its dome.

'That's magnificent,' commented Ben. 'I'm so

glad the council reversed its opposition to the clock tower.'

Everyone passed complimentary comments about the new building that would dominate the centre of Leeds.

'Thank goodness the architect built it to the back of the site and left plenty of room in front to form an attractive space,' observed Jack.

'What are those two smaller towers?' queried Dorothy.

'Ventilation shafts,' explained Dorian. 'I was puzzled when I saw them going up so I asked one of the workmen.'

'Don't the soldiers look smart?' said Rose admiring the ranks, in position for the arrival of the Queen.

The rumble of cheering that could be heard in the distance grew louder.

'She must be getting near,' someone said.

The clop of horses' hooves became clearer and in a few minutes the first of the cavalry appeared. Riding four abreast, swords held stiffly in their right hands and horses perfectly controlled, they made a magnificent sight as line after line rode into the square. The carriage procession was close behind and behind that another array of cavalry. The horsemen knew exactly the positions they had to take up. They wheeled their mounts and settled them, ignoring the cheering that rent the air at great volume when the Queen appeared. Wave after wave of sound broke across the square and resounded off the building she had come to open.

Everyone in Dorian's house strained to see as much as they could, trying to take in everything at once, thankful that they had such a privileged view. It was not until the Queen had descended from her carriage, been escorted into the Town Hall by the Mayor while a red flag was hoisted, and then a Royal Salute been fired to announce that the Town Hall had been officially opened, that they relaxed.

Everyone started to make comments until Freya silenced them. 'The Queen will be inside for some considerable time but please don't go. Stay to see her leave.'

'But we have imposed enough,' said Rose.

Her friends murmured their agreement and started to thank her and Dorian again, but Freya raised a hand and called for them to be silent.

'When Dorian's uncle suggested that you come, we were only too pleased to be able to give you a good viewing point. I also anticipated that you might like to see the Queen leave and prepared some refreshments. Please help us eat them or there will be a lot of leftovers.'

'We won't take no for an answer,' put in Dorian to emphasise his wife's invitation.

Everyone made their thanks and Ben added, 'This has been a most welcome surprise, all the more so because it was completely unexpected. Arthur had not said a word.'

'I wanted to surprise you all.'

'You certainly did that, and it was most acceptable,' said Barbara.

'Since you've given your maid the day off, we must help,' said Lizzie, and followed Freya to the kitchen where they were joined by the other young ladies.

As the men fell into conversation, Arthur went to the window, slipped a sketchbook and pencil from his pocket and in a few quick lines made an outline of the scene in the square.

'It could make a good subject,' said Ebenezer who had quietly come to his side.

'It might come in useful.'

'I'm sure it will.'

Arthur quickly made some notes on his sketch to remind him of colouring and angles of light. He could have gone on for a long time but when the ladies appeared carrying plates of sandwiches, scones and cakes, he pushed the book back into his pocket.

The time passed pleasantly. The joyful atmosphere of the occasion had lifted everyone's spirits. As the afternoon drew on, a wary eye was kept on proceedings outside. When Jack announced that things were beginning to happen everyone crowded to the windows again. They saw the Queen and her family emerge, make their farewells to the Leeds officials and, with cheers ringing out, leave for Wellington Street Station to continue the journey to Scotland.

It was something of an anti-climax when the girls insisted on washing up but that was offset when Ebenezer produced a final few bottles of wine that he had kept back for this moment. He raised his glass, toasted the Queen and insisted that the six bottles be finished. Everyone left in a merry mood and the friends who had set out together finished their week of celebrations at Arthur's and Rose's.

When the final guest had departed Arthur said

in a voice that was slightly slurred, 'I'm going to put some finishing touches to a picture.'

Rose gave a little smile. 'Oh, no, you're not, I've other things in mind.' Her eyes were bright and teasing as she came to him. She swayed. His hands came to her waist and steadied her. He looked down into eyes that had been made brighter by wine. He felt the suppleness and warmth of her body, and was lost. The painting he wanted to finish for Ebenezer could wait another day.

Chapter Ten

The strains of the piano drifted to Arthur as he was putting the final strokes to the painting he had neglected last night. He stood back and surveyed it with a critical eye. He came to the easel, made some adjustments to the tones on the side of the lady's dress, then stepped away again. A few moments later he gave a little nod of satisfaction and laid down his paints and brush. He hoped he had achieved what Ebenezer wanted. He would know tomorrow.

'Bring it through,' said his friend when Arthur walked into the shop the following evening.

In the next room, knowing what his friend wanted, Arthur put his painting on the easel and stepped away without a word. He waited anxiously while Ebenezer assessed the painting. Nervous tension gripped him, it always did whenever he awaited his friend's opinion.

'You learn fast,' commented Ebenezer over his shoulder, 'and that reveals a natural talent. This is good. You have embodied the techniques that you have displayed in your outdoor scenes, except of course, this does not have the atmosphere of night that you have created in those. The light here is just right for the subject. I can feel its illumination streaming in through the window and lighting the detail on the furniture, wallpaper, carpet, the pictures on the wall and the lady herself.' He glanced at Arthur. 'Rose. I see. Has she seen this?'

There was a touch of sadness in Arthur's eyes when he replied. 'Yes, but all she said was "Ooh, it's me. It's nice. Shall we hang it opposite my portrait?"'

'And?' Ebenezer prompted when Arthur hesitated.

'I told her I wanted you to see it, and that it was to be seen by Mr and Mrs Steel.'

'And her reaction?'

'"See that we get it back."'

'Well, at least she had that much interest.'

There was doubt in Arthur's answering grimace. Ebenezer wished that Rose were more enthusiastic, more supportive and inspiring. Arthur's work was already excellent but added vitality would make it exceptional. If only Rose took as much interest in Arthur's painting as Rowena Steel had, and still did, in Laurence's work. What would they say to Arthur's latest offerings?

'When you come from work tomorrow, we'll go to see the Steels.'

'Do they know?' Arthur asked.

'Yes. I left word for them and suggested they

contact me if it is not convenient. I've had no word, so presumably they will be expecting us.'

'I'll be late home today,' Arthur told Rose over breakfast.

'Ebenezer again?'

Arthur detected a note of antagonism in her voice. 'Yes.' he replied coolly. 'We are taking that painting I showed you, with two others that Ebenezer already has, to Mr and Mrs Steel's to see what they think to them.' His voice brightened on the idea that had suddenly occurred to him. 'Why don't you come too?'

She gave a shake of her head. 'There would be no point. I'd be bored while you four talked about art.'

'It's more than that. Mr and Mrs Steel are being good enough to give their time to criticise my work and help me improve. You might become interested.'

'I'd rather stay here and amuse myself at the piano.'

'I wish you would try to see what I want to do.'

'You want to improve your painting. I know that and it's all right.'

'It's more than improving. I want it to go on and on until I sell paintings regularly.'

Rose gave a little grunt of derision combined with annoyance. 'You go to the Steels' if you must but don't expect me to be enthusiastic about something that I can see taking up more and more of your time while getting you nowhere. Time that you should be spending with me.'

Arthur's eyes narrowed. 'Are you hinting that

I'm neglecting you?'

'Take it as you like.'

'What about your piano playing?'

'That doesn't take me out of the house.'

Arthur felt his temper rising. He forced himself to hold it on a tight rein. He did not want them to fall out. He hoped that would never happen. The joys they had shared last night swam before him. In their intimacy, his painting, her piano, did not matter. Their future was filled only with the ecstasy of sharing.

He stood up. 'I must go to work.' He looked hard at his wife. 'One day, Rose, you will be proud of me.'

She met his gaze firmly. 'I am proud of you now, you are doing well in your job.'

He kissed her on the forehead. 'I don't know exactly what time I will be in this evening. You get your meal. Ask Cook to leave me something cold.'

She said nothing but sat gazing at the door after he had closed it behind him. This would be the first time that they had not eaten their evening meal together. Was it a portent of things to come? She stiffened. She would see that it wasn't. She wished these people, who only seemed to be interested in art, wouldn't encourage Arthur and plant big ideas in his mind, ideas that would disrupt the comfortable life that lay ahead of them.

This confrontation, though he regarded it as a minor event, worried Arthur until he became engrossed in the forthcoming development of passenger services from Leeds. By the time he

reached Ebenezer's after work, he had submerged it in the thought that Rose would
become interested once he had sold a painting.

Ebenezer was as excited as he was on the way to
the Steels'. He could not stop chattering but
never mentioned art in any way; the subject
seemed taboo, and when Arthur's attempt to turn
the conversation to the latest exhibition at the
Philosophical Hall was dismissed out of hand,
Arthur knew what the trouble was. He made no
further attempt to break into Ebenezer's chatter.

Laurence and Rowena Steel were waiting for
them and as soon as they arrived invited them to
have a glass of Madeira. As he handed one to
Arthur, Laurence said, 'This is the civilised way
to view paintings. You've brought three, I see.'

'Yes, sir.'

'Painted since we last saw you?' asked Rowena.
'Yes.'

'Can we see them in the order you painted
them?' She indicated the easel.

Arthur placed his first painting for them to see.
'Park Row.'

Arthur was pleased that Rowena had instantly
recognised the subject.

She and her husband viewed it without speaking and after five minutes asked for the second
one.

'Boar Lane,' said Laurence.

Arthur caught Ebenezer's eye and saw him give
a little nod of approval that indicated he was
delighted that the subject had been recognisable.

'The third?' said Laurence after a few minutes.

Arthur's heart pounded. This was the painting

that was different in subject matter and lighting. What would they think?

The Steels took longer studying this picture than they had the others.

The moment he detected they had finished their consideration Arthur expected comments to be forthcoming but he was kept in suspense while Laurence said, 'We must recharge our glasses.'

His mind raced. He had tried to interpret their feelings from their expressions while they were looking at the paintings but had been unsuccessful. He had no more success now while watching the glasses being replenished.

Laurence took a sip of his wine, cleared his throat and said, 'Arthur, you have certainly improved.'

His heart raced at the praise but that did not tell him all he wanted to know. In his mind he urged Mr Steel to go on.

'I like all three, and am pleased that the third one differed from the other two. The atmosphere in the two paintings of Leeds is excellent. Do you prefer doing night scenes?'

'I don't prefer them but I like doing them.'

'That answer pleases me,' put in Rowena, 'because I liked the third one and if you enjoy that type of subject as well your art will be much wider and can develop more. You must keep both genres in mind. Now, that does not mean that all your landscapes have to be night scenes. You can produce daylight scenes and imbue them with the same bright use of colour as you have the third painting. And if you use moonlight or lamplight in scenes similar to the third painting you will get some very atmospheric moods. I think you have made marvellous progress.'

'Thank you, ma'am.' Arthur was thrilled with her criticism and guidance. He wanted to shout for joy. It appeared they had faith in his ability. He could sense that Ebenezer was as pleased as he was.

'I suggest that Ebenezer puts the two Leeds pictures in his window for sale,' said Laurence.

'Do you really think they will sell, sir?' asked Arthur, his voice faltering with excitement.

'I think they have a chance.'

'What about the third one?' Ebenezer asked.

Laurence smiled. 'I suspect that Arthur wants that for the young lady in the painting.'

Ebenezer looked quizzically at him. 'Do you?'

'Yes.'

Ebenezer was surprised but held his tongue.

'I like that one very much,' put in Rowena, 'and I think you could develop that type of portrait that shows something of the person in the background and setting as well as in their features and pose. I know the suggestion I am about to make can only materialise in, say two years, but it is something for Arthur to aim at and work towards. If he develops more paintings like those we have seen today, and also paints some country landscapes in the same style, we can have a one man exhibition.'

'What?' Arthur's cry was filled with astonishment. 'You really think so?'

'Yes. It will mean you have to spend a lot of time finding subjects and painting them. Will you want to do that?'

244

'Most certainly.' He glanced at Ebenezer who was grinning like a Cheshire cat. 'You'll help me, Ebenezer?'

'Try and stop me. To gain this accolade for my discovery from Mr and Mrs Steel is wonderful.'

'We'll all help,' said Rowena who received a nod of agreement from her husband. She paused then added, 'I must say one thing. My husband has influence but won't use that to promote you, nor must you. He and I will remain in the background ready with advice, should you want it. Our interest will only be revealed how and when we say. We will not be party to anything shabby or below standard. Laurence's reputation must not be damaged. So, Arthur, it is up to you to turn out work that we think is worthy of exhibiting. The more paintings we have to choose from the better, but that does not mean you should become slapdash. It will be quality that matters in the long run, and of course choice of subject matter. It is up to you.'

'Mrs Steel, what can I say? I am overwhelmed.'

'Then say nothing. It is our satisfaction to be of help to someone we believe will be an important artist one day.'

'My head is in the clouds.'

'Come down to earth. There is a long way to go before you can achieve what I detect is in your heart. That young lady in the painting is no doubt an inspiration to you.'

He caught Ebenezer's glance. Arthur knew his friend realised the truth but he was not about to reveal it to the Steels. Maybe he could make Rose change her mind and then she could become a real inspiration to him? In the meantime his drive

245

would come from turning out work that would establish his reputation and help convince his wife that his future lay in painting. In two years' time he hoped he would have achieved that.

Arthur and Ebenezer were in a state of high elation when they left the Steels'. All the way back to his shop Ebenezer was giving Arthur ideas of what to paint.

'Holding the exhibition in Leeds will attract local people who are making money on the back of the town's expansion. They will like paintings of their own surroundings. Transport is enabling people to reach further afield so there could be interest in pictures of places around Leeds as well.'

'And the coast is accessible by train,' Arthur reminded him.

'Ah, yes, you thought Scarborough and Whitby would make good subjects. I said I would have a look at them. I'll do that in the spring of next year. Certainly, if suitable, those places could be attractive to people from Leeds who have visited them. And do some more similar to your portrait of Rose. Gentlemen could be interested in similar portraits of their wives and daughters. There is great potential for this exhibition, but don't experiment with other styles. At least, not yet. Stick to the ones you like. This exhibition could give you a real foundation for future work.'

Arthur absorbed all this advice as he walked home from Ebenezer's shop. He wondered how Rose would take this news?

He heard soft gentle piano music when he opened the front door. He closed it gently behind him and stood listening. He recognised it as Rose's favourite piece, the Moonlight Sonata: it was a piece that she assiduously practised, ever striving to bring more feeling from the notes. He could not distinguish the subtle differences that came with her improvement, whereas he would have appreciated such things in a painting. Nevertheless he enjoyed hearing her play and this particular piece always seemed to put her in a good mood. He hoped that would be the case this evening.

He walked quietly across the marble floor of the small hall and gently pushed open the door of the drawing-room. Catching the movement, Rose looked up and stopped playing.

'Go on, love,' he encouraged.

She let her hands caress the keys and draw soothing sounds from the piano as he crossed the room. He bent over her from behind and kissed her on the cheek, at the same time squeezed her waist with a loving touch. She stopped and swung round on the piano stool.

'You must have had a good evening. You look like a cat that's just been given a bowl of cream.'

'That's exactly how I feel.' He pulled her to her feet and hugged her. Then, taking her by the hand, said, 'Come and sit down and I'll tell you all about it.' He led her to the sofa keeping hold of her hands. 'I'm going to have a one man exhibition,' he announced with the crisp sense of achievement.

'What? When?' Rose could only gasp the two words but she filled them with disbelief.

'About two years' time,' Arthur pressed on, his words ringing with pride. 'I'll have to do a lot of paintings so that we will have a choice when we know where the exhibition will be held and how many paintings can be displayed.'

Rose shook her head. 'Arthur Newton, stop teasing me. You've got that look you had when you used to snatch an apple from the pile I was carefully assembling in the shop.'

'I'm not teasing. It's perfectly true.'

She saw he was serious. 'But you? Exhibiting?' She frowned in disbelief.

'Why not? I told you I was good.'

'Is Ebenezer filling your mind with this nonsense?'

'It was Mrs Steel who suggested it.'

'What does she know about it?'

'You obviously haven't listened to what I told you about first going to meet them,' replied Arthur, slightly irritated that she hadn't taken more notice. 'She and her husband are well known in the art world.'

'So why are they bothering with you?'

'They think I have talent and, being friends of Ebenezer, want to help me.'

'I think it's all nonsense! They're filling your mind with impossibilities. All right, have this exhibition if you must, but don't get carried away with these foolish notions of becoming an important artist. That isn't for the likes of you.'

'Why not?'

'You have a respectable job – safe, comfortable and with every chance of promotion if you apply yourself.'

'You should be encouraging me,' snapped Arthur.

'I've said you could exhibit. It would appear it is going to take up a lot of your time and that I don't like. Two years? You'll get nowhere and then it will be two years wasted. And what if you do sell some paintings? It will be no guarantee for the future.'

'It will be a step in the right direction. It will make the chances of selling again more likely. People will have seen my work and talked about it. Who knows where it will end?'

'Dreamland.'

'Is it so wrong to have ambition?'

'No, as long as it's in the right direction, based on a good solid foundation. You have that in your work for the railway. Direct your ambition there and I know you will go far, maybe even right to the top. I could be of great help to you. You men think we have no ambition. Well, we have: the ambition to see our husbands successful and help them towards that end. How do you think my father would have done without Mother behind him? And I suspect that yours had a lot to do with your father gaining his promotion in the bank. I can do the same for you from the good start you have made at the railway.'

'But not for my art?'

'Direct you towards an uncertain future?' Rose shook her head.

'It wouldn't be like that.'

'You don't know. You'd best forget this exhibition and these people who fill your head with grandiose ideas.'

'I've got to have it! I won't know how far I can go until I've tried.'

Rose sighed. 'All right, have it, waste two years.' She gave a little pause. 'Maybe they won't be wasted if it gets this stupid idea out of your system.'

There was a steely determination in the way Arthur picked up his brush the following evening. Rose had unconsciously inspired him, maybe not in the way he had hoped but inspired nevertheless: to prove her wrong.

'Colette seems to have enjoyed this first year of photography,' commented her father when Miss Lund settled in front of the fire, having seen Colette and Adele to bed.

'She has indeed,' replied Susan, 'and so have I for that matter. I thank you for giving me the opportunity of sharing it with her.'

'It was to my own advantage for you to do so. I haven't spent as much time with her as I would have liked so it was a comfort for me to know that you were keeping an eye on her, especially when chemicals are involved.'

'She has ambitions for her photography. Sees it as a means of breaking out of the mould.'

'Your own radical views have not been tempered since coming to work here, I see.'

'I'm sorry if they oppose yours,' replied Susan, a little testily.

'No, not at all. I find them refreshing and think, in the way you present them, they are important to Colette's and Adele's education. Please don't water them down on my account.'

'Thank you for that vote of confidence.'

'I had that from the moment of your arrival

here, and from the way my daughters took to you and you to them. I realised I had found a gem in you.'

Susan blushed. 'I was equally lucky, if not more so. I had not had a pleasant life in Scarborough.' She changed the subject before she became wistful. 'Colette and I have been mostly using the waxed paper process.'

'That's the one where you can prepare materials a few days before you want to use them, and after taking the photograph can process the result up to two weeks afterwards?'

'Yes, that is correct, but the results are not as good as using glass plates with the Collodion process, which means using the plates while they are wet after being treated with the appropriate chemicals, so you have to work quickly.'

'And that is restricting you to portraits?'

'Yes, and both of us must be engaged in the work, one preparing the plates in the dark room while the other is getting the sitter ready in the studio.'

'So what is this leading to?'

'As you know Colette has always had a desire to record Whitby scenes and life.' He nodded. 'I believe that should be encouraged. I see signs that she is growing frustrated by not being able to do it with the quality of photography she wants.'

'I can see you are going to suggest something.'

'Yes.'

'Go ahead then.'

Susan dampened her lips and swallowed. 'You know there are portable darkrooms?'

'Of course. I've not encouraged her to consider

251

one because of the chemicals involved and the bulk of the equipment.'

'The portable dark room is becoming more and more manageable. In fact, it can be packed into a good-sized knapsack.'

'So you are suggesting that Colette should have one?'

Susan looked a little embarrassed. 'Yes. I think we shouldn't let the opportunity for her to photograph Whitby slip by. I can see it developing into a good business.'

'How?'

'She would be able to produce better prints and be able to repeat them time after time.'

'Why would she want to do that?'

'To sell them.'

'To whom?'

'To the people who appear in the photographs. They'd all like to have pictures of themselves. There will be further potential as the holiday trade grows, with people wanting photographs of the place they have visited.'

'You seem to have this all worked out, Miss Lund?'

'I have thought about it because I believe Colette has a gift for seeing a picture and translating it to paper by means of her camera. And it will give her some independence.'

'I'm not sure about turning this into a business, but if you think it would benefit her hobby then I'll get her a portable dark room for her birthday in the new year.'

'I'm sure she will be very grateful.'

'I'll tell her at breakfast in the morning.' He

eyed Susan seriously. 'There is only one thing: you must accompany her on these photographic expeditions.'

'I would not do otherwise, Mr Shipley,' she reassured him with equal seriousness.

'Good. And I wouldn't want you to neglect Adele.'

'I make sure that they receive equal attention. Tomorrow morning I will be taking Adele for a ride while Colette will be doing some written work that I have set her.'

Peter detected a touch of hurt in her voice, as if she thought he was criticising her. 'I'm not being critical, Susan. I couldn't be. I owe you a great deal for what you are doing for my daughters.'

She met his gaze then shyly looked away. He had used her Christian name! The first time since she had come here. Had he realised it? Pleasure churned inside her and she found herself embarrassed by it. Flustered, she stood up. 'I should go to bed.'

'Oh, dear, have I offended you? I didn't mean to. Don't go. Stay and have a glass of Madeira.'

'Thank you,' she said quietly and sat down again.

Later, as she lay in bed Susan counted her good fortune again and in her mind relived the evening when she and Peter Shipley became no longer employee and employer but friends on Christian name terms.

'Good morning, you two,' Peter said brightly when his daughters came into breakfast the next morning and bent to kiss him on the cheek.

'Good morning, Miss Lund,' they both said politely as they went to their places at table.

The governess returned their greeting with a smile.

Once everyone was settled, Peter cleared his throat. 'Colette, Susan and I were talking about photography after you had gone to bed last night.'

A serious expression laced with curiosity enveloped her face. 'Don't you mean Miss Lund, Papa?'

Peter gave a little start of embarrassment as his glance momentarily caught Susan's. Her Christian name had slipped out. 'I said Susan and that is what I meant,' he said gently by way of explanation. 'I think that Miss Lund has been with us long enough for me to treat her on equal terms, and call her by name. Now that is understood, I have something more to say to you, Colette.'

'This sounds serious,' she said in a deep voice and pulled a face at Adele.

Adele chuckled. 'You're in trouble, Colette!'

'She's not,' said their father. 'In fact, I think it's news that she will like.' His gaze settled on his elder daughter and he saw she was hanging on his every word. 'As I said, Susan and I were discussing photography last night and the outcome is that I will buy you a portable dark room for your thirteenth birthday in February.'

Silence. Colette just stared at him. This wasn't happening. She had only thought she had heard this.

'Well?' His prompting shattered the disbelief.

Colette jumped to her feet, almost sending her chair crashing. She rushed to him and flung her

254

arms round his neck. 'Thank you, thank you, thank you.' The words poured out as tears of gratitude filled her eyes. 1859 was going to be a wonderful year.

'Go and thank Susan,' he whispered in her ear, 'she talked me into it.'

Colette ran to her governess, hugged her and kissed her. 'Thank you.'

As she returned to her seat, Peter said, 'You must have Susan with you when you go out with the dark room. People will be curious. You are not to go out on your own. I look forward to seeing the results.'

'I'll be able to do so much more.'

'You are not to neglect your school work,' warned Susan. 'Are you all ready to do that written work while I take Adele riding this morning?'

'Yes.'

When Susan read the work later in the day she knew Colette's mind had not been fully focused on the task. She did not chide her, for she knew where her mind must have been. The excitement would pass.

Two weeks before Christmas Arthur headed for Ebenezer's shop. With the collar of his overcoat turned up against the biting wind, shoulders hunched against the chill, hat pulled well down, he was hardly aware of the window display. He reached the doorway and stopped. Something had caught his attention, something was different. He turned back to look in the window. There was only one of his paintings on display. *End of the Day, Boar Lane* was not there. Excitement flared in him but he quickly brought it under control. The fact that it was not there could mean anything. He didn't want his excitement to be met by disappointment.

He stepped into the shop and closed the door quickly to keep out the chill. Ebenezer was serving a customer so Arthur stood to one side, propped the picture he had brought against the wall and adjusted his overcoat more comfortably.

As the door closed behind the satisfied customer, Ebenezer grinned and said in a loud voice. 'Sold! Sold, my dear boy!'

'*End of the Day, Boar Lane?*'

'Yes! Yes!'

'Wonderful!' Arthur did a little jig.

There were footsteps on the stairs. Zilda appeared. 'I thought from that noise Arthur must have arrived. Nothing gets my husband more excited than selling a painting.' She smiled broadly and gave Arthur a kiss on the cheek. 'Well done!'

Ebenezer reached under the counter and brought out a bottle of wine and three glasses.

'He's had them under there for three days, waiting for you to come in,' Zilda explained.

Ebenezer filled the glasses and then raised his. 'To future success.'

When the immediate furore had settled, Arthur asked. 'Who bought it?'

'The owner of one of the shops in the painting. He said he wanted to hang it in the shop for all his customers to see and realise they were in an important shop, one that had been painted by a talented artist.'

'That will be good publicity for you,' said Zilda.

'It will be seen by a lot of people; paintings in private houses are seen by only a few.'

'I got three pounds for it,' said Ebenezer with a flourish.

'Wonderful!' cried Arthur.

Ebenezer took the money from a drawer and pushed it across the counter.

'You must take the commission we agreed on when you said you would sell for me.' Ebenezer waved a dismissive hand but Arthur would have none of it. 'Our dealings must be strictly businesslike. If not it could lead to trouble.'

Ebenezer tightened his lips in protest but slackened them when his wife intervened. 'Arthur is right, Ebenezer. It is the best way to avoid trouble between friends.'

'All right.' he agreed, and took his money. 'What have you brought to show us?'

'A present for Dorian and Freya for having us to see the Queen at the Town Hall.' He unwrapped the painting to reveal the scene from the window of their house.

Ebenezer and Zilda gasped and gazed at it with wondering eyes.

'That's magnificent,' said Ebenezer. 'You have really captured everything – and what an atmosphere of pomp and gaiety! You can almost hear cheering, and orders being shouted.'

'It's amazing. You improve with every painting,' said Zilda in admiration.

'I think I could sell some similar to this. Let me try and sell this one?' Ebenezer suggested.

'No,' replied Arthur emphatically. 'That is for your nephew and his wife. If I get a chance to do any more then you shall have them, but I am working towards the exhibition.'

Ebenezer gave a nod of approval. Arthur had his priorities right; his mind was on the exhibition, which, if his painting continued to improve as rapidly as was evident in his latest work, could mark an important point in his career. It could determine his future success and ability to become an artist whose works would be sought after. The sale of *End of the Day, Boar Lane, Leeds* had come at the right time; it would give added impetus to his work for the exhibition.

Arthur's eyes saw the world as a magical place as he walked home. He was unaware of the chill wind rippling the puddles left by the rain that had fallen while he had been with Ebenezer. He had sold a painting that would be displayed where hundreds, nay, maybe thousands, of people would see it! Nothing, not even the buffeting he was getting, could drown out the song in his heart. Rose must take note of this success.

She was busy with her latest embroidery when he walked into the drawing-room with a flourish that made her needle stop in mid-stitch.

'I've sold a painting!' His ebullient mood filled the room.

Her eyes brightened for a moment. 'Good, I'm pleased. Pocket money for you.'

'Pocket money?' He laughed at what he thought was her naïvety. 'It's a start. The rock on which my future ... no, our future ... will be based.' He sat down opposite her. Leaning forward with enthusiasm evident in every sinew, he gazed at her with

258

ambition burning in his eyes.

'Now, don't get carried away, Arthur. This is just one painting. You may not sell any more.'

Her attitude struck a chill to his heart. He had hoped she would be delighted. Instead she was pouring cold water, as sharp as the wind outside, on his enthusiasm.

'Ebenezer and Zilda think I will.'

'You're getting carried away again. Yes, if you sell a painting now and again it will be a very nice supplement to our income but as I've said before, don't let a simple success jeopardise our life.'

Naïve? Arthur laughed at himself. Rose wasn't naïve, she was very much the opposite. Now he recognised a determination in her that told him she would do all she could to achieve what she thought was right for him.

He pushed himself wearily to his feet and walked from the room without a word. He closed the door and stood with his back to it for a few moments. Then he strode across the hall to his studio, his body taut, fingers tight. They only relaxed when he picked up a brush. His first few strokes were vicious strikes across the paper, but they helped to calm him. He stood looking at the red slashes of paint, then quietly tore the paper from the pad and threw it away. But his determination had been heightened. He would prove that he was right.

Rose raised her eyebrows as the door closed. Such excitement over selling one picture! Oh, she could understand it, but it also carried a danger of upsetting their comfortable lives. She must be wary. Let Arthur paint if he must but she must be strong about not letting it take over as his profession.

Colette dressed quickly. This was the day when her photographic ambitions would gain a significant boost. She rushed into Adele's room but pulled up sharp. Her sister was not there. Her bed had not been straightened, something their father had insisted they should do before the maid came to make them properly. Clothes were scattered across a chair and the dressing-table was a mess. Colette gave a little grunt. 'Untidy girl.' Her sister must be downstairs already. She ran from the room, down the stairs and into the dining room.

'Happy Birthday!' three voices laughingly called at once. Her father, sister and governess stood at the end of the table facing the door with several parcels before them.

'Thank you!' Colette called as she ran over to them, her eyes widening at the sight of the gifts. She received their kisses and hugs and eagerly turned to her parcels. She started with the smallest and worked her way to the largest, for she knew what that one would be and, though she was anxious to see it, she wanted to save it until last. A necklace from her sister; a pale blue muslin dress from Miss Lund; three books from her father: *Emma*, *Cranford*, and *Rob Roy*; several small packets of various sizes containing ribbons, sweetmeats, an assortment of comfits, her favourite chocolate, brooches and bangles, some of them from the staff. She would go and thank them immediately after opening the big one. Her fingers twitched with excitement as she removed the wrapping paper to reveal a dark green knapsack. She slipped the fastenings loose and looked inside. Covers, trays, bottles ... everything she would require to process her pictures on location. 'Oh, it's all wonderful! Thank you so much.' She hugged her father.

'That's not all,' said Peter. 'There is something missing. Something Susan insisted on getting you.'

As he was speaking Susan was going to one corner of the room. She returned holding a substantial tripod. 'You'll need that on which to set the folding top that is in the knapsack.'

'Oh, Miss Lund, it's wonderful.' It was all too much for Colette. Tears of appreciation streamed down her cheeks as she hugged her governess.

'There was one with the dark room but Susan was adamant that you needed a stronger one and that she should buy it for you,' her father explained. 'Now the immediate excitement is over, go and thank the staff for their presents and then come and have your breakfast.'

When she returned Colette told them that Mrs Fenton said Cook had prepared a special tea. 'So I suggested that we don't sit down and that they and Charlotte, Hannah and Helen help us eat it.'

'That was very kind of you, I'm sure they will appreciate it.'

She joined them at the table. 'Can we go and try my dark room out, Miss Lund, please?'

Susan laughed. 'You've been too excited to look outside.'

Colette jumped from her chair and ran to the window. When she turned from it she gave a sharp shake of her head and snapped, 'Bother!'

It was snowing and there was already a thick covering. Though the trees wore a magical layer of dripping white, Colette did not see the beauty in it, only the hindrance.

It was a fortnight before she was able to try her new portable dark room. Susan was just as enthusiastic as she to try it out, and even Adele, who was not particularly interested in photography, became caught up in their enthusiasm and volunteered to carry some of the equipment.

'Are you coming, Papa?' Colette asked.

'I have two letters to write but I'll come along shortly. I wouldn't miss this first venture. I'll be there by the time you get set up. Where will you be?'

'Along St Ann's Staith or Pier Road. I want to take a picture looking upstream towards the bridge. Hopefully I'll be able to get some ships in it.'

Curious glances were cast in their direction while Colette set up her tripod and camera, but they became even more curious when the three young women started busily establishing a strange contraption with three sturdy legs supporting a table-like top on which they set out trays and bottles and over which they draped a large black cloth.

There were murmurs of speculation among the small crowd that had gathered round. A fisherman was bold enough to put the question everyone wanted to ask: 'What are you doing?'

'I am going to take a photograph, and then under that cloth I will develop and print it. If you wait you'll see it,' Colette explained.

She went to her camera and made some slight adjustments to achieve the composition she wanted. As she finished she was pleased to see her father hurrying towards them.

'Just in time,' she greeted him.

'You're gathering quite a crowd,' Peter said.

'I told you people would be interested.'

She took the picture and was quickly under the cover with the plate. Susan had everything ready and two minutes later they emerged with the print. Colette handed it to her father, who, with Adele also eager to see, let out an appreciative whistle. Colette could sense the heightened curiosity of the crowd.

'Very good,' Peter commented. 'I'm surprised at the ease with which you did it.'

'Well, I had help,' she pointed out as she passed the photograph to the fisherman and told him to show it around.

'What do you think, Susan?' Peter asked.

'It makes so much possible. The only drawback is having to carry all this equipment, but if it is helping to achieve what Colette wants then so be it. There will always be two of us so it should not present too many problems. I can see that some day it won't be necessary to do all this. Someone will find a simpler way. They're bound to in the name of progress.'

Meanwhile Colette had walked among the crowd and been answering their questions. She had been eyeing the curious fisherman as she was speaking to other people. His weather-beaten face, lined by the wind and the sea, eyes with their far-reaching vision, bushy but neatly trimmed beard, heavy gansey and high-crowned hat with its brim turned up at the back and sides, would make an interesting picture.

'Would you let me take your photograph?' she said boldly.

The man looked a little embarrassed by the request, but those who had heard it began to cajole him.

'Please?' Colette widened her attractive eyes with a pleading look that could not be denied.

'All right, lass,' he acquiesced.

'Would you mind coming over here?' She led him to the wooden rail that ran along the harbour side. 'If you would stand there and lean on the railing, please.' She stepped back and viewed the composition with a boat tied up on the opposite bank for background. She came to the fisherman and adjusted his stance, then went over to her camera, which she carefully positioned for the picture.

Reading her intention, Susan quickly prepared everything else so that within a very short time Colette had taken the picture, developed and printed it, and had passed it to the fisherman.

His eyes widened as he stared at the paper replica of himself. He looked up at Colette as if she had performed magic. 'It's me!' The words came as a long drawn out gasp of amazement. He thrust it at the person next to him for her to see. The picture was passed quickly through the crowd, bringing fresh comments of wonderment with its passage from hand to hand.

'You can keep it,' Colette said to the fisherman.

'Can I, miss?' There was grateful thanks in his question and, when she confirmed what she had said, he thanked her profusely. Concern showed on the fisherman's face as he glanced over the crowd trying to locate his photograph. He did not want to lose it or have it damaged. It was something he wanted to show his wife and keep as a precious memento.

'I don't want you to say that I am doing this for nothing. If anyone else wants their picture taking I must charge a copper or two to cover the cost of my materials,' Colette warned him.

'I understand, miss. And thank you again. You're a magician.'

Peter and Susan who had overheard this conversation exchanged knowing glances. 'She's got a business head on her shoulders,' whispered her father.

'She has a mind set on what she wants to do, and from what she has just said knows how to look after herself.'

'Watch over her, Susan, she's precious. They both are.'

'I will.'

'Don't forget we have Fred and Lizzie and Jack and Barbara coming this evening,' Rose reminded Arthur at breakfast.

He nodded and cursed to himself. He had forgotten and, on this last day of March, was preparing to take two paintings for Ebenezer to see this evening. He was anxious to know what his friend thought for he had tried to bring more depth to them. They would have to wait until tomorrow.

He made sure he arrived home in good time for he knew that Rose, having organised everything to her liking during the day, looked forward to relaxing with a glass of wine half an hour before their guests arrived. He did not want to upset her and change her attitude to his painting which had become a little more tolerant lately, though there were still times when she was tetchy and scathing about it, warning him not to be carried away by it. Without her realising it those moments only served to spur him on all the more.

The evening passed off well. They enjoyed a relaxing meal, played cards and were entertained by Rose at the piano. The guests left with a promise that they would have another evening together before too long.

Rose was first into bed. When Arthur came, she drew the bed-clothes back and opened her arms to him. He spread himself beside her and she drew him close.

'I've something to tell you, Arthur.' She gave the slightest of pauses, just sufficient to capture his curiosity and attention: 'I'm going to have a baby.'

There was an almost tangible feeling of shock when he heard that.

'What?' He shot up, propping himself on one elbow so that he could look down at her.

Her smile and bright eyes were framed by her hair which tonight she had allowed to spill freely across the pillow. They added enchantment to what she had said, but they were also welcoming, inviting him to come to her.

'Wonderful,' he whispered, and kissed her long and hard, imparting his delight at the news. The lovemaking that followed was special, tenderness and passion merged in every touch and gesture. Time stood still for them then and again the following morning.

'Can we keep this to ourselves for a little while?' Rose made the request as they went downstairs to breakfast. 'Let us get used to the idea first. There'll be a lot of fuss when we announce it to our families.'

'If that is what you want,' agreed Arthur.

'It is.' She stopped and kissed him. 'Let us enjoy our secret for a while.'

Arthur had a hard task to keep that secret from his friends at work, especially Ben, and even more so Ebenezer when he took the two paintings to him for criticism.

'Very good,' his friend said after studying them for a short while. 'I'm glad you chose two entirely different subjects. *The Old Leeds Bridge* is in the same category as the *Park Row*, the painting that is still in the window. If I don't sell it we'll put it in the exhibition. Keep doing more of Leeds. Oh, by the way, I'm planning to go to Scarborough and Whitby, but more of that later. Now for this second one! I'm glad you have followed up the portrait of Rose looking out of the window. In this one you convince me that the lady and small girl are really listening to the lady playing the piano. I like the triangular composition with its interplay of dark and light colours. The sombre background, even with all its detail is insignificant to the beautiful pale colours of the mother and child's costumes. I think the slight movement of the child within the stillness of the scene is a master-stroke. The balance is good with the darker dress of the pianist. Although the eyes of the people never meet, they are all entwined by the music.' He paused and then added with admiration as he looked at the mother and child. 'Don't they look relaxed and carefree?'

Arthur was delighted at this praise and that, coupled with the fact that he was to become a father, prompted his resolve to make even greater efforts.

A month later when Arthur took two more paintings to Ebenezer, the art dealer had just returned from three days on the Yorkshire coast visiting Scarborough and Whitby.

'I've a lot to tell you,' he said with great enthusiasm after they had exchanged greetings, full of pleasure at seeing each other again, 'but first I must see these paintings.' He studied them and Arthur was on tenterhooks awaiting his verdict.

'This one first. A similar picture to the one you did of Rose looking out of the window, but with a marked improvement in your technique and application. I think you have also given more thought to the composition. I am pleased that you have represented a different time of year, as it is evident by the light coming in through the windows. The title *Will it Rain?* is nicely conveyed in her expression and clothes as she looks out of the window.

'The second ... what can I say? The improvement of technique is marked. I would venture to say that this is the most recent painting?'

'It is,' agreed Arthur.

'It is not that that your technique is at fault in your previous paintings but in this one you have brought a splendid atmosphere of stillness and tranquillity to the lake. The evening light on the water makes it real but at the same time imparts a mystery that is heightened by the trees bending quietly towards their reflections on the far side of the lake. All this, and even the small dog looking up at her, heightens the solitude of the figure lost in thought in the foreground; the soft evening glow adds sadness to her pale complexion. Although a grey painting you have managed to impart a wonderful subtlety of colour; the slight deep crimson in her dress echoes the slight pink in the sky. I like the tip of a gas light in the far background reminding us that a bustling world awaits. It is quite beautiful, you are starting to get much more into your pictures. Keep this up, Arthur and we will have an excellent exhibition.' As he was speaking Ebenezer was wondering what had brought about the marked improvement in the young man's work. It was as if he was newly inspired by something, whether from within or from outside. But he did not seek an answer from Arthur. He was sure he would find out some time.

'You'll keep them here with the others?' asked Arthur.

'Yes, as we arranged.'

'And none will go on sale beforehand?'

'No. While it would be tempting to do so, it could mean that you might be put under pressure to find the right number for the exhibition, leading to your rushing your painting and thereby not presenting your best work. We have to exhibit the required number, we must not fall short, but we want them all to be of the highest standard. You are achieving that and I think will go on improving so we don't want any last-minute rush. See that you leave yourself enough time to avoid that. Don't let anything else get in the way.'

Arthur nodded but at the back of his mind was wondering how Rose's pregnancy would affect his work and, after the baby arrived, what effect it would have on his time? He was about to mention it to Ebenezer but held back and was thankful for it when his friend said, 'Now my visit to the coast,' and diverted Arthur's mind from possible problems ahead.

'You saw potential subjects in Scarborough and Whitby?' he asked, hoping that Ebenezer shared the same enthusiasm for the towns as he did.

'I did indeed. I know there are subjects all around us and that you could go on and on painting Leeds, but widening your scope is no bad thing. You could get some really atmospheric paintings in both places, in the manner of the Leeds canvasses. The old parts, in particular the harbours and ships, all cry out for such treatment. And of course, you should include paintings of the new developments especially in Scarborough, which I believe will become *the* seaside town on the Yorkshire coast. It is already attracting many visitors and there will undoubtedly be those who want to buy paintings of it. I suggest you should try to incorporate some paintings of both places in the exhibition.'

'I'll try to. I wish now that I had made some sketches when I was on my honeymoon.'

'You had other things on your mind then. Maybe you could suggest a holiday to Rose. You'll be due one this year, won't you?'

'Yes, but not until September. I'll see what we can manage.' Arthur knew it might be difficult persuading his wife who would want to stay near home, but he did not want to voice that to Ebenezer now. Maybe the summer after the child was born ... but that would not give him a lot of time before the exhibition.

'I also contacted art dealers in both places and they are willing to handle your work if it measures up to their requirements. I will try and arrange to take some work for them to see.'

Arthur seized on this. Could it be the excuse he wanted? 'If I could get three days off from work and persuade Rose to go to her mother's, I could come with you and find time to do some sketches.'

'A good idea! If you can arrange it, I leave the timing to you.'

I'll try and do it as soon as possible.' He knew the suggestion would not go down too well with Rose, especially if it was late in the summer or into the autumn.

'When I was in Whitby I was curious to see why a crowd had gathered around a particular young lady,' Ebenezer told him. 'On closer examination I saw that she was taking photographs. She had a camera set up on a tripod, and alongside she had what she told me was a portable dark room. She was able to prepare the plates, take the photograph and produce a print there and then. They were good, she had a real eye for a picture. She was selling them at a reasonable price. Naturally

271

many people were wanting their photograph taken but she did manage to take some views.'

'A young lady, you say?'

'Yes.' There was a slight pause then Ebenezer added, 'Ah, that surprises you, I see. But why in these days when female emancipation is much talked about?'

'I suppose it is,' conceded Arthur. 'There's no reason why a woman should not be as good at photography as a man, I agree.'

'You shall see for yourself. I bought one. I'll get it.'

Arthur heard him go upstairs and in a few moments he was back.

'This is good,' he commented when he saw the picture, and continued looking at it thoughtfully. 'You know, Ebenezer, photographs like this could be very useful to an artist. He would have less need to rely on sketches. Of course, photographs could only give him the composition of the scene, the placing of things in relation to each other. He would still need his sketchbook for noting colours, angles of light, degrees of shadow and so on.'

'Apart from which, the equipment is cumbersome. You would need help to hump it around. There were two of them required to shift the apparatus I saw.'

'Still, interesting.'

'You've something on your mind, Arthur.' Rose laid down her knife and fork and placed her hands on the table in front of her as much as to say, 'You'd better tell me, I'm waiting.' She fixed him with a steely gaze.

272

He dampened his lips, searching for the right words.

'Ebenezer has been to Scarborough and Whitby and has contacted an art dealer in each place who would like to see some of my work. He is going to take some paintings and wants me to accompany him.'

'What about your other work?' she said icily.

'I could take three days off, I'm entitled.'

'Could you get them soon?'

'I could swap with Ben or Fred if necessary.'

'Then if you can you may take the pictures ... and I'll come with you.'

Arthur stared at her in amazement. 'But – the baby?'

Rose started to laugh. 'The baby's not due until the middle of November, so I'll be all right to come to Scarborough. In fact, it would do me good. You fix the dates then write to Mrs Symonds and see when she can take us.'

'Can we afford that luxury again?'

'I'm having your child, you'd better pamper me.'

Ten days later they received a reply from Mrs Symonds. Dates were fixed and arrangements made with Ebenezer who was pleased to let Arthur take the paintings. He explained where the art dealers had their galleries and wrote letters of introduction should Arthur require them.

'This is like a second honeymoon,' commented Rose when they reached the house on St Nicholas Cliff.

'Hardly. You are in a rather different condition

now,' Arthur smiled with a mischievous twinkle in his eye.

'And that's not going to stop us having a good time,' she promised, kissing him in such a way that he could not misinterpret her intentions.

As they were changing from their travelling clothes, Rose said, 'We haven't a lot of time so I suggest you go to see the art dealer here tomorrow morning, then we can have the afternoon together. The following day you can go to Whitby, then we'll have one day free before we go home. I will be perfectly happy here while you see to your business.'

'If you are sure?' Arthur did not want to raise any false objections. Rose's suggestions suited him perfectly. He would see the art dealers and be able to do some sketching also. Was Rose softening in her attitude to his art? Maybe she had seen that it was this that had led to their second visit to Scarborough, a place he knew she liked. If so maybe she saw that it could be beneficial in the future. If she really did see it that way then so be it, let her interpret things in this way if she desired. He would not mind so long as it did not stand in the way of his ambitions, to become a painter of note.

Chapter Eleven

The following morning according to Ebenezer's directions, Arthur found the local gallery owner who, seeing the potential in the growing popularity of Scarborough as a seaside resort, had combined an interest in art with that of book-selling, just like Ebenezer.

Lionel Ross, a man in his mid-forties, was thin-faced which made his nose appear more beak-like than it was. This, coupled with a naturally super-cilious expression, made for a slightly forbidding exterior, but any customer interested in art soon found that this was merely a form of self-defence he had not been able to shake off since childhood. When Arthur introduced himself and the con-nection was made with the art dealer from Leeds, he detected that beneath the brusque exterior Lionel Ross had a more amiable personality, if not one to which Arthur could readily take.

Ross made no comment on the paintings for five minutes, even brushing away, with an irri-tated wave of his hand, an enquiry one of his assistants dared to make regarding a book. He still did not reveal his feelings for the work when he asked sharply, with a snap of his fingers, 'Your sketchbook.' He flicked through the pages, pausing briefly now and again to give a little more attention to a particular sketch. Then he closed the book with a snap and thrust it back at Arthur.

'I'm very interested and willing to display your paintings for sale on the terms I discussed with your representative in Leeds. I like your style and can see that Scarborough would offer you untold subjects. That is what I would like to sell here.' He gave a short pause. 'These I take it, are of Leeds?'

'Yes.'

'Come back with some paintings of this town in the same style.'

'It will not be until after my exhibition in

275

September next year,' explained Arthur.

Lionel gave a grimace of annoyance. 'I was hoping for some before then.' He gave a shrug of his shoulders. 'But if that's the way it is, I'll have to wait. Thank you for coming. Good day to you.'

Arthur, a little taken aback by this sharp and sudden dismissal, muttered his thanks and left the shop. He was irritated by the sudden change in Mr Ross's demeanour. It rankled with him until he realised that, although the man had made no comment on his paintings, he must have liked them or he would not have said he wanted to see some of Scarborough and, without committing himself, appeared to be willing to wait.

The interview had not taken long and Arthur seized his chance to do some sketches of Scarborough's old town and harbour that he could work into the promised paintings. Highly satisfied with his morning, he spent a pleasant afternoon with Rose walking on the South Cliff in the gardens there, though he did wish she had been more receptive to his account of what had transpired with Lionel Ross. She was more interested in telling him that she had paid a subscription for them to attend a ball in one of Scarborough's assembly rooms in Long Room Street.

'Are you sure it's wise?' asked Arthur with concern.

'It soon won't be. I intend to make the most of it now!'

They returned to their rooms that evening in high spirits after a most enjoyable ball.

'I hope you haven't overtired yourself?' cautioned Arthur as he climbed into bed.

'I haven't,' Rose replied as she held out her arms to him. 'I can rest tomorrow while you are in Whitby.'

Arthur was up early the next morning in order to catch the first coach. He was thankful that it was a day of cotton-wool clouds, sunshine and light breezes. It would make the journey pleasanter. His travelling companions were two young ladies who he learned were going to stay with an aunt in Whitby, and a gentleman returning there from a visit to London, who expressed a hope that the railways would soon come to his home town. Revealing himself to be a railroad employee, Arthur was able to reassure him that a line from Scarborough to Whitby was under consideration. The final occupant of the coach was a middle-aged man who revealed that he was part-owner of a merchant ship sailing out of Whitby and was going to a meeting there with his partner. Arthur got into earnest conversation with him when he revealed that, as well as his employment by the railway, he hoped to become an artist and was on his way to make some drawings of the town to be exhibited in his one-man exhibition in Leeds the following year.

'Maybe, with your permission, sir, I could draw your ship and use that for one of my paintings?'

'Certainly. I would be most interested to see it. The ship is the *Wandering Star*. She'll be at her quay on the east bank. If you do paint her, let me know. If it is a success other shipowners could be interested. I would put in a good word for you.'

'Thank you, sir. I'm most grateful.' Arthur took

his sketchbook from his pocket and scribbled Ebenezer's address on it. 'That is my representative's address, sir, if ever you wish to get in touch with me.' He thought it would be more impressive to mention Ebenezer in this way rather than give this gentleman his home address.

'Thank you. My name is Richard Mulready. I live in Mulready House, The Crescent, Scarborough.'

Arthur made a note of it in his sketchbook. His exhibition was over a year away but he did not believe in missing any opportunity that might help him towards making art his full-time occupation. And who knew what this chance encounter in the coach to Whitby might bring?

Disembarking at the Angel, he said goodbye to his fellow travellers and made his way to Skinner Street and the art dealer Ebenezer had contacted.

'Mr Redgrave?' Arthur made the tentative enquiry of a small rotund man who looked up from his desk on which he was carefully laying a sheet of tissue paper.

He peered at Arthur from round eyes set in a round face. In fact, everything about the man seemed to be circular, even the round red cheeks.

'Yes, Mr William Redgrave. I have a brother, Mr Richard. Which of us do you want?' His words were clipped but did not carry any note of annoyance. Arthur was soon to learn that this was a characteristic of Mr Redgrave's speech.

'I would like to see Mr William...'

'That's me. And who might you be?'

'Arthur Newton, sir. Mr Ebenezer Hirst saw you on my behalf a few weeks ago.'

'Newton? Newton? I know no Newton. Hirst? Hirst?' He was looking more doubtful so Arthur interposed quickly, 'Mr Hirst saw you about my paintings. You said you might be interested in selling some of my work in Whitby. I've brought a painting and my sketchbook for you to see, sir.'

'Ah, yes!' Mr Redgrave raised his hands as if thanking heaven that he had remembered. His smile made his face seem even rounder, and filled it with friendliness. Arthur was immediately struck by the marked contrast with Lionel Ross in Scarborough. 'Just let me get this out of the way.' He was extremely particular in the way he handled the watercolour which he had been carefully covering with tissue paper. 'Sold that yesterday,' he informed Arthur. 'Be with you in a minute.' Carrying the watercolour with reverential care he went through a door at the back of the shop.

Arthur looked around him. His first impression was that it was in a muddle but he soon realised that this was organised chaos and no doubt Mr Redgrave knew exactly where everything was. There were paint boxes here, paint boxes there, pads of paper there, pads of paper here, brushes and pencils everywhere. All new, except for those on the desk which, along with some jars, appeared to be Mr Redgrave's working tools. The walls carried a number of paintings, marked for sale, and in the shop window were two more standing on easels to catch the eyes of passers-by.

Mr Redgrave reappeared, fussing as he came back to his desk, which Arthur now realised was really a large table. 'Mr Richard won't come.' William passed on the information with a touch

279

of irritation. 'He's always like this, says he's shy. Poppycock! Ridiculous in a man of his age.' He gave a shrug of his shoulders. 'He works in the back, leaves the shop to me. We do restoration work and touching up so it keeps him out of sight. Maybe just as well ... he'd annoy customers, of that I'm sure.' He gave another shrug. 'Ah, well, don't let's go into that and spoil the day. Put your painting on the table.'

Arthur, amused by William's assessment of his brother, did as he was told.

'No, no, no. What am I talking about? It's that brother of mine, he's sent me into a fluster. I mean, put it on that easel.' He gave a wave of his hand in no particular direction but as there was only one easel that was not occupied Arthur placed his painting there. He then realised that it must be the easel's permanent position, for it was so placed as to give a perfect viewing point in this crowded room.

William was never still. He made little movements back and forth in front of the picture but his eyes were on it all the time. Now and again he would give an almost inaudible grunt from which Arthur could deduce nothing.

'Your sketchbook, please.'

Arthur handed it to him, received a 'Thank you', and sat down on a chair, as invited by Mr Redgrave with a quick point of a finger and nod of the head. The art dealer went to his own chair on the opposite side of the desk and immediately started turning over the pages one at a time, looking at each picture for a few moments. Arthur was struck again by his apparently meticulous care in contrast to the way the art dealer in Scarborough had flicked over the pages.

When Mr Redgrave had finished he slid the book across the table to Arthur. 'I am very impressed, young man. I think you have great potential especially if you go on improving in the way this sketchbook shows you have been doing. No doubt the pictures there are mostly of Leeds, as is the one on the easel?'

'Yes, sir.'

William gave a wave of his hand. 'Please, dispense with the sir.'

'Er, yes, si–' Arthur gave a little grin as he stopped himself. 'Nearly forgot.'

Mr Redgrave smiled. 'I would certainly like to try to sell your paintings in Whitby. I like the atmosphere you create and the moonlight treatment especially. Now, if you can transfer that to Whitby subjects I feel sure they will sell. That doesn't mean that all the paintings have to be in darkness or moonlight, of course. I am sure you are quite capable of developing subjects in other directions while maintaining the technique you are happy with.'

'It may be a little while before I can...'

Mr Redgrave raised a hand to stop him. 'Mr Hirst explained about your exhibition and that you will be devoting most of your painting time to that. However, time will pass quickly. I look forward to seeing you and Mr Hirst whenever you feel the time is right.'

'Thank you. And thank you for seeing me today.'

'A pleasure.' William rose from his seat. 'Is it

back home for you now?'

'I am staying in Scarborough with my wife. We have the day there tomorrow and return home the following day.'

'You have some time to spend before your coach leaves for Scarborough?'

'Oh, yes, but I am going to take the opportunity to do some sketches of Whitby.'

'You'll find plenty to occupy you.'

They shook hands and Arthur left the shop. He made his way to the bridge that linked the two sides of the town across the river. From the bridge he surveyed the quays on the east bank and saw two ships at their berths. He reached the East Side and turned along Church Street in the direction of the ships. The first one he saw was the *Wandering Star*. He made a few quick sketches of various aspects of the ship and some notes alongside them. Satisfied with his work, he made his way back to the West Side of the river and found a position from which he gained a satisfactory background to the ship. He made his sketch and then drew an overall picture of the *Wandering Star*. The one he would paint was already forming in his mind.

He walked back to the bridge, made a sketch looking downstream towards the piers and then walked along St Ann's Staith in the direction of the West Pier. His eyes were ever probing the scenes around him, taking in colours, atmosphere and the arrangement of buildings, the position of ships, and the direction of the sunlight, which is so important to any painter. And having absorbed them all, Arthur in his mind's eye suffused the scenes with moonlight.

He then became aware of a group of people ahead of him. There were ten or twelve of them, locals by the appearance of their dress, fishermen and housewives. The centre of their attention was a young lady – well, little more than a girl really, they grew up so fast these days. Her attire was smarter than those around her except for one lady who seemed to be accompanying her. Arthur wondered if these were the persons from whom Ebenezer had purchased his photograph of Whitby? It was only then that he saw the camera on its tripod and another contraption close to it.

He moved nearer and listened. The young person was showing something to the crowd and explaining in simple terms what she had done. 'If any of you want your picture taking, come back tomorrow. I must take some pictures looking across the river now, the light is just right. If I don't do it now I probably won't get it like this again.'

Arthur glanced across the water. The roofs on the East Side glinted red in the sunlight. Indeed the buildings climbing the cliffside, scrambling one on top of the other, did make an attractive picture. His fingers itched to paint it. He took his sketchbook from his pocket, started to draw and then stopped. Ebenezer had purchased a picture from this young lady. Maybe he could get her to take the one he wanted and so save himself from making the sketch, though of course he would need to make notes of colours to jog his memory when he got down to the actual painting.

The crowd had dispersed except for a couple who leaned on the rail nearby to see what the young lady was doing. Arthur watched her repositioning her camera. Her movements had a certain grace that emphasised her slim figure. Her concentration did not mar the pleasing symmetry of her oval face. She looked as though she found pleasure in what she was doing. As she had dressed simply for the task, there were no frills and fancies to get in the way; she wore no bonnet, but had tied her fair hair loosely on the top of her head. Her blue eyes had the alertness of someone who was always seeing views and people in terms of the camera which Arthur deemed unusual in one who looked so young; yet gave the impression of one much older than her years. There was innocence in her ivory complexion and Arthur experienced a sudden desire to draw her.

The fact that she had adopted a pose seemed to indicate she was satisfied with the set of the camera. She spoke quickly to her collaborator who disappeared beneath the cloth-covered tripod, which Arthur assumed held the darkroom of which Ebenezer had spoken. The lull in proceedings prompted him to approach her.

'Good day, miss.' He raised his hat. 'A friend of mine purchased a picture from you. I wonder if I might do the same? You appear to be about to take a view in which I am interested.'

She smiled. 'Of course you may. I will be taking it in a few minutes if you care to wait. Are you sure that is the one you want?'

'It would seem so. From the way you have aligned your camera, that is.'

'Might I ask what is your particular interest in that view?'

'I intend to paint it. I was going to make some sketches but, seeing you, I thought a photograph would save me time and, while I will not slavishly copy the photograph, it will serve as a guide to my positioning of the buildings.'

'Ah.' Her eyes twinkled. 'So an artist makes use of photography when, from what I read, many of them deride it.'

'My dear young lady, I don't think either of us has the time to enter into that sort of discussion.'

She smiled. 'Maybe you are right. Do you live in Whitby?'

'No, Leeds.'

'Alas, I shall not be able to see your painting then.'

'Who knows? You might. Mr Redgrave on Skinner Street may handle my work, but won't be displaying any for a while, I am working up a collection for an exhibition in Leeds next year.'

'Nevertheless, I hope to see it sometime. So your name, please, and then I can look out for it.'

'Arthur Newton. And you?' Somehow it seemed perfectly normal to be asking this young lady her name.

'Colette Shipley.'

'You live in Whitby?'

'Yes, and am pleased that I do because it holds an attraction for me as a photographer.'

'An unusual occupation for such a young person.'

Arthur found himself enjoying this conversation and was sorry when the young lady's companion reappeared.

'I'm all set, Colette.'

285

'So am I. This gentleman wants to buy one of the pictures I am about to take.' She glanced at Arthur. 'This is Miss Lund. We share an interest in photography.'

Susan acknowledged Arthur and then said to Colette, 'We had better do this now, the light is changing.'

'So it is.' Colette went to her camera, made one final check and called out to Susan. In a matter of moments Colette had the plate Susan had prepared, had taken the picture and passed it back to her partner to develop and print.

Arthur stood and watched, admiring the precision with which the two friends worked and commenting on it to Colette as they awaited the result.

'Once my father had bought me this portable dark room Miss Lund and I practised so that there would be no fumbling when we came outdoors to take photographs.'

When Susan presented him with the photograph he was amazed at its quality and the skilful composition of the picture. 'Just what I want,' he said with delight. He was prepared to pay double what she was asking, but Colette and Susan would have none of it.

'We have our set prices according to what we are taking and will not deviate from them unless it is strictly necessary.'

Arthur made his goodbyes.

'I will keep a look out for your paintings in Mr Redgrave's,' said Colette. 'It has been a pleasure talking to you. Good luck with your exhibition.'

Arthur was not sorry when his companions in the

coach on the way back to Scarborough were not inclined to talk beyond a cursory acknowledgement of each other once they had settled down. He was lost in his thoughts. Initially they were of the young woman taking the photographs. He pictured her face and imagined interpreting it on paper. He gave a small smile, realising it would never be possible and chiding himself for being so attracted by her. He drew his sketchbook from his pocket and chased the thoughts of Colette from his mind by studying the sketches he had made, deciding how he might treat them on the bigger canvas. He became so absorbed that he did not realise they had reached Scarborough until the coach was pulling to a halt in the coaching inn's yard.

He made his way quickly to St Nicholas Cliff and found his wife dressing in preparation for their evening meal.

Rose recognised his good mood and knew his day had gone well. Nevertheless she had to enquire. His reply was as she'd expected and she hoped she was not going to have to endure a lecture about art over their evening meal. To her relief it did not come. He merely told her that he had seen Mr Redgrave who was interested in his work. Arthur made no mention of Miss Shipley and afterwards wondered why.

The following day he was careful to allow Rose to dictate how they should enjoy themselves and was pleased that she had an enjoyable time, promenading on the South Cliff and shopping in the new town. So, although regretting having to leave Scarborough, she was in good spirits when the train pulled out for the start of their journey to Leeds. With a carriage to themselves, she settled close to him and linked her arm through his.

'Thank you for bringing me,' she said in an appreciative tone. 'I enjoyed every moment of it.'

'Good. I did too. *Every* moment.' He gave her a mischievous wink.

She gave an amused chuckle and dug him with her elbow. 'We'll have to come again after the baby is born. We'll get Mother to look after her.'

'What about him?'

'I'm sure it will be a girl, and I'm certain Mother would rather look after a girl than a boy. After all she's had me, so I think I'd better make sure that it is a girl.'

Arthur laughed. 'You'll be very clever if you can do that!'

But Rose was right. A fine healthy girl was born on 20 November 1859, but Rose had had a hard time and was in a serious condition for a week after the birth. Once she got over that her health improved and she regained her strength.

Two weeks later when Arthur returned home from work one night he was met by a serious-faced Mrs Duggan.

'What is it? Is Rose all right? She hasn't had a relapse, has she?' Alarm filled his voice as he shed his coat and hat and started for the stairs, not waiting for his questions to be answered.

He took the stairs two at a time and burst into their bedroom. He found Rose sobbing with her head buried in her pillow and the bedclothes askew.

288

'What's wrong, love?' he asked as he sat down and placed a comforting hand on her shoulder.

She twisted round, sat up and flung her arms round his neck. 'Oh, Arthur,' she gasped between racking sobs, 'I'm no good, no good.'

He held her tight. 'What on earth are you talking about?' he asked soothingly.

'I can't have any more children, the doctor's just told me.'

Though the information came as a shock to him, Arthur controlled his immediate reaction. 'Oh, love, don't take on so.' He rubbed her back gently with one hand, while holding her tight. 'You are more important. As long as you are well in every other way, what does it matter? We have a fine healthy daughter and can give her all our love and attention.'

'But...'

He eased her from him so he could look into her eyes. 'No buts, no regrets.' He kissed her on the forehead, smiled at her and said, 'And now I must kiss those tears away.' He gently kissed each eye and then her lips.

Rose gave a little whimper and a wan smile, trying to drive the tears away. She lay in the comfort of his arms until the sobbing had completely stopped and the tears run dry.

Arthur looked deep into her eyes again and said, 'I love you, Rose. No more tears. We have each other, and we have Marie.'

She bit her lip and nodded.

He eased her back on the pillow, straightened the bedclothes, and kissed her again. 'Try and get some sleep. I'll ask your mother to come and sit with you while I get something to eat.'

'No,' she said. 'Mother's taken it hard. She could only have me and she was looking forward to having more grandchildren.'

Arthur nodded. He realised that Mrs Duggan's attitude, after being told the situation by the doctor, had further upset her daughter.

When he went downstairs he was confronted by his mother-in-law whose face was contorted in despair. 'Oh, Arthur, this is shattering.'

'Hardly shattering, Mrs Duggan. A blow, but not shattering. Rose and I have a wonderful daughter, and a marvellous future to look forward to. We must not let this passing sadness mar that.'

'But...'

'There are no buts,' he interrupted.

'I'll go to her.' Moira rose from her chair.

'It might be better if you didn't.' Arthur's words were kindly but firm. 'Rose is all right, she's trying to get some sleep. I am home for the weekend now so we can manage. If you wish you can return to Mr Duggan. We are extremely grateful to you for being here, we couldn't have managed without you. Your presence was essential when Rose was so ill, but she'll be up and about again in a couple of days.'

'Well, if you are certain ... I know Mr Duggan is wondering when I'll be going back. But you be sure to let me know if Rose wants me again, if she has a relapse or is unwell.'

'I will. Now, dine with me. Not knowing you would be going home, Cook will have prepared plenty. Then I'll walk you home.'

'Oh, thank you. Mr Duggan will have eaten so

290

if I may dine with you it will save trouble when I get back.'

They enjoyed a meal of roast lamb followed by fruit pie, after which Mrs Duggan said, 'There is no need for you to see me home, I'll be perfectly all right.'

Arthur shook his head. 'I can't allow you to walk home in the dark on your own.' He brushed any further objections aside.

Rose smiled her thanks when he looked in on her and, seeing she was awake, told her what he was doing. She took his hand for a moment. 'Thank you, Arthur. Don't worry about me. I will be all right. I feel much better for that sleep. I will be up tomorrow.'

This was the first positive sign that he had seen in her since the baby was born, and he was pleased. It was a step to getting back to a normal life. Normal but changed now there was a new member of the family.

As he walked back from the Duggans' his thoughts turned to his painting and how it might be affected by this change to their life. His world had suffered during the last few weeks of Rose's pregnancy and had been virtually nonexistent since Marie was born, but he must try to re-establish it soon. He had worked on some of the sketches that he had done in Whitby and was particularly pleased with his interpretation of the *Morning Star*. He'd placed the ship sailing down the river towards the sea, with the East Side of Whitby in the background. He had been tempted to make it a sailing by moonlight but decided that it would be better as an evening scene so that he could use bold colouring to show the lowering sun flaming the red roofs of the houses climbing the cliffside, and could detail the church and abbey on the cliff top against a thin layer of broken cloud.

But the painting that he had found gave him most pleasure was that which he did from the photograph he had purchased from the pleasant young lady. While he was interpreting this picture as a moonlight scene, he had a feeling he was being urged on by something more than wanting to prove himself to Rose. It was as if he was inspired to do a good painting because of the young lady's interest in the same scene.

Rose's observations when she saw these paintings were, as they were about any others, disinterested and inane. Was that the reason, Arthur wondered, why he had never shown her the photograph or was there some other reason that he would not even acknowledge to himself? But with the birth of the baby approaching and then throughout the subsequent weeks all such thoughts had disappeared.

'Are you sure that you should be up today?' asked Arthur, eyeing his wife as he dressed the following morning.

Rose smiled. 'Don't fuss, Arthur, I'm so much better. Besides the nursemaid starts work today. I should be up to see that she understands what we want of her. And again, I must give some thought to Christmas.'

Arthur raised his eyebrows. 'Good gracious, I'd forgotten it's so near. What do you want to do, love?'

'I want just the three of us to spend the day here. I know my parents and your parents will want us to go to them but I want to be here. We'll invite both families for Boxing Day. Then maybe we'll split two days at New Year between them.'

'If that's what you want then that's how it will be.'

On his way to work Arthur's mind dwelt on the coming weeks. He could see that they were going to be full and that there was going to be little time for painting.

Try as he would to snatch even a few minutes sketching he found it nigh on impossible and, while he enjoyed Christmas Day as a tiny family followed by a much livelier New Year, he was pleased when the holiday passed and he and Rose settled into a routine.

Now that Rose had a baby to be considered and nursemaid to be supervised as well as the household to run, Arthur found that he could seize more painting time. He knew he must take up his brushes again in earnest. Time would fly by and then the exhibition would be upon him.

Chapter Twelve

Though at times she was irritated by the hours that Arthur spent painting, Rose held her tongue. Get this exhibition in September out of the way and life could settle down into the way she wanted it, with comfort and security and more time spent together as a family. She felt sure that disappointment at not selling would curb Arthur's ambitions, which she still saw as a nonsensical dream.

He was aware of her irritation though she did not openly criticise him for the time he spent in his studio. With a plan in mind he kept his special news to himself until one day, at the beginning of May, his arrival brought the comment from Rose, 'You look very pleased with yourself.' She linked arms with him after he had shed his outdoor clothes in the hall.

'I am,' he replied with a bit of a swagger. 'I was promoted six weeks ago.'

'What?' There was a mixture of surprise, delight and annoyance in her expression. 'You didn't tell me. Why not?'

He held her round her waist and laughed with teasing eyes as he held back his explanation. 'Aren't you pleased?'

'Of course I am.' She flung her arms round his neck and kissed him. 'But why keep it a secret until now?' She leaned back against his arms so that she could look directly into his eyes.

'I applied for ten days' holiday when I was told so we could celebrate. I didn't want to tell you until I had it all arranged.'

'Tell me, tell me!' she cried excitedly.

'We're going to Scarborough.'

'Oh, Arthur, how wonderful.' She hugged him tight and kissed him again. 'What about Marie?'

'She comes too.'

'But...' Rose wasn't sure if she was pleased or not. Not able to have any more children, she doted on Marie and was delighted that Arthur wanted her with them in Scarborough but realised it would restrict the freedom they had experienced the last time they were in the resort.

'The nursemaid comes, too, to look after her.'

'Oh, Arthur, to have Anita with us will be very costly.'

'Remember I said I had got a rise? I've been putting that aside to pay for her.'

'Oh, you've planned it all so cleverly! Anita will be thrilled. I don't suppose she has ever had a holiday, let alone been to Scarborough.'

'You're happy with her even though she is only seventeen?'

'Oh, yes. She is so pleasant and very capable. I don't know who trained her but they did a good job. She adores Marie and Marie seems to love her.'

'Good, then it's all settled.'

When Arthur told Ebenezer of his plans, the art dealer was pleased. He knew that Arthur had been working hard at his painting for the exhibition. A break at the coast would do him good.

'I worked it that way, Ebenezer,' Arthur explained, 'so that Rose would be happy and I could get some more subjects.'

'No painting! Sketchbook, maybe, but no painting. You need a break from it for a few days. You'll come back refreshed and that will help when you pick up the brushes again. The paintings that you have done so far are very good. As you know, Mr and Mrs Steel are pleased with them and with your progress. I was talking with them the other day and they, like me, thought that you needed to leave it for a while. I was going to tell you but you have provided the answer yourself. We can discuss other possible subjects and what gaps need filling to make this exhibition a comprehensive representation of your work. But start after the holiday.'

When they left for Scarborough Arthur knew he should return with sketches of ships in an active harbour scene, Scarborough Castle, Whitby Abbey, its harbour, and piers. Ebenezer had suggested a mixture of night scenes and moonlit subjects. He also thought that it would be a good idea to have some paintings in which the human figure was prominent maybe in garden or house settings. With all this in mind, Arthur set out with his family determined to have a relaxing holiday as well.

He accompanied Rose on her outings with Marie and was proud when people stopped to admire the baby and remark on how beautiful she was. While Rose promenaded on the South Cliff he escaped to slip into the gardens and sketch the flowers, composing a background for paintings in which a lady would be prominent. He also noted the colour and patterns of dresses on the ladies that walked by. One afternoon, when Rose had arranged to meet some friends with whom she had become acquainted while strolling across the Spa bridge, Arthur went to the old town and harbour, returning highly satisfied with the drawings he had made.

This particular outing fired his desire to return to Whitby. He made the suggestion of visiting the port only to receive a cold reply.

'You know I didn't like the place, Arthur. Why

do you want to go?'

'Ebenezer suggested Whitby subjects to complete my exhibition.'

'Can't you make do with Scarborough?' asked Rose irritably.

'No. Whitby has a different personality.'

'Personality? Places don't have personalities.'

'Oh, they do.'

'Poppycock.'

'Atmosphere, if you like. Whitby's is so different from Scarborough's.'

'I'll agree with you there! Whitby's is horrible. But if you must go, then go tomorrow. I'll be seeing some friends.'

Arthur said no more. He had got what he wanted. He only hoped tomorrow would be a fine day.

After the usual courteous acknowledgements of his fellow passengers, Arthur lapsed into silence and let his thoughts drift, trying to understand the excitement that had enveloped him. Was it because he was alone and could please himself? He had been alone in Scarborough but hadn't felt like this. Was it because he was returning to Whitby even though it was only a day visit? Had the town-cast a magical spell on him, luring him back? Or was it because...? His thoughts startled him. The young lady photographer had come into his mind. Why? He tried to shake off the thought but without much determination. He tried to remember her name, tightened his lips in annoyance and cursed his memory. Then in a sudden flash – Colette! But Colette who? No, the 'who' didn't really matter.

Nevertheless he kept repeating her Christian name in his mind, trying to attach a surname to it. Then it came to him ... Shipley. Colette Shipley. He savoured it silently. Without conscious effort he stayed in this half-dream and was startled to find that she still occupied his mind when the coach rumbled to a halt in Whitby.

He hurried to St Ann's Staith, hoping he might see her. He walked along Pier Road. Still no sign of her. His disappointment deepened. He stopped and looked across the river but was not really seeing anything. He started and then shook himself out of his thoughts. Why was he acting like this? Why had feelings of disappointment and despair almost overwhelmed him? It was ridiculous the way he had allowed her to occupy his mind. He turned sharply and walked briskly towards the West Pier, stopping now and again to look back at the bridge. On one occasion he stopped longer, surveying the scene. This was just about what he wanted. He moved slightly to his left. This was it! The rail along the harbour wall ran at an angle to the right leading the eye to Pier Road which angled back, carrying the eye to the bridge. He could take in the river slightly left of centre, bring in some buildings on the east bank while those along Pier Road could also be made eye leaders along with the road itself. Should he paint it by moonlight, as a night scene, or as he saw it now in daylight? Well, he would see.

Satisfied with his plan he turned in the opposite direction and walked a few yards so that he attained a position from which he could make an attractive painting of the piers and lighthouses.

His pencil moved quickly for he remembered that Ebenezer had suggested an abbey painting might be worthwhile. He slipped his sketchbook and pencil back into his pocket and walked at a brisk pace until he had crossed the river to the East Side.

Reaching Church Street, he turned in the direction of the Church Stairs, the one hundred and ninety-nine steps leading to the old parish church on the cliff top near the ruined abbey. Fascinated by the narrow street with its shops, inns and houses, he slowed his pace better to take in the potential for more drawings and paintings. He paused at the small square market place that opened off to the left and was dominated by the town hall. Though the abbey was the object of his expedition to this side of the river, he could not but help open his sketchbook to draw this unusual building of hewn stone. Four pillars on each side supported a hall above. The building was surmounted by a domed clock tower.

With his impression down on paper Arthur continued on his way along Church Street, noting the narrow yards that led to rows of houses climbing the cliffside or, on the opposite side of the road, leading down to the river. He had not time to examine them but, from the appearance of the people entering and leaving these yards, he was aware that some were more salubrious than others. He hoped that he would be back some day to observe them more closely and capture their special atmosphere on paper.

He found climbing the Church Stairs strenuous and had to pause now and again to catch his breath. In those moments he turned to look back across the red roofs to the west side of the river. Pictures! Paintings! He really must come back for a prolonged visit, but would he ever get Rose to agree? He was tempted to stop and sketch the church but decided it must wait. Ebenezer wanted a painting of the abbey.

Passing beyond the church, he stopped to survey the ruin. Even from the remaining stonework he could marvel at what must have been a magnificent building with wonderful arches, pillars, carvings and stained glass. In his imagination he could picture the sun streaming through those windows, sending their sacred colours to form a moving carpet across the stone floor. Oh, to have time to put it all down on paper and canvas! But now he would only be able to do one sketch with maybe a few quickly drawn details. He must decide from where he would like to portray this ruin that had stood inviolate near the edge of the cliff for centuries, defying the vicious elements, but had been unable to contest the greed and vandalism of man. Could he possibly get all this atmosphere and meaning into one painting?

He started to circle the ruins to find a vantage point from which to make his sketch. As he passed beyond a wall more of the spacious nave and chancel came into view and with it two figures setting up some equipment. Arthur stopped. His heart started to beat faster. He stood staring at them, not quite believing that they were there. This was ridiculous – why did such pleasurable excitement grip him? He walked towards them.

When they became aware that there was

someone else in the abbey they stopped what they were doing and cast an enquiring glance in his direction.

'Good day, ladies,' Arthur called pleasantly, including them both in his smile.

'Good day.' The civil greeting faded. There was a brief pause as recognition dawned. 'Why, it's Mr Newton.'

'You remembered my name.' Why did he derive pleasure from the fact that the younger lady had done so?

'Indeed I did, and I have often wondered if you ever did a painting from the photograph that you bought?'

'I did, Miss Shipley.'

'Ah, you too have a good memory for names.'

'I have, and I remember your friend is called Miss Lund.'

'I am flattered, sir,' returned Susan.

'It is easy to remember two such pleasant people who were kind to me on my last visit to Whitby.'

'You are here to find more subjects for your painting?' asked Colette.

'Yes.' He gave a little chuckle. 'It seems that we both chose the same viewpoint.'

'Well, that is understandable. Artists and photographers must both have an eye for a picture,' said Susan.

'And you have picked a good position.'

'Not me, Mr Newton. It is Miss Shipley who really has the eye for what will make a good picture.'

'You do yourself a disservice, Susan,' protested Colette, blushing at the praise. She added quickly,

'Would you like a photograph taken from here, Mr Newton?'

'Indeed I would, Miss Shipley.'

There was an awkward silence while Colette and Susan set up their equipment and Arthur made some notes about the scene in his sketchbook.

In a few minutes he was in possession of the scene he would painstakingly have drawn. 'That is wonderful, Miss Shipley. And thank you, Miss Lund.' He withdrew some coins from his pocket.

'Have it with our compliments, Mr Newton,' Colette offered.

'That is kind of you, Miss Shipley, but it is no way to run a business. You were businesslike the last time we met so I insist on paying your asking price now.'

Colette smiled. 'Ah, you have me there Mr Newton.' She accepted the coins graciously. 'I wish you well in your painting of Whitby Abbey.'

'Thank you, Miss Shipley. I am sure this photograph will help enormously. Now I must be away, I cannot afford to miss my coach to Scarborough. Good day to you, Miss Shipley. And to you, Miss Lund.' He turned and hurried away.

Colette watched him go, her gaze intent. For a few moments Susan watched her then she too turned her gaze to Arthur.

He reached a point where he knew he would lose sight of them. He stopped, turned back and waved. He saw Colette raise her hand and a fraction of a second later Susan waved too.

All the way back to Scarborough Arthur's thoughts drifted back to that meeting. He wondered if they would ever meet again. Kept fingering the photograph in his pocket as if that would help him memorise the two ladies, and especially the younger one. Once again he felt an intense desire to paint her. Maybe in one of his paintings for the exhibition.

'Was it a worthwhile visit, Arthur?' asked Rose amiably when he reached their rooms on St Nicholas Cliff. There was a tinge of mild interest in her voice and Arthur knew that she had had an enjoyable day.

'Yes, it was. I drew sufficient sketches to complete my exhibition.' He did not mention the photograph or his meeting with the lady photographers. 'And you? Have you had a good day?'

'Excellent, thank you. I walked Marie this morning for an hour then, when Anita took over, did some shopping. After my rest I walked on the South Cliff. I got into conversation with a most pleasant couple of about our age. They are staying at the Crown Hotel, that big one. You know it, we've passed it.'

Arthur nodded.

'They are here to find a house as he is opening a jeweller's shop on Cliff Terrace. They've invited us to dine with them tomorrow evening at seven. Isn't it exciting?'

'That's all very well, Rose, but when are we going to be able to reciprocate?'

'We shall have to come to Scarborough again and then we can do so. I have given them our address and they have promised to let me have theirs when they get settled. So, you see, we shall

303

be able to return the favour. I'm sure you will like them.'

'Who are they?'

Rose laughed. 'Silly of me. In my excitement I haven't told you. Fanny and Oliver Brooks. They live in Harrogate at the moment.'

'I look forward to meeting them.'

The following evening, after spending a pleasant day together during which Arthur bowed to his wife's every wish, they experienced the splendour of the Crown Hotel and enjoyed the company of Rose's new found friends.

Arthur found their company exhilarating, and their obvious love of life and good nature made the evening memorable. He could see why Rose had enjoyed their company the previous day and was pleased. They were open about their coming business venture in Scarborough, indicating that it was an off-shoot of one they had in Harrogate which they were going to leave in the hands of a capable manager. They were good listeners, too, showing interest in Arthur's work with the railway, as it was described by Rose, and he found a common interest in Oliver's love of cricket. It seemed to draw the couples closer together.

'Rose told us that you were in Whitby yesterday,' commented Fanny. 'Was that for something special?' She gave Arthur a questioning look, then added quickly, 'Oh, dear, I shouldn't pry.'

'That's perfectly all right,' her reassured her. 'I went there to do some sketching.'

'You enjoy that?' Amused by her query she gave a little smile. 'Obviously you do otherwise you wouldn't have gone.'

'I was gathering material for an exhibition I am having in Leeds in September.'

'Then you are a serious artist?' said Oliver. He glanced at Rose. 'Is he good?'

She gave a dismissive shrug of her shoulders. 'He paints nice pictures,' was her only unenthusiastic comment.

Oliver exchanged a quick glance with his wife and knew from her look that he should drop the subject. Fanny had detected that Rose and Arthur did not see eye to eye about his painting. Pursuing the subject could spoil the evening. She did not want that to happen because she had taken to the two of them and had been sympathetic to Rose's liking for Scarborough. She remembered her comment of yesterday: 'You're very lucky being able to move here. I wish we could too.'

Fanny turned the conversation to the books she had read recently and was reading now. 'If you haven't read it, Rose, you must read Thackeray's *Vanity Fair*, and I'm sure you would like *Frankenstein* by Mary Shelley, Arthur. If you like fearsome stories!' Discovering their mutual love of books and the fact that Fanny also played the piano drew the couples even closer together. They were sorry that they were parting tomorrow but promised that they would keep in touch.

As they walked back to St Nicholas Cliff, Rose asked, 'You liked them?'

'Yes.'

'It is a pity that we don't live nearer,' she said with a touch of regret in her tone. 'But we must come to Scarborough again. Apart from liking it we now have friends here.'

305

Arthur made no comment but locked those words in the back of his mind. If his exhibition went well he certainly would return for more subjects here and to Whitby.

Throughout the summer Arthur played a delicate balancing act between his family, work, friends, cricket and painting. His work slotted into certain hours each weekday and he was able to combine cricket with meeting friends. Care and delicate manipulation were needed when his painting impinged on family life, especially on time that Rose claimed. He parried her criticisms when she complained that painting was taking too much of his attention by promising that, once the exhibition was over, he would take her to Scarborough again.

When he took time for painting, often late at night, he worked hard with a will and determination to succeed. Whenever he completed a painting he took it to Ebenezer for criticism. Absorbing that, he endeavoured to improve with every brush stroke he made. Ebenezer was delighted with the progress and keenly drew Mr and Mrs Steel's attention to it. With three-quarters of the paintings for the exhibition in his possession he arranged for the Steels to view them without Arthur's knowledge. They had seen some of the earlier paintings and Ebenezer was keen for them to see how Arthur had taken up their suggestions.

They arrived at Ebenezer's shop one evening eager to see the work of the young man whom they thought would have a great future as an artist, yet keen not to let this personal judgement

306

of him colour their criticism of his paintings. It was essential that he got this exhibition right.

Ebenezer had the paintings arranged so that they could view them in the order in which Arthur had painted them. After welcoming them with a glass of wine he made no comment, allowing them to study and form opinions as they willed. They made no remarks to each other but jotted notes in their notebooks.

Laurence was the first to speak. 'This young man has improved enormously and I would suggest that the first four paintings be eliminated from the exhibition. I am not saying that they won't sell, they probably will because they are competent enough, but they are not of the same calibre as the rest and I feel they would detract from the whole.' He glanced at his wife to see how she was reacting to his comment.

She saw the query in his eyes. 'I agree with you. It would spoil the impact of the others if they were included.' Rowena paused a moment, viewing the fifth painting with a critical eye. 'You can see a marked improvement at this stage. In this painting, *The Park*, you can see he has got to grips with space. Before this his spatial handling was shallow; afterwards the depth he conveys gives more weight to his paintings.'

'You are right, Rowena,' Laurence agreed, 'and we can both see that Arthur has continued to exploit and develop that ability in subsequent works. I am also very attracted to the variety of the subjects he chooses, though he does have a leaning towards moonlight or night scenes.'

'The collection is no worse for that,' Rowena

pointed out.

'Agreed.' Laurence gave a gesture of surrender to her judgement, but then countered, 'Maybe a couple of still-lifes ... and for the other two, I would suggest they be of people. What do you think, Ebenezer?'

'They would give more balance. I'll pass on your views to Arthur.'

'I think perhaps similar to the painting of the girl looking out of a window, obviously admiring the view across the river at Whitby for we can see the abbey through the window. She's a beautiful girl ... is she someone in particular?'

Though he had recognised Colette when Arthur had brought the painting to him, Ebenezer had made no observation and was not about to make one now. 'She must be someone he came across when he went there to do some sketching for the Whitby scenes.'

'I particularly like this one, looking along the river towards the bridge. The use of perspective is excellent, and the atmosphere created by the use of moonlight coupled with the shadows and the reflections of the lights in the water really gives the feeling of walking along by the river,' commented Rowena. 'Ebenezer, we have the venue for the exhibition – the Town Hall. Would you like me to organise everything else?'

Ebenezer could not hide his delight at this offer. 'Are you sure?' he added to his thanks.

'Of course I am. I've had experience of them in London and see no reason why, with the growing interest in art in Leeds, we can't match them. I have some ideas and would like to discuss them with Arthur. It might be best if he met me in the room we are to use for the exhibition as the hanging of the pictures will be important. Can you arrange that for next Saturday morning at eleven o'clock, Ebenezer?'

'Certainly. He may have a cricket match but that won't be until the afternoon.'

'We'll be finished in time for that.'

When Arthur called at Ebenezer's on his way home from work that evening, the art dealer told him about the Steels' visit and passed on their comments. Arthur was disappointed that they had advised eliminating his four earlier paintings but he understood their reasoning when Ebenezer explained it to him. He studied the paintings and had to agree that the improvement in his subsequent technique was obvious. He would have to work a little harder now in order to complete the required number of canvasses.

'Mrs Steel has become caught up in this exhibition and has offered to organise it from now on,' Ebenezer explained.

Arthur was ecstatic, for he had been wondering about publicity and was meaning to bring it up with Ebenezer. Now there was no need. 'I'll certainly be there,' he enthused when Ebenezer told him about meeting her on Saturday morning. 'I have a cricket match but that won't interfere.'

'Good. I look forward to your telling me what she proposes.'

Arthur was in high spirits as he walked home, eager to tell Rose the Steels' opinion of his paintings.

Her reaction was mildly interested but came

with the grumble, 'Four to replace on top of those you still have to finish! It's going to take up all your time. I'm never going to see you, and you'll not get to know your daughter properly.'

'It won't be for long. The exhibition will soon be here.'

'Thank goodness. We'll just get it over and then we can get down to a more civilised life.'

'It hasn't been that bad, love.'

'Maybe not for you. You go and shut yourself away. These last few weeks I've hardly seen you except when we come with you to a cricket match. Oh, that reminds me. Grace came by this afternoon with a message from Fred.'

'He's not in the office this week – he's been sent on a job at York,' Arthur offered by way of an explanation why he had not seen his friend.

'So she said. She wanted to let you know that the match on Saturday has been rescheduled as a one-day game starting at twelve.'

'Oh, no!'

'What's wrong?'

'I have to meet Mrs Steel at the Town Hall at eleven.'

Rose frowned at this news. 'What for?'

'Something about the exhibition. She's going to do the organising from now on.'

'Oh?' Arthur did not notice the touch of suspicion in his wife's voice. 'You'll have to cancel it.'

'I can't, it's important. I'll just have to hope we are through quickly. I'll go straight from the meeting to the match.'

Rose said nothing. She knew from the determination in Arthur's voice that he would not put off this meeting and she wondered why. Was there more to it than he was saying?

Although Saturday dawned with grey skies, by ten o'clock breaks in the cloud had appeared and were getting bigger with the passing minutes. It promised to be a good day for the cricket match.

When Arthur came to say goodbye, Rose made sure he was aware that she had noticed he was wearing his newly acquired jacket and matching trousers. 'You are looking smart.'

'It was awkward making a choice, having to change again at the match, but I thought I'd better wear these for the meeting.'

Rose made no comment, merely raising a judgemental eyebrow that was lost on Arthur whose mind was occupied with the coming meeting with Mrs Steel.

'I'll see you at the field,' said Rose. 'Don't be late.'

'I hope not to be.' He kissed her on the cheek, picked up his cricket gear and left the house.

Rose found herself questioning his motive as she watched him leave.

Reaching the Town Hall, Arthur hurried to the room that was to be used for the exhibition only to find it empty. He strolled round studying the wall space and the way the light fell from the windows, trying to visualise which would be the best locations for his paintings. He became so absorbed that when he looked at his watch and saw that a quarter of an hour had passed he got a shock. Where was Mrs Steel? Had she forgotten?

Surely not, she wasn't that type. She had always struck him as being so efficient. Being late did not fit her personality. Had she had an accident? He found himself growing concerned for her. Maybe he should make some enquiries, but where? It would mean having to visit her house then he would be late for the cricket match. His lips tightened; he would be in any case. Maybe he should take it that she had forgotten and leave for the game now. But if he did he would have a guilty conscience. What if she was in trouble and he had done nothing? He was still trying to decide his course of action when he heard the tap of hurrying feet on the marble floor. He turned to the door as Mrs Steel rushed in. She drew a deep breath and was immediately in control of herself.

'I'm so sorry, Arthur, there was trouble in the town, an accident, and we had to wait until the road was cleared.'

He admired the way in which she gave the impression that nothing had happened. He knew she had been flustered from those hurrying footsteps but she gave no evidence of it now. Nothing was out of place, not even a single hair when she slipped her small bonnet from her head. Her complexion had maybe reddened a little but that seemed to have given a fresh glow to her beauty.

'It is perfectly all right, Mrs Steel. I have been studying the wall space.'

'Arthur, we are going to be working more closely between now and the exhibition. I would rather such formality were dropped. Call me Rowena, please.' She gave him a glance that made him feel it would be boorish to go against her wishes.

'Very well, if that is the way you would like it.'

'It is. I will feel more comfortable.' She gave a small pause and then said, 'I have studied the paintings that are at Ebenezer's and you will have some others to add.'

They discussed the paintings in relation to hanging and found that they were quickly in accord.

'That is good,' commented Rowena, 'it means that as soon as this room is available I can arrange for the paintings to be brought here and can supervise the hanging without bothering you. If necessary you can go on painting until three days before the exhibition and we will still have time to make any final adjustments in the positions. Are you happy with that?'

'Yes.'

'Good. Now, Arthur, I am sure that the quality of your paintings will make this exhibition a success but it can only be successful if people know about it, so this is what I propose to do. I will take out adverts in the *Leeds Mercury* and *Leeds Intelligencer*, and have posters distributed in the busy parts of the town. The night before the exhibition is open to the public we will have a preview night to which admission is by invitation only. I will send out specially printed invitations to prominent members of the cultural and business communities and persuade the Lord Mayor to declare the exhibition open.' She paused a moment then added, 'If there is anything you do not agree with, or want to add, please say so.'

Arthur looked at her in amazement. 'M– Rowena. I'm overwhelmed. I had no idea that my exhibition would merit such attention. I am deeply grateful for what you are doing.'

She smiled and patted him on the arm. 'Arthur, Laurence and I feel that, through Ebenezer, we have uncovered a new talent that will be widely recognised. We find joy and satisfaction in bringing that talent to the notice of the public. This is the best way to do it.'

'Thank you. I only hope that my paintings live up to your expectations.'

'They do.'

'I hope the public think so too.'

They left the Town Hall together. Arthur thought he should be courteous and offered to escort Rowena home.

'That is kind of you,' she replied with a smile of appreciation. 'I would have said yes but I have two more calls to make in town.'

Arthur felt a touch of relief. He had noted on coming out of the Town Hall that it was the moment when the cricket match would be starting.

'Arthur not with you?' Fred showed some concern when Rose arrived at Chapeltown Moor with Marie and her nursemaid but no Arthur.

'He had an appointment in town,' she explained. 'Said he would come straight here. I thought he would have been here by now.'

'I hope he's not delayed,' said Fred. 'I must go and find their captain and make the toss.'

Rose settled herself on a seat while Anita pushed Marie in her pram around the moor but she was not as calm as she outwardly appeared. Where was Arthur? Why was he late? The game would be starting in a few minutes. Was Mrs Steel the attraction? Why had he got involved with her? She hoped her disquiet was not showing when Lizzie and Grace came to sit with her, especially when she had to explain Arthur's absence. Her irritation mounted when she saw the match get underway and Lizzie remarked, 'It's a good job Fred won the toss and elected to bat. It gives Arthur a chance to get here before he is wanted.'

Ten more minutes passed and Rose was finding it hard to keep her annoyance from showing when Grace exclaimed, 'Here he is.' She had spotted Arthur hurrying across the moor from the horse-bus.

'Sorry I'm late,' he called out to make his remark embrace everyone.

'It's all right,' Fred called back. 'Thankfully I won the toss.'

'I was relieved when I saw we were batting as I got off the bus.'

'What kept you?' asked Rose, giving him a cold look.

'There was a lot to discuss,' he offered lamely and went off to change into his cricket clothes.

'I'll bet there was,' thought Rose, but knew she would receive no further explanation until they were alone. She resolved if one were not forthcoming she would demand one.

Arthur had detected annoyance in his wife and was a little puzzled as to why that should be. He had only been late in arriving and that had not affected her. He soon forgot her attitude as he became absorbed in the cricket match in which he did rather well, scoring fifty runs and taking four wickets. He hoped his success and the praise he received from his team mates and spectators would thaw Rose's attitude. Fred wanted to celebrate their win and extended an invitation to meet later. Arthur was in favour of doing so but Rose blocked his enthusiasm with the excuse that there was Marie to see to.

'What's wrong with you?' demanded Arthur when they were alone at home, Anita having taken Marie to prepare her for bed. 'You've been sulky all afternoon and then you refused Fred's invitation.'

'Why were you so late?' snapped Rose.

'Why should that put you in a bad mood? It couldn't be helped. Rowena was held up.'

'Ah, so it's Rowena now? It was Mrs Steel when you left home!'

As the enormity of what he judged his wife was implying struck home, Arthur cursed his own mistake in using the Christian name. But it irked him to think that his wife considered him capable of that sort of relationship and, by implication, drew Rowena into that sphere too. 'What are you getting at?' His face darkened angrily.

'If the cap fits, wear it,' she retorted.

'No! If you have any suspicion say so.' His words were crisp, eyes intent. He watched her closely with an expression that told her she had gone too far, but Rose found she could not hold back.

'What else does it look like? You have a liaison with a married woman with whom you now reveal you are on Christian name terms and who causes you to be late for an important appointment. Where has this damned art of yours led you?'

Incredulity clouded his eyes: his expression was one of disbelief. 'What are you implying?' he asked coldly.

'How many other times have you met her that I don't know about?'

'Don't be so ridiculous. Mrs Steel – no, I'll call her Rowena – and her husband – yes, she has a husband as you well know – have helped me with my work. Rowena has taken it upon herself to organise this exhibition...'

'For what purpose?' Rose sneered.

'Certainly not what you choose to think without so much as a shred of evidence. Sully my name with your falsehoods if you must but don't sully hers.' As he was speaking Arthur had moved closer to his wife.

Rose tried to look away but something in his eyes held her with its earnest, deep-seated authority. Doubt edged into her mind. Had she judged wrongly? Had she been dazed by a haze of suspicion that had no foundation? 'There's nothing between you then?' she asked in a low tentative voice.

He stood for a moment staring at her. Did she really have to put that question? Did it not reek of the suspicion still lodged in her mind? He stiffened and made a fierce effort to prevent any reply that could damage his relationship with Rose forever. The word 'Nothing' was delivered with such intensity that the truth behind it was unmistakable. His eyes fixed on Rose for her reaction.

He saw her face soften with a mixture of regret, a plea for understanding of what had caused her to make such accusations, and the desire to be forgiven. She reached out to hold his arms. 'Arthur, I'm sorry. Please forgive me?'

He felt a tremor in her fingers. He knew she was hurting from causing this confrontation. He did not speak but held her eyes with a gaze that penetrated deep to her soul.

'Please, Arthur, forgive my jealousy?'

'Jealousy? You have nothing to be jealous about.'

There was silence between them. She hoped that it was a sign of forgiveness; he that her suspicions had been wiped from her mind. Their eyes held and silence brought a sudden desire. His arms came round her waist and pulled her roughly to him. She came willingly and with a relief that softened her. Their lips met with a passion that drove the confrontation from their minds. Only one thing more was needed to purge them of the anger that could destroy. When their lips parted they left the room and hurried up the stairs.

Chapter Thirteen

Arthur was breathless with excitement. In three hours' time his first exhibition would be opened by none other than the Lord Mayor himself. He felt as if he was walking on dizzy heights. He had dressed for the occasion early and now could not settle. He paced the house making excuses to himself to go into various rooms. He entered the bedroom, followed Rose into the drawing-room, went to dampen his dry mouth with a glass of water, did everything but relax.

'Arthur, do settle down! You'll make yourself ill if you go on like this and then you'll miss the exhibition.'

He knew there was wisdom in her words but they did nothing to ease his tension. He sat down, on her instructions, but it was only for a few moments, then he was up again.

'Arthur,' she said in exasperation, swinging round on the stool in front of her dressing table, 'if you can't settle then go to the Town Hall now. At least then you'll stop wondering if everything is all right.'

'But...' He started a weak protest. Maybe Rose was right. One anxiety would be out of the way; though what could have gone wrong in the past twenty-four hours he couldn't imagine. Everything had been in place when he had last visited the Town Hall.

'I'll come later. You've ordered a carriage so I'll be all right.'

'I don't like leaving you.'

She gave a dismissive wave of her hand. 'Go on, off you go. Let me get ready at my leisure.'

'Well, if you think so.'

'I do.'

With a little sense of relief he went to Rose and bent to kiss her on the cheek. 'You're sure?'

'Yes, yes, stop fussing.'

'All right. I'll see you later. Don't be late.'

'I won't.' Rose breathed more easily when the bedroom door closed behind him. She eyed herself in the mirror. 'You'll be glad when this is all over, won't you?' she said to her image. 'Then he can forget his art and we can settle down to a normal life.' She tightened her lips as she thought back over the past few weeks when she had seen very little of Arthur. He left for work, and when he returned home spent his time completing the paintings for the exhibition. Although she knew he must have met Mrs Steel again, because she would need his approval for the publicity campaign she was conducting, Rose kept her own counsel and never mentioned her name, not even when he showed her copies of the newspaper announcements Rowena had placed.

Rose was meticulous in her own preparations. She wanted to look her best because she knew from the list of invitations Arthur had shown her that there could be many distinguished people present and she was not going to miss out on mixing in such company. She believed there would not be another such opportunity.

Arthur walked briskly, finding this surge of activity relieved the anxiety he had experienced at home. The past few weeks had been hectic, trying to find time to finish his paintings, receive Ebenezer's approval and keep in touch with Rowena about her publicity campaign. He had met her on four occasions, on one of which he'd scanned the list of people to whom she was sending invitations. With her agreement he'd added his own family, Rose's mother and father, and his friends from work and cricket. Yesterday he had taken a day off in order to meet her and Ebenezer and hang the paintings. Though Arthur had a preconceived idea of what should go where he bowed to their suggestions when they ran contrary to his and agreed with their reasoning.

The hanging was finished and they were standing back to view their work when Laurence Steel arrived. He nodded to them. Arthur was about to greet him when Rowena laid a hand on his arm to silence him, gave a little shake of her head. The three friends sat down without speaking and waited patiently while Laurence concentrated on the paintings. Arthur found his anxiety mounting as the minutes ticked away. He almost jumped when Laurence swung round and said sharply. 'Excellent, excellent. An attractive exhibition. It should do well and open the eyes of some Leeds worthies.'

Now, on the way to the Town Hall, Arthur recalled the sense of relief he had felt at Laurence's comments and hoped that his predictions proved correct.

When he reached the Town Hall he found the exhibition room locked but, once he had located the holder of the keys, was quickly admitted. He stood in the quiet of the room, his eyes moving slowly across the paintings. 'Did I really do all these?' He moved closer, singling out one for particular attention. He had automatically moved to the work that had given him most pleasure, though he had not voiced this fact to anyone. He stood assessing his work on the picture he had merely called *Admiring the View*, but his eyes concentrated on Colette and he found himself wondering what she was doing now, wishing she was here to see this painting and speculating what she

321

might say about it. He was jolted out of these thoughts by the sound of footsteps. He turned round to see Laurence and Rowena entering the room.

Greetings were exchanged. 'It looks well,' commented Laurence.

'It does indeed,' Arthur agreed. 'The arrangements of flowers in the corners of the room add a very nice touch without detracting from the paintings. Thank you.'

Rowena smiled. 'As we came in I confirmed the instruction about serving wine.'

'This is far more than I expected,' said Arthur, thinking, 'I hope I make enough money out of the exhibition to pay for all this!'

'I wanted no half measures in launching the career of a new artist for whom we see a great future,' said Rowena. 'Let us get a glass of wine each and relax while we wait. Would you?' she added, indicating to her husband to get the drinks.

'A pleasure,' he said and started for the door.

'I would like to put a Not For Sale notice on *Admiring the View.*' The request was out almost before Arthur had realised it. It just seemed the right thing to do. He did not want anyone to have it but Colette. He was bemused when he questioned himself as to why.

'Are you sure?' asked Rowena, wondering why he had not said so before. 'It is one of your better paintings. In fact I would say that it is the best one here, it has so much life and feeling about it. I think it would fetch a good price if you let it go on sale.'

'No. I promised Mr Redgrave in Whitby that I

would let him have a painting of the town after the exhibition and I would like it to be that one.'

'There are others of Whitby,' Rowena pointed out.

'I want it to be that one.'

'Very well. It is your decision.'

Laurence arrived with the drinks.

'Just put mine on the table,' said Rowena. 'Arthur wants me to put a Not For Sale notice on *Admiring the View*.'

Laurence made an attempt to persuade Arthur otherwise but he was adamant. Rowena returned with a small label.

'You are sure?' she queried.

Arthur nodded. 'Certain.'

A few minutes later they heard a movement and turned to see a figure in the doorway looking a little apprehensive.

Arthur jumped to his feet. 'Rose.' He hurried over to her.

She gave him a wan smile. 'I'm in the right place?'

'Yes,' he said warmly to put her at ease. 'Come and meet Mr and Mrs Steel.' His touch as he took her by the elbow was reassuring and Rose dismissed her own uncertainty. She must not show nervousness in front of Arthur's friends from the art world.

'Mr and Mrs Steel ... my wife Rose.'

'I am pleased to meet you.' Laurence took her hand and raised it towards his lips as he bowed graciously.

'And I you, Mr Steel,' she returned quietly and then turned towards Rowena. 'Mrs Steel.'

Rowena took Rose's outstretched hand and she could not but be aware of the desire to be friendly in her touch. 'Mrs Newton, I am delighted to meet you at last.'

'It is my pleasure too.' Rose's head was swimming. Could she blame Arthur if he had been bewitched by such a beautiful creature? This person must surely turn any man's head. Her eyes, two limpid pools of delicate blue, sparkled like the smile that would draw people to her. Her slim figure was held erect and with an air of assurance. Rose felt sure that Mrs Steel would never harbour one moment of doubt in her own ability in any situation. Her air of self-confidence, though not intrusive, was palpable and made Rose envious.

Laurence returned with a glass of wine for her which she accepted graciously.

'Let's you and I sit down over there,' Rowena suggested, 'and leave the men to it. We'll have a few moments to ourselves.' She led the way to a seat saying as they went, 'I do admire your dress, Rose ... you don't mind if I call you Rose? It is so much less formal and more suited to this modern age.'

'Not at all, Mrs Steel.'

'Oh, my dear, Rowena, please. The colouring of your dress suits you most admirably.'

'My mother made it, specially for this occasion.'

'She has graced it well with her choice of material and design. I'm afraid I was never taught dressmaking. I wish I had been.'

'It's never too late.'

Rowena smiled. 'I know, but I get interested in so many things that I find I haven't the time.'

'You have put so much effort into organising this exhibition. We are grateful, but Arthur should not have encroached on your time and good nature.'

'When I first saw his work I knew there would come a time when he should have an exhibition. Laurence and I keep a look out for new talent and we have experience of finding it from our time in London. We were only too pleased to be able to do this.'

Before Rose could probe any further, a footman, one of several available for functions held in the Town Hall, hurried in and, seeing Mrs Steel, came straight to her.

'Excuse me, ma'am, the first guests are arriving.'

Rowena thanked him and, turning to Rose, said. 'Please excuse me? We'll talk again later.' She rose to her feet and left the room.

Laurence, seeing his wife leaving, hurried after her. Arthur went to Rose and sat down beside her.

'All right?' he asked.

She nodded. 'She's so beautiful.'

He leaned closer and said quietly, '*You* are my beauty.'

In the context of this setting his remark made her blush. She looked around the room in awe. 'It certainly looks a grand display.'

He smiled his appreciation. 'You must look at them more closely. But, from here, which do you like best?'

She hesitated, letting her gaze sweep across the paintings. 'Oh, I don't know, they're all nice.'

'Nice? Don't you see more in one than in the others?'

'They're just pictures to me, but I must ask you

why you paint so many gloomy night scenes? I can't understand what people see in them. I don't think I'll ever appreciate paintings, but what does that matter so long as you're making money from them?' Her eyes wandered around the room again. 'I must say they do look well, so impressive when seen together. I'm proud of you, Arthur.'

He smiled. 'There is an art even in hanging paintings so that they do not impinge one on the other. They need to be viewed individually so that, although the viewer may be aware of another close by, it will not impair his judgement of the one he is looking at.'

'Oh, I thought you just hung them anywhere on a wall.'

'Oh, no! Rowena has an excellent eye for what is just right.' He sensed Rose bristle just a little. 'Rose, you have no cause...'

The sentence was never finished, for a voice called out, 'Hello, you two.' Rose's mother and father were coming over to them, all smiles. They were followed in a few minutes by Arthur's parents, and in a very short time the room seemed to be full of friends and strangers. Conversation buzzed, introductions were made and paintings looked at, though only in a casual way as the Lord Mayor, Rowena by his side, was hovering by a dais that had been erected in one corner of the room. A gong was struck and silence descended on the room.

'Ladies and gentlemen,' Rowena's voice rang out loud and clear. It drew everyone's attention immediately. 'It is a pleasure to welcome you all to this exhibition by a new artist, a young man whom I am sure will make an impact on art in Leeds. I now welcome the Lord Mayor and thank him for agreeing to open this exhibition. Without saying any more, I would like to introduce His Worship the Lord Mayor of Leeds.'

Applause rippled through the room. The Lord Mayor cleared his throat. Silence reigned once more.

'Ladies and gentlemen, I have as yet only had a casual glance at these paintings but I know that a closer inspection is going to prove most enjoyable and hope that you will all feel the same. We have among us a young man, Arthur Newton, who has an exceptional talent of which we in Leeds should be proud. London has always been the centre of the English art world and it would appear that to date few have taken art in the provinces seriously, but that has been changing recently thanks to a number of artists in this town who are beginning to make a wider impact. They are making people throughout this country realise that we have talent here that can hold its own with the best in the capital. The more we can encourage our own artists, the better it will be for us. I hope this exhibition by a young man of remarkable talent will not only encourage him to go further, while remaining a true son of Leeds, but will also lead others to develop their own talents and be unafraid to display them.

'I would like to see the business and cultural community of Leeds encouraging all aspects of the arts for the benefit of our noble town. Industrially we are expanding and the future looks exceptionally prosperous. Let us make our cul-

tural background equally prosperous by developing the talents of people like Arthur Newton.
Ladies and gentlemen ... Arthur Newton!'

He turned to Arthur who, having been brought
on to the dais by Rowena at the start of proceedings, was standing beside him. Everyone in the
room now took up the Lord Mayor's applause.

As it died down Arthur caught Rowena's eye
and she indicated that he should say a few words.
He began nervously. 'Your Worship, ladies and
gentlemen, I would like to thank you all for
coming this evening. I owe a debt of gratitude to
Mrs Steel for organising this event so splendidly.
But my thanks extend much further than that,
for she and her husband, the noted Leeds painter
Laurence Steel who is with us this evening,
encouraged me, as did Mr Ebenezer Hirst. In
fact if it hadn't been for him I may never have
met Mr and Mrs Steel. I would also like to thank
my wife Rose for the support she has given me. I
only hope that the results prove worthy of your
attention. Enjoy yourselves.'

Renewed clapping broke out around the room.
Conversations buzzed. People began to move
and paintings came under eager scrutiny.

Rose saw Arthur speaking with the Lord Mayor
and Mrs Steel. He turned as if he was looking for
someone and she was aware of him signalling her
to join them.

The Lord Mayor, the signs of good food and a
liking for wine evident in his broadening body
and florid features, beamed as she reached them
and welcomed her with a robust flourish. 'My
dear Mrs Newton, it is my privilege to meet the

wife of such a talented young man. You must be justly proud of him. This is such a wonderful exhibition! Mind, I've only had a cursory look as yet. I must make a closer examination and decide which one to purchase for my chambers.'

'It is an honour to meet you, sir,' returned Rose a little nervously, almost overwhelmed to find herself in his presence. This man had entertained the Queen, and here he was speaking with her and actually wanting to buy one of her husband's paintings! Was he just being kind? Did he feel obliged to? Or did he really think they were worth buying?

'Do you paint too, Mrs Newton?'

Rose had let her mind wander and was startled by the question. 'Oh ... no...' she spluttered. 'I've no talent in that direction, but I do play the piano.'

'Ah, yes! A fine occupation for you ladies. Ah, here's Laurence. He is going to conduct me round the paintings and advise me on making a good choice. Excuse me.'

As he moved away, Rowena smiled at Arthur. 'Your first sale. And if he's as good as his word and hangs it in his chambers, it will be seen by many. You must be pleased, Rose?'

'Er ... yes. I am.'

'I hope many more paintings are sold this evening. Oh, there's someone I must talk to. Please excuse me.' Rowena glided away.

'I did not expect so many people,' whispered Rose.

'I knew Rowena had sent out a lot of invitations but I didn't think the room would actually be crowded.'

There was little time for further conversation between them as people kept coming to talk with Arthur, to congratulate him, to ask about his painting methods and how he'd achieved certain effects, where and when hc had painted certain scenes. His mother and father expressed amazement. Rose's parents said that they'd had no idea he had done so many paintings, and all four of them made known their surprise at the number of influential people who were present. Ebenezer and Zilda admired the way the paintings were displayed and were excited about the comments they overheard while walking among the guests.

More and more people sought some of Arthur's time and he became separated from Rose who gravitated to her parents.

After an hour the Lord Mayor came over to Arthur. 'Young man, I am impressed and hope you go on to greater things. I purchased one of the *Roundhay Park* paintings, a favourite place of mine.'

'Thank you, sir.'

'I must be going.' He glanced around the room. 'I don't see your charming wife. Please say good night to her for me.'

'I will. Good night, sir.'

Laurence winked at Arthur and escorted the Lord Mayor from the Town Hall.

As they moved away, Rowena took the opportunity to capture Arthur's attention. 'Let's walk round the paintings again,' she suggested. 'But you may have seen enough of them?'

'No. I always see something different in them even though I painted them.'

'You still view them with a critical eye?'

'Oh, yes, always looking for something I should have done, something that would have improved a canvas. A figure here or there, a different angle of light.'

'Are you ever satisfied?'

Arthur paused briefly and then said, 'Never.'

But Rowena had caught that brief moment. She knew there was a painting that had satisfied him. She wondered which it was? Then she remembered the painting, which he had said was not for sale. Could that be it? If so, why had it satisfied him? Was it the technique he had employed or was it the subject matter? It could be a combination of the two but Rowena guessed it was chiefly the latter. She wondered about the identity of the girl in the painting, but she would not pry. 'I am pleased,' was all she said. 'That augurs well for your future.'

Caught up with her parents and in-laws, Rose noted her husband and Rowena deep in conversation as they went from picture to picture. Jealousy gnawed at her again though she knew it should not. She would have made an excuse to break up the discussion but was prevented by Ebenezer and Zilda asking her to come and meet Dorian and his wife who had entertained them so kindly during Queen Victoria's visit.

By the time she was free everyone was beginning to make their way out. Rowena was not to be seen and Arthur was coming over to his wife.

'Are you ready for home?' he asked.

'Yes.'

'Rowena saw you were engaged so asked me to

say goodnight to you. She looks forward to seeing you tomorrow.'

'Tomorrow?' Rose looked a little bewildered.

'Yes.' Arthur noted her expression. 'Oh, I thought she had asked you? I must have misunderstood. We are invited to the Steels' for lunch tomorrow and to stay on for tea. The way she worded it, I thought she had already spoken to you.'

'And you said yes?'

'I did.'

Rose felt a little annoyed but hid it. 'Very well,' she agreed. 'I'll get Mother to look in on Marie and Anita.'

'Good. Ebenezer and Zilda will be there too. I think it is a celebration of how well today went. I sold five paintings as well as the one the Lord Mayor bought.'

'Well done! That will make a nice supplement to your wages.'

'It will take us to Scarborough as I promised you.'

'You really meant that?'

'Of course I did.'

Rose linked arms with him as they walked home. Well, there was something to be derived from his hobby if it brought extra visits to Scarborough! And not only that, she had been moving among the gentry of Leeds this evening, and tomorrow she was going to dine with the Steels, whom she had learned this evening were well known in the art world and had connections in London. There was something to be said for this 'high' life, and if by his hobby Arthur was able to provide them with extra money then she had better take a little more interest.

'When will we go, Arthur?' she asked.

'As soon as the exhibition comes down, in a fortnight. Then I'll be able to take some paintings to Mr Ross in Scarborough and Mr Redgrave in Whitby. I'll make the bookings for then.'

'Something to look forward to,' his wife said with an excited tremor in her voice.

That excitement was heightened two days later when she announced to Arthur on his return home from work that she had received a letter from the Brooks telling her that they had made the move to Scarborough and were hoping to see them when they next visited the resort. 'They'll get a surprise, it will be sooner than they think!'

When Arthur went to collect the remaining paintings at the end of the exhibition he found Rowena and Ebenezer already there. They greeted him with the news that two more had been sold during the fortnight that they were on display.

'Eight paintings altogether out of the twenty on display. That is good, Arthur,' commented Rowena with obvious pleasure. 'I hope you are pleased?'

'That is more than I expected,' he enthused. 'I am going to Scarborough for a few days so I'll take two there and two to Whitby.'

'Is that in addition to the one that was not for sale, *Admiring the View?*' she asked.

'Oh, yes, that was done with Mr Redgrave's request in mind,' he explained, but Rowena still doubted it was the true reason.

'That will leave seven,' put in Ebenezer. 'I'll take some and keep changing them over in the window. Which will you take, Arthur?'

He made his choice.

All the paintings were taken to Ebenczer's shop where he wrapped Arthur's with care. They would be collected on the day that he and Rose were departing for Scarborough.

'Good day, Mr Redgrave,' said Arthur brightly when he entered the shop in Whitby. He had taken the opportunity to visit the art dealer on the second day of their visit to Scarborough when Rose was happy to be out on a shopping expedition with Fanny Brooks.

Mr Redgrave looked up from the painting he was wrapping. 'Ah, the young artist. How are you?'

'Very well, Mr Redgrave. Mr Hirst sends his regards.'

'Thank you.' He eyed the packages that Arthur had manoeuvred into the shop. 'Work for me to see?'

'Yes.'

William Redgrave gave a smile of pleasure. 'This is the part I like, seeing a new painting.'

Arthur unwrapped the first one. William made no comment but his little grunts seemed to express delight. 'The next one, young man, the next one,' he urged.

Arthur smiled and did as he was bid. William seemed positively ecstatic as he viewed this one. 'They'll sell, my boy, be sure of that.'

'I hope so, Mr Redgrave.'

'The third one, the third one! Don't keep me in suspense.'

Arthur unwrapped it and waited. 'Wonderful, wonderful! It is most unusual way of depicting Whitby, through the window. *Admiring the View*. Aptly named. That young woman...' He stopped and then fixed his gaze on Arthur. 'That's Miss Shipley.' He looked back at the picture. 'Yes, yes, it is. She was in here only yesterday.'

'This is not for sale, Mr Redgrave.'

A look of sheer disbelief was cast at Arthur. 'Why not? It's the best of the three.'

'I want you to give it to her the next time she comes into your shop. I do not know where she lives and besides would not want to embarrass her with my presence when she receives the picture. Please do that for me, Mr Redgrave.'

'Well, er, this is most unusual, but if that is what you want me to do then I will. Do I say it is from you?'

'I think she will guess that from my signature on the painting.'

'Of course.' He nodded. 'Now, what about the price for the other paintings?'

'Mr Redgrave, you are an honest man and know more about the prices they may bring so I leave that up to you.'

'If that is the way you want it then I'm happy to evaluate them.'

'Good,' said Arthur in a tone of satisfaction, 'then that is that.'

'Not quite, young man.'

Arthur looked surprised. 'What is it, Mr Redgrave?'

'I want to know what other paintings you will bring me?'

'Are you commissioning me?'

'No, but I will tell you what I think will sell here in Whitby. That is, if you want to do business this way?'

'Certainly, Mr Redgrave. I will paint to your requirements so long as you understand that I will also be painting to my own desires and inclinations and in my own style.'

'I would not want you to do otherwise. I would hope that one would not be to the detriment of the other.'

'Very well, we have an understanding.' They fell to discussing what William Redgrave would like to see and, when, he left the shop, realising he had time to visit some of the sites indicated by Mr Redgrave, Arthur hurried away to do some sketches.

He was in high spirits on his way back to Scarborough. Mr Redgrave wanted more, as and when they were ready, and the previous morning Mr Ross also had asked for more in his supercilious way. Arthur had a busy time ahead but was determined that for the next three days he would relax with his wife and friends.

When he told Rose about his meeting with Mr Redgrave she was pleased for him but bemoaned the fact that meeting the orders of the two art dealers was going to take up a lot of his time. She also pointed out that although they had asked for more paintings it did not mean that they would sell them.

Arthur made no comment on the cold water

336

she had cast on his excitement. He silently agreed there was no certainty of any sales but believed the men would not have asked for more if they did not think they would sell.

'I spent a most enjoyable day with Fanny,' Rose said to change the subject. We are dining with them this evening.'

'You've booked somewhere?'

'Yes. It was our turn. We are going to Donner's Hotel.'

'Well thought of, I believe.'

'More than that.'

So it proved to be. They were given every attention in luxurious surroundings and the food and wine were excellent. It was highly conducive to the good mood they were all in from the moment they had partaken of a glass of Madeira at the Brooks house in The Crescent.

'Your business here is well established now?' Arthur asked Oliver when the ladies lapsed into discussing the latest fashions.

'It certainly is. And I see it growing all the more with the expansion of this town as a holiday resort, and of course with people coming to take the waters. You know, I'll be surprised if Lionel Ross doesn't do well for you. By the way, how did your exhibition in Leeds go?'

'Very well indeed. I was more than pleased. I sold eight,' Arthur smiled. 'Including one to the Lord Mayor himself. He probably felt obliged to buy it, seeing as he opened the exhibition. I brought two for Lionel Ross to sell here and he wants more.'

'That's good. He must feel pretty confident.'

337

'I took two to Mr Redgrave in Whitby also, and he too wants more.'

Oliver eyes widened. 'Good for you! You'll be giving up your railway job to paint.'

Rose caught the last remark and immediately broke off her conversation with Fanny. 'Don't put that idea into his head! We couldn't live with the uncertainty. Arthur's present job is secure. If he wants to paint let him do so but let it put the jam and cream on the certain bread and butter.' She turned back to Fanny. She had made her point and did not want any further discussion.

Arthur and Oliver exchanged knowing glances. Later, when the ladies excused themselves, their host put in quickly, 'If you think you can make a living by painting, I'd say do it, Arthur. You'll be able to devote more time to it and then it could provide the bread and butter as well as the jam and cream! I was in a similar position myself once regarding the jewellery trade. I'm not sorry I took the plunge and made it my full-time profession. You think about it, Arthur. You're selling. People must see potential otherwise Lionel Ross and this fellow Redgrave wouldn't have such faith in you. And of course you'll start selling more in Leeds now after your exhibition. You think about it seriously, Arthur. I gather I shouldn't say anything in front of Rose?'

Arthur smiled. 'You're right. She likes her comfort and I can't blame her. We are nicely settled. I have a job in which there is certain promotion...'

'But you long to be an artist,' put in Oliver. He saw the ladies returning then so quickly whispered. 'Do it, Arthur. Do it at the right time.'

Chapter Fourteen

Ebenezer paced up and down outside the railway offices. The day had been bright but the spring afternoons of 1861 still turned chilly. He tightened his lips. He really should curb his impatience. He couldn't expect Arthur to leave work before time. Someone came out of the door. Not Arthur. Two more unknowns chatting, hurrying off, escaping from work to a night of leisure. A few more then the trickle became a rush. Ebenezer peered at every person who emerged on to the pavement. Then out came Arthur, laughing, with Fred and Ben. Ebenezer moved towards him.

'What are you doing here?' gasped Arthur when an agitated Ebenezer reached him. His immediate reaction on seeing his friend was that he was a bearer of bad news, but then he saw excitement in his eyes.

'Mr Hirst,' Ben and Fred acknowledged him.

'Good day, young men! Can I tear Arthur away from you?'

'Of course you can. We're glad to get rid of him.' With a laugh they dodged the playful punch Arthur aimed at them. 'See you tomorrow,' they called over their shoulders as they made off.

'What is it Ebenezer?' asked Arthur

Ebenezer took hold of his arm and started to walk with him.

'You know I spent the last three days in Scarborough and Whitby with the prime purpose of keeping up contact with Mr Ross and Mr Redgrave?' Arthur nodded. 'Well, they have sold the paintings you left with them and are anxious for more. I told them you were working on them.'

'Marvellous! I'd better work a bit faster.'

'That's not all.'

'What more can there be?'

'When I got back today Zilda barely had time to greet me. She's sold four of your paintings from the exhibition.'

'What?' Arthur gasped, his eyes widening in astonishment. 'This is unbelievable. Which ones?'

'Those that concentrate on nature.'

'Why those especially?'

'Well, it seems the gentleman purchaser she was serving originated from Leeds but now lives in London. He was visiting relatives here and heard about your exhibition from them – wool merchants who live about two miles out of town by the River Aire. He was delighted when he saw the four paintings, bought them all, saying he was sure that his friends would be interested in them too. Apparently there is a market for such subjects among the middle classes in London who want to look at something to help them escape the claustrophobia of the city, its dreary smoke and fog. He said your detailed pictures of the countryside, especially the two with figures working in the fields would remind them that there was still a world untouched by the march of industrial progress. He is sure we will hear from his London friends. It looks like you have another market!'

Excitement had been growing in Arthur with

340

Ebenezer's every word. He let out a whoop grabbed his friend and forced him into a little jig. They both burst out laughing when they saw passers-by stop and stare. Then they set off arm in arm at a brisk pace that was full of joy.

When they reached Ebenezer's Arthur did not hold back. He went straight to Zilda, grabbed her round the waist and kissed her.

'Oh, my goodness, Arthur, what's got into you?' she cried with pleasure, knowing full well what his exuberance was all about.

'You've made my mind up,' he cried enthusiastically. Ebenezer knew immediately to what he was referring. A serious expression came to his face. As much as he did not wish to dampen Arthur's elation he knew he must issue a warning. 'Arthur, we had better have a chat.'

'What for?'

'I think I know what you are going to say.'

'That I'm going to leave the railway to paint?'

'Yes.'

'Then you are right.'

'Hold on a minute, Arthur, you must consider this seriously.' Ebenezer's expression was grave. He shot a glance at his wife and saw that she too was concerned. He knew he had an ally there.

'I am regarding it seriously,' replied Arthur.

'You're swept along on the euphoria of the moment. You haven't thought what this bold step might mean.'

'It was going round in my mind as we walked here.'

'But that was hardly enough time to study it,' put in Zilda.

'It was all I needed.'

'You need to think more seriously about the practical side of this.'

'I give up my job and concentrate on my painting. Sounds quite sensible to me.'

'Far from it,' Zilda pointed out. 'You have a wife and child to think of.'

'Rose will agree.'

'I don't think you really believe that.'

That observation from Zilda jolted Arthur. She had put her finger on the kernel of doubt that still lurked in the back of his mind.

'See, you haven't an answer.'

'Surely when I tell her about these new sales she'll see reason?'

'It is you who are not doing that,' said Ebenezer.

'But these sales prove...'

'Little,' cut in his friend. 'Yes, you've sold and sold well. Maybe too well at this stage. You are ignoring the fact that Ross and Redgrave might not sell any more. I might not. We might never hear again from our London client.'

'I think you are being very pessimistic,' said Arthur. 'Or is it that you have lost faith in my ability?'

Ebenezer threw up his hands in despair. 'That's not so.' His eyes narrowed and bored deep into Arthur. 'Don't you ever think that of your friend.'

'I'm sorry, Ebenezer, truly I am.' Arthur wished he could bite back his words but they had been said.

Ebenezer gave a little nod. 'Think carefully. At the moment everything looks rosy. Yes, you will paint the pictures your patrons request, you will execute them well and they will sell. But be careful of selling your soul on the altar of needing to prove you are right, wanting to show Rose that you can make a living from painting.'

Arthur looked puzzled. 'What do you mean? Isn't this what you've always wanted? Didn't you want me to sell my work?'

'Of course I did, and do, but with the commissions that have poured in since the exhibition you are in danger of producing only what is wanted now, what sells now. I had, and still have, a vision of your becoming a great artist, someone producing inspired works that will be looked up to by anyone who understands art.'

'I can still do that. I'll have more time if I leave the railway.'

'And in that extra time you'll be tempted to paint only the pictures that are wanted by people who see them merely as pretty possessions. That sort of customer will always be there. It will be very tempting for you merely to supply their wants and be well paid for it.'

'They'll provide my bread and butter just like the railway does now. At other times I can aim towards what you believe I can become.'

'I can see that you are determined to go through with this,' put in Zilda, 'but on your way home, think hard about what Ebenezer has said.'

'And remember, Arthur,' said his friend in all seriousness, 'that it is in your paintings of Whitby that I see the real quality that can lead you to greatness.'

As he walked home Arthur had much to think

about but his resolve had not weakened by the time he reached his own front door. He paused there, drew a deep breath and acted as he had decided on the way home.

He rushed across the hall, burst into the drawing-room, grabbed Rose by the hand and pulled her from her chair, sending the book she had been reading clattering on the floor.

'Arthur, what is it? What's the matter?' Alarm tinged her voice.

'Get your coat and bonnet,' he called as he rushed her into the hall.

'Why? Where are we going?'

'Just get them. We're going to your mother's.'

'Why?'

'You'll learn when we get to my parents'.'

'Your parents'? I thought we were going to mine?'

'We are, and we are going to take them to mine.'

'What's this all about?' Rose demanded as she tried to keep pace with him.

'Just wait.'

'Slow down, please.' She tugged at his arm.

Arthur slackened his pace but only a little. His mind was a whirl of excitement. They reached the Duggans' shop. He was relieved to see no customers inside. Mr Duggan was busy bagging up some sugar.

'Hello, you two, what brings you here at this time? And you look as though you've been rushing.'

'Get your hat and coat and bring Mrs Duggan. You must come with us.' Arthur put all the urgency he could into his voice.

It was not lost on Conan. Puzzled, he looked sharply from one to the other. 'What's up?'

Rose's shrug of her shoulders told him that even she did not know.

'Arthur, I cannot leave the shop.'

'Close it then.'

Conan bristled at this curt demand. A frown of annoyance furrowed his forehead. 'I can't just walk out. There might be customers.'

'This is important,' pressed Arthur. 'Put a notice on the door "Back in an Hour".'

'I've never done that in my life.'

'There's always a first time.'

'Arthur, don't you...'

'Then you'll miss something important.' He turned to Rose. 'Get your mother.'

'Now see here...' began Conan.

'No,' cut in Arthur roughly. 'If you won't come then I hope Mrs Duggan at least will.'

'Where are you going?'

'My parents' house. I want you all to hear what I have to say.'

Conan saw the determination on Arthur's face and knew there was no chance of learning what was in his mind now. It must be something serious. He grabbed a sheet of paper and started to write.

A few minutes later a bewildered Mrs Duggan, clad in her outdoor clothes, appeared with Rose just as Conan was putting his notice in the shop window. As he turned he saw the questioning look on his wife's face. 'I know no more than you,' he snapped, still irritated by Arthur's demanding attitude.

He ushered them from the shop and waited while Conan locked the door. Not a word was spoken as Arthur hurried them to his parents' home.

They had just finished their meal and were surprised to see the unexpected visitors.

'Is something the matter?' asked Enid.

At the same moment Harold said, 'Nice to see you all,' though his expression queried why they were there.

'I know nothing about this, none of us does,' replied Conan sharply. 'Your son rushed us over here without telling us what it's all about.'

All eyes turned to Arthur. 'I think we had better go into the drawing-room and sit down.' His brother and sister looked at him in a manner that asked if they were included. 'Aye, you two may as well hear what I have to say.'

In the drawing-room Arthur took up a position with his back to the fireplace so that he could see everyone sitting in an arc in front of him. Behind his back his hands twisted fiercely together as the moment of revelation neared. He licked his lips nervously and cleared his throat.

'Well, get on with it, lad, I'm losing trade,' grunted Conan.

Moira, sitting next to him, tapped him on the knee, a sign she always employed when she wanted him to calm down. He set his lips in irritation but said no more.

'I'm giving up my job tomorrow!' Arthur almost astonished himself with his sudden burst of words. The silence that descended on the room was filled with shock and disbelief. Then the uproar began.

'You're what?'

'No!'

'Are you mad!'

'You don't mean it!'

'Arthur!' Rose's cry was stricken. 'Please, no! Say you don't mean it?'

He wanted to spare her pain but couldn't if he was to be true to himself. 'I do, Rose. I want you to understand and give me your support.'

She stared at him in bewilderment. Words choked in her throat and tears started to stream down her cheek.

'Look what you are doing to my daughter!' shouted Conan.

'What are you going to do instead?' demanded his father.

'Paint!'

There were further outbursts of incredulity.

He held up his hands to quieten the furore. 'Just listen to me.' He went on to explain about his recent sales and the commissions he still had to fulfil.

'You can't be sure this will continue,' his father put in.

'Be careful, son,' warned his mother. 'You've a wife and daughter to support.'

'Never forget that,' Harold bolstered his wife's comment. 'You've got a good job that is bringing you a good living, don't throw it all away.'

'He'll be throwing more than that away,' growled Conan. All eyes turned on him. What could he mean? 'I had plans for Arthur,' he went on. 'And Moira approved them. We only have Rose so she will inherit my shop. In another couple of years, after he'd had more experience dealing with people, I'd intended to take Arthur into the business with me, show him the ropes, and then we could have opened another shop, and another, and another.' A vision of future Duggan Emporiums criss-crossing Leeds filled his mind, as he expounded his ideas.

'That is most kind of you, Mr Duggan, but it's not for me, I'm afraid. I want to paint.'

'Paint!' Conan exploded. With an angry red tide mounting his neck, he glared fiercely at his son-in-law. 'Where will that get you 'eh? You'd throw my offer back in my face in order to satisfy a whim?'

'Hardly a whim,' answered Arthur coldly. 'A life's ambition.'

'Arthur, think carefully about Con's offer,' prompted Harold. 'It is a wonderful opportunity.'

'It is, but I doubt if I would ever be happy in that trade.'

'What about my happiness?' The words came quietly from Rose but everyone heard them.

'I always have that at heart,' replied Arthur.

'It looks like it,' she mocked.

Enid, who sympathised with her son's dilemma and saw that Conan's fury was about to boil over, quickly interceded. 'I think we had better leave this to Rose and Arthur to decide. It is their future at stake here. It is obvious that Arthur had not discussed this with her before you all came here. I think it would have been better if he had. So I think it best we all say no more for now and let them go home to discuss things.'

Moira sensed her husband did not want it that way. She tapped him on the knee, a little more sharply this time. He knew he would have her to answer to if he said any more. He scowled but remained silent.

Enid stood up. Looking at Arthur and Rose, she said, 'Come along, I'll see you out.' In the hall she took out a clean handkerchief from her sleeve and handed it to Rose. 'Wipe your tears, love. Life can't always be smooth and comfortable. You'll work things out between you.' She gave her daughter-in-law a hug, which told Rose that she had her sympathy and support, whatever decision was reached. She imparted the same feeling to Arthur as she embraced him and said quietly, 'I realise you have your dreams, Arthur, but don't forget your responsibilities. Rose and Marie are precious to us all.'

He nodded, too full of emotion to speak; instead he gave his mother an extra squeeze, thanking her for her understanding.

As they started along the street Arthur placed his hand gently on Rose's arm. 'Please try and understand, love.'

She shook his hand off angrily. 'You think only of yourself,' she hissed.

'No, love, I think of us. I know I can build on what has happened and make a good living doing something that I love.'

'Do it by all means but don't give up your job.'

'I have to if I want my painting to progress. I need to spend more time at it.'

'You'd jeopardise our future, mine and Marie's,

for that?'

'Rose, trust me. Believe in me.'

She lapsed into a hostile silence and he said nothing in the hope that by the time they'd reached home her anger would have subsided.

He could tell it had not by the way she threw down her coat and bonnet on the chair in the hall and strode into the drawing-room without a word to the maid who had greeted them on their arrival and informed them that Anita had taken Marie to her room. Arthur followed his wife. He could have gone upstairs and avoided a confrontation but it would have to be faced sometime and he thought it better to do so now.

Rose was leaning against the mantelpiece, the fingers of one hand displaying the irritation she was trying to control by nervously tapping the wood. She stood upright when she heard the door click shut and faced her husband.

'Please don't do this, Arthur.'

'I've got to, love.'

'No! You haven't *got* to!'

'I need to. With the sale of these latest paintings and the strong likelihood that I can sell some more soon, I must take the chance that is offered me.'

'What about my father's generous offer and the opportunity *that* presents? We'll be well off, will want for nothing. Doesn't that mean anything to you?'

'Of course it does but I don't want to take it. I want to do what *I* want to do.'

'There you go,' she snapped. 'What *you* want. What about Marie and me?'

'You are everything to me.'

'Then give up this mad idea.'

'I can't. It's gnawing at me. I must do it. If I don't I'll regret it for the rest of my life. Always wonder if I could have made a success of my painting.'

She gave a little sneer of contempt. 'Don't come to me for sympathy when you fail.' She was striding towards the door as she was speaking.

He grabbed her by the arm when she went to pass him and turned her roughly to him. She tried to shake off his grip but he held her tight. He grasped her other arm, pulled her close and looked down into her hostile eyes. 'I love you, Rose, I need you with me in this.'

'If you take this step, you do it on your own. You'll get no help from me. You'd better sell enough to keep me and Marie in the style in which your wage from the railway kept us. I can see there will be no more jam and cream now.'

'How wrong you will be!'

'That's what you think,' she sneered.

She started to pull away but he would not let her. His eyes were fired with determination. He stared deep into her eyes. 'One day, when my work is well known, you'll be proud of me.' She struggled to be free from his grasp. His grip tightened. 'Remember that you refused to support me, and remember how even then I confirmed I loved you.' His lips came down on hers in fierce possession. Rose struggled for a few moments more but eventually succumbed. For now. She knew she would never forgive him for throwing away both a good job and her father's offer in order to follow his own selfish dream.

'I suppose you've done it?' said Rose when her husband returned from work the following evening. She had spent her day preparing for this moment. If Arthur really had gone through with his idea then she would have to live with it. What would be would be. She would have to make the best of it, but she would never let him forget his obligations to his family. She had told herself this over and over again, her outright hostility assuaged by their lovemaking last night.

'Yes, my resignation shocked them all. I have to work a week's notice.' She nodded; it was what she had expected. 'And another thing – I've sold this house.'

'You've *what?*' Rose couldn't believe what she had heard.

'I've sold this house.'

As much as she had primed herself to be calm this unforeseen announcement brought fury rising to the surface. 'Now you take the roof from over our heads! What do you expect us to do? Go to Mother's?'

'No,' he snapped. 'Just give me time to explain. It's something I think you'll like...'

'Like? What could you possibly say to please me after selling my house?'

'We have three weeks to find a new one in Scarborough.'

'Scarborough?' squeaked Rose, not knowing whether to be delighted or antagonistic.

'Yes. I knew if we were to move from Leeds you would like to live in Scarborough. I have sufficient sketches of Leeds to work from but I want to do

352

more paintings of the Yorkshire coast and thought you'd rather it be in Scarborough than anywhere else. You've always enjoyed it there and we already have friends in the Brooks. Besides, in the light of my decision, we'll be better away from our families.'

With this news of a move to the place she liked, Rose found herself coming round to this idea of Arthur's. 'Maybe you're right about leaving Leeds. It is easy to come back and visit now there is the railway...'

'And I'll need to keep returning because I want Ebenezer to keep handling my work. I'll have to go and see him and acquaint him with all this after we have eaten.'

'You are later this evening?' commented Ebenezer when Arthur arrived.

'I went home first because there was something I wanted to tell Rose before I saw you.'

'You've left the railway?'

'Yes.'

'I thought I hadn't talked you out of it yesterday.'

'You did your best but my mind was made up. I handed in my resignation today.'

'Well. I wish you all the luck in the world.'

'So do I,' said Zilda, and kissed him on the cheek.

'Remember two things, Arthur. First you make your own luck by working hard. Second, I will always be here to help you. And I hope our agreement. made what seems a long time ago now, still stands?'

'Of course it does and always will. I owe a lot to you and will never be able to repay you.'

'Just be a success, that will be payment enough.'

'There is one more thing.' He went on to tell them of the proposed move to Scarborough.

Ebenezer's immediate reaction was one of disappointment. 'Then we shan't see so much of you,' he said, but on reflection thought it might be a good move and one that, of course, gave plenty of scope for a wide variety of new subjects.

'Whenever you bring paintings for Ebenezer and are not returning the same day or staying with your family, there is always a bed here for you,' Zilda offered.

'Thank you. I have such good friends,' replied Arthur.

The news that they were leaving Leeds shattered their families, particularly the Duggans who dreaded the loss of their only child. It would have created a rift in a long standing family friendship if it had not been for Enid and Moira's determination to remain close.

'They could be going to the other end of the world, and then we would never see them again, whereas in fact they are only going to be a short train journey away,' they pointed out to their husbands who on one occasion had nearly come to blows because of the vehemence with which Conan blamed Harold's son for taking his daughter away from them.

It was a hectic three weeks for Arthur and Rose. At the end of the first his friends at the office gave Arthur a farewell party. On the Monday of the following week he and Rose went to Scarborough, stayed two nights, and found a house close to their friends. The Brooks were delighted to hear of their move to Scarborough. Arthur hoped having friends close by would help Rose to settle in. Anita agreed to come with them, which greatly relieved both Arthur and Rose.

Packing their belongings, deciding what needed to be taken and what they could dispense with, did not make for an easy few days. With their belongings finally despatched by carrier, leaving an empty house, Conan relented in his opposition to the move and let the young couple, with Marie and Anita, stay with them their last two nights in Leeds.

The Duggans and the Newtons made a tearful farewell at the station. As Conan took Arthur's proffered hand he stared seriously at him and said. 'You look after my daughter, see that she always has the comfort she could have had if you had not embarked on this foolhardy course.'

Arthur ignored the jibe. 'Rose will not suffer because of my actions.'

'See she doesn't.'

Arthur embraced Mrs Duggan. 'Rose will be fine. Come and stay with us soon.' Moira was too choked to say anything.

He turned to his father next. There was warmth in Harold's handshake. 'Do well, son. Remember we are here if there is ever anything...' His voice broke.

'Thanks,' replied Arthur, and turned to his mother.

Enid held out her arms to him and, as he

stepped into them and felt her loving embrace, he knew she understood. 'Be true to yourself, love,' she whispered in his ear.

He gave a little nod. 'Come and see us, Ma.'

'I will. I know you will be a success. Work hard and take a pride in what you do. I will always be thinking of you.'

'And I of you.' He gave her a special hug that they were both reluctant to break.

'All aboard, all aboard!' With that shout came the last few hectic moments of departure. Arthur saw Anita and Marie into the carriage as last kisses were showered on the baby. He urged Rose on to the train. Having made her tearful good-byes, she still had damp eyes and cheeks. He climbed on board himself, turned and called his last farewell. His eyes rested on his mother. He saw her tears had dried and in their place was a look of encouragement that he knew he would carry with him into the future.

Arthur kept up a running conversation to divert Rose's mind from all they were leaving, encouraging her to look forward to their new life in Scarborough. She was quiet for a while, trying to come to terms with the changes ahead and not to think of what life would have been like if they had stayed in Leeds with Arthur still in his secure job. Anita was excited, absorbing every aspect of her first journey by train, and beyond Leeds. She continually encouraged Marie's interest in what was passing by the carriage window.

The carrier was already there when they arrived at their new home. Having left a key with the Brooks and instructed the carrier where it could be picked up, the Newtons were pleased that a lot of their furniture and goods were already in the house.

It took Rose four weeks to arrange things as she wanted them. Her constant change of placements preyed on Arthur's time and mind, until one day he protested: 'For goodness' sake, leave things as they are. You'll soon be protesting there's no money coming in. If you're constantly changing things, I can't get on with my painting.'

'You want your home to be nice, I expect!' she snapped.

'Of course but...'

'Then you'd better earn something.'

Arthur gave up. He could not do right for doing wrong. He knew Rose still had not forgiven him for leaving the railway on what she saw as a foolhardy whim. He was thankful when she seemed to have got the house to her liking, and doubly thankful that it was a good summer so that she could get out and enjoy her promenading.

He began to work fast to try and make up for lost time, heeding particularly the demands of Lionel Ross who saw a good chance of selling summer visitors pretty pictures of Scarborough. Arthur turned out competent work but had little time to experiment or develop the accomplished technique that had marked his exhibition in Leeds.

He realised that the demand might lessen in winter but he would take his opportunity then to stockpile canvasses for the following summer. He also wondered how Rose would take to a winter in this town. He'd bowed to her desire to go to

Leeds to spend Christmas with her parents but in the event snow lay heavily inland and with the lines blocked no trains were running. Knowing that she was disappointed, Arthur went out of his way to make a Christmas that revolved round her and Marie. He also knew that the inclement weather had shown Rose a new side of Scarborough that was very different from that she had experienced at better times of the year. Living here permanently was different from coming for a holiday in the summer.

Occasional barbs were still thrown by her: 'We'd have been better off staying in Leeds'; 'You'd better sell something soon or money will become a problem'; 'I'll not lower my standards ... what would Fanny and Oliver think?'; 'You should never have given up your job. Go and see if you can get a job on the railway here'.

Arthur took the criticism without comment until it became more frequent. His retaliation when his patience snapped was sharp and fierce, and Rose dissolved into a flood of tears. 'Nag, nag, nag! Is that all the encouragement you can give me? Can't you see I'm doing my best? A little faith from you would help.'

Such episodes grew more frequent until Arthur found he feared what each day might bring and locked himself in his studio to paint fiercely, catering for the demands of Lionel Ross. He also needed to do some studies of Leeds for Ebenezer or his friend would think he was being neglected, and a London gallery owner had contacted Ebenezer wanting more nature studies.

With these commissions Arthur pointed out to

Rose that their financial situation was in fact improving but all he got in return was, 'They would have provided the jam and cream if you had a job with a regular income.'

He knew she was right, but as long as he was making a living with his painting he would not consider doing anything else.

He knew there was the possibility of reopening the market in Whitby through Mr Redgrave but with his Scarborough and Leeds outlets he had not had time to revisit the port. Besides he dare not risk an uncertain venture in the present climate. He had to continue to paint where the money was. Sometimes, though, his mind would drift to Whitby and he would wonder if Miss Shipley was still taking photographs there and if she had ever received her painting. She must be growing into a fine young woman – three years could make a significant difference.

Chapter Fifteen

William Redgrave looked up and peered over his spectacles to see who had just entered his shop. 'Good day, Miss Shipley.'

'Good day to you, Mr Redgrave.'

'Still no word from Mr Newton?' she asked as she glanced round hoping to see some of Arthur's works. A look of disappointment came over her face when she saw him shaking his head.

'I'm sorry. I can't understand it. He let me have

two more paintings but they were delivered by a stranger. That was over two years ago. I have not heard of him since and there has been no further contact from his representative.'

'You never found that address.'

'Sadly, no. As I told you before I can only conclude that my brother threw it out when, against my wishes, he did some tidying up while I was out.'

'What do you think could have happened to Mr Newton?'

William shrugged his shoulders and spread his hands.

'I still feel awful at never having been able to thank him for that wonderful portrait he gave me.'

'It was indeed wonderful,' agreed William, recalling it vividly. 'It was more than a good likeness of you. There was real feeling in it too ... for Whitby, of course. The way he depicted a glimpse of it through the window.'

'And the detail in the room made me feel I was actually standing there.'

'Indeed.'

'I wonder if he did any more painting?'

'He had real talent. No, it was more than that, it was a gift. It would be a great pity if he did not make good use of it. Maybe he has had to give up painting.'

'Oh, I hope not.'

'So do I. Or maybe he has moved away from Leeds.'

'As I have said before, do let me know if he appears again.'

'I most certainly will, Miss Shipley.'

When Colette reached home she found her sister, in the drawing-room, sitting on the window seat, reading. Colette raised her eyebrows and shot Adele an enquiring glance when she saw the title: *Lady Audley's Secret.* 'Does Father know you are reading that sensational novel?'

'Yes.'

'Didn't he object?'

'No, he views it as part of our education so long as it is supervised by Miss Lund.'

'Where is he, by the way?'

'He and Miss Lund went for a walk.'

'They seem to be spending a lot of time together recently.'

'Do you object?' asked Adele seriously.

'No, no,' Colette replied quickly.

'What if it led to something more serious?'

Colette sat down beside her. 'You mean, marriage?'

'Yes. Do you think that would be disrespectful to Mother?'

Colette looked thoughtful. 'No. It's nine years since she died. I know how terribly Father missed her and it hurt him for a long time. If Susan has eased the pain in any way then I'm grateful to her. Father deserves some happiness, and if he can find it with Susan then I think he should.' She saw a relieved expression on Adele's face.

'I'm so pleased you think that way. I feel the same, and if we are both of the same mind it will be easier for him if the relationship does come to anything.'

'That's settled then,' said Colette, rising from her seat. 'Sorry I interrupted your reading.' She went upstairs to her bedroom and stood looking at the painting that Mr Newton had given her and for which she had never had the chance to thank him.

She recalled the unbelievable surprise she had received when Mr Redgrave had given it to her together with the message from Mr Newton. When she'd brought it home, her father, sister and Miss Lund, were not only surprised by the gift but amazed by the quality of the painting. Like Colette they felt drawn into the picture; they were there with her looking out of that window towards Whitby. Her father had wanted to know more about the person who had painted it and even queried the possible motive behind the gift, but his worry and doubt were pacified when he learned that Miss Lund had met the artist. She assured him that she was convinced the painting was a gift because he shared Colette's interest in Whitby.

Now, as she looked at the painting, she found herself wishing she had taken a photograph of the man who had made her such a gift and had been so pleasant on the two occasions they had met. They seemed so long ago.

With the winter weather easing into the spring of 1864 Arthur took the opportunity to take four paintings to Ebenezer in Leeds.

'Good day, old friends, it is good to see you again,' he said brightly as he greeted Ebenezer and Zilda, but they knew that behind his tone lay desire for the frequent contact that they had once enjoyed. They had gradually realised over the intervening years that, in order to meet Rose's demands for a comfortable living, his work was becoming more commercialised.

'We are pleased to see you too,' replied Ebenezer as they exchanged a warm handshake.

'You know we are delighted to see you every time you visit,' said Zilda as she embraced Arthur and kissed his cheek. 'You'll stay?'

'Thank you but no. I didn't see my parents last time I was in Leeds and I really must visit Rose's, though that will be a quick call.' He added the last remark with a touch of regret.

'Conan is still resentful?'

Arthur's lips tightened with regret. 'I'm afraid so. I shattered his dream and took his daughter away. Thankfully my father has not allowed Mr Duggan's attitude to me to mar their friendship. I think he sees himself as a stepping-stone to a possible reconciliation between us. Forgive me. I must away. I'm staying the night at home so I'll call in the morning to see if you are satisfied with the three paintings I've brought.'

'We look forward to seeing you tomorrow.'

The door had hardly closed when Ebenezer and Zilda set about unwrapping the paintings. When they had positioned them for viewing they stood looking at them without speaking for nearly ten minutes. Then they looked at each other and could see that each had reached the same conclusion.

It was Ebenezer who voiced it. 'Very competent. They'll sell. I'm only sorry they don't sparkle like those he did for the exhibition. There was a lot of promise there. The Steels saw it and regret what is happening to Arthur now.'

'As you say, they're competent and will sell, but they won't be going to people who would come back for more and become collectors of Arthur Newton's work.'

Ebenezer frowned. 'Oh, why didn't he heed my words of advice about throwing up his job?' Annoyance crept into his tone. 'He's painting to satisfy Rose's ambitions. I don't blame her for wanting her security but she doesn't realise the effect it has had on his work.'

'There are certain sections of these three paintings where you can still see his exceptional talent – it is as if it is waiting to surface – but I am afraid Arthur is not aware of it. In different circumstances he would be and then his true talent would emerge again and he would become the artist you expected,' said Zilda. She slid her arm through her husband's as they continued looking at the paintings. 'I know how much you thought of his painting in the early days. Saw a great future for him. Don't give up hope. Something could happen that will make him change course.'

'Then I wish it would soon.'

She patted his hand. 'It will, it will.'

Ebenezer gave her a wan smile and said, 'Thank goodness I have you to bolster my dreams.'

Zilda passed her fingers across her forehead and pushed some hairs behind her ears.

'You look thoughtful, love?' he commented.

'These are paintings of Leeds. What does he do for Ross?'

'Scarborough.'

'Cast your mind back to the exhibition. What were the outstanding canvasses?'

364

Ebenezer's reply was immediate. 'Those of Whitby, and especially the one he entitled *Admiring the View*.'

'Exactly. They all had that extra something. Since he went to Scarborough he has never done any more of Whitby. Why? It's just along the coast.'

'Because he is fully occupied with paintings of Scarborough for Lionel Ross who, because of the ever-changing clientele that the town attracts, finds he can sell all that Arthur can supply. He does Leeds as well, along with the nature subjects for London, because he knows he can sell them and is motivated now by the need to make a living.'

'What you say is perfectly true,' agreed Zilda.

'So what are you getting at?' asked a puzzled Ebenezer.

'Ask him to do some paintings of Whitby for us. Say we've had enquiries from someone who saw his exhibition and liked the studies of Whitby.'

'Won't he wonder why this person hasn't come forward before?'

'Oh, Ebenezer, make up some story that he has been away and has just returned to set up home here. Anything to get Arthur interested. But point out that they have to be of the same standard and technique as those in the exhibition. And also say that there is no time limit, it is quality that is demanded here, so he can work them in with the paintings from which he makes his living.'

'You seriously think that Whitby is the subject that will motivate him?'

'Well, it did once, and I believe that was reflected in the works he did of Leeds at the same time. If it wasn't Whitby itself then it was something he saw in it ... someone even.'

'You are thinking it could be the young lady in *Admiring the View?*'

'Why not? I never thought for one minute that she was a figment of his imagination though I never said anything because it was Arthur's business.' As she was speaking she had noted her husband's eyes half close as if she had touched on a point he had kept secret. 'Ebenezer Hirst, you know something?' When he hesitated she knew she was right. 'Come on, out with it. We've never had secrets.'

'She's a young lady living in Whitby. A photographer. Arthur met her when he went there to do some sketches of subjects for the exhibition. But that was all.'

Zilda cast him a wry side-glance. 'Yet he put her in a painting?'

'Can't that happen without people thinking there is more to it?'

Zilda shrugged her shoulders. 'Perhaps. But do as I suggest ... ask him for more paintings of Whitby.'

The next morning Ebenezer was ready with his approach to Arthur who had left home in time to share a cup of chocolate with his friends, before taking the train.

'I could do with some paintings of Whitby,' Ebenezer announced. 'You haven't done any since your exhibition.'

'I've been too busy with Scarborough and Leeds, as you know.'

'Well, I have an interested party.'

'Who particularly wants Whitby views?'

'Yes.' Ebenezer went on to explain what was wanted.

'You'll have to visit and do some more sketches which will give you the opportunity of contacting Mr Redgrave again. It is a pity that connection was allowed to drop, you could do with another outlet.'

'Did you have a successful trip, dear?' Rose asked when she had exchanged the customary welcoming kiss with Arthur on his arrival in Scarborough.

He knew that the two chief concerns behind her query were an interest in what money he would be receiving and whether he had seen her parents. How he wished she would talk about his paintings and what Ebenezer had thought of them! But she never did and he had become resigned to the fact that she probably never would. As long as they were living in reasonable comfort he knew she was broadly satisfied. But there were other times when she would not miss the opportunity to remind him how much better off they would have been with two incomes.

'Your mother and father are well. They send their love.'

'The business is still thriving?' This question was always put on his return from visiting them. He knew it was asked as a reminder of the way he'd turned down her father's generous offer.

'And does Ebenezer want more paintings?' Again, a regular question on his return.

'Yes, but he wants some of Whitby this time. He has had a request from an interested customer.'

'I suppose that means you will have to go there?'

'Yes. I'll need to find some different aspects.'

'Well, go if you must. But don't expect me to accompany you and have to hang about in that dreadful place.'

Arthur shrugged his shoulders but did not contradict her by expressing his own feelings that Whitby was more attractive than Scarborough as well as having an atmosphere that was more conducive to his work.

For the next four days Arthur worked hard at two paintings he had to complete for Lionel Ross. Then he found it a relief to relax in the early-morning coach to Whitby. After the initial greeting of his fellow passenger he fell into silent contemplation, from which even the rough jerks caused by unavoidable potholes made only a brief distraction. He anticipated the sights, smells, sounds and feelings generated by the port. His thoughts of Whitby became overlaid by a face ... that of the young lady who was *Admiring the View*. He held the vision for a while and began to wonder if she had changed since he last saw her three years ago in 1860. Was Colette still pursuing her photography? He had never for-gotten her name. The recollection startled him. Why was he thinking of her now? Why was he hoping he would see her again? She might not even be living in Whitby still! He bit his lip. Why did that thought disturb him so?

The coach rolled into Whitby. The horses,

under the expert hands of the coachman, were guided to the Angel where all became hustle and bustle with passengers to be taken care of, horses to be unhitched and stabled, luggage to be unloaded, messages left and received.

Arthur left it all and made his way to Skinner Street. He must renew his acquaintance with Mr Redgrave immediately in the hope that the friendliness the art dealer had shown him two years ago would remain the same. Would Redgrave have news of Colette? Had she received his painting, and what had she thought of it?

There was no one in the shop when Arthur walked in but the tinkle of the doorbell soon brought William Redgrave hurrying. He came to a sudden halt on seeing Arthur, throwing up his arms in surprise. The ticking off that came with his initial surprise was quickly lost in a broad welcoming beam.

'My dear, boy! How delightful to see you again.' He held out his hand.

Apprehension over his reception fell from Arthur who smiled and shook the proffered hand. There was warmth and friendliness in the men's greeting and pleasure in their expressions.

'I am sorry I have neglected you, Mr Redgrave, but I have been extremely busy.' Arthur told him about his move to Scarborough.

'And no doubt painting for Lionel Ross?'

'Yes.'

'He can be very demanding, I gather, because he has the custom of wealthy people coming to take the Spa waters.'

'You are right. With what he and my

369

representative in Leeds wanted I had to neglect Whitby, but now Mr Hirst has a customer who is looking for paintings of this town. So here I am to do some sketching and to apologise to you.'

'No need to apologise.' William dismissed Arthur's words with a wave of his hand. 'If you have time to do some paintings for me, you know I will always welcome them.'

'I will, and I promise I won't neglect you again.'

'Arthur, I'm going to have to rush you away,' William said regretfully. 'I have someone coming to see me in a few minutes, but do come back later. What time does your coach leave?'

'Four o'clock.'

'Come back at half-past two, then we can talk about the scenes I would like.'

'Very well! I'll look forward to our chat.'

Arthur reached the door and hesitated. He almost turned back but then opened the door and stepped outside. Mr Redgrave had not mentioned the painting he had left for Miss Shipley. Was there some reason for this or had it slipped his mind? Perhaps he would ask him when he saw him later.

William waited for a few minutes after Arthur had left. He rubbed his chin thoughtfully then, his decision made, picked up his hat and cane and left the shop.

Arthur spent a successful few hours sketching, working quickly but purposefully. These drawings gave lightning impressions that would unlock the observations stored in his brain. As he wandered through Whitby he found himself half expecting, indeed hoping, that he would come across Colette and Miss Lund but he did not catch sight of either.

He did not wish to inconvenience Mr Redgrave by being late for his appointment so made certain that on the stroke of two-thirty he was opening the door of the shop in Skinner Street.

'Had a good day?' William asked.

'I have indeed.' Arthur pulled his sketchbook from his pocket. 'See what I have been doing.'

William turned the pages over slowly. 'They should all make very good subjects, handled in the style you were executing when I last saw your work.'

'That is how I intend to tackle them,' replied Arthur, pleased at this comment, for even in this short visit to Whitby he had felt its atmosphere urging him to devote more time to the old style he had almost neglected in his quest to make a living wage from his painting.

'No doubt it will have improved?'

Arthur was saved from making a reply as the shop door opened. William looked up and a smile tinged with relief crossed his face.

'Good afternoon, Mr Redgrave.'

Arthur tensed. He knew that voice. A mixture of excitement, embarrassment, pleasure, delight, and eagerness to meet her again ran through him. 'Miss Shipley.'

She gave a little nod. 'Mr Newton.'

'It is a pleasure to see you again. Are you still taking photographs?'

'Indeed I am. I hope you are still painting?'

'I have never given up, but because of other

371

demands on my time I have neglected Whitby these past two years.'

Neither of them noticed that Mr Redgrave had quietly slipped away to the room behind the shop.

'I wondered. I was anxious to thank you for the delightful painting you left with Mr Redgrave for me. It was a wonderful present, so brilliantly executed. It hangs in my bedroom.'

'I'm flattered.'

She could tell by his tone of voice that he was underestimating his own achievement. 'Don't play down your talent, Mr Newton. You paint extremely well. You certainly have an eye for presenting a subject in the best possible manner, attractive and sometimes unusual. I hope your painting has continued to develop?'

'You will have to be the judge of that when I bring some more canvases for Mr Redgrave.'

'Is that why you are here?' She noticed the sketch book that lay on the table. 'Yours?' she queried.

'Yes. I came to renew my acquaintance with Whitby and do some sketches, which I hope to develop into paintings.'

'May I?' she queried, glancing from the book to Arthur.

'Of course.'

Colette picked up the book and started looking at his sketches. He watched her, transfixed by her serenity and beauty. His fingers itched to capture this moment on paper. He also saw her obviously deep interest in the contents of the book, which pleased him.

'They are only rough,' he offered.

'But nevertheless they reveal an eye for a picture, and an ability to capture a mood in a few strokes of the pencil. These sketches would stand on their own without further development, but I have no doubt that you will execute paintings that bring out everything you feel about their subjects.'

'You are too kind.' He glanced at her, wondering if these were thoughts she really felt or she was just being charitable.

She caught the question in his eyes. 'I really mean it.' She emphasised her words so that he was left in no doubt.

'Then I must thank you again.'

She closed the book slowly as if she saw it as something precious and had to take every care of it.

An embarrassing silence settled between them. It seemed to stretch an age as each of them sought what should be said next. It was in fact only a matter of seconds. Yet in that silence there came a shared understanding.

'I must be going.' The fact that they both said exactly the same words at the same moment not only emphasised what had passed between them, it also brought laughter.

'I have a coach to catch,' Arthur explained.

'You have a long journey to Leeds.'

'No. I live in Scarborough now.'

'Then maybe we will see more of you in Whitby?' she ventured.

'Certainly, it is easier to get to and I will have Mr Redgrave to satisfy with new paintings. Maybe we will meet when you are taking photographs and I will see what you have been doing.

Does Miss Lund still help you?'

'She does, and so does my sister Adele on occasion.'

'It sounds as though you keep busy?'

'We do. The demand for photographs is growing. I hope it does not do so to the detriment of painting.'

Arthur gave a little smile. 'It won't ever do that, Miss Shipley. Photography will never be able to capture the atmosphere of a place as a work of art can.'

'I think you are mistaken there, Mr Newton.'

He was about to take up the argument when Mr Redgrave appeared. 'I'm sorry to have left you, Miss Shipley.'

'That's all right, Mr Redgrave, I was just going.' She smiled her thanks and turned to Arthur. 'It has been pleasant meeting you again, Mr Newton. Goodbye.'

As the door closed, Arthur picked up his sketchbook. 'I too must be off, or I will miss my coach. I will let you have something in due course, Mr Redgrave. Thank you for receiving me again after all this time.'

'It has been a pleasure, my boy. I look forward to seeing your new paintings.'

They shook hands and Arthur left. As he walked to the Angel, where he would board the coach for Scarborough, his mind turned to Colette and the pleasure he had derived from seeing her. How in their few minutes together she had shown a genuine interest in his work. With his thoughts came an observation and a query. She had carried out no transaction with Mr Redgrave. Had he arranged for her to call at the shop, knowing that she wanted to make her thanks for the painting delivered after his exhibition? Arthur smiled to himself. If there had been intrigue behind that 'chance' meeting, he was glad.

Reaching home, he found Rose playing with Marie in the drawing-room. He kissed his wife and hugged his daughter.

'Has she been good?' he asked.

'No bother,' replied Rose. 'Anita had her all morning while I visited Fanny. We decided to have a look round the shops and while we were out we paid a visit to Oliver at his shop.'

'They were both well?'

'Yes, Oliver was busy. His shop is thriving. He had sold two diamond necklaces just before we arrived so was very pleased with himself.'

'And this afternoon?'

'I spent it with Marie after she woke from her nap. I gave Anita the rest of the afternoon off.'

'Good. The little change will do her no harm. She has settled well.'

'It is a relief that she has done so. She is so good with Marie.'

The child stirred in Arthur's arms. 'You want to be with your toys?' He put her down on the carpet.

As he straightened, Rose asked, 'Did your day in Whitby go well?' Her tone gave the impression that she had put the question as if fulfilling an obligation.

'Yes. I drew a number of sketches that I can work into paintings. Would you like to see them?' He held out the sketchbook to her.

Rose took it and, without any undue enthusiasm, flicked through the pages. She made no comment except to say, 'Very nice,' as she handed the book back.

'If only she would show half the interest Colette did,' he thought as he took the book, but said only, 'I saw Mr Redgrave.'

'Mr Redgrave?' She looked puzzled.

'I last saw him three years ago and was going to do some paintings for him but I got too busy supplying Mr Ross and Ebenezer.'

'Oh, yes, I remember now. But Mr Ross was so much handier especially when we moved to Scarborough. Mr Redgrave recalled you?'

'Oh, yes. He was pleased to see me and still wants some paintings of Whitby.'

'I suppose that means you'll be going again.'

'He assures me he can sell whatever I supply so long as they are of a particular standard.'

'Doesn't Mr Ross require a particular standard, as you put it?'

'Yes, but he looks for quantity at a certain standard, and, being able to sell them, does not look beyond that, whereas Mr Redgrave will always be looking for an improving style.'

'But if you are painting what people want in the way they want it, why look beyond that?'

'Any artist worth his salt is always striving to do better, to develop that something extra that will lead to improvement in each painting.'

'Isn't he then just painting to satisfy himself, and risking the prospect that his work might not sell? Isn't it better to do what other people want?'

'Not really, though he may have to do that to

make a living, particularly if he has family obligations.'

Rose stiffened. Was Arthur indicating that she and Marie were burdens, hindering him from what he really wanted to do? 'You mean we hold you back?' she snapped.

'No. No,' he hastened to mollify her.

'You should have thought of that before you married me.'

'I thought you would come round to my way of thinking, see what I wanted to achieve, and help me by your encouragement and understanding.'

'Understanding? What is there to understand? You paint pretty pictures. What more can they be?'

'There should be atmosphere, character, soul, in every painting that a true artist does. These factors can disappear if he is just painting commercially. And of course, work with soul in it can still sell.'

Rose threw up her arms in despair. 'I can't pretend to understand all that twaddle. As far as I can see, you either paint or you don't. But I'll tell you one thing – you'd better not let anything get in the way of providing Marie and me with a good living and the comfort we would have enjoyed from your railway job.'

Words sprang to his lips to counter her threat but he curbed them. He walked from the room.

'We will be eating in half an hour,' she called as he was closing the door.

Chapter Sixteen

Colette was thoughtful as she walked home, her mind dwelling on the encounter with Mr Newton. Why had her pulse raced when she stepped into the shop and saw him? Was she just excited at the prospect of being able to thank him for the painting? She was sure it had been no coincidence that Mr Redgrave had called that morning and asked her to be at his shop at two-thirty-five. He had insisted that she should call precisely at that time. He must surely have set up that meeting and, wanting to surprise her, had declined to give a reason. She smiled to herself, recalling his intrigue, but she was pleased of it. She had been delighted to be in conversation with Mr Newton and looked forward to the prospect of talking to him again.

As she approached the house she felt an urge to go straight to her room to look at *Admiring the View*. She saw it every day so why the intense desire to do so now? She could not answer the question with any conviction. Was it because she had just seen the artist again? Did she feel it would bring him closer? She knew nothing about him; did she think looking at the painting could reveal something? What could it, except that he was a good painter? But even as that question came to her, she knew she would always see there an expression of Mr Newton's feelings. Did she really need to know more?

Her hopes for solitude were dashed as she entered the house. Adele came rushing into the hall.

'I'm glad you're back, I saw you through the window,' she said, excitement bright in her eyes. 'There's a surprise for you.' As her words poured out she was hurrying her sister out of her outdoor clothes.

'What is it?' asked Colette, puzzled by Adele's exuberance.

'Not what ... who?'

A little startled and annoyed that there was a visitor just when she wanted solitude, Colette nevertheless glanced in the mirror, patted her hair into place and smoothed her dress.

Impatiently, her sister urged her to hurry, although Colette's attention to her appearance had taken only a few seconds. She raised a questioning eyebrow but the only reply she received was an eager smile. Finally Adele opened the door to the drawing-room and allowed Colette to walk in.

Her father and the young man to whom he was talking rose from their chairs. The young man, tall, slim, dressed impeccably, gave Colette a smile that was full of pleasure and admiration.

'My dear Colette.' He stepped forward and held out his hand to her.

Bewildered by his unexpected appearance, Colette automatically offered hers. He took it and raised it to his lips as he bowed without taking his eyes off her.

'Bernard! Bernard Clayton! What are you doing here?'

He laughed at the wide-eyed look of surprise she gave him. 'I'm sorry if I've shocked you.'

She gave a disbelieving shake of her head and glanced at her father and Adele as if seeking an explanation. It came from Bernard.

'We've come to live in Scarborough, only last week. I had some business in Whitby today so took the opportunity to call on our dear friends the Shipleys.'

'Sit down, my dear, Bernard will explain,' said her father. 'Adele, I think Colette could do with a glass of Madeira to help her get over the shock.'

She sank into a chair, grateful for the glass of wine. She looked enquiringly at Bernard who had sat down opposite her.

She saw a handsome young man, with clean-cut features. She'd last seen him ten years ago when he was ten and she was eight. The families had lived within two houses of each other and all the children – he had two younger sisters – had grown up together. Colette always had a special affection for him, seeing him as the brother she'd never had. Bernard had been lanky then. Now here he was with a self-assured air to him. His alert pale blue eyes drew attention to him. His hair, inherited from his Norwegian mother, was neat and fair.

'How long, Colette?' he queried in a soft 'company' voice. She smiled to herself when she recalled the raucous tone he'd sometimes displayed in play when he was leader of their pirate gang.

'Must be ten years,' she replied. 'We've grown up,' she commented wistfully. He wondered why she sounded as if she would like to turn back the years. Did she long for childhood? Miss her mother? Or were there years in between that meant more to her?

'It is good to see you looking so well.'

She acknowledged his comment with a shy inclination of her head.

'Tell her what you were telling us,' prompted Adele.

'Well, a couple of years ago Mother was not too well so Father brought her to Scarborough to take the waters.'

'They did her good?' asked Colette.

'Well, whether they did or not we can't be absolutely certain but her health certainly improved over the following six weeks. She completely recovered to become her former self again. They had both liked Scarborough, found it bracing by the sea. Father judged that, with all its attractions, the town was going to expand so he decided to sell his business on Teesside, buy land in Scarborough and build desirable dwellings. He has just started to build his first houses.'

'So you'll be living there permanently?'

'Yes. Father built our house first, on the South Cliff.'

'You said you had come to Whitby on business?' Mr Shipley put in.

'Yes, sir. Father can see the tourist trade to Scarborough increasing and has plans to build two high-class hotels there. In one he wishes to display items with country associations, in the other maritime artefacts. It is the latter that I seek in Whitby.'

'You will be here a few days then?'

'Yes. I am booked in at the Angel for four days.'

'My dear boy, you should have stayed with us.'

'Sir, that is generous of you, but I could not appear out of the blue and impose on you. Besides, I would have disrupted the smooth running of your household.'

The door opened and Miss Lund came in. She drew up short when she saw a stranger. 'Oh, I'm sorry. I did not know you had a visitor.'

The two men had risen from their chairs. 'It's all right, Susan. Come in.' Peter made the introductions. 'Mr Clayton, a dear friend of ours ... Miss Lund, our governess.'

Adele had risen to pour some wine for Susan.

Bernard was politeness itself but his mind raised questions he could not ask aloud. Colette and Adele were surely past the governess stage and Mr Shipley had most unusually used her Christian name when she'd entered the room. Adele had served her with wine. It was as if she was one of the family. The smiles that were exchanged between Mr Shipley and Susan Lund were not lost upon him, and he sensed there was also an easy relationship between her and the two sisters. The air of warm, pleasant contentment that filled the house could only be created by people living in love and harmony, respecting each other.

'You should show Bernard some of your photographs, Colette,' said Adele.

'I don't want to bore him,' she replied, embarrassed that her sister had put this idea forward.

'Photographs?' Bernard instantly showed curiosity. 'I'd love to see them.'

'I'll get some, Colette.' Susan Lund sprang to her feet. 'You shouldn't hide your light under a bushel.'

'Susan plays her part in this too,' Adele offered as the governess left the room.

'Tell me more?' Bernard urged.

By the time Susan returned he had all the facts. Susan Lund handed the photographs to Colette who moved to sit in a chair next to Bernard. She passed them to him one at a time. He was astonished by their quality but even more so by her interpretations of Whitby scenes.

'These are excellent. Can you print in a bigger size?'

'Yes, but if you go too big you begin to lose quality. Susan has become the printing expert.'

Bernard looked to her for further explanation when he said, 'I think some of these, particularly those with ships as part of the scene, would look well in the rooms of the new hotel when it is completed. We would have to judge the optimum size. In the meantime could you do enlargements of those two to give me some idea how big you can go without losing quality?' He glanced at Colette. 'If this works we could be in business.' He pulled himself up. 'Maybe I'm making an assumption? Are you doing this commercially or is it merely a hobby?'

'She sells pictures,' put in Adele hastily, 'but mainly of people.'

'Let me see those two enlargements and then maybe we could discuss further what I would like for the hotel.'

'I will see what views I can take of ships from a variety of angles,' said Colette. It was something she had not concentrated on though she'd had it in mind to do so. Ships had only appeared so far as part of the overall picture or as background to a personality. Now she had an incentive to interpret Whitby's lifeline.

'There's more come out of this visit to old friends than I expected,' Bernard enthused. 'But I must be going. I have taken up enough of your time as it is. First let me invite you all, and that includes you, Miss Lund, to dine with me tomorrow evening at the Angel. Say seven o'clock?'

'That is most generous of you, Bernard. We will be delighted to accept.' From the expressions on everyone's faces, Peter knew he was saying the right thing.

'Good, then tomorrow evening it is.' He made his goodbyes and Colette escorted him from the room.

They reached the front door where Bernard paused. 'It is good to see you again, Colette. You have grown into a beautiful young lady.'

She blushed and gave a dismissive wave of her hand.

'You have,' he confirmed. 'There was a time when I thought you an ugly duckling, but that was looking through the eyes of a boy who did not know that ugly ducklings can sometimes turn into beautiful swans.'

She smiled. 'Well, look at yourself. When you played the rescuing prince in our games, I thought, the prince should be handsome!'

'And now?' He looked wryly at her. 'Do you need rescuing?

She met his admiring gaze for a brief moment then turned her eyes away. 'Until tomorrow.'

He bowed and left the house.

Colette did not return to the drawing-room. Instead she went up the stairs, her mind dwelling on the past and old friendships which had returned to their lives.

She crossed her room to stand in front of the painting. Her latest meeting with Mr Newton came back into her mind. She recalled how glad she had been. Was it because she had been able to thank him for this picture? Was it because she liked talking to him? Or was there something more? She recalled how after his two previous visits, whenever she had been around the town taking photographs she had looked for him until, with the passage of time, she ceased to do so, believing he would not visit Whitby again. Then, today, her heart had raced and she had experienced joy in the knowledge that he would be returning.

She saw reflected in the picture a feeling for her on his part too. Or was that wishful thinking? Why should he have any affection for her? What did he really know of her? What did she know of him? Did such knowledge matter if two people realised what lay between them and it had strength enough to overcome anything else?

Now Bernard had re-entered her life. She gave a little twitch of her eyebrows betraying amusement as she recalled their first kiss when he was ten and she eight. He had been playing the prince and she the Sleeping Beauty. He really had grown into a handsome prince now.

Only at the thought of their ages did she realise there must be a greater gap between her and Mr Newton. How wide? She could not guess but, it surely was not enough to make a difference to their attitude to each other. What did age matter between compatible minds?

Colette's mind was a whirl of confusion. She pulled her fanciful thoughts to a halt. This was ridiculous. She was actually beginning to imagine these two men were rivals for her affections. Annoyed with herself for entertaining such wild surmise, she changed her dress and smoothed her hair before rejoining her family for a quiet evening together.

The following morning, when light streaming through the sash window woke her, Colette rubbed sleep from her eyes and eased herself into a more comfortable position. It brought *Admiring the View* into her vision and that immediately made her recall her meeting with Arthur yesterday. She remembered the gentleness in his eyes which also held the vigour and alertness of an artist. Could she ever capture that on a photograph?

That thought reminded her of her promise to Bernard. She slipped out of bed and went to the window. She saw a clear sky, and a glance at the trees told her that there was only a light breeze. A good morning on which to look for suitable ships and take their photographs.

She announced her intention to her father and Adele at breakfast. Susan, with some jobs to attend to, had already had hers.

'Can you go with her, Adele?' her father asked. 'Susan and I have an appointment with Mr Copley.'

'The solicitor?' queried Adele with a look of surprise.

'Yes,' came the answer, unusually sharply for their father. It was as if he was a touch embarrassed to admit it. He got on with his breakfast and they knew he did not wish to be asked the questions that had sprung to their minds.

The sisters exchanged glances and grimaces that indicated neither of them knew what was afoot. It immediately became their first topic of conversation when they stepped out of the house later with the photographic equipment.

'What do you think that is all about?' asked Adele as they set off towards Flowergate and the river.

'I have no idea. I'm as curious as you but it is no use our speculating. You know Father, he'll tell us when he thinks it's right. If there is anything to tell.'

'There must be something behind it, or why take Susan? But let's forget it for now and concentrate on the photographs. You heard what Bernard wants.'

'Seeing him was a surprise after all these years,' commented Adele. 'He's grown into quite a handsome man. Remember the gangling boy you rather liked?'

'I did not!' protested Colette.

'You did,' replied Adele with a grin. She enjoyed teasing her sister.

'He was like a brother to us.'

'So you say. Well, he could be more than a brother now.' She took a sly glance at Colette. 'You're blushing.'

'No, I'm not,' snapped Colette. 'Now stop talking about him.'

Adele smiled to herself. She knew when to stop and this was the moment, but she wondered if she had hit a nerve.

'You didn't tell them any more?' Susan asked as she and Peter walked to Baxtergate where Mr Copley had his premises.

'No, it was not the appropriate time. I had not intended to tell them anything until after we had seen Mr Copley but was forced to ask Adele to help Colette when she announced she was going to take photographs today. She would have expected you to accompany her otherwise.'

'You must tell them soon.'

I know, but I wanted to alter my will first.'

'It isn't necessary.'

'Oh, but it is. You have come to mean so much to me, and that is no disrespect to my late wife.'

'Peter, I know the circumstances. I have wanted nothing more than to share your life as you saw fit. You have been kind and generous to me.'

'No more than you deserve for the companion-ship you have given me and the way you brought up my daughters.'

Reaching the building in Baxtergate, they were shown straight to Mr Copley's office.

With greetings over, and seeing his visitors comfortably settled, Mr Copley took up his seat. He leaned forward, his clasped hands resting on the desk. He was a man of medium build, whose thinning hair revealed a bald patch at the back of his head. He was neatly dressed in a black three-quarter length jacket and matching trousers. A grey tie was knotted at his stiff white collar. His sharp face held brown eyes that seemed to be constantly on the move as if he must take in everything at once and miss nothing.

'I have all your papers and documents here, Mr Shipley. Since you made the appointment and indicated that you wished to change your will, I have studied them in advance. I will advise you when I have heard exactly what it is you want to do.' Mr Copley pursed his lips. A swift glance at Susan, whom he knew had been engaged as a governess and had stayed on after her wards no longer needed one, made him wonder why she was accompanying Mr Shipley now. But his was not to question, he was only here to carry out a client's wishes and advise when advice was requested.

An hour later, with matters finished, he said, 'I will have everything drawn up in the way you requested and would be obliged if you will call in a week today to look over the new document and sign it in front of two witnesses whom I will enlist.'

'Thank you, Mr Copley. I shall be here.'

The solicitor turned to Susan, who had made only the odd remark throughout the negotiations. 'Good day to you, Miss Lund, it has been a pleasure meeting you.'

After he had seen them out and had returned to his office, he wondered just how deep a relationship existed between those two. Though he was curious he would make no enquiry, nor would he say anything about the other matter that had been revealed.

'Let us walk on the West Pier,' Peter suggested.

Susan respected his silence as they turned up

Cliff Lane and cut through Bakehouse Yard to Haggersgate. He still had not spoken by the time they had traversed Pier Lane and reached the West Pier. Away from the buildings and the protection of the cliff they felt the breeze. Light though it was, it made Peter quicken his pace. Determination came into his step and she knew he was trying to eliminate the turmoil from his mind.

Reaching the end of the pier, just beyond the towering Doric-columned lighthouse, he stopped, he stiffened and drew in several breaths of pure sea air. His eyes stared far into the distance as if seeking answers. Susan stood beside him, silent, waiting.

Slowly, he turned to her and looked at her with compassion. 'I'm sorry,' he said quietly.

She knew that he was, for her and not for himself. 'You have nothing to be sorry for and need not be sorry for me. I count myself most fortunate in knowing you and your family. That is something I will always treasure.' She reached out and touched his arm with a gentleness that had the power to affect him. She saw a new light come to his eyes then.

'I don't want to cause you any more hurt but I must tell you that I have come to love you, Susan. I know Margot would approve and there is no less place in my heart for her now that you are there also. You made me feel young again. Gave me heart when, because of your kindness, understanding, and the love you gave them, Colette and Adele did not suffer the loss of their mother as much as they might have. I have much to be grateful for in you.' He kissed her on the cheek.

There were tears of gratitude in Susan's eyes as she fingered the place where his lips had been. She would remember this first time. She looked up at him in the new understanding that passed between them and kissed him passionately on the lips, imparting the feelings she had held back for so long. 'I love you and always will,' she murmured.

'Then we should...' he started.

She raised her fingers to his lips quickly to halt his words. 'Don't say it, Peter, please. It will be better if our relationship is left as it is, otherwise there will be too much sadness.'

As strongly as he wanted to contradict her, he did not. He knew she was right. All he said was, 'I'll say nothing to Colette and Adele until tomorrow. I don't want to cast a shadow over tonight's enjoyment at the Angel.'

'Thank goodness we no longer have to process your pictures out here,' commented Adele as they crossed the bridge to the east side of the river, she carrying the tripod and a bag with the necessary pre-waxed paper that had been coated with light-sensitive chemicals beforehand and enabled Colette or Susan to process the pictures some time later. Colette carried the camera and a second bag of paper.

'It makes things a lot easier,' she agreed.

They crossed the bridge, each carefully guarding their equipment lest the jostling crowd, bent about its business, accidentally jolted it to shatter on the ground. They turned off Bridge Street into Grape Lane, thankful that it was quieter.

391

Reaching Church Street, they turned to the quays where ships were tied up. The scene was a hive of activity: labourers were carrying bales and boxes of various sizes filled with all manner of products bound for distant shores across what Colette hoped would be calm seas. Moving as she had often done among the sailors and other people who earned their living in this busy port, she had grown to have a sympathetic under-standing of the dangers they faced and with it came an increased desire to record these people for posterity. This morning she would turn her attention to the means of this trade.

She was glad the tide was coming in, mingling with the river water to fill the harbour above and below the bridge, sending eddies shimmering in the sunlight that streaked the water with strings of brightness. It would make a captivating back-ground.

'We're on the wrong side of the river to get a full view of the ships,' Adele pointed out.

'We'll get one or two of those on our way back. I'm looking to do something different to straight-forward photographs. I want to capture the feel-ing of this scene. By photographing ships' details, the studies will be more expressive.'

Adele gave a little shake of her head as if she did not understand and said resignedly, 'I suppose you know what you're doing. You're the one with the eye for a picture.'

Reaching the first ship, Colette stopped to study it and then, her decision made, started to set up her tripod with Adele's help. A few people stopped to watch them; others called greetings as they passed or went about their jobs. Colette had become a familiar figure among them.

By the time she was ready for home she had photographed figureheads, ropes, rigging, nets, bows, sterns, sacks, and ships' names. Another day she decided she would come and photograph people at their work, rather than just posing for a portrait.

When they recrossed the river they stopped to take some general views of the shipping.

Highly satisfied with their morning's work they made their way home in time for luncheon. They found their father and Susan already there.

'Did you have a good morning?' Peter greeted them cheerfully.

'We did. The weather was just right.'

'What have you been taking?' asked Susan.

'Photographs I hope will interest Bernard Clayton.'

'Would you like me to print them this afternoon?' Susan offered.

'No, not today. It's too fine a day to be inside. Besides I intend to take some more and I gathered yesterday that Bernard is not concerned about getting them immediately.' Colette glanced at her father. 'Was your meeting with Mr Copley satisfactory?'

He nodded. 'It was.'

The manner of his delivery told her not to pry.

Colette and Adele exchanged glances and both knew that the other was thinking the same: what was so important that their interest should be brushed away so curtly? Was the matter so private it could not be voiced? And why had Susan accompanied him?

They both speculated in the quietness of their rooms and only pushed the questions to the back of their minds when they all left for the Angel. Nothing was going to spoil a special evening, getting to know Bernard and talking about old times and the years between.

Colette sensed that at the beginning of the evening Susan was strained. Had something earlier in the day upset her or was it that she just felt an outsider when they talked of the past? She concluded it was probably the latter because as the evening wore on Susan became much more relaxed under the good-humoured attention that Bernard afforded them all.

When she entered the dining-room the next morning for breakfast everyone was already there. Colette sensed a slight tension but when she eyed her sister all she got was a slight shake of the head and an expression that told her Adele did not know what was happening either.

Little was said during the meal except to comment on the pleasant evening they had spent with Bernard. As breakfast drew to a close their father rose from his chair and said, 'When you two have finished, will you come to my study?' Susan, not wanting to face any questions, swiftly followed him from the room.

'What's this about?' Adele asked as the door closed.

'I don't know,' replied Colette, 'but it sounds serious.'

'I'm not waiting any longer,' said her sister.

'Nor I,' Colette agreed.

The sisters laid their napkins on the table. When they entered the study they found their father standing with his back to the fireplace and Susan sitting on a chair to his left. Though heavily panelled, with one wall covered in bookshelves, it was a room in which Colette had always felt comfortable but this morning the unease here was palpable and that was heightened in her mind when the conversation between her father and Susan ended abruptly as she and Adele entered.

'Sit down, I have something important to say to you.' Peter indicated the sofa to his right, which they both noted had been turned from its usual position to face him more directly. He waited until they were seated before he continued. 'As you know I went to see my solicitor yesterday and Susan accompanied me. There was a purpose behind that. Susan has been with us many years, past the time when you really needed a governess. But she had become one of the family and I thought it best she stayed with us. She was only too delighted to do so.'

In the slight pause after that, Susan murmured, 'It would have broken my heart to leave you two.'

'And we would have missed you,' said Colette, a feeling that was reiterated by her sister.

Their father cleared his throat and continued. 'Susan and I became close and we have shared many happy moments together – nothing more than that, a pleasant companionable relationship. Though I should say that, as Susan now knows, with no disrespect or loss of love for your mother, marriage might have been proposed had not certain unfortunate circumstances arisen.' His voice almost broke at this point.

Colette sensed his emotion and a feeling of dread came over her.

'I have been seeing the doctor for the past six months.' He saw the alarm register on his daughters' faces and held out a hand as if to spare them what he was about to reveal. 'Three days ago he confirmed that I have an incurable disease.'

'Oh, no!' As one they jumped from the sofa and flung themselves to his side. He took one girl in each arm and hugged them close.

'It's not true!' cried Adele. Her father couldn't die.

'There's been a mistake,' said Colette forcibly.

Her father shook his head. 'I'm afraid not. I have six months.'

Both girls, feeling draining from them, sagged against him.

'You must be brave about this, we all must. We must live as normal a life as possible.'

'How can we?' cried Adele.

'We have to try. Please, for me. Let us enjoy the time left together, all four of us.'

This remark focused Colette's attention on Susan. She must be suffering as they were. She saw tears streaming down the beloved face of this woman who had become more than a governess to them. Slipping from her father's arm Colette went to her, knelt down beside her and offered her arms. They embraced in the love they had for each other and for the man who loved them all.

Peter eased Adele away. 'I have one more thing to tell you and then let's think of happier things.'

Colette and Adele returned to their seats and he went to sit on a chair next to Susan.

'My purpose in going to the solicitor was to change my will. I felt I should make some provision for Susan.' He took her hand in his and gave her a little smile. 'She did not want me to do so, but I thought it only right. I have left her a small legacy that will provide her with a regular income. The rest of my estate is divided equally between you two. I have requested that you allow Susan to stay in this house as long as she wants. If you want to sell the house before she has had her time in it then you should provide her with adequate accommodation. This particular property will be in your names, and once Susan has finished with it you may do with it what you please. If you have any questions about all this in the future then see Mr Copley. He is fully aware of the wishes recorded in the will.' Peter paused. A poignant silence filled the room.

Colette could not believe that this healthy-looking man standing before them had only six months to live. There appeared to be nothing wrong with him, but she had to face up to his announcement.

Adele seemed unable to think clearly. The numbness that gripped her would break under the engulfing wave of reason but would fail utterly to calm her mind.

Susan had shared her employer's knowledge of the doctor's diagnosis for the past three days. It was something of a relief that now someone else did too. Deep regret that such happiness had been snatched from her weighed heavily on her but she forced herself to be grateful for the happy times she had spent with this family. She must be strong for the sake of Peter's daughters.

He coughed. 'Come now, there's another day to be lived. Do what you were going to do and don't let this occupy your minds.' He walked briskly from the room.

Susan stood up and held out her arms. Colette and Adele came to her and they found comfort in their love for each other.

Chapter Seventeen

'I'll be going to Leeds tomorrow,' Arthur announced. 'I have two paintings for Ebenezer.'

'Very well. I hope he has sold some of the others,' commented Rose. 'Will you be staying the night?'

'Yes.'

'So you'll have time to visit my parents?'

'Yes.'

'Give them my love and tell them I hope they will come and stay next summer. Get them to make a date. Time will soon pass once the new year arrives in eight weeks.'

'I'll do my best but you know what your father is like about leaving the shop.'

'Tell him Rose says he needs a holiday. The shop will still be there when he gets back.'

Arthur would deliver the message but he had no intention of pressing his case for his father-in-law, though always civil, had never forgiven him for turning down his offer.

'And next week I shall go to Whitby. I have two paintings for Mr Redgrave and must get them to him before inclement weather cuts off the town.'

'Will that be a one-day visit?'

'Yes. It will just be a case of delivering the paintings and catching the afternoon coach. I'll go back in the spring to do some more sketches.'

Rose nodded but made no comment. If this was the way life was then so be it. Arthur spent most of his days in his studio turning out work for Mr Ross and Ebenezer and now Whitby had to be visited again, but if it was bringing in a little more money then she could tolerate the absence. She did make it clear to Arthur that he should not neglect their friendship with the Brooks, a point with which he was willing to comply if it made his wife more happy and amenable. Besides he liked and got on well with both Oliver and Fanny. Their company was always lively and well-informed, and for some reason imbued him with new enthusiasm when he took up his brushes again the next day.

'Wait a moment, Arthur. I'll get Zilda. As it happens the Steels have called. It will be good for you to let them see your paintings as well.'

Arthur had just arrived from Scarborough and was eager for Ebenezer to see his work. When he had completed these paintings he had felt more satisfaction than he had of late. When he had tried to analyse the reason for this he always came back to the same answer: his renewed enthusiasm seemed to stem from his visits to Whitby. Was it the atmosphere he always felt when he was there or was it because he had renewed his acquaintance with Colette Shipley?

'That's good, now I'll have four opinions to listen to.'

Ebenezer left the shop and when he returned again, with his wife and the Steels, greetings were exchanged quickly amidst the general enthusiasm to see Arthur's work.

For the first painting he had taken up position on Scotch Head on the west bank of the river. It had given him a view of the old town on the east bank dominated by the parish church and ruined abbey. He had brought a special atmosphere to the scene with strong shafts of light breaking through the clouds, highlighting the masts and rigging of a vessel lying at a quay close to his viewpoint. Arthur's brush strokes emphasised the oncoming clouds that forced the sailors to quicken their activities of unloading their cargo. Nets were being draped over a rail and Arthur had given the passers-by a lack of detail that suggested their hurrying steps to escape the rain that looked sure to come. He had given a feeling of real life to the scene.

Though not a word was spoken, he sensed exhilaration enter the room. He unveiled the second picture.

He had depicted a scene from the bridge looking down river towards the piers and the lighthouses. He had used the evening glow of the setting sun to bring the scene vividly alive through strong colours. Ships were tied up along the quays

400

on the west bank. He had put more activity into this picture by depicting sailors checking sails, and coiling ropes, and children at play while their mothers chatted nearby. The whole scene had an atmosphere of oncoming night, though, in spite of the brightness and richness of the palette.

When not a word was spoken Arthur began to grow anxious. Ebenezer shot him a glance and saw his anxiety and immediately relieved it with, 'Splendid, Arthur, splendid. You are recapturing the significant work you did for the exhibition.' Arthur saw Zilda agree with her husband with an emphatic nod of her head.

'These two paintings delight me.' Rowena said with enthusiasm. 'I agree with Ebenezer, they would stand alongside any of those you did for the exhibition. I am glad you have recaptured the spirit of those previous paintings. Don't let it slip again, Arthur.'

'I won't.' He was too overwhelmed by her praise not to take notice.

'I agree with them,' put in Laurence. 'May I make one or two suggestions?'

'Of course.'

Arthur listened intently as Laurence said he thought the first picture would have been enhanced had he made the cirrus cloud more high-lying and went on to explain how to do this. He had liked the use of figures in the first painting but was less enthusiastic about them in the second and showed Arthur what he thought would have been a better use of them in the composition. 'What I have said is not meant as criticism but only to give you something to think about in the future. I certainly look forward to seeing your next work. I am so glad you have thrown off the mantle of commercial painting.'

Arthur thanked them all again and then excused himself in order to call on the Duggans before going to his parents.

The Steels left a few moments later. As the door closed behind them Ebenezer swung round excitedly to find his wife with a broad grin lighting up her face as she held out her arms to him.

'We did it!' she cried.

'No, *you* did it. It was your suggestion.' He grabbed her round the waist, her arms came to his neck and they did a jig in the shop.

Laughter rang round the room and floated up the stairs to fill the whole house with the joy of success.

'What do you think did it, Ebenezer?' she asked. 'Whitby or the girl in *Admiring the View* or both?'

'I don't know and I don't care as long as it goes on. Arthur Newton, painter, has been reborn!'

Elated by the excitement and enthusiasm of his friends, Arthur was eager to get home and then go to Whitby. He hoped Mr Redgrave's response would equal that he had just received.

As the coach rumbled its way to his destination, Arthur kept chiding himself for being impatient. The journey seemed longer today yet he was sure they were keeping to time. Why this overwhelming eagerness to be there? Had the enthusiasm for his new paintings aroused a desire to get on with more or should he admit to himself that he really wanted to get to Whitby to see and talk to Miss Shipley again?

Mr Redgrave waxed lyrical about the paintings. The three years' wait had been worth it. He had no doubt he would soon sell them both, for the essence of Whitby was in the scenes. He could almost feel the pulse of an active river coming from them. They were paintings that would constantly bring joy and from which something different could be captured every time the owner looked at them.

'Are you doing some more sketching before you return?' he enquired.

'Yes, as long as the weather holds.'

'I think it will. In fact, if I read the signs correctly it will improve as the day goes on.'

'Is there any subject you might be looking for especially?'

'Details of ships imposed on a Whitby background.'

'I have used ships before but not in detail. It could make for some interesting compositions.'

Arthur was about to leave when Mr Redgrave halted him. 'May I make a comment?' He looked warily at Arthur.

'Of course.'

'These latest paintings are of a quality above that which I know Mr Ross requires. With all due respect to him, for he knows what he wants and what he can sell, his clientele will not be looking for this type of work.' He inclined his head towards the paintings Arthur had brought. 'I can sell more of this standard, and your income won't drop if you forego the more commercial aspects of the trade. Your painting rises above that. I suggest that next time you visit me you include a painting of Scarborough in this manner.'

'I'll do that, Mr Redgrave.' As he walked to the harbour Arthur mulled over what the art dealer had said. He was delighted by his opinion. Twice in three days his latest work had been praised and its enhanced quality commented upon. He would be glad to leave behind the more skimpy, commercially motivated style in favour of this.

He went with the flow of people crossing the bridge using a broad-shouldered man in front of him to carve a path in the press of folk coming in the opposite direction. He made his way to the quays along the east bank and positioned himself beside some crates waiting to be taken on board a nearby ship. He took out his sketch-book and started to put pencil to paper. No one took much notice of him; only casual glances from passers by were cast in his direction while the dockers were too busy, under the watchful eyes of their gangers, to take much notice of him. He became so absorbed in his drawing that he was all but unaware of the life of the busy port going on around him. He was lost to sound and movement until a voice said quietly in his ear, 'Good day, Mr Newton.'

The soft tone sent a thrill through him. He sprang to his feet. 'Miss Shipley! How good to see you.' He almost dropped his pencil and book in the confusion and excitement that engulfed him.

'Oh, dear, I've interrupted your drawing,' she apologised. 'I shouldn't have stopped.'

'No, you haven't. And I'm glad you did.' Arthur realised he wasn't making much sense. He

404

glanced beyond her. 'You are on your own?'

'No, but I sent my sister ahead to locate a good vantage point for some photographs.'

Arthur's mind seized on this information. Had Colette done that on purpose? Had she wanted to see him alone? He rebuked himself for entertaining such thoughts. They belittled Miss Shipley.

'You have something special in mind?'

'Details of ships. I have a client who is opening a new hotel in Scarborough and is interested in using them there.'

'I am pleased for you.'

'Thank you. And what brings you to Whitby again?'

'I have brought some paintings to Mr Redgrave and he, like your customer, suggested I should paint some ships to reflect the atmosphere of a busy port.'

'It seems we are on similar missions.'

'If I may suggest it,' said Arthur tentatively, 'we could exchange notes and ideas, especially about locations? Two minds are better than one. Or perhaps I should include your sister and say three.'

Colette smiled but he detected something in it that disturbed him. Her smile today was not as he'd remembered it. Then there had been laugher and joy in her eyes and on her lips, a pleasure in and enjoyment of life. Today her eyes lacked sparkle. He thought he could detect sadness behind them, and her smile seemed strained. Questions raced through his mind. What had upset her? Was she not well? Suffered some loss? Dare he ask her?

Since her father's announcement Colette had

405

tried to do as he had asked, but how could she behave as if nothing had happened, knowing that in the not-too-distant future they faced a devastating loss? Although she, Adele and Susan all sensed the scythe hanging over the household they tried not to show their feelings. Each of them sought to find solace in their own way and all agreed that activity through photography helped. With Bernard's requirements in mind they strove to capture better and better pictures, spending much of their spare time along the quays where the coming and going of so many different vessels gave them a wide range of subjects.

As she and Adele had reached this particular quay on the east bank she'd seen Mr Newton at work and her heart skipped a beat. He was practically a stranger to Colette and yet ever since their first meeting she had basked in pleasant thoughts about him and these had never faded, even during the three years he had not come to Whitby. Now it seemed as if those years had not happened; it was as if he had never been absent. Her mind cried out silent thanks when she saw him and she was engulfed by a strong desire to speak to him on her own. So it was that she said to her sister, 'There's Mr Newton. I'm going to have a word with him. You go on and find a good subject for the photographs.'

For one brief moment Adele was about to protest. Why shouldn't she speak to Mr Newton as well? But she saw her sister's expression and for a moment the sadness had disappeared from Colette's eyes.

Now Colette found herself desiring to pour out

her troubles to him. Why had he had this effect on her? She thrust all such thoughts from her mind and said. 'Will you be coming to Whitby more often after Mr Redgrave's request?'

'Yes. As long as he sells my paintings I will constantly have to revise my subject matter, look for different scenes, different angles, new ways of conveying Whitby's atmosphere, and as that is constantly changing I will need to come more often.' Arthur surprised himself by his enthusiasm to impart this information, as if he wanted to be sure she knew. It also sounded to him as if he was mapping out good reasons that would enable him to see Colette again and again.

'Then no doubt we shall meet again.'

'I look forward to it.'

'So do I.'

Their eyes met and from the look they exchanged, which they made no effort to disguise, both could read a deeper meaning behind their last exchanges. But even then Arthur noted that touch of sadness.

'I had better find my sister.' She started to move away.

He wanted to stop her and ask how he could help her but it was not his place to pry. Instead he found himself saying. 'I will be here the day after tomorrow,' not knowing why he had said it, for he had made no such plan.

When he reached home that evening Rose made what she regarded as her obligatory query. 'Did you do well today?'

'Yes,' Arthur replied, thinking it had gone better than he could say. 'Mr Redgrave wants more, in particular paintings involving ships. It will mean I have to go to Whitby more frequently ... I hope you don't mind? There will be more money even though I will stop painting for Mr Ross.'

'You've had a steady income from Mr Ross. Don't throw that away as you did the railway job,' Rose warned.

'I said, it would mean more money,' Arthur snapped.

'But how can it? They're all just pictures.'

'The ones Mr Redgrave wants are better executed and can fetch more.'

'I suppose you know what you're talking about, but see that Marie and I are not neglected.'

He knew she was hinting that there should be no lack of funds. 'You won't be,' he replied, annoyed by his wife's mercenary attitude to his painting.

Two days later, on the coach for Whitby again, Arthur could not settle his thoughts. They drifted between the subjects he wanted to sketch and the girl he hoped to see. She had indicated that she wanted to see him again but had she really meant it? He had told her he would be on the same quay today. Would she be there? He was startled by the strength of his feeling. His longing to meet her had all the fervour of a schoolboy for his first love. He had to remind himself that he was a married man. He debated whether he should tell Colette that. He didn't want to, for if he did he was certain that would end a relationship he wanted to continue. Maybe it would be best if he went elsewhere in Whitby?

That thought was in his mind when he stepped

out of the coach at the Angel. Nevertheless he made straight for the bridge and crossed the river. As he headed for the quay where they had met two days ago, his eyes searched people embarked on their everyday lives. He could not see Colette. His hope faltered. Disconsolate, he took up his place on the quay and started to sketch. The vessels of two days ago had sailed. Different ships lay beside the quays, discharging their cargoes via muscular backs and arms. There were subjects a-plenty here and Arthur knew they could direct his future painting and bring him to Whitby as many times as he wanted, but that would depend on...

'Good day, Mr Newton.'

He spun round smiling as he did so. 'Miss Shipley.'

Their eyes met and each knew that this was the moment they had been waiting for.

She saw him look beyond her and that he had noted she had no photographic equipment. She gave a little smile. 'I am on my own, Mr Newton, and am not taking photographs today.'

His mind ran on. Had she planned this? Had she wanted to see him on her own? He heard her offering an explanation. 'My sister and Miss Lund decided to go riding when I said I would not be taking photographs. It is not right that I take up all their time when I know they like to ride. Father was resting so I slipped out.'

It seemed the answer to his two questions was yes. 'You don't ride, Miss Shipley?'

She shook her head. 'I don't like horses. Do you, Mr Newton?'

'I have no experience of them. I think I would

prefer to keep it that way, just as I would prefer you to call me Arthur, if you don't mind?'

'I have no reason to mind, but if I am to do that then I would like you to use my Christian name.'

'Colette.' He savoured the word. 'A pretty name.'

'I am pleased you think so.'

'Colette, should we walk instead of standing talking on the quay among all this movement and noise?'

'But what about your sketching?'

'That can be done another day. I have plenty to keep me busy for a while.' They started to walk along the quay before crossing to the other side of Church Street.

'Then you had no real need to come today?'

'To draw? To be honest, no.'

'Then why?'

Arthur hesitated but felt compelled to say, 'To see you.'

'But you could not be certain I would even be here?'

'When we last parted I thought it possible. Nor could you have been certain that I would be.'

'I thought like you.'

'And because of that you came alone?'

'Yes. Was that so wrong of me?'

'In my eyes, no! I'm glad you did. If you hadn't I would not now be walking with a beautiful young lady who I see will cast convention aside if it is not to her liking.'

She bowed her head and blushed a little with embarrassment. 'Is that how you see me?'

'Yes. I also see a kind, thoughtful and gentle

person, but now I detect a sadness that was not there when I first met you. You are trying to hide it but you are not wholly successful. It has dulled your eyes a little but becomes more evident when your thoughts stray to something that worries you. I noticed it when you mentioned your father.' Arthur stopped voicing his observations. 'I shouldn't have mentioned this, I'm sorry. Please forgive me. I was not prying.'

She was silent for a few moments, deciding whether to tell him or not. He shouldn't be burdened with her troubles, not someone who was almost a stranger, yet he did not seem that way in her mind. He had never been that. There had been a palpable empathy between them from the first moment he had approached her two years ago, even though at that time the age gap, for she had recognised that he was older than her, seemed wider than it did now. She felt an overwhelming desire to talk to him about her father. There was a deep need to speak to someone other than Adele or Susan. She drew strength from the support they gave each other but an outsider's perspective was lacking. And she felt it would help her if she could acquire it.

'You are very perceptive, Arthur, and I never entertained the thought that you were prying.'

'I am relieved. If you want to talk about it, I can be a good listener.'

She had turned off Church Street and started the climb to the Abbey Plain. He did not question where she was going but automatically followed her. She knew this part of Whitby; he did not. He respected her silence, realising she needed time to

411

decide whether she should reveal what troubled her and, if she did, how much she should tell him. His thoughts, concentrated on admiring this young woman who walked beside him, were shattered by the blunt announcement she made next.

'My father is dying.'

It stopped Arthur in his tracks and brought a sharp intake of breath. He felt an instinctive desire to take her into the comfort of his arms but etiquette prevented that. All he said was, 'I'm so sorry.' The words seemed lame and inadequate to him but Colette recognised from his tone that he sensed what she was suffering and that he wanted to help. 'What more can I say?' he went on, feeling helpless to relieve her pain. He reached out and let his hand rest gently on her arm, an automatic gesture that brought understanding and comfort.

She slipped her arm through his, wanting the contact he had made to continue, for in his touch she found consolation and the ability to speak about her father.

Knowing that it would help, he let her talk without interruption. By the time she had run out of words they had reached the Abbey Plain. The ruined abbey stood stark before them, a reminder of the past upheaval when the monks were forcibly expelled from their home. It seemed a link with the turmoil that had overtaken Colette's life, and yet offered hope that the future could be faced with resolution.

They came to a path near the cliff edge and turned towards the ruin. The sky was blue, white clouds floating before a gentle breeze. A sea the colour of pewter tinged with blue, was breaking gently on the rocks far below. It was too perfect a day to harbour unhappy thoughts.

Arthur stopped and turned her to him. 'Oh, Colette, what can I say? I am so sad for you. I want to help you but I feel so inadequate.'

'You have helped, by listening.' She looked deep into his eyes and said, 'Please keep coming to Whitby.'

He met her searching gaze and asked gently, 'Are you sure? You know nothing about me.'

'I don't need to know any more than I do. You are a kind and gentle person. I don't seek to know more, it might spoil things. Please don't desert our friendship?'

'I won't.'

Chapter Eighteen

Commissions were Arthur's excuse to Rose for spending so much time in his studio. He painted quickly but with no lack of technique. In fact, his paintings became more vibrant, particularly in his bold use of colour and brush strokes. He continued to indulge his liking for evening and night scenes and made particular use of moonlight. He was creating an individual style that was becoming known and at last the London market that had promised to open up to him but had remained dormant finally showed signs of stirring in 1865. It was on the back of this that he was able to make his excuses to visit Whitby more often. As time passed there was never a week went by but he contrived to be there.

He could always be found drawing the first ship berthed on the east side of the river upstream from the bridge. Colette knew this. Sometimes she would manage to come on her own, when he would leave his sketching and walk with her. At others, when she was on a photographic expedition with either her sister or Miss Lund, she would manage to find an excuse to talk to him. She was aware on these occasions that they were conscious of the attention she paid Mr Newton and knew that one day it would be mentioned.

It was Susan who raised the matter one day after they had not seen him. 'You looked disappointed that Mr Newton was not there today?'

For a moment Colette was prepared to protest at what Susan was implying but she knew she would make a poor attempt.

'I find him an interesting person. An artist of note, I would say.'

Susan smiled and winked at Adele.

'Oh, come, sister, I think there is more than an interest in art at stake here. It wouldn't surprise me if on the days Susan and I go riding, which I might say have become more frequent, you visit that quay.'

'And what if I do?'

Susan's expression changed. She eyed Colette seriously when she said. 'He is older than you. What do you know of him?'

'He is a gentleman, a kind one, and I find his conversation most agreeable.'

'But what do you know of his background?'

'What do I need to know?' retorted Colette, annoyed that she should be given this inquisition.

'Well, you never know what it might be. Have you told your father about him?'

'No.'

'Don't you think you should?'

'Father is a sick man. I don't want to give him any reason to worry. And you know he would if I told him about Mr Newton.'

'Are you in love?' Adele came out with the blunt question.

'Of course not!' replied Colette indignantly. 'Don't be so silly.'

But Adele reckoned she knew her sister better than Colette did herself. Besides, the heightening blush told its tale.

'I don't want either of you to say a word to Father,' she insisted, glancing from one to the other. 'Promise me?'

They both did so and, knowing them as she did, she was certain they would not break their promises.

'These photographs are superb!' Bernard was most enthusiastic about the work he had just seen. 'I have only gone through them quickly, but the quality and artistic interpretation have amazed me. We will go through them together slowly and I will pick out those I believe will complement the decorations we have in mind for the new hotel.

'It is coming on apace. The sooner it is finished the better. There is a growing number of visitors and we wish to take advantage of this as soon as possible. Father has persuaded the builders to take on more men.' He realised he was getting carried away. 'Ah, well, time will tell. Now, the photographs!'

He made his choice after long deliberations over some of them, and added, 'Keep on taking more because I visualise changing them every so often and that will be a good way of attracting customers for you. It won't be everyone who wants a large-format picture so why don't you produce some of a smaller size? I'm sure our customers would love to take one home as a souvenir of their visit or send them as postcards to their friends.'

The three women were swept up in his enthusiasm as he expanded on his idea. 'You could have the makings of a lucrative business here, especially if you were willing to take photographs beyond Whitby.'

'Why not?' enthused Adele. 'We could do that.'

'It's well worth thinking about,' Susan agreed.

Their eyes turned to Colette. After all, it was she who had first become besotted with photography.

'I think we should,' she agreed. 'We'll look at other possible presentations too.'

Bernard was glad his ruse had worked. He had planned it during luncheon. He had arrived from Scarborough that morning to see what the photographers had for him. He had accepted their invitation to lunch, and sensing gloom in the household, saw the reason when he met Mr Shipley. But, being the polite person he was, he made no comment and gave no sign that he had noticed. Instead he planned what he might do to lighten the lives of his old friends.

Having chosen the photographs he wanted, he asked Colette if she would walk with him. 'Maybe I can spot something that would be a suitable subject for my purpose.'

Colette knew that would mean visiting the quays. Would Arthur be there? She had no means of knowing. If he was what would he think, seeing her in the company of such a handsome young man?

Her heart was aflutter as they approached the bridge. Discomfort sent a shiver up the back of her neck and her features were tight with nervousness. They turned towards the quays. Her eyes tried to penetrate the press of people to reach the place that Arthur would occupy. When she succeeded relief swept over her. They walked on, she barely hearing what Bernard was saying as she wondered at her own behaviour. Why had she not wanted Arthur to see her walking with another man? Did she fear what it might do to their friendship? Did she prize that above all else? She started. 'Sorry, Bernard, my mind wandered. What did you say?'

'I pointed out that figurehead. If the ship is still here tomorrow I would like a photograph of it.'

'Yes, certainly. I'm sorry my attention drifted off.'

'Don't worry about it. It is understandable under the circumstances.'

She stiffened. What did he know about Arthur? He couldn't

'How long has your father been ill?'

So that was what he thought had distracted her. 'You noticed?'

417

'I couldn't help but do so. I haven't seen him for a while. You see him every day and, although you must be aware of the deterioration, it won't seem as marked as it did to me.'

When she had finished telling him that her father had not long to live, his sympathy and concern were marked. 'If there is anything I can do, anything, please call on me.'

'Thank you, Bernard. You are a dear friend. It is good to know the past still means something to you.'

'It does and always will where you are concerned, Colette.' He wanted to say more but with this shadow hanging over her he knew now was not the time.

'Come and see the two paintings I am taking to Ebenezer tomorrow.' Arthur held out his hand to Rose. She took it and he helped her from the chair.

'You never said you were going to Leeds tomorrow.'

'It depended when I finished the paintings.' He led her into his studio. Each of the paintings was standing on an easel.

'They're of Scarborough. The South Bay, and the other the lighthouse and harbour. Very nice. I can see how your painting has improved.'

Arthur caught this comment. Was Rose at last beginning to take more interest in his painting?

'Can Mr Hirst sell these, even though they are not of Leeds?'

'Oh, yes. It is the quality of the painting that counts, not the place depicted, though there are people who like a combination of both. Look, this next one I'm working on is a commission from London through Ebenezer.'

'But it's just rocks, stunted trees and grasses. Why would anyone want that?'

'As I say, the quality of the painting, and the way the subject is interpreted. This is just a nature picture, of nowhere in particular, but people in London see such subjects as an escape from the smoke and the grime. With buildings closing in on them this sort of picture reminds them that there are open spaces beyond the metropolis.'

Rose looked puzzled for a moment as she considered this explanation then said, 'I think I can understand that.'

Arthur took renewed heart from this. Were his continual efforts to get Rose more interested in his work at last beginning to bear fruit?

'If you are going to Leeds, Marie and I will come with you,' she said. 'It's time she saw her grandparents again. We can spend a few days there.'

'You can if you wish. I can't. I have other pictures to take to Whitby on Thursday.'

'Then they'll have to wait until next week,' she said, tightening her lips in exasperation.

'They can't. They've been done to commission. They are going to be presented by the buyer to a member of his family at the weekend. I've got to go.'

'Whitby! Whitby!' she snapped. 'You're spending more and more time in that awful place.'

'It's where the money is,' he pointed out.

'It's a wonder you don't want to live there.'

'I would if I could.'

'Don't expect me to agree to that. And as for this visit to Leeds, I shall come. If you *have* to come back and go to Whitby there is no point in my returning with you. I may as well stay with Mother and Father for a week. No, maybe I'll make that two weeks. Having made the journey, I may as well make it worthwhile.'

'Just as you wish.' Arthur did not make his agreement too obvious, but he was already relishing the thought of having a whole fortnight at liberty to go where he liked, meet whom he pleased.

Arthur left his paintings in the carriage he had hired at the station when he escorted Rose and Marie into the Duggans'. He knew it was no use taking the canvasses in for his parents-in-law to see; they would only serve to raise their ire. Arthur thought the better part of valour was merely to say that he must go on and see his representative. They were pleased their daughter was going to stay a fortnight and expressed no regret that their son-in-law was having to return to Scarborough.

He was relieved to escape the tension by visiting his parents that evening and taking a message from Rose that she and Marie would visit them later.

On his way back to Scarborough he pondered Ebenezer's comments about his Scarborough paintings. They'd arranged he would bring the painting for London when he came back to Leeds to escort Rose and Marie home.

'Make it special,' advised Ebenezer. 'Now that London interest has stirred again and your work has improved, I'm sure more will be wanted. Your new work has such vibrancy. It pulses with atmosphere. Keep it up, don't let it slip.'

Praise indeed, thought Arthur. While executing his last few paintings he'd felt there was a new sense of life in his work. Now Ebenezer had seen and commented on it too. He looked for answers but always came back to the first he had offered in explanation. Each of these paintings had been executed as if he was painting it for Colette. Although he could always picture her in his mind, he needed constantly to renew contact with her. He told himself she provided the support and stimulation he required to blot out Rose's indifference, though his wife seemed to have started to show more interest recently...

The following morning he left Scarborough for Whitby. He was thankful that it was a dry day, though dull, but that would not affect his drawing. But first he must deliver the two paintings to Mr Redgrave. He had only gone a few steps when he stopped. He pondered for a few moments and then turned back to the inn. The jovial landlord was supervising his staff, seeing to the needs of the coach passengers.

'Good day, sir,' he greeted Arthur. 'Can I help you?'

'Could I have a room for twelve days?'

'Indeed, sir.' He had seen Arthur arrive by coach before but never once had he booked a room. The man was curious. 'I have a very fine room available that overlooks the river.'

'That would be splendid,' replied Arthur, realising that it would give him the opportunity to sketch some views from the window.

'I would be obliged if you would sign the visitors' book.'

Arthur took the pen he offered, dipped it in the inkwell, signed his name and added his address.

The landlord glanced at the entry. 'You have not come far, Mr Newton. Taking a well-earned break?'

'I come to work, landlord, I am an artist. These are two of my paintings which I am delivering to Mr Redgrave.' He indicated the carefully wrapped packages he had propped against the wall.

'Ah, I thought your name meant something to me. I have seen your signature on paintings displayed in Mr Redgrave's window. It is an honour to have you here, sir. I'll have you shown to your room.' He signalled to a boy standing by at the foot of the stairs. 'Show Mr Newton to room twelve.' He saw the boy look round about him. 'You have no other luggage, sir?' asked the landlord.

Arthur smiled. 'No. I made the decision to stay as I got off the coach. I will buy what is necessary.'

'Will you want to dine here in the evenings?'

'Yes. It will be easiest.'

'Very well! I will arrange a special corner table for you so that you will have a view of the whole room.'

'Thank you,' replied Arthur. 'Careful with those paintings,' he added as the youngster picked them up. He followed the boy to his room, tossed him a coin and, when the lad had left, stood looking round him. The room was cosy with a chest of drawers, a wardrobe, a comfortable looking bed draped with a colourful patchwork quilt, and a wing chair positioned near the window. He crossed to survey the scene outside for a few moments. Oh, yes, there was much he could sketch from here. In his mind's eye he already saw the paintings that could be developed from those sketches.

He turned from the window, realising he was wasting time.

He left the Angel with a quick step. Colette knew, what time the coach from Scarborough arrived. She could be on the quay now. Why do folk get in the way? he thought irritably to himself as he side-stepped through the flow of people. It was particularly awkward on the bridge today and he found his progress no easier as he hurried along Church Street to the part of the quay he and Colette had accepted as their meeting place.

His eyes probed the distance. Then he saw her and his heart leaped. Her expression was one of disappointment. He was glad; it showed she cared.

Disconsolate, her head bowed, she walked slowly away from their meeting place. Then she looked up and saw him hurrying towards her. Her whole expression changed to one of delight.

'Colette!' He held out his hands to her.

She took them and felt his joy to see her in his touch.

'Walk with me?'

She nodded and they crossed the road. 'Was the coach late today?'

'No.' He went on to explain his delay in reaching the quay. 'I took time to book a room at the Angel.'

'You are staying in Whitby?'

'Yes, for twelve days.'

He offered no further explanation and she did not seek one. But she felt her heart race with joy. He was here at the time she needed him. 'Father is not well,' she said quietly. 'The doctor has carried out another examination and says perhaps a month.' Her voice faltered.

'I'm sorry. I shouldn't be intruding on your life at this time.'

'You aren't. Please don't think that. You give me strength.'

'I hope I can do that, but please, if ever you believe I am in the way, tell me.'

'You will never be that.'

Arthur's conscience pricked him. He felt like a fraud, a charlatan. He should tell her the truth about himself, but the real truth, the truth that now lay at the heart of his being, was that he wanted to go on seeing her.

They walked on and after a few steps were lost in a world of their own. They shared silences of their own making in which they experienced a closeness neither of them had felt with anyone before. They talked, ranging across all manner of subjects but chiefly they spoke of photography and art, arguing their merits, promoting their own particular interest, yet concluding that each could help the other.

They spent the twelve days in this way, each enjoying more than anything else the presence of the other. So that suspicions weren't aroused in Adele and Susan, Colette devoted four days to taking photographs and arranged that Arthur would meet her in different parts of Whitby on those days.

The day before he was to leave they walked on the cliffs beyond the abbey. Neither seemed inclined to talk. Sadness seemed to be in the air. The gentle breeze touched their cheeks like the comforting fingers they wanted to feel. The sun reflected off the sea with a brilliance that wanted to drive the shadow of parting from their minds. The path dipped into a hollow. Arthur stopped and turned Colette to him there. They looked into each other's eyes and saw love there.

'Thank you for spending time with me,' he whispered.

'It was a joy for me too.'

'And thank you for being the inspiration behind my paintings.'

'I hope I always will be.'

He bent slowly towards her. She waited expectantly and trembled when his lips met hers. They parted then met again in a fiercer passion. They clung to each other, reluctant ever to let go.

He wanted to say so much but knew if he did their world would be shattered. He found so much in Colette, which he did not want to lose, things that were missing from Rose.

She wanted to ask him so many questions but was afraid to do so. The answers may disperse a dream she wanted to keep intact. To lose it so close to the time when a precious life would be taken from her would be devastating. She was content for the relationship to go on as it was until Arthur wanted to tell her more about himself.

They strolled on wanting to draw out the time

together as much as possible. But time does not stand still and a parting had to be made eventually.

'Come again before long,' Colette whispered sadly when they reached the west side of the river.

'I will.' Arthur's eyes too were touched with sadness. He pressed her hand and hurried away.

During the ride to Scarborough he recalled the amount of drawing he had been able to do, the lauding of his paintings by Mr Redgrave and the three commissions he had received, then allowed his mind to fill with memories of time spent with Colette.

He was planning his journey to Leeds tomorrow when he arrived home but found his plans need not materialise.

'Rose! You're back,' he gasped when he walked in to find his wife having a cup of tea and Marie playing on the floor.

'Yes,' she replied haughtily. 'Marie began to witter to come home. It upset Mother so I decided it was best to return. That was the day before yesterday. I expected you to be here, but what did I find? The only time you have been home was the day you returned from Leeds. Where have you been, Arthur? What's going on?'

'Nothing's going on,' he replied sharply. 'I took the paintings to Mr Redgrave and on the spur of the moment decided that, as you were in Leeds, I'd stay in Whitby.'

She gave a sharp nod, an indication that she was still annoyed he was not here when she returned.

'It saved journeys and gave me more time to devote to my sketching. I got a lot done,' he added.

'I hope you did, considering the expense you must have incurred.'

'Is that all you can ever think of, money?' His voice was harsh. His mind conjured up images of Colette and he knew her attitude wouldn't have taken this course. 'Let me tell you, it resulted in three commissions from sketches I did during my stay. There are promises of more. It is a good way to work: let the customer see the sketches from which he can pick the scene he would like to receive as a painting. In fact, it would be advantageous for us to move to Whitby.' The last sentence was out before he realised it. He cursed himself. If Rose agreed, his meetings with Colette would be more difficult, if not doomed. But in the back of his mind he knew she would not agree. So it proved.

'Move to Whitby? Never!' Rose placed her cup and saucer on the table next to her chair with a determination that caused them to rattle. 'Never! Do you hear me, Arthur Newton? Never!' Then came a remark that took him completely by surprise. 'If as you say you got more work done by being in Whitby and it means more money, why don't you get somewhere to live there?'

Arthur couldn't believe what he was hearing. 'You mean, I should go and live there? But what about us?'

'I don't mean permanently, just somewhere where you can have a bed and a studio when you need it. You say being there saved you the journeys and gave you more time to work. You'll be able to fulfil your commissions more readily if you spend more time on your visits.'

427

'I'll have to give it some thought,' he replied, not wanting to appear over-enthusiastic. But the idea of seeing Colette every day almost overwhelmed him. To have a kindred spirit so close to him would surely be an inspiration.

'You know what commissions you are likely to get. You know whether we can afford a place for you in Whitby.'

'There is no question about that. My work is selling.'

'Well, it's up to you. There is only one proviso I make, and that is that purchasing a place in Whitby does not undermine the standard of living I expect for myself and Marie.'

'You won't suffer any loss,' replied Arthur. He knew it would not be easy to match the criterion she was laying down but meet it he would. With that came a fresh resolution that he would not turn back to commercialising his work but would succeed through the sheer quality of his paintings. And the quality he was sure would only increase with Colette close by.

It was two weeks before he could get to Whitby again.

Chapter Nineteen

The wind blew bleak across the churchyard beside the parish church on top of Whitby's East Cliff. The group of people round the open grave turned up their collars or hunched a shoulder against the chill that came out of the North. The parson intoned his burial prayers as the coffin was lowered slowly into the ground. Colette's tears did nothing to relieve the pain inside. On one side she felt Adele's hand slide into hers, seeking comfort and to comfort. On the other, Susan sought the same.

As she watched her father come to his final rest Colette resolved not to remember his last four days when life had worn him away. Instead she would always recall his vitality, his pleasant, gentle manner and his wisdom. His kindly presence and his love for his beloved Margot, which he never disguised, had been gifts she would always treasure.

The cleric's voice drained away. Only the sough of the wind reminded her that it would never die and life had to go on. There was a movement close to her and she realised someone was holding a small trowel towards her. She glanced at it, hardly seeing the soil that rested on it. Automatically she reached out, took some in her hand and sprinkled it over the coffin. Dazed, as if she did not know what to do next, she waited while Adele and Susan made their last gestures. Then the pressure of Susan's fingers indicated she should move aside. She looked down one last time to where her father lay then reluctantly turned away. The three women walked away slowly to a convenient place where they could await the mourners and thank them for attending the funeral.

It had not been a big one. The Shipleys were not Whitby-born, nor had they been in the town very long. Nevertheless they had made some good friends who had come to pay their last respects. The staff too attended the last rites of an employer they'd loved, and who'd treated them with kindness and consideration. They hurried off to prepare for the mourners who would come back to the house in New Buildings. And, as always, there were others who felt it their duty to be present at a funeral even though they did not know the deceased.

'I am so so sorry.' Bernard Clayton held out his hand to the ladies.

'Thank you for coming,' replied Colette.

'I could do no other. May I escort you ladies to your carriage?'

After a brief word with the vicar, they walked to the waiting carriage.

'You must ride with us, Bernard. There is room,' offered Colette.

'That is most kind,' After he had seen them settled, he climbed into the coach and took the vacant seat beside Susan.

Over the past few weeks he had visited Whitby on a number of occasions, using the photographs as an excuse to meet Colette. He enjoyed being with her but was careful not to impose too much on her time. He wanted to build a deeper relationship than a purely business one and such things took time.

When they reached their home they found several mourners waiting to offer their condolences. It was a silent group that watched Colette, Adele and Susan, followed by Bernard, enter the house.

Susan hurried to the kitchen to inform Mrs

Fenton and Mrs Vasey that they were back. When she returned a few moments later she found Colette and Adele in the drawing-room attended by a solicitous Bernard. She eyed them with concern. The pallor of their complexions seemed to have heightened under the severe black of their mourning dresses. 'Are you prepared for this or would you like me to make your excuses to people?'

Colette gave a little shake of her head. 'We must receive them.' She glanced at her sister for confirmation.

'Of course we must,' agreed Adele.

They seated themselves in different parts of the room so that the mourners would not feel cramped for space.

It was nearly three hours later when the last of them left. Colette breathed a sigh of relief. The strain of accepting expressions of sympathy, trying to identify people, speaking to strangers about their father, had taken its toll.

'Now, you two, come with me.' Susan had taken charge. 'On occasions like this your strength becomes sapped and because you are talking to people you get little to eat. We must put that right.' She led them to the dining-room where the remains of the refreshments provided for the mourners were being tidied by two of the maids while a third was setting four places at the table. Susan sat the two girls down, glanced at Bernard. 'You too, Bernard. You were too busy to eat.' He smiled and sat down opposite Colette. Susan fussed for a few more minutes and then joined them.

431

No one really felt like eating but sitting together to share a meal gradually relaxed the atmosphere. They were grateful that Bernard was there and they were not thrown in on themselves. The conversation, desultory at first, began to flow a little more freely. Colette and Adele, at nineteen and eighteen, had thought that recollections of their father would tear their hearts out but found just the opposite and were pleased to recall him.

As they returned to the drawing-room, feeling better for having eaten, Colette said, 'What time does your coach leave, Bernard?'

'I'm not returning to Scarborough today. I have booked a room at the Angel. I thought the three of you might like some company, especially this evening. I hope I have not been too presumptuous?'

'Not at all. It is a very kind thought.'

'I can stay a few days if you would like me to?'

'You are being so considerate, but we could not presume on your kindness any longer.'

'I know that you may well want time to yourselves to adjust in your own way, but if there is anything I can do, I beg of you don't hesitate to send a message to me.'

'Thank you.' Colette smiled. It was a wan smile with sadness behind it and Bernard wished he could erase all trace of that.

'I'm going up to my room, I'll be down in a few minutes,' said Susan, turning away from Adele whom she had accompanied to a seat in the window.

'Bernard has just told me he is staying at the Angel tonight so he'll be with us this evening,'

432

Colette informed her.

'I'll tell the kitchen there will be one more.' When the door closed behind her, Bernard put his question a little tentatively, 'I don't want to pry. Understand I only ask this out of concern. If you think I don't deserve an answer I will understand.'

Colette looked questioningly at him. Adele turned her unseeing gaze from the window to focus on him momentarily.

'Will you be staying in this house?'

The sisters exchanged a quick glance but in it Adele gave her approval to Colette.

'Oh, yes! Father made provision for the three of us. We will all be living here. If at any time the circumstances change they are covered in his will.'

'Miss Lund too?' Bernard was a little surprised that Colette had said all three of them.

'Of course. Susan couldn't be left out. She has been with us so long and Father regarded her as one of the family.'

'Quite right.' Bernard felt sure it was correct to agree. 'I'll say it again: if ever you need help in any way whatsoever, do call on me.'

'Thank you. We'll not forget.'

'And when the hotel is finished you must all come and stay as my guests.'

'That would be fun,' said Adele.

'And bring your photographic equipment. You might find a market in Scarborough.'

The thought of staying there brought Arthur into Colette's thoughts. As she wished he knew of her father's death, she experienced a desire to have him by her side, supporting her with the kindness

433

and compassion she knew he would show.

Two weeks after Rose's suggestion that he should find somewhere in Whitby where he could have a room and a studio, Arthur was in the coach heading for the port.

During those two weeks he had pondered her suggestion and the more he had thought about it the more he liked it. He had studied his financial position and was satisfied that he would be able, with careful consideration, to afford something better than just two rooms, one for living and the other for a studio. He was making money from his art, selling more and commissions were lining up. The main purpose of this visit was to make some sketches of the abbey for a customer in Leeds. But Arthur also had other objectives in mind: to see Colette, tell her about his proposed move to Whitby and enlist her help in finding a suitable house.

He was brimming with excitement and anticipation when he dismounted from the coach and was welcomed by the landlord of the Angel for the night, something Rose had approved of when he had explained that he might need two days to get the variety of sketches he wanted of the abbey.

'Good to have you again, sir.' Seeing Arthur, the landlord put on his most jovial manner, anticipating possible future custom. 'More paintings for Mr Redgrave, sir?' he asked, indicating the two packages that one of his boys had carried in from the coach.

'Yes, and I hope he has more commissions for me.'

'Since your last visit I've made it in my way to look in his shop window. He's had two of your paintings on display and they have both gone.' Arthur's eyes brightened at this news. 'Mind you,' the landlord went on, 'that doesn't mean they've been sold but I would think it more than likely.'

'I hope you're right.'

'Show Mr Newton to room twelve! It's the same one you had last time. I thought it would make you feel at home.'

'Very thoughtful of you,' said Arthur. 'No, leave those,' he said to the boy who was picking up the paintings. 'Run up to my room with this bag and then you can carry one of those to Mr Redgrave's for me.' He glanced at the man behind the desk. 'That is if it is all right with you, landlord?'

'Of course, sir! Hurry along, boy, don't dawdle.'

Mr Redgrave greeted him warmly. Arthur passed a coin to a grateful boy who ran from the shop with his prize grasped firmly in his hand.

'Now, let me see what you have brought me.' Enthusiasm was sharp in William's voice.

'Wait.' Arthur dampened his eagerness. 'I understand you have had two of my paintings in the window and they are gone?'

William peered over his glasses and put on an air of hurt solemnity. 'Have you someone spying on me?'

'No! No!' protested Arthur quickly, concerned that he had upset his friend. 'The landlord at the Angel became interested in my work during my last visit and he has been looking in your window.

435

He told me.'

William laughed. 'Thought you had offended me? Arthur, it would take more than that. He's right, I sold them both.'

Arthur let out a whoop. 'How much?'

William raised an eyebrow. 'Getting mercenary now?'

'No, I just want to know. It might enable me to buy somewhere to stay when I come here to Whitby, save travelling each day to Scarborough.'

'To live permanently?'

'No, I can't leave Scarborough.'

He offered no further explanation, thinking it better not to. William expected a reason would be forthcoming but when it was not he said no more on the matter. He was not going to pry. Instead he said. 'Fifty pounds.'

'Good. Twenty-five each?'

'No. Fifty each.'

Arthur stared at him in astonishment for a moment then let out another whoop. This would certainly make getting a house easier. 'That's wonderful.'

'You keep painting to the quality you are showing presently and there'll be no difficulty selling. Now let me see what you have brought.'

Arthur unveiled his two paintings. Mr Redgrave studied them thoughtfully. He pointed to one of a rough sea breaking round the West Pier. Arthur had used a hazy moon as his sole source of light. It not only added a special atmosphere to the whole scene but it enhanced the lustre of the foam on the breaking waves. He had used moonlight here to convey the power and majesty of the sea.

'You can feel and hear it pounding! You must have done quite a few sea paintings, why haven't I seen them before?'

'This is the first I've done.'

'What? You're a near genius.'

'I practised and experimented for a while before I was satisfied.'

'You can be more than satisfied,' said William knowingly. 'I'll sell that tomorrow. You must have sixth sense! I have a good customer who has bought two of your paintings. The last time he was in he suggested I ask you if you could do a seascape. He is particularly interested in them. And here you are with one. You must have known. He'll certainly buy that one.'

'He specialises in seascapes?'

'He has been showing an inclination that way: talked of turning his collection into a specialised one, concentrating on Whitby and the sea. Do some more and we'll see his reaction.'

'I certainly will. What about the other?'

'*A Busy Scene at the Angel?* There's plenty of vitality in it. A real slice of Whitby life. I'm surprised you didn't show it to the landlord.'

'Sales in Whitby are made only through you, Mr Redgrave.'

'Thank you, my boy.'

'We made an agreement, I don't propose to break it. Put it in the window. I'm sure he'll see it. Might even be tempted.'

William chuckled, wondering how much he could get out of the landlord.

'I must be away, Mr Redgrave. Got to go up to the abbey, a customer in Leeds is interested.'

'Good for you! Keep up the good work.'

'I will.'

Arthur started for the door but came up sharp when Mr Redgrave pronounced solemnly, 'It was sad for Miss Shipley that her father died.'

Arthur spun round, concern clear to see on his face. 'When?'

'Ten days ago.'

Arthur's mind was a confusion of thoughts; quite soon after he had last seen her. How she must have suffered. He wished he had been there to offer support. She must still be desolate. He should hold her in his arms and offer comfort, should be with her, but of course he did not know where she lived. She might be on the quay. But no, not so soon.

'Mr Redgrave, where does she live?' He saw hesitation in his friend's manner. 'I should offer her my condolences.'

'I'm not in the habit of giving customers' addresses to anyone.'

'Mr Redgrave, I'm not anyone. You know me.' The pleading in Arthur's voice touched the gallery owner and brought with it a recollection of that painting of Miss Shipley that Arthur, through him, had presented to her. Both the painting and his present concern revealed a lot but he kept that to himself and knew he always would unless a relationship was to come into the open. He could not refuse Arthur now. He gave him the address in New Buildings.

'Thank you, Mr Redgrave.' He hurried from the shop, leaving William looking at the door and wondering where that evidence of love he had

438

seen in Arthur's face would lead?

All thoughts of sketching in the abbey had vanished. Arthur's stride was long and purposeful as he made his way to New Buildings. William had described the house to him but he was not prepared for the look of wealth and opulence that confronted him as he walked through the well-kept garden to the front door. He almost hesitated, thinking he might embarrass Colette by calling unexpectedly, but the desire to see her and be with her at this trying time overwhelmed him. He tugged hard at the bell-pull.

After a few heart-fluttering moments the door opened to reveal a black-clad maid.

'Good day. I would like to see Miss Colette Shipley, if she is at home.'

'I will see if she is receiving visitors, sir. Whom shall I say is calling?'

'Mr Arthur Newton.'

'Yes, sir. Will you please step inside?'

Arthur did so but moved no further after the maid had shut the door. She hurried across the hall and disappeared. A few minutes later, footsteps drew his attention. The maid appeared but did not even glance in his direction. He lost sight of her as she proceeded along a corridor, which he presumed led to the rear rooms. He stood nervously twitching his fingers. What was happening? Had she forgotten him?

He heard the faint swish of a skirt, the light skim of shoes. His heart started to race. Colette came into the hall and stopped on seeing him. Their eyes met across the space between them and eliminated it. There was no barrier. They were together again.

'Arthur!' She moved towards him, her hands held out for him to take.

He came forward. There was no need for words; their touch said them all.

'I'm sorry to intrude. I...' His voice faltered.

'Don't be. I'm glad you are here. How did you know? How did you find me?' She had started to lead him to the drawing-room.

'Mr Redgrave told me about your father. I'm so sorry. I just had to see you so I asked him for your address. He wasn't going to tell me but I pressed him until he had to give way and here I am. It would have been sooner had I known.'

'Thank you. I wished for you to be here but, not knowing where you lived, I could not inform you.'

'But you? How are you?' he asked anxiously, his eyes searching for telltale signs. He was mesmerised by the beauty that still shone through in spite of her loss.

'Trying to accept the fact he is gone is hard. Adele and Susan suffer too but we offer each other support and draw strength from each other. There is a void but time will bring acceptance.'

'I know it is easy to say but you must look forward. Keep your memories, but I'm sure your father would not want you to spend all your time looking back. There is a bright future for you. Take up your photography again.'

'I realise you are right. We are all trying to look ahead and we will take up the photography before long.' He detected a note of determination in her voice. 'But what about you, Arthur?'

'I'm well.'

'Are you just here for the day?'

'I'm staying the night at the Angel. I want some sketches of the abbey.'

'When will you do those?'

'I'll go there when I leave here and if necessary do some more tomorrow before the coach leaves.'

'If you are going when you leave here, may I come with you?'

'Nothing would give me greater pleasure if you think you should and feel up to it.'

'I need to start getting out again. Adele and Susan are out now, walking on the West Cliff.'

'And you didn't go with them.' His statement held the question: Why not?

'I didn't feel like it, but you have changed that.' She rose from her seat. 'We'll go now before they get back otherwise we'll be held up.'

They went into the hall where he waited while Colette got her pelisse and bonnet. Her mourning dress was beautifully cut, the bodice coming tight to the waist before flaring slightly to ankle-length. The only trimming was a small edging of lace around the collar. He was immediately struck by how much black suited her and enhanced her beauty rather than subdued it. He felt an intense desire to paint her as she was now.

She put on her outdoor clothes, gave him a small smile and said. 'Ready?'

He opened the front door and they stepped outside.

'Have your paintings been selling recently?' she

441

asked as they set off.

'Yes, indeed,' he replied and went on to tell her in more detail, hardly noticing passers-by as they crossed the bridge to Church Street and turned in the direction of the Stairs. He was solicitous for her welfare among the jostling crowd, which gradually trickled away to almost nothing when they started the steep climb to the cliff top and abbey. He automatically placed his hand on Colette's elbow, as the natural thing to do to lend her support while negotiating the steps. She accepted his thoughtfulness with silent gratitude.

The climb wasn't easy and they paused now and again to get their breath. They looked back across the river to the West Cliff and beyond, to the sweeping strand of sand that was lost at the foot of distant soaring cliffs. Seeing the view with the eye of an artist Arthur commented on its various aspects, hoping that he would stimulate her desire to take up photography again as soon as possible.

They reached the top and walked past the church. When Colette automatically turned towards the abbey he stopped her.

'Let us walk a little further,' he suggested.

'I thought you needed to sketch the abbey?'

'I do, but I'll do it on the way back. There is something I want to tell you first.'

She looked at him with curiosity. His voice sounded so serious. She waited for him to continue but he was silent as he started to walk again. It was as if he was trying to find a way to say what was on his mind.

'Just come out with it, Arthur,' she prompted, quietly.

He gave a nervous smile and, with a little nod, convinced himself that that was the best way. 'I am looking for a house in Whitby.'

She stopped and stared at him. Her mind raced with all the possibilities this could imply. What had he in mind? How should she react? 'You are going to live in Whitby permanently?'

'No I cannot do that, but with more commissions for Whitby pictures I thought it best to have a place here so that I do not waste so much time travelling.'

'That seems a good idea, but why not live here permanently?' Almost caught unawares, Arthur sought another plausible explanation. 'My mother is settled, it would not be good to give her the upheaval of moving again. Besides I need my connections with Leeds. In fact, some of the Whitby paintings are bound for there, and it is easier to get to Leeds from Scarborough because of the railway.'

'That makes sense, I suppose.' Colette hid her disappointment and scolded herself for entertaining the thought that Arthur might have something else in mind.

'I thought so.'

She started to walk again.

He stopped her and turned her to him. 'It does mean we can see more of each other, though. That is, if you want to?'

She placed a hand reassuringly on his arm and said softly, 'Of course I want to.'

His expressions of grateful thanks lingered in her mind long after they had parted.

As the morning proceeded in the pleasure of

each other's company they walked and talked and she watched with interest as he made his required sketches of the abbey. Time was lost to them both. It came as a shock when they realised how quickly it had passed.

'I should get back. Adele and Susan, will surely be home by now and be wondering where I am.'

They hurried down the Church Stairs, along Church Street and across the bridge. As they headed for New Buildings Colette said, 'I don't know how much you want to pay but there is a pleasant property for sale in Well Close Square.'

'Come and see it with me tomorrow before I return to Scarborough?'

She gave a knowing smile. 'That might not be wise. Tongues could wag if we are seen viewing it together.'

They had reached the gate to her home. 'Until tomorrow,' she said. 'I'll be at our usual meeting place on the quay at ten o'clock.'

'You have not forgotten it?'

'How could I? It holds special memories.' With that she was gone, hurrying up the path. He watched her until she had disappeared inside.

Arthur walked thoughtfully back to the Angel where he had cheese, bread, fruit and a glass of ale to fortify himself for the afternoon. He had decided that there was no point in pondering the decision about buying a place in Whitby. He was here. Colette had mentioned Well Close Square, so he may as well have a look before he did some more drawings of the abbey. He enquired of the landlord the whereabouts of the square.

'Simple, sir! You know Mr Redgrave's shop in Skinner Street? Continue past there and you'll come to Well Close Square on the left-hand side. Can't miss it.'

Arthur found himself in a small square of elegant Georgian houses. He was attracted by the quiet feeling of the square but feared that property here might be beyond his means. However he would not be put off until he had more facts about the house which he was thankful to see was the smallest in the square. His enquiries led him to be shown round and he was pleased to find that it would suit his needs with one room he could turn into an adequate studio. He declared he had no need of any more time to consider the matter and asked that the necessary documents be drawn up as quickly as possible.

Delighted by what he had done, he walked briskly through the town back to the Church Stairs. This time the climb did not seem to sap his energy as it had done that morning; there was a new spring to his step. He pulled out his sketchbook and drew quickly, finding that his impressions of the ancient abbey had taken on new life, one which he felt sure he could transfer to canvas.

Satisfied with what he had accomplished, he found a spot near the cliff edge where he could sit down and stare out over a tranquil sea. He wished Colette was sitting beside him now, listening to his plans for the house in Well Close Square, but he would have to forego that pleasure until tomorrow.

Arthur slept easily in the knowledge of having purchased a house in Whitby. Towards dawn his

445

subconscious took over and held him in eager anticipation of seeing Colette. He woke early. Knowing sleep would not come again he rose, dressed, ate a good breakfast and left the inn.

He paused to survey the river flowing steadily towards the bridge and beyond, to narrow between the piers and merge with the sea. The cool light of the early morning was being suffused by the warmth of the rising sun, colouring the tiled roofs that crowned the town. He made some quick notes in his sketchbook and then moved on towards the bridge. Soon it would be filled with people passing from one bank to the other, going about their daily lives. At the moment their numbers were few and in his mind's eye, Arthur saw them as ghostly figures he would insert into a painting, looking downstream to the sea's horizon where the light of a new day was announced by the cold streaks of dawn. He paused on the bridge and, glancing upstream, noted the position of the vessels at their quays. There were many pictures here to an artist's eye and he only wished he could spend all his time interpreting them on paper and canvas. Well, he'd have more opportunity now he had the house in Well Close Square.

He crossed the bridge and cut through Grape Lane to Church Street. He went straight to the place to which he knew Colette would come. In the ships, different from those that were berthed the last time he had been here, he saw a fresh challenge and set about rising to it. He became so engrossed in his work that he was not aware of how time was passing until he heard his name. He jumped to his feet, all sketching forgotten.

'Colette.' His pleasure was clearly evident in the way he let her name slip from his lips. He held out his free hand which she took in hers, allowing her touch to express her pleasure at seeing him. 'We'll walk,' he said. 'I have much to tell you.'

'You have sketches of the abbey to do,' she reminded him.

'Then we'll walk that way,' he replied. 'But not just yet, we must go back across the bridge.'

'Why? You must get...' She looked troubled.

He smiled reassuringly. 'All in good time! Come.' He started off and she fell into step beside him.

They crossed the bridge, turned alongside the river and headed for the West Pier. Before reaching it he turned away and escorted her to the top of the West Cliff. He paused and looked back to the east side.

'You want a drawing of the abbey from here?' she queried.

'I might one day. It is good to have this view in mind. But for now we have a little further to go.'

When they entered Skinner Street she said, 'We are going to Well Close Square, aren't we? You've been teasing me, bringing me a long way round.'

Arthur smiled. 'Well, I didn't want it to be too obvious.'

'You want me to point out the house I mentioned?'

'I thought it might be an idea to see it together.'

They turned into Well Close Square. 'We can only walk past it. We can't go in,' she warned.

He did not answer.

After a few more steps Colette stopped. Her face

clouded over with disappointment. 'Oh, dear, the *For Sale* notice has gone. The house must have been sold. I'm sorry for wasting your time.'

'You haven't. It will suit me very well.'

For one moment Colette did not grasp the significance of the words so casually delivered, then their meaning struck her. She pulled up sharply and gasped, 'What?' She stared hard at him, her eyes wide. 'You've been inside?'

'Yes. After we parted yesterday.' He laughed at her amazed expression. 'I thought there was no sense in wasting time.'

'You certainly didn't.' She started to walk again, her eyes fixed on the house. 'Is it comfortable inside?'

'Yes. It has been well looked after. It's not big, but big enough for my needs. Most importantly, it has a room that will make a good studio.'

'I'm pleased for you. When will you take it over?'

'The present owner is moving to Sleights, and has already taken most of his furniture and belongings there, but the final settlement might not be for three weeks.'

'Are you happy with that?'

'Yes. Thank you for telling me about it.' He stopped and laid a hand on her arm. 'I will always be grateful. Apart from saving time, it will open a new world to me.'

Their eyes met and she saw his express so much more that he wanted to say. 'I think we had better get to the abbey, you've sketching to do.' Colette set off and he could do nothing more but fall into step beside her.

For the rest of the morning their conversation kept away from the house in Well Close Square. It was as if neither dare voice what it might mean to them. Instead they talked about art and photography, aspects of Whitby that would make good subjects, and in general about life and their interests. They also shared silences as only two people falling in love can, and in those moments when their eyes met, Colette's smile was so radiant with pleasure that there was no doubt it came from deep within her heart. At those moments Arthur felt a prick of conscience.

He felt it again on the coach during his ride back to Scarborough. There was guilt at living a lie. But he had never before experienced the feelings he had for Colette, not even for Rose. She was the family friend whom everyone had expected him to marry and he had been caught up in the tide of that expectation. This was different. His heart sang when he knew he would be meeting Colette again and those moments could not come quick enough for him. Time spent with her was time in another world, a place where two like souls found joy in each other. With a house in Well Close Square those moments could be more frequent. But he knew that to enjoy them fully he would have to shut out the guilt he felt and be prepared to live a lie.

Chapter Twenty

Arthur's arrival brought Marie running into the hall to greet him. 'Daddy! Daddy!' Her face was wreathed in broad smiles as she rushed to him. He stooped, swept her into his arms and lifted her high in the air. She threw her head back in laughter and he felt joy in its ringing tones. Immediately he was touched anew by guilt but he thrust that from his mind without further consideration. He lowered Marie to the floor. 'Where's Mama?' he asked.

'There.' She pointed to the open door.

Hand in hand, they went into the drawing-room. Arthur went over to Rose who stood up to receive his kiss and return it. Marie ran to the toys she had laid out on one of the window seats. She lifted up two dolls and ran from the room.

'I hope the weather in Whitby was as good as it has been here. If so you will have done a lot of sketching.'

'It was and I did,' he replied as he shrugged himself out of his outdoor clothes.

'So it was worthwhile?'

'In more ways than one,' thought Arthur but said, 'Oh, yes! I've a good selection to work on for Ebenezer, and Mr Redgrave said he would be able to sell one of the paintings I took him immediately. And he was sure that same customer would want similar seascapes.'

'So that means more time in Whitby?'

'I'm afraid so. Because of that likelihood I followed your suggestion and found a small but adequate property to act as a studio.'

Rose was taken aback. 'You've lost no time,' she said sharply.

'Didn't see any reason to with commissions looming.'

Rose nodded. She felt a pang of regret that she had ever made the suggestion but quickly dismissed it. If this was the way for Arthur to make money then so be it, but... She voiced her concern. 'Whatever you do, don't neglect me or Marie. You know how she adores you.'

'Nothing like that will happen,' he reassured her.

'So, tell me about this place you have bought?'

'It is a small house in Well Close Square. Ideal for what I want. A good room for a studio and one which is adequate enough to live in.'

'What about furniture? Will you take any from here?'

'No. I only want a bed, table and chair. I'm not going to be there for any length of time. It's merely to save me the travelling. The time saved on that will be spent painting, and more works will mean more money.'

'I'm sure you'll see that it does.'

Although Arthur was anxious to get the house in Whitby to his liking as soon as possible he curbed his desire for three weeks until the transaction was completed. During that time he painted seascapes at every possible moment, concentrating on tranquil waters suffused by moonlight or the setting sun. They bore the hallmark of a man possessed. Deep down Arthur knew that they were all inspired by his desire to see Colette again and for her to see these paintings.

When he stood back to survey the second canvas he was pleased with what he had done.

'Want to see what I will be taking to Whitby the day after tomorrow?' he asked, wiping his hands as he came into the drawing-room.

Rose turned from the window.

'Can I see, Papa?' cried Marie, excitedly jumping to her feet, leaving the book she had been reading on the floor.

'Of course, love.' He held out his hand to her.

'Why the day after tomorrow?' asked Rose as they walked from the room together.

'I thought all three of us could have an outing tomorrow.'

'That would be a treat. Thank you, Arthur.'

They strolled on the South Cliff, walked through the gardens, skirted the Spa and crossed the sands towards the Harbour. Marie raced around, calling to her parents as she did so.

'Watch me, Papa, watch me!' she shouted, then skidded in the sand, rolled over and leaped to her feet to do it all over again. Her laughter rang with joy.

'She'll get in an awful mess with that sand,' commented Rose, without much desire to admonish her. She doted on the child, finding in her a companionship that filled her time when Arthur was away.

'She's all right,' he replied. 'It will do her good to run wild.'

'Papa, are we going to see the ships?'

'If you want to.'

'Oh, yes!' Marie shouted with excitement. 'I always like to see the ships.'

Rose noted the light that always shone in Marie's eyes when Arthur approved of anything she said. 'She idolises you, Arthur. Frets for a day when you go away.'

He made no comment but Rose's observation tugged at his conscience and heightened the guilt he knew he would feel on leaving his wife and daughter tomorrow.

'Hurry back, Papa,' Marie requested as she and her mother came into the hall, to bid Arthur goodbye.

'Your father may be away a little longer than usual,' Rose informed her.

'Why?' Marie wailed, her face filling with disappointment.

'He has some special paintings to do in Whitby.'

'Can't we go with him?'

'No,' put in Rose quickly. 'You wouldn't like it. You wouldn't be happy there.'

Arthur saw more protests coming from his daughter and put in quickly, 'I promise, I won't be long. Be back as soon as I can. Now, give me a big kiss to remember you by.' He bent down. Marie flung her arms round his neck and gave him a long kiss on the cheek.

'There,' he said, 'now you'll be in my mind all the time.' He turned to Rose. 'You'll be all right?'

'Of course.' She kissed him. 'See that you do some good paintings.'

'I will. I know it.'

As he sat back in the coach these words came back to Arthur. How did he know he would? A painting could just as easily go wrong as right. But he was convinced his painting could only be enhanced by Colette's closeness in Whitby. Then those thoughts were marred by memories of his daughter's pleas and guilt returned.

It disturbed his mind for a few miles but the thought of setting up a studio in his new house quelled the battle that was threatening within. That studio meant a new life that could lead to even better paintings. His fingers twitched, eager for a brush to impart to the canvas all the rich and varying tones he was eager to exploit.

Reaching Whitby, he went straight to William Redgrave. 'Seascapes,' he announced when they had exchanged greetings.

'Come through, come through.' William fussed, eager to see the paintings. 'My brother is away but I'll get my wife. She helps when Richard is away. You've never met her, have you?' He hurried to the door that led to the rear of the premises, returning a few minutes later. 'Genetta, this is Arthur of whom I have spoken. He has brought some seascapes.'

'Hello, Arthur,' she greeted him with a pleasant smile. 'I've heard a lot about you from my husband. You have a great talent, I understand.'

'I wouldn't say that, Mrs Redgrave, but it does allow me to meet some interesting people, yourself among them.' He liked the look of this

454

small well-built woman who looked to be an ideal partner for Mr Redgrave.

She laughed. 'You know how to flatter, Mr Newton! I like that. Now, let us see these paintings.'

Arthur placed them on the easel one at a time. Within ten minutes they had considered the two and had nothing but praise for them.

'Splendid, my boy, simply splendid! My client will leap at these. And he'll want more.'

'I see real vitality in this work,' commented Genetta. 'I can feel the power of the waves in that one, but in this the sea is so peaceful that I'm sure it would calm me every time I looked at it.'

'Then maybe I should purchase it and place it where you can see it all the time,' quipped William. He gave Arthur a wink. 'How long are you here, my boy?'

'Ah, now I have some news for you. The last time I was here I purchased a small house in Well Close Square.'

'You're coming to live here permanently?' asked Genetta.

'No, I can't leave Scarborough, but I thought if it was necessary to spend more time here painting, I would be able to cut down on the travelling.'

'Splendid,' cried William again. 'We'll see more of you then.'

'I'm going to get things organised there now and convert one of the rooms into a studio. So, Mr Redgrave, I require some things from you.'

'Of course, my boy! You will have them at cost, and the easel shall be a starting present from Genetta and me.'

'I couldn't...' Arthur tried to protest, but

William stopped him.

'You can and you will,' he said, so emphatically that Arthur knew it was useless to protest any further.

'That is most kind of you, and I thank you both.' In his mind Arthur was already planning to execute a seascape for Genetta similar to the one she'd liked.

After everything had been selected, William insisted on accompanying Arthur to Well Close Square. He was delighted with the house and suggested that he send Genetta round to measure for curtains that he was sure she would be glad to make. He conducted Arthur to the best place to obtain furniture and by mid-afternoon the house was habitable and Arthur had set his mark on it. He wished Colette could see it. She could not even know he was in Whitby; that would have to wait until tomorrow morning when he would be in his usual place on the east quay.

He was there early. He did not want to miss her. Though he tried to do some sketching his mind would not concentrate. He knew it never would until he had told Colette what had transpired yesterday.

His heart beat a little faster when he saw her coming. He could not take his eyes off her, and once again felt an intense desire to paint her in a different setting from the previous one.

With polite greetings exchanged, he suggested that they walk together. Reaching the end of Church Street, they found a path that ran by the river.

'The house is all furnished,' he announced.

She looked at him in surprise. 'When? How?'

'I arrived yesterday.' He went on to tell her about William and Genetta's generosity and help. 'You must come and see it,' he finished with a note of enthusiasm in his invitation, then added, 'though I would understand if you thought it unwise. I would not want to be instrumental in starting any gossip that might tarnish your reputation.'

'That would be my affair and no one else's. I would love to see it.'

Arthur felt a surge of delight at the prospect of showing her his new house and studio. 'Would you like to go now?'

'Why not?'

They retraced their footsteps, crossed the bridge and made their way to Well Close Square via Skinner Street.

He stopped in front of his house.

It seemed to be smiling down, silently saying, 'Welcome. You will find happiness here.' A shiver of delight ran through Colette. 1865 had been a year of tragedy and elation but this house promised that the joy would be carried into 1866 and beyond.

Arthur escorted her to the front door, unlocked it and stepped aside for her to enter.

'It is only sparsely furnished at the moment but is quite adequate for me,' he explained as he led her from room to room. Reaching the last he said proudly, 'My studio,' as he swept the door open with a movement that said, 'This is where I really belong. This is where my work will blossom beyond even the wildest dreams I entertained

457

before I met you. This is where I will make you proud of me.'

His thoughts were interrupted by the soft tones of Colette's voice. 'This should be ideal, not too big, not too small. The table is handy for your easel which I see you have rightly placed to catch the northern light.' She smiled at the questioning look he shot her. 'A photographer studies light too, you know. That north-facing window is just right.' Her voice heightened with excitement. 'Oh, Arthur, I hope you are happy here.' Her hand was on his arm as if to emphasise the sentiment she'd expressed.

As he turned and reached out to her he said, 'I will be, so long as I can see you.' His arms came to her waist and he drew her gently to him. All the time his eyes were fixed on hers. Colette came to him willingly.

'Of course you can,' she whispered.

Their lips met and lingered in an expression of love that spanned all time. Each knew that the silent touch had created a bond that would ever be revived and savoured in memory, time and time again.

Colette was reluctant to end these happy moments, when her heart sang with joy, banishing her period of mourning. Outwardly she would still observe the correct etiquette, but inwardly she would rejoice for the love she had found. 'I think I should be going so you can get on with your painting.'

Arthur held her a moment longer and kissed her again. 'I suppose I should,' he agreed reluctantly. 'Call again this afternoon?'

She nodded.

Though he felt a void after she had gone, Arthur also felt invigorated. He set up his canvas, picked up his palette, assembled the necessary paints, chose his brush and with swift strokes brought a picture to life. He became lost in his painting as he added detail and colour to produce the atmosphere that had become synonymous with his work. The abbey, with dark threatening clouds behind it, glowed by the light of the setting sun.

As he stood back to view what he had judged would be his final alteration, he heard a knock at the door. He went through to the hall and was taken aback when the clock told him it was nearly four o'clock. He opened the door to find Colette standing there with a basket on her arm. He moved to one side and she stepped into the hall.

'I don't suppose you've eaten,' she commented as she passed through to the kitchen.

'No, I had no idea how time had gone on.'

'I guessed rightly that you'd start painting when I left and become absorbed in it. Well, you can come and sit down while you have what I have brought.' She placed the basket on the table, untied her bonnet, and put it to one side along with her cape.

'You shouldn't have bothered but I am exceedingly grateful. I've only just realised how hungry I am.'

Bread, ham, cheese, pickle, an apple pie and a bottle of wine appeared as if by magic. 'This is the best I could do.'

'There's no need to apologise,' he returned.

459

'This is wonderful. Aren't you joining me?'

'No there'll be a meal later at home and if I don't eat reasonably well questions might be asked.'

He nodded.

'How long are you going to be in Whitby?'

'Another two days.' He guessed where this conversation was going so he added quickly, 'You must not compromise yourself by bringing me food. I'll look after myself. Where did you get this?'

'From shops in Skinner Street.'

'Then I can do the same or go to one of the inns.'

'See that you don't neglect yourself.'

'I won't.'

'What happens to your mother while you are away? Is she able to look after herself?'

'To a certain extent, but a kindly neighbour keeps an eye on her and takes her meals.'

'She'll miss you.'

'Yes.' Arthur was wary of where this might lead so he changed the subject. 'Have you taken up photography again?'

Colette was rising from her seat as she replied. 'I'll tell you in a moment. I'm going to see what you have been working on that kept you so busy today.' With that she was on her way to the studio.

Arthur went on eating. Silence from the studio flowed into the kitchen enveloping him, binding him to Colette as he awaited her verdict. He felt the intimacy of her quiet consideration.

She was held enthralled by the picture, which managed to be both lively and mysterious.

'This is wonderful, Arthur,' she called finally. 'Just wonderful.'

He felt deeply gratified by her assessment, and pleased that she had been moved by it; he could tell by the tone in her voice.

'A commission?' she asked.

'Yes,' he called. 'My art dealer in Leeds, Ebenezer Hirst, has a customer.'

'Good. And more?' She came back to join him.

'Yes.'

'I'm pleased for you.'

'Thanks.'

'So you'll be busy? I should not disturb you.'

'I'll be sorry if you don't.'

She met his gaze, read the meaning behind his words, and was pleased.

'You still haven't answered my question about your photography,' he pointed out.

'I've done none since Father died.'

'You should start again.'

'I intend to.'

'Don't just intend to, do it. You have talent, I've seen that. You have a gift. Use it. Your father would want you to. I know there is something missing from your life. It is hard, but you must step forward again, and the hardest part is taking that first step. Let that painting in there be an inspiration to you. I had to put the first brush stroke on the canvas and that to me is always the hardest part. Once I have done that I am away. You go out and take your first photograph and you'll find you quickly become absorbed again. Then we can meet and go out together, you photographing, and me sketching. Do it, Colette.'

Half an hour later when she left he said, 'I'll be in our usual meeting place tomorrow morning. I

461

hope to see you arrive with your camera.'

'If I do I'll have Adele or Susan with me. If not they'll think it strange.'

'So be it,' he replied, 'but you must take up photography again. I don't want to be the cause of your not doing so.'

His words were food for thought as Colette walked home. Arthur was right, her father wouldn't want her to neglect her photography. Should she tell Adele and Susan about Arthur now? They would have to be told sometime. She pondered that question and finally decided, 'Not just yet.' Let the meeting tomorrow appear accidental.

When she announced that she was going to start taking photographs again Adele and Susan were delighted. They had recognised that it was Colette who had suffered most from the death of Peter and had begun to fear she had retreated too much into thoughts of the past. Adele and Susan had suffered too but in different ways from Colette. While Adele would never forget the past that she had shared with her father, or Susan an employer who had come to mean more than that to her, they had not allowed sadness to dominate them as Colette had. Pleased by her decision, they wondered what had brought about this sudden change, the throwing off of the cloak of mourning that had laid heavily on her.

The next morning, feeling anxious about the weather, Colette was awake early. Looking from her bedroom window she studied the sky, remembering the signs her father had taught her to look for. She decided that the early-morning mist that rose from the river and enveloped the town would clear with the warming sun and leave a fine day. Clouds may gather in the afternoon but they would not be threatening. On the whole, she judged, it would be a pleasant day.

She dressed in a mood of excitement. Arthur's purchase of a house, though principally for a studio, seemed a portent of a more permanent relationship. She reined her thoughts in sharply. She must not let such ideas run away with her, must compose herself before facing Adele and Susan across the breakfast table.

Their first query after she had walked into the dining-room was, 'You haven't changed your mind about the photography?'

'No,' she replied. 'Why should I?'

'Good,' Adele approved and then added, 'we'll both come with you.'

'Very well.' Colette was non-committal in her agreement.

'Have you anything particular in mind?' asked Susan

'I thought I might expand the ship theme.'

'But you won't neglect portraits?'

'No. I can see a possible extension of that in studio portraits of families, but I would also like to build up a reputation for scenes of Whitby and the surrounding district.'

They did not linger after finishing breakfast and, once they left the house, allowed Colette to lead the way as it was obvious she had somewhere in mind.

She took them to the quays along the east bank and set up her equipment there with their help.

They had completed their task and Colette was positioning her camera for her first composition, an interpretation of the *Sea Fury*, when she heard Adele say, 'Good morning, Mr Newton.'

Colette, her heart racing, turned. Their eyes met as they exchanged polite greetings, trying to sound and look surprised.

Both Adele and Susan had caught that brief moment of meaningful exchange but, not wanting to upset nor embarrass Colette, held their counsel then and afterwards. They would wait and see what this association brought.

Thus began an idyllic time for Colette and Arthur. During each of the succeeding eight weeks he spent two days in Whitby. She visited him each afternoon, to watch him paint or to relax together, talking about painting and photography and their respective places in the world of art, regretting how quickly time passed, putting off parting as long as they dare.

Arthur talked little about himself and avoided being led on the subject despite Colette's occasional attempts to do so. She never pursued the matter with more forthright questions, content with things as they were. She wanted nothing to destroy a relationship that held two people together in such mutual respect and love. Time spent together was a joy to them both. They shared moments of laughter that heightened the growing bond between them as only laughter, in its subtle way, can. They were happy.

Guilt only bothered Arthur when he returned to Scarborough but he drowned that in the knowledge that he was not neglecting Rose or Marie. He further submerged it by painting furiously both in Scarborough and Whitby. That did not mean that his work became slipshod, rather the opposite. His paintings were imbued with new life. The atmospheric style he had developed was still there, it always would be, but now it displayed a final touch of vitality that had been absent before. It lifted his paintings beyond the merely competent.

That was duly noticed by Ebenezer in Leeds and Mr Redgrave in Whitby. Their praise became glowing and they constantly plied Arthur with fresh commissions. His decision to throw up his railway job and become an artist had clearly been vindicated, and he knew the inspiration behind his new found success came from Colette. From their discussions about his painting, her instinctive understanding of what he wanted to achieve and why he needed to express himself through painting. Arthur wanted her to be proud of him.

Colette was glad for him, too, and ever ready with constructive criticism, encouragement and praise. He wondered what he would have achieved if he had experienced such support from the start of his career, if Rose had adopted this same belief in him? No matter – now he had Colette and dare not contemplate the possibility of losing her. If only he could make their relationship permanent.

Bernard Clayton had visited Colette whenever he

was in Whitby, becoming more and more concerned about her lacklustre demeanour, but today, as soon as he was shown into the drawing-room where she was engaged in some delicate needlework, he sensed a change in her. There was a new light in her eyes, a sparkle and real pleasure in her expression when she greeted him.

She ordered hot chocolate and they chatted amicably while they enjoyed it. He was pleased that she had taken up her interest in photography again and enthused over the recent photographs that he insisted she show him.

'I would like copies of these,' he said, setting six aside. 'They will display nicely in the hotel. And you are to let me pay for them.'

Colette shook her head. 'No. As a dear friend you shall have them as a gift from me, in thanks for your support and concern.'

'But you cannot do that if you are to make photography your business.'

'I can and I will.'

'Then I shall see that you are duly acknowledged as the photographer and hopefully that will lead to sales for you.'

'That will be payment enough.'

He glanced towards the window. 'It is a fine morning, will you walk with me?'

'I will be delighted. I was thinking about having a walk when you arrived. It will be good to have company. I have none when Adele and Susan go riding.'

'Then I'm lucky in the timing of my visit.'

They walked on the West Cliff where strollers who knew her as Mr Shipley's eldest daughter, nodded, bade her 'Good morning' and wondered about the identity of the handsome man who accompanied her.

Bernard chatted enthusiastically about whatever topic arose. Colette was equally articulate, which pleased him because it confirmed his feelings that she had adopted a new perspective on life. They passed beyond the new houses that were expanding the town along the West Cliff and were soon alone on the cliff top. Here they stopped and gazed across a tranquil sea, sharing a silence that was only broken by the faint lapping of the waves on the sand far below.

Colette was lost in thoughts of Arthur when Bernard's whispered words reached her like thunder.

'Marry me, Colette. I have loved you all my life. Sadly our ways parted but I never lost my love for you. Now, with no father to ask for your hand in marriage, I ask you to be my wife.'

The hope she saw in his eyes was like a blow to her heart. She did not want to hurt this man whom she had known so long, whom she admired and loved, if in a different way from the love she had for Arthur. Yet what did she really know of Arthur? She was certain he loved her but he had never expressed it in so many words. There was real empathy between them, so different from the joking relationship between her and Bernard. This was friendship. Her feelings for Arthur were so much more. Her mind raced. What should she say?

Her eyes were damp as they met Bernard's. 'Oh, Bernard, I'm so flattered but I'm not certain... This is so unexpected.'

'I'll not rush you for an answer if you wish to think about it.' There was a sorrowful look about his eyes, though, as if it hurt him that she had not responded with a joyful yes.

She laid one hand gently on his arm. 'You are a kind and considerate man, Bernard. Be patient with me.'

'I'll wait for eternity if necessary. My love for you is so deep that there can never be anyone else.'

'Oh, Bernard, please don't impose an obligation on me that way,' she cried.

'I'm not. I would never do that. It is meant merely as an expression of my unbounded love.' He kissed her gently on the cheek. 'I'll be as patient as I have to be. May I go on calling on you whenever I am in Whitby?'

'Yes, Bernard, please do. You are dear to me and I would be hurt if our friendship faltered because I have not immediately given you the answer you wanted.'

'Then I will live in hope.'

Chapter Twenty-one

'Colette, you are quiet and appear troubled,' commented Susan, laying down her knife and fork as she looked seriously at this young woman for whom she felt responsible after Peter's death. She sensed her charge stiffen. 'I don't want to pry. You are an adult, can run your own life, but I did promise your father I would be here if you needed advice.'

Colette grimaced at the thought of all that had happened and her own confused reaction.

'We are here to listen if you want us to,' prompted Adele.

Colette looked down at her half-eaten meal which she had merely picked at. In that moment Adele exchanged a look of concern with Susan and knew, from the nod she received in return, that Susan approved of her trying to elicit a further response from her sister.

'Is it Mr Newton?' she asked.

Colette looked up slowly. 'Yes and no,' she replied, the vagueness in her voice matching her words.

'It must be one or the other,' said Adele impatiently.

Colette hesitated a moment. 'I've had a proposal of marriage.' A stunned silence came into the room and she met their astonishment by saying, 'While you were out riding I had a visitor.'

'Mr Newton?' said Susan. 'We guessed you had been seeing him. You seemed to know when he was coming to Whitby. On those occasions you always wanted to photograph ships. We guessed it was prearranged so you knew he had arrived. And you always walked out alone those afternoons.'

'Was it so obvious?' cried Colette, blushing with embarrassment that her conduct had been so transparent.

'Only to we who are near to you,' Adele assured her.

'My visitor today wasn't Mr Newton,' said Colette quietly.

'So who was it?' snapped Adele.

'Bernard.'

'Bernard?' gasped Adele, exchanging a glance of surprise with Susan.

'Yes.'

'And?' prompted Susan.

'He asked me to marry him.'

'We guessed that from what you said.' Adele's retort was charged with irritation. 'What was your answer?'

'I turned him down.'

There was a moment's silence while Adele and Susan grasped the implications of this refusal.

'In favour of Mr Newton?' asked Susan tentatively.

'Arthur, please,' said Colette shyly.

'In favour of Arthur, then?' snapped Adele, annoyed that her sister was not being more forthcoming.

'I'm in love with him.'

This still was not what Adele wanted to hear. 'Has he proposed to you?'

Colette hesitated and then revealed that he had not.

'Do you expect him to?' asked Susan.

'He loves me.'

'Are you sure?' Susan pressed.

Colette nodded

'Then why hasn't he proposed?' asked her sister.

'I don't know.'

'What do you know about him apart from the fact that he is a painter whom you met by accident?' asked Susan protectively.

'That I like to be with him. That we share the

same creative interests though his are focussed on his painting and mine photography. There is a lot of common ground.'

'But you must know more about his personal life? Where he comes from? What family he has?'

'He comes from Leeds originally and lives in Scarborough with his mother.'

'Is that all you know?'

'Yes.'

'Has he ever suggested you should meet her?'

'I gather she is a bit of a tartar. He's an only child and she rules his life. He has indicated that she would be upset if I were to meet her.'

'I think what he really means is that she doesn't want him to marry,' put in Adele.

'Beware of sons ruled by their mothers,' Susan warned. 'Such relationships can play havoc with marriages. I think you should find out more about him.'

'I think you should marry Bernard.' Adele put her own opinion more forcibly.

Colette met her sister's commanding gaze. 'Would you marry someone with whom you weren't in love, as I believe man and wife should be?'

'Yes, if that man loved me, as Bernard must you since he has asked you to marry him. And if I held him in the same high esteem as I know you hold Bernard.'

'You are right about my regard for him but my love lies elsewhere. If you loved someone as I love Arthur, I'm sure you would alter your view.'

Colette saw a small flare of anger touch the corners of her sister's eyes but Adele did not respond with words.

'You should find out more about Arthur,' Susan advised, averting a possible conflict between the sisters with words of good sense. 'Don't take anything for granted, Colette. Be sure of the facts.'

Colette had time to ponder those words during the next week for it was not until seven days later that she learned Arthur was back in Whitby. She had continued her photography with enthusiasm and, whenever she had time alone, would walk through Well Close Square looking for the telltale signal of open curtains that signified Arthur was in Whitby.

She formed all sorts of questions to ask him, but when he opened the door to her and she stepped inside they all faded into insignificance. What did these matter when they were immersed in their love for each other?

Arthur helped her out of her coat and took her bonnet. Not a word was spoken as he laid them carefully on a chair beside the door. When he straightened and turned back he found Colette waiting. The look in her eyes was enticing. She held out her hands to him. He took them in his, their soft warmth trembling with emotion.

'I've missed you more than ever this week,' she whispered, still locked in his embrace after their lips had parted.

'Even while lost in your photography?' he said teasingly.

'Even then! I suppose your painting over-whelmed any thoughts of me?'

'Come and see, and judge for yourself.' Hold-

472

ing her hand, he led her to the studio.

On an easel placed to catch the best light was a painting of Well Close Square in which Arthur's house was prominent.

'It is for you. Our house,' he told her.

'Oh, Arthur, it's wonderful. Thank you so much.' Colette flung her arms round his neck and kissed him. 'It shall hang in this house in a prominent position, a reminder of our love for each other.'

'Do we need a reminder?'

She gave a little laugh. 'I suppose not, so maybe it should be a symbol of our future?'

If Arthur recognised the hint behind that statement he did not remark upon it and the moment was lost while he replaced the picture on the easel with another.

Colette gazed at it in wonder for a few minutes and then allowed her praise to come quietly. 'That is wonderful … such a tremendous atmosphere in that sea. I can practically feel the swell of the water and it is telling me something.' She paused a moment. He waited for her to go on. 'In spite of the fact that there is strength in it, there is also tranquillity. You have imparted a feeling that life can offer peace of mind if only we will look for it and accept it in whatever form it comes.'

Arthur contemplated the canvas a moment longer. His mind flashed back to the few moments before he left Scarborough when he'd showed the same painting to Rose. Her remarks had been, 'It is a very nice painting of the sea, but it should have a ship or something on it to make it more meaningful.'

473

'I'm so glad you read that into it, Colette. That is what I hoped I had achieved.'

'Oh, you certainly have.'

'Then let us go and see if Mr Redgrave sees it that way too. I painted it for his wife in thanks for helping with this house when I purchased it. She commented on a painting I did for a possible commission so I thought I would do a similar one for her.'

'I'm sure she will love it.'

'Come on, let's see what she thinks.'

'Are you sure you want me to come?'

'Of course.' He pulled his enthusiasm up sharply. 'Oh! I see what you mean. You think tongues might wag? I don't think the Redgraves will be like that but I don't mind if you don't. I can't see word getting back to my mother from here.'

'Would it bother her if it did?'

'Yes. She's very possessive.'

Colette was silent while he got the pictures ready. Was she going to have to wait until something happened to Arthur's mother? Should she insist, in a gentle way, that she meet her? She wished she knew more about his private life. But would that upset their relationship? She did not want that. Maybe it was best to go on as they were and enjoy the idyllic times when they were able to be together?

'I'm ready.' His voice interrupted her thoughts.

William Redgrave greeted them enthusiastically when they walked into the shop. Their coming in together, exuding joy at being in each other's company, confirmed his earlier opinion that there could be more to this relationship. Genetta would sense that better than he so he called her to come, using the excuse that he wanted her to see the paintings.

'I too would like her to see them,' approved Arthur. His wink at Colette when William went for his wife brought a smile to her lips.

'Mr Newton!' Genetta was already making her greeting as she came through the door. Then she saw Colette. 'And Miss Shipley too! This is a nice surprise.'

William's eyes were bright when he said, 'Two paintings! Come, Arthur, don't hold out any longer.'

Everyone smiled at his enthusiasm.

'Calm, William, calm,' said his wife gently.

Arthur unwrapped the first painting and placed it on the easel.

'Your house in Well Close Square,' Genetta identified the subject.

'That is excellent,' commented William. 'You have a new sparkle to your paintings and a new depth. There'll be no problem in selling that.'

'I'm sorry, Mr Redgrave, it's not for sale.'

'Not for sale?' William started indignantly. He saw his wife shoot him a glance and let his comment fade into, 'Oh, I see.' He quickly brushed off the embarrassment he was feeling, 'Now, for the other.'

When Arthur placed the seascape on the easel he felt tension and wonder come over William and Genetta. He waited while they absorbed the impact of the painting. Judging his moment, he said quietly, 'It's not for sale either.'

He couldn't have said anything more shattering to William. 'What! You don't mean it! You can't!'

Arthur smiled but said in all seriousness, 'I do.'

'But...' William started.

'It is a present for Mrs Redgrave.' His statement brought a stunned silence to them both. Then Arthur added, 'I hope you will enjoy it too, William.'

'It's a wonderful painting,' said Genetta, quietly in awe. 'But I couldn't accept it.'

'You can and you will, as thanks for all you did when I bought the house in Well Close Square.'

Genetta gave a low moan of appreciation. Her eyes were damp with gratitude as she said, 'What can I say except thank you? And that is barely adequate.'

'I think Arthur will be satisfied if you tell him what you see in the painting,' put in Colette.

Genetta studied the painting and then explained what she saw and how it affected her emotions.

As she finished Arthur raised his eyebrows at Colette. Genetta's feelings for the painting were almost identical to hers. He thanked Genetta and added, 'That is payment enough. You have seen exactly what I was trying to express.'

'I'm sure it is worth more than that, but I do appreciate your kindness.'

Arthur smiled and gave a slight shake of his head. 'No, I'm grateful for what you and your husband have done for me.'

William slapped him on the shoulder. 'I'm glad you came into our lives. Never fail to visit us when you come to Whitby.'

'I won't, and there'll be more paintings to sell.'

William looked at Colette. 'Maybe we could sell some of your photographs, Miss Shipley?'

'Do you think you could?' Her appreciation of the suggestion was evident.

'We can but try.'

When Colette and Arthur left the shop they walked with a new sense of light-hearted purpose. Life was good. Laughter was on their lips but each had forcefully to dismiss intrusive thoughts, hers of Bernard and his of Rose.

'What do you think?' asked William when the door closed behind Colette and Arthur.

'I think it is a wonderful gift,' replied Genetta.

'You know what I mean,' he replied. 'What do you think of those two?' He inclined his head towards the door.

'I think they are very much in love and not afraid to show it, though this is the first time they have been to the shop together.'

'I wonder if he will leave Scarborough and move into his house in Well Close Square permanently?'

The same question dwelt in Colette's mind but she was afraid to approach Arthur with it for fear of upsetting their relationship. Why risk doing that when she was happy with the way things were? She ignored any pressure that came from the occasional question from Susan, 'Have you learned any more about him?'

Over the next weeks they lived a blissful life whenever Arthur was in Whitby.

Inclement weather set in during November and

made it impossible for him to reach the town. He painted in Scarborough but every time his brush touched a canvas his thoughts were with Colette and he could feel the power of her influence in every stroke.

On the days when the weather of late 1865 relented a little, Colette ventured forth with her camera. She wanted to capture Whitby in its mantle of winter white and through the icicles hanging like jewels glistening in the cold sunlight. She thought of Arthur and wondered how he would interpret these scenes. No doubt he would welcome using some of her photographs as a basis for painting winter pieces. She longed for the weather to ease with a yearning that tore at her very being, but that did not happen until late February.

As soon as she knew the road from Scarborough was passable she started to take her walks via Well Close Square but it was not until the second week in March that she saw the curtains of the house had been opened. The sign pulled her up sharp but it was only a momentary hesitation. With pounding heart she hurried to the front door. Thoughts raced through her mind. What would Arthur say? Would four months' separation have changed him? She wondered if he had missed her as she had missed him. Desire welled inside her. She longed for the door to open. It seemed an eternity since she had tugged at the bell-pull. Maybe he had gone out. Maybe he had taken some paintings to Mr Redgrave. All sorts of possibilities raged through her mind.

But the minutes were not as long as she'd

thought. The door opened. He was there, his face wreathed in a smile of untold pleasure, and she answered him with an expression of the joy she felt.

'Arthur!'

'Colette!'

Their words were scarcely above a whisper but they expressed a joyous easing of the tension each had endured throughout the winter.

She stepped inside.

He closed the door.

Their eyes met. The outside world no longer existed for them. They were together. Alone. Nothing and no one else mattered. There was no need for words. Their understanding of each other's love overrode any obstacles; it was in the longing they shared, in their touch when they reached out to each other. Their lips met, charged with desire.

Colette said nothing as she turned away towards the stairs. With her fingers tightly entwined in Arthur's he could do nothing but follow. The longing, heightened by the enforced parting, was so strong in them both that it could not be denied.

He banished a qualm of conscience when they reached the bedroom door. Colette refused to dwell on what Adele and Susan would think. Each refused to harbour doubts, safe in the knowledge that they were about to express a deep and devoted love for each other.

'No regrets?' Arthur said quietly as he lay with Colette nestling in his arms later.

She gave a small shake of her head. 'None.'

There was joy in her voice. 'When do you go back?'

'The day after tomorrow.'

She knew it was no good protesting. Instead she twisted round so she could look into his eyes. 'Then, love me again now and all tomorrow, from the moment I arrive until I am forced to return home, for appearance's sake.'

He smiled his love and, encircling her in his arms, drew her close.

Two days later she forced back the tears as she said goodbye to him. 'When will you be back?'

'Next week and every week,' Arthur replied without proper consideration.

She realised that he had done so and uttered a warning. 'Is that wise? Your mother might become suspicious. Maybe it would be better and easier for us if you told her.'

'I will when the time is right.' Arthur gave a short pause and added, 'Maybe you are right. It's probably better if I come when I can and you keep a check on the curtains.'

'Make it as often as you can.'

He could not ignore the pleading tone in her voice, besides he did not want to. 'I will,' he promised. 'I want to be with you as much as I can. When we are apart there is a void in me crying to be filled. I imagine you walking the streets of Whitby, climbing the Church Stairs to photograph the abbey or the roofs through the smoke haze curling skywards from the chimneys. I see you setting your camera to photograph the shop fronts, or the yards and their houses climbing the cliffside. I want to be with you, sharing every experience, for in sharing there is a closeness to transcend all others, and in that lies joy.'

His hands had settled on her waist as he was speaking. She gave a little shiver of excitement at his touch. He drew her to him then, his eyes never leaving hers, and she revelled in the love she read there.

During the second week in May Arthur alighted from the coach and lost no time in reaching the house in Well Close Square where his first action was to draw back the curtains. He went to the studio and opened the curtains there so that the north light could fall upon the painting on which he had been working last week. He surveyed his work for a moment before going to the hall and placing the paintings he had brought for Mr Redgrave in a convenient place. They must wait until he had contacted Colette. He would not venture from the house in case she called while he was out. He went back to his painting and started to work but his mind was not fully on it.

He recalled Rose's words when he had announced that he would be going to Whitby again soon and that he was likely to be away three nights. She had observed that he was visiting the town more frequently, and that now he proposed to be away an extra night. He wondered if he had grown careless but drew comfort from the fact that she had seemed appeased by being told that he was engaged on an important commission, which would bring them a sizeable sum. But he warned himself that he would have to be more

481

cautious in the future. If his relationship with Colette were marred in any way he would be mortified and that could have a disastrous effect on his work. He fully recognised that every time he took up a brush he was not painting for a client, only for Colette. She had become his severest critic but every word was constructive. He recognised her worth and knew he would never receive praise from her unless it was warranted.

He heard a knock on the door, dropped his brush and flew through the hall. He jerked open the door. As he held her in his arms he kicked it closed. Their kiss was long and passionate, making up for the time they had spent apart and pointed a way through the summer.

The knock on the drawing-room door was followed by the appearance of Betsy. Rose raised her eyes from her sewing and gave the maid a questioning look.

'Two ladies and two gentlemen, are asking to see you, ma'am.'

'Well, who are they?' asked Rose a little tetchily because she had had to put the question when Betsy was quite capable of following the rules she had set down about announcing visitors.

Betsy's face crimsoned at the rebuke in her tone. 'I don't know, ma'am. They would not say. Said they wanted to surprise you.'

Rose's lips tightened. She was on the point of refusing to see them, deeming it ungentlemanly, and certainly not ladylike, to arrive unannounced and refuse to identify themselves, but she was piqued by the possibility of a surprise. 'All right,

I'll come.' She certainly wasn't going to let strangers beyond her hall. She laid her sewing down carefully.

'I'm coming too, Mama,' said Marie, sliding from the window seat where she had been reading. She followed her mother into the hall where Betsy scurried past them to open the front door. Four people stood on the step, laughter on their lips and merriment in their eyes.

'Surprise! Surprise!' they all called at once.

The two women stepped into the hall and swept an astonished Rose into their arms.

The two men shouted their greetings and then looked at the bewildered child. 'You must be Marie,' one of them said as he held out his hand which she automatically took. The other gave her a broad smile and winked, and then contributed to the uproar that filled the hall.

Rose had still not got over the shock. 'Lizzie! Grace! Fred! Ben!' Her eyes ranged from one to the other yet took them all in at once. 'Oh, it's good to see you all again. Come in, come in.' She ushered them to the drawing-room. 'What are you doing here?'

'We thought we'd take a September holiday, set us up for the winter!' replied Lizzie.

Marie's bewilderment was swept away by her mother's joyous mood. She smiled up at Fred when he took her hand again.

'Betsy,' Rose called over her shoulder, 'some tea, please.'

'Yes, ma'am.' Pleased to see her mistress in such a good mood, Betsy hurried to the kitchen where she acquainted the rest of the staff with the news.

'Sit down, find a chair,' called Rose with a wave of her hand that encompassed the room.

Fred found himself an armchair and perched Marie on his knee when he sat down.

'Flirting again, Fred, and we've only just arrived,' teased his sister Lizzie.

'You have quite a reputation yourself,' chided her husband Ben light-heartedly.

'What's flirting mean?' asked Marie, looking coyly at Fred.

He grinned. 'It means I like you.'

She cocked her head on one side. 'Then *I'm* flirting with *you*.'

Peals of laughter rang round the room.

'Now tell me all about yourselves,' said Rose, putting a brake on the hilarity.

'All in good time,' said Ben. 'Where's Arthur? He may as well hear it too.'

'He's in Whitby. Won't be back until the day after tomorrow.'

The four visitors looked disappointed. 'Then we'll miss him,' said Grace. 'We return to Leeds that day.'

'No, we won't,' put in Fred brightly. 'Do you know where he'll be in Whitby?'

'He has a small house in Well Close Square that he uses for a studio. He receives a number of commissions for Whitby scenes and it seemed a good idea for him to have a studio there, not waste time travelling.'

'Good. We'll all go to Whitby tomorrow and surprise him, and you and Marie will come too.'

Rose was about to protest that she didn't like Whitby but saw the light in her daughter's face

484

and knew she would be disappointed if they did not accept this invitation. Besides it would be throwing kindness back in the face of dear friends if she refused. 'That's kind of you.'

'Not at all. And what's more, we have a lot to talk about so you and Marie are invited to dine with us this evening.' Fred saw the protests rising to Rose's lips. He held up his hand to stop her and said, 'We won't take no for an answer.' Everyone else murmured their agreement.

There were three other people for the coach the following morning. The two gentlemen offered to ride outside while the young woman, who was travelling to see her parents, was able to ride inside when Fred offered his knee to Marie.

It was a pleasant ride filled with eager conversation into which the five friends drew the young lady travelling alone.

As the coach was drawing into Whitby, Rose said to the young woman, 'If your parents live in Whitby you must be familiar with it. Can you direct us to Well Close Square?'

'I am going near there myself. If you walk with me I'll direct you.'

'That is most kind.'

Leaving behind the bustle that always accompanied the arrival of a coach at the Angel, the young lady guided them to Skinner Street where she pointed out Well Close Square. They made their goodbyes and a few minutes later were standing outside Arthur's house, all of them charged with excitement at the surprise they were going to cause him.

Chapter Twenty-two

The early September warmth flowed into the house in Well Close Square when Arthur opened the door to Colette. There was rapture in her eyes when they kissed but before she could disclose her joy, he took her hand and started towards his studio. 'Come,' he said, teasing laughter in his eyes.

'A new painting for me to see?'

He did not reply but, on entering the room he asked her to sit down.

She looked at him questioningly but did as she was bid.

'Turn your head a little to the left.' He stood back to observe as he said, 'I'm going to draw you.'

She laughed, 'Why waste time on me?'

'It's something I've wanted to do ever since I first saw you, but now our relationship has developed in such a way that I read much more into your expression and I must capture it.' When he was satisfied that the position was to his liking he picked up his sketchbook and pencil.

Not wanting to disturb his concentration she kept silent.

An hour later he was finished with his sketch. It had been one of the most fulfilling hours he had spent.

'Can I see?'

As she came to him he wrote across the bottom of the page 'Colette. 8th September 1866'.

The rap on the front door brought a questioning glance from Colette. 'Are you expecting anyone?' she asked, her eyes filling with worry.

Arthur was on his feet. The knocking came again. As he opened the door to the hall they could hear voices outside. More than one person. In fact, it sounded like several. Colette was curious. She too rose from her chair and went to the door, which Arthur had left open. She waited just inside the room. All she could discern from the enthusiastic shouts that came from the visitors was that they were friends of Arthur.

'Surprise! Surprise!' Six voices shouted at once.

'He's speechless!'

'We aren't ghosts.'

'Hello, love. They persuaded me to come.'

That greeting froze Colette. Who had addressed Arthur in that way? Who was that woman? But the next voice tore at her heart.

'Papa! Papa!'

The child could only be shouting at Arthur. If she was the daughter of one of the newcomers there would be no such excitement.

'Well, aren't you going to ask us in?'

Colette recognised the voice as that which had used the term of endearment. Panic gripped her. She had a strong urge to disappear but there was nowhere for her to go. She was trapped. She retreated from the door, her body tense, her mind numb, her eyes fixed on the doorway, unable to tear them away.

The woman who appeared stopped on the

threshold. She stared in disbelief at Colette. As the others crowded in behind her, their jocular conversation faded into curiosity and bewilderment.

Rose immediately interpreted the situation and had it confirmed by the flush that suffused Colette's face. She clearly bore the embarrassed look of someone who had been caught in a compromising position. Rose's body and mind were numb with shock. She had the almost overwhelming desire to break down, but drew strength from deep inside and took up a formidable stance as she faced a woman who was much younger than herself. And yet there was a look of bewilderment about this stranger, as if she did not quite know what was going on. Rose realised that this person may not know the true situation. She knew that she had to strike without preamble. She drew herself up and fixed Colette with eyes that left her in no doubt that she was about to hear the truth. 'Good day to you. I am Arthur's wife!'

The words thundered in Colette's mind. Betrayed! Duped! Tears welled in her eyes but she fought them back. Determined there would be no scene in which she would belittle herself, she scooped up her coat and bonnet in one sweeping movement and made for the door. She strode past Rose and a clear way automatically opened between the people crowding the doorway. With head held high, she ignored them all. Only when she reached Arthur did her step falter for a fraction of a moment, time enough to say, 'How could you?' with all the contempt she could muster. He could not meet her accusing eyes. She swept out of the house without bothering to slam the door.

As she walked from Well Close Square towards Skinner Street she heard the door close. It marked the end of a life in which she had loved with all her heart. As she realised the bitter truth Colette cried.

She turned towards the West Cliff. Fewer people would be there and eventually there would be no one. She kept her head bowed, hiding the way she dabbed at her eyes with her lace-edged handkerchief. Her horror at what had happened, her shame, and regret, were mastered by the time she found herself alone. She walked on and with each step purged the memories of the times she and Arthur had walked this way. Those happy times were gone for good, besmirched by his betrayal, and she determined that by walking here now she would eradicate them forever. She had her future to consider, and in that future there would be a child and Arthur must never know. Never!

But that determination brought a problem, for Adele and Susan would become embroiled and Colette wanted no stigma attached to them, nor did she wish to hear them say, 'We warned you.'

Her thoughts remained confused as she sought a solution. Until the path dipped into a small hollow and she was reminded that she had also walked this way with Bernard.

Rose never knew who actually closed the door of the house in Well Close Square but she immediately took charge of the situation. She was not going to be shamed further in front of her friends from Leeds. Arthur had been caught out: that was sufficient humiliation for him for the moment. She certainly wasn't going to create a scene now, one that would bring more harm to Marie than to herself. Children's minds were sharp, they took things in, and though they may not understand them at once, incidents like this dwelt in receptive minds and pushed themselves forward later, with possibly disastrous results. Now she must protect Marie from witnessing such unpleasantness.

She sent Arthur a glance of withering contempt and was pleased to see his total embarrassment in front of his friends. He did not know what to say or do. So Rose took charge.

'The key to this house, Arthur, please,' she said, an authoritative note in her voice. She knew that, in front of everyone, he could do no else but comply.

He fished in his pocket and without a word handed the key to her.

'Now, everyone, as our day has not turned out as expected, I think it would be best if we hired a coach and returned to Scarborough immediately.'

'Maybe you would prefer it if you and Arthur returned alone,' suggested Grace.

'It does not matter to me,' she replied briskly, 'but I don't want to spoil your day. If you would like to see something of Whitby, you must stay and return later.'

'That might be the best,' said Lizzie. 'Why doesn't Marie stay with us?'

'Would you like to stay with Auntie Lizzie and

Auntie Grace, love?' asked Rose.

'Yes, may I?' replied Marie. She sensed something was wrong, though she didn't know the details except that it must have had something to do with the lady who was in the house when they arrived to surprise her father.

'Of course you may.'

'We'll have a splendid time,' said Lizzie, putting her hand on Marie's shoulder.

'Will you hire a carriage from the inn where we disembarked on arrival?' asked Fred.

'Yes.'

'Then we shall walk that way with you, find the time for our coach and then you will know what time we will arrive back in Scarborough.'

'Very well,' agreed Rose. 'We will all dine together this evening. I will have booked somewhere by the time you return.'

Lizzie was surprised by this suggestion. 'Are you sure?' she asked, perturbed that prolonging their association at this time might prove awkward for her friend.

'Of course I am.'

Lizzie caught the look of despair that Arthur shot his wife, as much as to say. 'Please don't pile on the agonising embarrassment any further.' She knew Rose had deliberately made the suggestion exactly to do that, and smiled to herself. Lizzie would play along just as she knew the others would. Arthur deserved as much. He had obviously betrayed his wife and that would take some forgiving. He had played a loose game. If he wanted to do that he should have been careful enough to remember the maxim, 'Don't get caught.'

Not a word was spoken until the hired carriage had climbed out of Whitby. It was Arthur who could stand the silence no longer.

'I'm sorry,' he mumbled.

'Don't apologise, Arthur,' said Rose, her tone severe enough to send a chill through him. He knew she would hold his behaviour over him like the Sword of Damocles. He would ever wonder when she would cut the thread and destroy his life. 'Just tell me who she was?'

Arthur's silence was morose.

'Tell me!'

Arthur knew from her delivery that he could not avoid it. 'Her name is Colette Shipley. She's a photographer who lives in Whitby. We became interested in each other's work and...'

'That will do,' Rose interrupted. 'You never told her you were married. I could tell that from the astonished look on her face when I announced who I was. That poor girl!'

Arthur was taken aback. He had never expected Rose to sympathise with Colette. That struck him hard. It would have been easier had she ranted and raved at him, but to punish him with understanding Colette's feelings pierced him to the heart. He did not know what to say except, 'How did you find me?'

She gave a little mocking laugh. 'You told me yourself when you bought the house. Did you not intend to? Was that a slip? "Be sure your sins will find you out".'

He cursed himself silently. After a few minutes

he asked. 'Why did you have to invite them to dine with us tonight? The evening can only be fraught with embarrassment.'

'They are our friends, here on holiday. It is up to us to make them welcome.'

'But how can we act as if nothing had happened?' he said testily.

'I will, and you had better because that is how the future is going to be for us.'

Rose warned him of that point again when they were ready to go to meet their friends at a hotel on the South Cliff where she had booked a table.

First she went to say good night to Marie. She kissed her daughter who flung her arms round her mother's neck and said, 'Who was that lady in Whitby?'

'A friend of your father's.'

'Will we be seeing her again?'

'No.'

'Does that mean we won't be going to Whitby again?'

'We will all go when your Father has pictures to deliver, but it will only be for the day.'

Marie nodded.

But Rose saw a puzzled frown come over her daughter's face and quickly said, 'You don't have to worry about anything. It will be all right.' She heard footsteps behind her and saw Arthur coming into the room. She said nothing more but stepped to one side.

'Who's my girl?' said Arthur, using the expression he always did when he said goodnight to Marie.

'I am,' she said, but did not smile tonight.

Arthur sensed she was puzzled. He kissed her on the forehead. 'Sleep sound. All is well.' As he turned he took Rose's hand in his, making it obvious to Marie, a gesture to assure her his last statement was true.

Rose made sure that the embarrassment everyone felt when they met that evening was quickly dispelled. She saw the conversation remained lively. Their friends responded in kind. They talked of happy times in Leeds, of the cricket matches, their excursions to Kirkstall and surrounding area, recalled Queen Victoria's visit, and of course their families.

It did not take Arthur long to realise what Rose was doing. She had no intention of bringing up his relationship with Colette again. As far as she was concerned it was a thing of the past, a momentary hitch in their marriage, and by ignoring it Rose knew she was inflicting punishment on him. Talking about Colette, even in disparaging terms, was something she was determined not to do because it would only heighten his affection for her, only help to keep her in his mind. She would never know, indeed could never know, if thoughts of Colette were ever eradicated from his mind completely but of one thing she was certain: she would not encourage them by so much as mentioning her rival's name. She wondered, had he loved her? But even as that thought came to mind Rose dismissed it as of no consequence; she was his wife and she would never let him go.

With that determination came the resolve that their life, in every aspect, would remain as it always

494

had been; she would hold back in no way, even though there was no likelihood of another child. Maybe there had been times when she'd let that disappointment become too obvious to Arthur. She saw his misdemeanour as a signal that maybe she had let their marriage go stale by not being as responsive as she should have been. Now she could put that right. Tonight would be the start of a new life for them, brought about by an innocent visit from their friends. She looked round them all as they sat at their table and silently thanked them. Finally her eyes came to rest on her husband at the opposite end of the table. He looked up and met her gaze. It said, 'I am your wife, Arthur. I love you, don't ever forget it.'

He read her unspoken message, clear and strong. The conversation flowed around him unheard He realised his wife was trying to eradicate all thoughts of Colette from his mind, but she could never do that. He could always keep her memory alive. She would always be there. But how he wished that he could talk to her, try to explain, tell her what she had meant to him. Still did. He pictured Colette, trying to remember her beauty, the charm that was reflected in her eyes and smile, but all that he saw was the horror on her face and the condemnation in her eyes as she fled their house in Well Close Square.

He realised from Rose's behaviour and frame of mind since the encounter in Whitby that she expected a normal life to be resumed, and God help him if he didn't fall into line. For one moment he was on the point of rebellion but he caught that look from her and knew he could never do it, for she would never let him go and in that look he also read, 'Don't you dare break Marie's heart. My child is precious to me and she had better be just as precious to you.'

As he brought his glass of wine to his lips he made a silent toast: 'To you Colette, may you be happy in your future. Forgive me.'

As soon as she came in from walking on the West Cliff, Colette went straight to her room and without a second thought took down Arthur's painting of her. It could not be part of the future she envisaged now. She slashed it savagely with a knife, venting all her pent-up feelings against him. She found one of the servants then, telling her to get rid of it and tell no one. Next she found Adele and Susan in the drawing-room and made an announcement that took them by surprise.

'I have been to the Angel and have booked three seats for us on the coach to Scarborough tomorrow.'

'But...' started Adele, eyes widening with curiosity.

'Why?' asked Susan, a little more suspicious as to the motive behind Colette's action.

'I thought it time we took up Bernard's open invitation to visit now that his hotel is finished.'

'But shouldn't we have contacted him first, to make sure it will be all right to go?'

'I have already done that,' replied Colette with a smile of satisfaction that hid the pain that still tore at her. 'I paid for a rider to take a message to him and return with an answer. He'll do so later today. If it's not convenient I can cancel our seats on the coach.'

'Why so quick? Why now?' asked Adele.

'Impulse, dear sister, impulse. But it will give us the opportunity to show Bernard some more of my photographs.' She started for the door. 'I suggest we all pack for the visit. I said we would take three rooms for a week.'

As the door closed, Adele and Susan looked askance at each other.

'What's brought this on?' said Adele

'I don't know,' replied Susan. 'Do you think she has changed her mind about Bernard?'

Adele gave a shrug of her shoulders. 'Is Arthur in Whitby?'

'Not that I know of,' replied Susan. 'Why? Do you think that he's invited Colette to see his mother?'

'If that was so I think she would be visiting Scarborough just for the day, not staying a week.'

'And Bernard wouldn't come into that.'

'Do you think she's changed her mind about his proposal?'

'I wouldn't have thought so, but anything is possible. Maybe something has happened between her and Arthur.'

'I'll ask her.' Sisterly curiosity had been stimulated and when that happened Adele could be terrier-like and never let go until she knew the truth.

Susan knew this and quickly advised, 'You'd better not tackle her. If there is anything that she wants to tell us, she will. We'll get to know more if she does it in her own good time.'

This turned out to be true. Colette had decided

that she would feel better for telling Adele and Susan what had happened and so, over the evening meal, she informed them of the morning's event. They heard her through without interruption, only silently displaying their shock until she had finished. Then they were not critical of her, or her behaviour, but horrified by Arthur's deceitful conduct. She brushed their sympathy aside, saying that she had learned a lesson and that she was not going to let what had happened mar her life.

They had just finished their meal and were crossing the hall to the drawing-room when a maid came hurrying from the kitchen to say that a horseman was at the back door and had brought this message for Miss Colette.

Colette read the note quickly, looked up and smiled as she announced, 'We can go.' She turned to the maid. 'See that the rider has something to eat and tell him there is no answer.' As Susan closed the door after they had entered the drawing-room, she said brightly, 'This is the start of a new future for you, Colette.'

She tried to keep that in mind as she went to bed. She had determined on the path she would take and the start had been her decision to go to Scarborough but, snug in her feather bed, in the quiet of her room, Arthur crept back into her thoughts. Hurt as she was, confounded by his deceit, she still recalled the happy moments they had shared, time when they'd seemed one in thought and drew strength from each other. But should her suspicions have been aroused by his reluctance to let her meet his so-called mother?

She had trusted him, and shouldn't trust be the cornerstone of any true, loving relationship? But it needed honesty as well, and finally the truth had come out. Shocked and hurt as she had been, she knew that there would always be a corner of her heart set aside for Arthur. Married or not, she knew that he had loved her. But she also knew there was nothing she could do about it, for she had seen, as Rose's hostile expression had faded into sympathy, that his wife would never let him go and that was not only because of her love for him but was also to safeguard their daughter.

With this last thought Colette drifted off to sleep, having returned to her resolution that there was a future for her there and she had made the first step on a new road.

The following day, Bernard greeted them kindly without being overpowering. He was considerate of their welfare on their journey, solicitous to see that the care and attention that they received from his staff was second to none. The rooms he had allocated them were first class and he had assigned his best maid, Peggy, to be there for them at all times. As he left them to settle in he told them they were to dine with him that evening as his guests.

'He's out to impress you, Colette,' observed Adele. 'I think he hopes you have reconsidered his proposal. After what has happened, I suppose...'

'It is my decision that counts,' Colette interrupted. 'You will hear that when I decide what is right.'

They had taken up seats in a window in the

large lounge from where they had a view of the South Bay and of the harbour with the ruined castle behind on its rocky promontory.

'Don't either of you breathe a word about Arthur and what happened. That is all in the past and should never be allowed to mar the future. Promise me you will never, ever say anything that will hurt Bernard?'

They both gave her their word.

Susan looked seriously at her then. 'I must say this, Colette. If you have come here with the purpose of altering the answer you gave to Bernard, be careful of doing so on the rebound. Hasty decisions embarked on in such a way often spell disaster.'

'Susan, I appreciate what you are saying but...'

'I am not going to be drawn into discussion. You know the situation better than I. All I'm saying is, think about what you are doing.'

Colette leaned forward and took her hand. 'I will, Susan. Thank you for your concern.' She gave a wry smile. 'Besides, he may not ask me again.'

But Bernard did just that. He had taken Colette to a concert at the Spa. Both Adele and Susan had graciously refused to accompany them. When the crowds thinned as they left the Spa, Colette sensed an impulse between them, one that draws two people to each other in mutual understanding. Seeing they were alone, he stopped walking and took her hands in his. Bernard's expression was serious when he said, 'I have lived in hope since I proposed to you in Whitby. I stayed away for fear of crowding you. When you sent me that note saying you would like to come and stay my hopes rose again. Was I wrong to let them?'

She gave a little shake of her head. 'No, you weren't.'

'Then there is...'

'I will marry you, Bernard.'

For one moment he stared at her as if he could not believe what he had heard, then with all the joy that surged through him he swept her into his arms and kissed her long and passionately. When he drew away but still held her, afraid to let her go in case she vanished and his dream was shattered, he said, 'You have made me the happiest person in the world.'

'A night I will always remember,' Colette whispered. She turned so that she could snuggle close to his side with his arm around her and look out across the sea, its gentle undulations shimmering in the moonlight. 'Beautiful,' she said, her voice hushed. 'And so peaceful.'

'As our future will be,' he promised. 'When shall we be married? Or do you want a long engagement?'

'I don't,' she replied. Though her tone was quiet her words were forceful. 'Why waste precious time?'

'Exactly my sentiments,' he said. 'I don't want to risk losing you.'

'You won't, Bernard. Let's get married four weeks from today.'

'So soon?'

'Why not? Is that too much of a rush?'

'No. It can be done. Would you like to marry here in Scarborough? It will be easier for you. We can have the reception at the hotel so that can be arranged straight away.'

'Oh, Bernard, that is splendid! We'll go and book the church tomorrow morning, then I'll know it is all in hand before we return to Whitby.'

He turned her to him and said, 'We'll remember this night always.'

'We will, my love,' she said.

A month later they were married in the parish church not far from the castle. That morning Arthur was roaming the old town in search of vantage points. He carried a folding stool in one hand and the other rested on a satchel slung over his shoulder containing art supplies. A commission for a painting of Scarborough's South Bay had brought him here.

He neared the parish church and saw among the number of carriages drawn up on the roadway that one was decorated in wedding ribbons, waiting to welcome the newly married bride and groom and carry them off into the future. He was going to pass by but then hesitated. Here was an opportunity to do some quick impressions of the departing wedding party that might come in useful. He set his stool down a little distance away so that he would not be intrusive and started to draw carriages, horses, and the men in charge. He worked quickly for he knew he might not have long before the ceremony was over. He was satisfied with his efforts and had one more carriage to complete when he heard voices and laughter and knew the wedding party must be leaving the church.

He looked up and his whole being froze. He felt

utterly numb and helpless. Only his voice seemed real and that was only a whisper, barely audible. 'Colette!' He stared unbelievingly yet drinking in her beauty. Memories of her returned full force as he saw the lovely original. There was laughter on her lips, brightness in her eyes, and they combined to express happiness. Arthur was hardly aware of the man standing beside her except that he was lovingly attentive. For the one moment that he observed the bridegroom Arthur knew that Colette was in good hands, had married a man who adored her. He was thankful, pleased and jealous all at the same time.

The carriage began to move off. There were shouts, laughter. Colette threw her bouquet high in the air above the crowd. It fell. She saw it caught by Adele. She turned to Bernard to make some remark but it was never uttered. A figure with sketch-pad in his hand, sitting on a stool, seemed frozen in time. Their eyes met. Arthur saw her lips silently mouth his name. Then the carriage had passed him. He saw her look back over her shoulder as if she wanted to make certain whom she had seen.

He did nothing, made no gesture, still struck with astonishment that he should have been there at the precise moment she left the church. Hastily he gathered his things and moved away before Adele and Susan, whom he now recognised, should see him. He walked home slowly, all desire to draw gone. Visions of days spent with Colette tumbled through his mind and, though he had subdued them by the time he reached home, he knew he still loved her.

Colette carried the sight of that man sitting on the stool as far as the hotel. It disturbed her, though she hid her unease and automatically joined in Bernard's exuberant happiness. She too was happy and let that be seen though she knew now that she still had some love for Arthur. By the time they had reached the hotel she had resolved upon one thing and the opportunity to express it came more readily than she'd anticipated.

During the wedding breakfast Bernard whispered to her, 'You haven't told me what you would like as a wedding present and this day should not pass without your telling me.'

'But you bought me this pearl necklace,' she replied, fingering it around her neck.

'Yes, but that was so you would always remember today's ceremony. You must have something to make you recall the whole day. Haven't you anything in mind?'

'Well...' She hesitated.

'Come on, out with it,' he pressed.

She gave a little shake of her head. 'It's too much to ask.'

'I'll be the judge of that. Besides, nothing is too much for my beautiful Colette. Tell me.'

'I would like to live in Whitby.'

'Is that all? Then you shall.'

She looked at him in amazement. 'Just as easily as that?'

'Yes.'

'But what about this hotel?'

'I've a very good staff. I don't need to be here all the time. We can have a room set aside for us for the few occasions we shall have to come. So

Whitby it shall be.'

Colette felt a huge relief. It had not crossed her mind until today that there was more likelihood of bumping into Arthur in Scarborough than there was in Whitby, for she guessed his wife would keep a tight rein on visits to William Redgrave's.

Even among the buzz of the reception Bernard let his mind consider more deeply Colette's request. Just before the speeches started he put his idea to her. 'How would you like to live in your old home in Whitby? Though it's hardly old, you've barely left it.' He smiled at the bewilderment on her face. 'I mean it.'

'But what about Adele and Susan?'

'I saw Adele and a young man at the wedding making a great fuss of each other, as you can see now.' He indicated the couple at a nearby table.

'Jeremy Wentworth,' she said. 'He has been escorting her to some functions in Whitby.'

'And she caught the flowers you tossed.'

Colette laughed. 'You don't believe in those old superstitions, do you?'

'They are romantic.'

'Maybe, but we may have to wait a long time for them to work...'

'I don't think so.' He cast another look at the couple.

She followed his gaze and saw them holding hands, heads close together in deep conversation. Colette wondered why Adele hadn't said how close her relationship with Jeremy was getting.

'You see what I mean?'

She nodded. 'But there's Susan'

'Yes. I've thought of her. With you and Adele married, the house will be rather big for her. So what I propose is that I buy their shares in it. That will enable Adele and Jeremy to find a home of their own and Susan to find somewhere more suitable to her needs and close at hand, for I know you would like her to be near if we are to be in Whitby.'

'Bernard, you are a wonder. If all that works out it will be marvellous.'

Chapter Twenty-three

'I have two paintings ready for Mr Redgrave,' Arthur announced to Rose two weeks later.

'Very well, we shall go the day after tomorrow. I've been thinking over what should be done about paintings for Mr Redgrave. You have a collection of sketches of Whitby?'

'Yes.'

'Good. On this occasion we will deliver the finished works, but you will give him to understand that in future they will be delivered by carrier, and from now on commissions will be arranged by letter.'

'But...'

'There are no buts,' Rose broke in sharply. 'These are my terms and they will be adhered to. While we are in Whitby we will arrange for the house in Well Close Square to be sold.'

Arthur felt dejected but knew there was nothing he could do. The consequences of not falling in with Rose's proposals could be catastrophic, especially for Marie. He was not going to jeopardise his daughter's happiness.

Two days later, as they made their way to the coach, Marie was excited at the prospect of the ride and seeing Whitby again. She did not fully understand the events that had taken place on their arrival at the house in Well Close Square. It had involved a stranger, a lady, but beyond that the outcome had not really impinged on her mind. It was the time she had spent there with their friends from Leeds that she remembered.

Arthur saw the excited light in his daughter's eyes as they got their first glimpses of the town and wondered if Whitby had made the same first impression on her as it had on him.

As Arthur turned to help her from the coach, Rose said, 'We'll go straight to Mr Redgrave's then come back here to the Angel to dine and await the coach for our return.'

'Can't we see the ships, Mama?' The pleading in Marie's voice and eyes could not be denied.

'Very well, Marie. We'll see them on our way back to the Inn.'

Arthur was a little apprehensive when he led them to Mr Redgrave's. The last time he had seen William and Genetta he had had Colette with him. What would be their reaction today?

They were examining a painting and looked round when they heard the shop door open. Their faces lit up and their eyes showed pleasure at seeing Arthur, but there was also curiosity about the lady beside him. He realised he must take the initiative.

'Mr and Mrs Redgrave. I'm pleased to see you again,' he said quickly, 'May I introduce you to my wife Rose and my daughter Marie?' He saw them swiftly disguise their surprise.

'We are pleased to meet you, Mrs Newton.' Genetta inclined her head in greeting.

'The pleasure is reciprocated,' replied Rose. 'I must thank you both for all the encouragement you have given my husband through selling his paintings.'

'My dear lady,' said William, spreading his hands in dismissal of the thanks, 'it is we who are privileged to sell his works. Long may we go on doing so.'

'I hope so too,' replied Rose.

'Let us have a look at what you have brought us today.' William edged towards the door to the next room.

'Come this way,' Genetta invited, then turned her attention to Marie, 'Do you draw too?' she asked with a pleasant smile.

'Yes, but I'm not as good as Papa,' she replied brightly. She liked the look of this lady and gentleman.

'Maybe you will be one day.'

'If I am, will you sell my paintings too?'

'Certainly, if we are still here,' said Genetta, exchanging a smile with Rose.

The paintings were placed on two easels and Rose was a little taken aback when William and Genetta waxed greatly enthusiastic about them, mentioning points that she had not even con-

508

sidered. She listened carefully to what they were saying but soon got lost in their analysis and comparisons.

'These will sell immediately,' said William.

That was something Rose understood. 'And you could sell more?'

'Oh, yes. Arthur's work has always sold readily here, as you will have realised. There is something special about an Arthur Newton painting, no matter what its subject. I hope you will go on encouraging him to send more work to us?'

'Oh, certainly, I shall, but I should tell you that in future we will send them to you by carrier.'

William was thunderstruck. He glanced at Arthur who wore a look of resignation. 'I'm sorry about that but if that's the way you want it...'

'It is, Mr Redgrave,' replied Rose firmly so that William and Genetta, who was equally taken aback, knew it was no good trying to persuade them otherwise.

William nodded, a look of disappointment on his face. 'We shall miss the personal contact. I hope this does not mean an eventual cessation of our dealings?'

'Not at all! Hopefully it will mean more work. Arthur will be saving time by not travelling. He can paint new canvasses for you, and if you have any fresh commissions you can let us know.'

Arthur made no comment on this, knowing the value of personal contact.

Genetta had felt the slight tension come into the room at the mention of these new arrangements. She wanted to counteract it, so quickly said, 'Have you come straight from the coach?'

'Yes,' replied Rose.

'Then let me get you some refreshment? Forgive me for not offering before.'

'That is kind,' replied Rose. 'Just a drink. We will be dining at the Angel before taking the coach back to Scarborough.'

'Very well! Hot chocolate?'

'Splendid.'

Genetta started for the door then stopped. 'Would you like to help me, Marie?' She had noticed that the girl was bored with adult talk.

'Oh, yes! May I, Mama?' cried Marie, pleased to find a loophole that let her escape, for a short while, the uninteresting exchanges.

'Yes, but don't get in the way.'

'I won't.' She eagerly followed Genetta who encouraged her to chatter.

When the door closed behind the departing Newtons, William and Genetta stared at each other dumbly until William broke the silence with an astounded, 'Well! What do you think of that?'

Genetta gave a mystified shake of her head. 'I was flabbergasted. There had never been a hint that Arthur was married.'

'And with a child of that age!'

'I thought he and Colette Shipley were...'

'That's just what I thought,' agreed William.

'I wonder if she knows?'

William shrugged his shoulders, then gave a little gasp as if he had just realised something. 'Maybe she does. Maybe Arthur's wife found out about her. That could be the reason for the new arrangements.'

510

'You could be right, but whether Colette knows or not, we are not to say a thing if she comes into the shop.'

That did not happen for two months.

William Redgrave had just taken a mid-morning delivery of two packages from Scarborough. He judged they could possibly be from Arthur and had excitedly called for his wife. She was coming down the stairs into the shop when the Street door opened. She stopped in mid-step when she saw Colette accompanied by a man. Genetta quickly restored her composure and continued on her downward path, wondering who this tall handsome gentleman could be.

William, who had also been surprised by the appearance of Colette, turned from his desk to greet them. As he did so he caught his wife's eye and in the exchange of glances there was the same query.

'Miss Shipley, how delightful to see you.' Genetta had reached the bottom of the stairs by now and gave Colette a warm smile.

'Miss Shipley.' There was pleasure in William's greeting as he bowed to her.

Colette smiled and a mischievous light glinted in her eyes as if she was deriving delight from what she was about to say. 'Mr and Mrs Redgrave, it is no longer Miss Shipley. Meet my husband, Mr Clayton – Mr Bernard Clayton.'

William and Genetta showed their surprise. 'We did not know, Mrs Clayton, but if it is not too late, may we offer our congratulations? And to you too, sir.'

Bernard swept his hat from his head and nodded politely to his new acquaintances. 'It is my pleasure to meet you both, my wife has spoken of you.'

'Bernard has been a dear friend from early days. We married two months ago in Scarborough but have come to live in my old home here in Whitby.'

'We hope you will both be very happy,' said Genetta warmly. Her mind had taken in the significance of that 'two months' and linked it closely with the time that Arthur had introduced his wife to them.

'We are having a rethink about the paintings in the house,' said Bernard.

'And you would like to see what I have on offer?' said William. 'Have you anything particular in mind?'

'No.'

'First, may I ask if you are an artist yourself?'

Bernard laughed. 'No, sad to say, I am not, but I love looking at paintings, seeing what I like about them and trying to discover what lies behind the artist's technique. His choice of viewpoint, colours chosen and what he is likely to be saying through his painting.'

'Very well, let's see if I can tempt you with anything I have in stock. I can always have canvasses commissioned to your requirements.'

'That is good to know.'

In the next hour they looked at several paintings and had decided on three landscapes by a painter who lived in the Esk Valley. William had noticed Colette searching much harder than her husband, moving rapidly from one painting to another. He guessed she was looking for some of Arthur's work. He had hesitated to mention it but when he saw the disappointment on her face, as it seemed she and Bernard had made their final choice, he offered, 'I've just had two paintings delivered from Scarborough. I was about to unpack them when you came in. Would you like to see them?'

He saw a touch of hope come into her eyes. Colette said casually, 'May we, if it is not too much trouble?'

'It is no trouble at all, Mrs Clayton.' He started to unwrap one of the packages while his wife attended to the other.

Genetta held hers back so that the two paintings did not impinge on each other.

William placed his on an easel and stood back. Silence gripped the room. While the Redgraves were charged with the excitement of seeing Arthur's latest painting, which they immediately judged had surpassed anything he had done before, they wondered what effect it would have on Colette for surely she would realise it was Arthur's work.

The instant she saw it she recognised it as a painting, one of several, on which he had been working before their cruel parting. Before her eyes were all the feelings of those days encapsulated in a canvas, even though this was a painting of the abbey. She felt numb; her heart cried out with longing.

'That is truly wonderful.' Bernard broke the silence. 'Such a delicate handling of the light to gain a haunting atmosphere! Even though they

513

aren't there you can feel the ghostly presence of the monks which in its turn creates a feeling of lives long past.' He stepped closer to the painting.

When Colette saw him stoop to read the signature she felt relief that she had destroyed the one Arthur had done of her. Bernard had seen nothing to connect her with this painter.

'Arthur Newton,' he read. As he straightened he asked over his shoulder, 'Do you know anything about him, Mr Redgrave?'

William, wondering what to say, dampened his lips. He saw worry cross Colette's face and realised her husband knew nothing of her association with Arthur. 'He is a Leeds artist whose work has developed so much that I have a constant demand for it.'

'Is this one reserved for anyone?'

'No.'

'Then we shall have it.' Bernard made his decision swiftly but his expression changed to one of apology as he looked at his wife. 'I'm sorry. Colette, I should have consulted you first. Would you like it? It's such a terribly good painting.'

She met her husband's questioning gaze firmly. 'I would love to have it,' she replied.

'Good. We'll take it, Mr Redgrave.' He looked at the painting that Genetta still held so that no one could see it. 'Could that be another by the same artist if they arrived together?'

William removed the painting from the easel to allow his wife to place the other there. A young lady sat on a garden seat; her full dress of light blue was partly overlaid by thin muslin, which matched the drape around her shoulders. The only decoration she wore was a plain black necklace tight to her throat. Her brown hair was frizzed and cut short to her neck. One hand rested on the back of the seat, her other rested on her lap. The garden was exquisitely drawn, its detail brought out by meticulous brush strokes and with colours that complemented the sitter's complexion.

'That is a fine painting,' commented Bernard. 'In the first one, although it is a landscape, I detected a work of love – and by that I mean a love for someone. I wondered who it might be? Now I think it might be the sitter in this second picture. Should we have that one as well, Colette?'

Her answer sprang to her lips but she held it back. She did not want to display hostility. She looked at it for a few moments with a thoughtful expression on her face then said, 'That is only your supposition and the two paintings don't necessarily have to be displayed together. I much prefer the first one.' Colette too had seen the love in the painting of the abbey and knew for whom it was expressed. In the second she recognised the sitter. Although she had glimpsed her only for a few moments on that fateful day, she realised that Arthur had depicted his daughter, Marie, as an adult. She did not want reminding of that, only of the love that she realised from the first painting would always be stored in Arthur's heart. She gave a minute nod to confirm her words. 'Just the first one please, Bernard.'

'Two months,' mused Genetta, when Colette and Bernard had left.

'What's that, love?' asked William, his mind still on the sale he had made.

'Colette said they had been married two months. Well, that would be about the time we had that visit from Arthur and his wife.'

'What are you surmising?' asked William, doubting his wife's speculation even before she had made it.

'Well, I wonder if Colette, after finding out that Arthur was married, turned to a childhood sweetheart?'

'Ah, I see what you are getting at. Love on the rebound?'

Genetta nodded but as she made her way up stairs she muttered to herself, 'Maybe there's more behind it than that.'

Six months later a six-pound healthy boy was born to Colette.

Chapter Twenty-four

'I'll fetch the letters,' Marie announced on hearing something drop through the letterbox.

Her mother smiled and nodded.

Marie slipped from her chair at the breakfast table and hurried from the room.

'There are three,' she informed them when she returned. 'One for you, Papa, and two for Mama.' She handed the letters over and resumed her place at the table where she gave serious attention to her breakfast.

Arthur slit his envelope open with a knife, withdrew a sheet of paper and unfolded it. 'It's from Ebenezer,' he said. His eyes sped across the writing. 'He wants two more paintings of Leeds but would like to discuss them.' He looked up at Rose. 'Aren't you going to open yours?' he prompted, seeing his wife was still handling the letters. He sensed a reluctance to do so.

'This one's from Father. I wonder what he wants?'

'There's only one way to find out.'

'But he never writes. Mother always does that.'

'Maybe he wants...'

Rose was shaking her head to dismiss whatever suggestion Arthur was going to make. 'There's something the matter.' Her fingers were trembling as she broke the seal and smoothed out the paper. The movement of her fingers seemed to unveil the words and, as they did so, the colour drained from her face. 'Oh, no!'

'What is it?' queried Arthur.

'Mama!' There was concern in Marie's voice at the sight of tears welling in her mother's eyes.

Rose swallowed hard and forced herself to keep calm even though her mind was pounding with the words she had just scanned quickly. 'Mother is seriously ill. I must go at once.' She started to push herself from the chair but stopped and picked up the other letter. Her husband and daughter stared at her in silence, waiting for her to tell them who had sent it. 'It's from Lizzie. She wonders if I know about Mother.' Now she pushed herself from the table and was immediately in charge. 'I will get the next train. Send one of the maids to find out its time of departure. Marie, go and tell Betsy I want to see her.'

Marie leaped from her chair and ran from the room. Rose started for the door but Arthur caught her arm and stopped her.

'We'll all go.'

'There's no need.'

'You cannot go alone. You need someone with you.'

She met his gaze. 'That is most considerate of you, Arthur.' He noted the stony quality in her voice. It was always thus at serious moments when even a little tenderness would have been so much better. It was as if she constantly wanted to remind him how he had hurt her through his association with another woman. He had to have this out with her, even if it was a difficult time.

'Have I ever neglected you during these past five years?' Rose hesitated to reply. 'Have I?' he repeated

'No.'

'Then I'll not start now.' He released his hold.

Rose walked from the room without another word.

They arrived at the shop in Leeds to find her father in a despondent state. Rose's first words of enquiry were filled with concern, for she sensed that the situation was worse even than she had expected. There were tears in her father's eyes as he embraced his daughter and she knew from the shake of his head that he feared the worst.

The faint smile that came to Moira's lips was obviously an effort, and there was no strength in her fingers as she took Rose's hand in hers. There was a sense of doom about the whole house. Madge Hobson had stepped in to help run the shop but she could do little but serve the customers and take deliveries. As these fell off with Conan's inattention to ordering, it was decided to close the shop, at least for the time being.

When that decision was made four days after the arrival of Rose, Arthur and Marie, Conan grumbled, 'This would never have been necessary had you not taken up that foolish idea of being an artist and accepted my offer of a partnership instead.' Arthur was taken aback that the elderly man should still bear him a grudge after all this time. He must have seen his putative empire of shops as a reality and brooded on its loss all this time. Arthur felt sorry for him.

'That's unfair, Father.' Rose sprang quickly to her husband's defence. She caught his eye and saw appreciation there. 'Arthur has done very well. His paintings are in demand and we are reasonably well off. I don't think his heart would ever have been in the grocery trade.'

Conan grunted his belief that this was not so and that he was right.

'We are here to ease your days now and to look after Mother, so let's have no more animosity.'

Conan did not reply but bowed his head in resignation to what he knew was not far off and kept his thoughts to himself.

The inevitable happened four days later.

With all the mourners and sympathisers gone from the house, Rose retreated to her room to seek a few minutes in thoughtful contemplation. She was sitting beside the window when the door opened quietly and Arthur stepped in as if reluctant to intrude on her solitude. He set another chair beside her and sat down.

'Rose, I've been giving serious thought to the future during these last few days. I don't know if your father has given you any indication what he intends to do?'

She shook her head. 'None. He's been in too much of a daze.'

'Do you think he'll want to stay here?'

'I don't know. Mother played an important part in running the shop, though much of what she did was behind the scenes. She kept her eye on the stock and did all the ordering to replenish it. Well, you've seen what has happened since she was no longer doing it. I'm worried about Father too. He's hopeless about the house, I'm afraid he'll neglect himself.'

Arthur nodded. This was the same conclusion he had come to. 'How would you like to come back to Leeds to be near him?'

The suggestion came as a shock to Rose. She looked sharply at her husband with enquiring eyes, wishing to know more.

'I am not suggesting he should live with us. That wouldn't work. As you've seen he is still annoyed at me, and besides he would never take to the fact that I was painting.'

'So what are you proposing?' prompted Rose when he hesitated.

'That he sells the shop and buys a house from the proceeds. He won't need a big place and from what he gets for this house and shop, which could thrive again, he would be comfortably off. We would get somewhere nearby and then you and Marie would be able to keep an eye on him.'

'Arthur, that sounds a wonderful idea!' There was heartfelt appreciation in her eyes and for the first time since their arrival in Leeds a new brightness in her eyes. 'I'll be sorry to leave Scarborough, though, I like being there.'

'Then as long as I am making good money, we'll keep our house there and use it as a retreat whenever we feel in need of a change.'

'Do you think all that is possible?' she asked doubtfully.

'We can but try.' He stood up. 'Think it over.' He started for the door.

'Arthur.'

He stopped and turned round. She rose from her chair and stood close to him, looking up into his eyes. 'I've no need to think it over but I'll have to persuade Father.' Her voice lowered, her eyes became misty. 'Thank you.' Rose slid her arms around his shoulders and round his neck. She raised herself on her toes and kissed him with a warmth he had not felt from her for a long time. 'We've loved, Arthur, but something that once was there has been missing. Can we put it back?'

He did not reply but tightened his grip around her waist and kissed her with passion as if that would wipe all memories away.

But memories and dreams can never be erased so easily.

It took Rose a week to persuade her father that Arthur's scheme would be the best way forward for him, though she thought it wise not to mention that it had been his son-in-law's idea. She worked steadily on him without letting up so that on the seventh day when he came down to breakfast and announced, 'It will be good to have you near,' she was delighted to see she had been successful.

During that week Arthur paid a visit to Ebenezer. It had been six months since they had last met and his old friend expressed delight on seeing him again.

'You'll be seeing more of me in the future,' replied Arthur, and went on to tell him of the plans afoot to move back to Leeds and the reason for them.

Ebenezer expressed his sympathy and then got down to serious discussion of Arthur's work.

'I must be frank with you, Arthur. Over the past five years your work has stood still. In fact, I would say it has taken several backward steps. The spark is not there any more. Oh, your paintings are competent and still sell but not as readily as they used to. People who once sought your work because they liked it and those who wanted your work as an investment have fallen away. They still come looking but do not buy as readily as they used to.'

Arthur was only slightly shaken by this information. He had noticed that he had been painting less and less to commissions from Ebenezer and those from William Redgrave had all but disappeared. 'Maybe there is not the same money about?' he offered lamely.

Ebenezer shook his head. 'No, that is not the case. Your paintings lack that sparkle, that something special they once had ... something that came from true inspiration. As I have said before – find it again, Arthur. Find it again.'

He was thoughtful as he walked back to the Duggans' house. Though he had always tried to push it to the back of his mind he knew exactly what Ebenezer meant. There was only himself in his paintings now, there was no sense of Colette. And, of course, nothing he could do about it. Find her and he would destroy too many lives. He would go on being merely a competent painter, one able to support his family but no more than that. He began to wonder what might have been; what heights his paintings could have reached if only he... He dare not contemplate that scenario any further lest he destroy himself in a morass of self-pity.

Two months later they were settled in a house that stood in its own grounds in a pleasant part of Leeds. The choice had come down to two but as Rose pointed out this one had a room that was extremely suitable for a studio. Her observation took Arthur by surprise as the other had a better garden, until she pointed out practically that he was the breadwinner. The shop sold quickly to a local couple who had knowledge of the trade, with the result that Conan was soon settled in a modest house of his own, big enough for his needs, and within easy walking distance of Rose and Arthur.

The move back to Leeds had come too late for Arthur to resume close ties with his own family. His father had suffered serious injuries in an accident in the middle of Leeds when he was rushing home from work, after staying back to receive news of a promotion. Arthur had offered to help at the time but his mother and father had chosen to be near their daughter Celia who had married and moved to Dewsbury, while his brother Oswald had emigrated to America where he was certain he would make his fortune.

Life settled down and Arthur was glad when it did, for now he could get into a routine and concentrate on his painting.

A year later when he took his two latest paintings to Ebenezer he said, 'I hope these two bring a better price than you have been receiving lately.'

The dealer did not answer immediately but went on unwrapping the two paintings. He stood back, surveyed them for a moment, grunted, picked them up and said, 'Follow me.' He led the way up the stairs. As he reached the top he called out, 'Zilda, can you come a minute?'

She came from the kitchen, wiping her hands on a towel as she did so. She stopped when she saw Arthur. 'Hello,' she greeted him pleasantly.

'In here,' called Ebenezer, entering their living room.

He placed the two paintings against a wall on which hung one of Arthur's Whitby paintings. He glanced at his wife. 'Zilda, do you think these two will fetch a better price than we have been getting?'

There was sadness in her voice when she answered, 'I don't, no.' She saw her husband indicate for her to continue. 'Arthur, the two paintings you have just brought are the work of a competent journeyman painter. The artist who created the one on the wall was inspired. That painting promised great things for him. For six years we've been waiting to see that promise fulfilled.'

Arthur said nothing. He knew she was right. His work was adequate, above mediocrity, but held none of the promise it once had. Try as he might to recapture the earlier excitement in his paintings, he always failed to bring that something special to them.

He knew the reason why he failed, knew where the inspiration was and knew he could do nothing about it, nor ever tell Ebenezer and Zilda the reason why.

'I'm afraid I must go to Scarborough, love. The change of management needs my attention at the hotel. It will seem strange going without you but I will be back as soon as I can.' Bernard's glum expression betrayed his wish that he had not to leave Colette.

'I'm sorry too, Bernard,' she offered, 'but I think, with Edward not too well, it will be better if I stay.'

'Take care of him, he's very precious. As are you, my love.'

Bernard left later that day. Colette did not venture out for the next two, wanting to be there if Edward needed her. On the third day there was a turn for the better and, feeling immense relief that her son would recover, Colette took the chance to get some fresh air while leaving him in the care of a nurse.

Reaching the West Cliff, she paused to gaze across a sea that ran fast before the wind. The waves, flecked with white, moved in line towards the long curve of sand that reached the cliffs beyond Sandsend. In the opposite direction the stone piers protecting the river mouth defied the searching waves, repelling their onslaught in surging foam and spray. Colette breathed deep on the exhilarating air, enjoying the fresh chill it brought to her lungs. She glanced round. She was alone. She pulled at the ribbons of her bonnet and swept it from her head. She revelled in the feel of the wind through her hair and with it came a sensuous recollection of Arthur sending it streaming down her back. She forced such thoughts from her mind. That was long ago and should be a distant memory. She chided herself for entertaining it at all. Nevertheless there had crept into her mind the thought, 'I wonder what happened to him?'

Whether that prompted her steps she never really knew, but she found herself looking in the window of Mr Redgrave's shop. There were several paintings on display. None caught her immediate attention, something she always relied on when forming an opinion. She felt a sense of disappointment that none stimulated her imagination and let her eyes drift across them again, taking in second impressions. She gave a little start. That one to the right-hand side of the display must be one of Arthur's. Though it was of only mediocre execution, there were unmistakable aspects of his work that she recalled. She felt disturbed. Once, Arthur's painting would have commanded an exclusive display in this window.

She turned to go but was held back by a moment of indecision. Then she pushed the door open and stepped inside.

'Mrs Clayton, how nice to see you. It's been some time.' Mr Redgrave greeted her with pleasure.

'I'm afraid my photography has been neglected a little of late but the way is becoming clearer to pursue it again. Would you be interested in selling my photographs once more?' She had allowed her photography to take a back seat to devoting her life to Bernard and Edward, but the possibility of taking it up again had been in the back of her mind for a considerable time. She had not thought of mentioning it when she walked into the shop but found herself using it as an excuse to be here when the real reason she had come in was to make an enquiry.

'I most certainly would,' replied William enthusiastically. 'They used to sell well. I always admired your eye for a picture.'

'Thank you, Mr Redgrave, that is a kind observation. I think I learned some of that from Mr Newton.'

'I'm sure you already had it. I don't think it can be truly learned. I think a person either has that gift or hasn't. It can be developed and enhanced but it has to be there in the first place. And even if you have it, you have to put something special into it to make it outstanding. You only have to take Mr Newton's work as an example.'

'That is one of his in the window, to the right?'

'Ah, you noticed it. Yes, there are still characteristics that make it a Newton but it lacks that something special we are talking about.'

Colette nodded her understanding. 'But they still sell?'

'Yes, though not in the way they used to nor at the prices I used to get. He is still a good painter but something went missing from his work and he has never recovered it.'

'Does he still come to Whitby?'

'No. Any work for me arrives by carrier from Leeds, now.'

Sad thoughts about Arthur not realising his true potential dominated Colette's mind as she walked home.

With Bernard's return and Edward's recovery, Colette's life settled back into its pleasant routine that only changed when she broached the subject of resuming her photography on a more businesslike basis. Though she had no need to do so from a financial point of view, Bernard recognised that it was a means of expressing herself, expanding her interests, and using a talent that should not be hidden. He was a forward-thinking man. And so he readily agreed to her suggestion. He realised also that it would reaffirm the previous close relationship with her sister Adele, who had married Jeremy Wentworth, and with Susan who, while not expressing it openly, had seemed regretful that the photography had fallen away. Now all three could take joy in it again.

Both Adele and Susan were delighted at Colette's decision and were only too pleased to be involved, though they gave her to understand that they did not want to be considered as partners, only as helpers.

They were soon to be seen, at least once a week, photographing the town in all its moods, and the ever-changing scenes of Whitby life. Colette's reputation as a first-class photographer spread beyond the town and she began to move further afield, to depict other coastal towns and villages as well as the surrounding countryside.

Arthur settled to his painting in Leeds. He found escape from himself in the hours he spent with brush in hand. He painted principally for Ebenezer, less so for William in Whitby. His work still sold, keeping them comfortably off, and because of that Rose offered no criticism. She'd always appreciated his decision to return to Leeds and did not hold back on her love for him now.

They were both proud of Marie's development not only into a beautiful young lady but also an artist in her own right. Arthur recognised in her the talent he'd had at her age and hoped it would never be thwarted by events as his had been. He hoped that when she married it would be to someone who appreciated her talent to the full. He encouraged her in her efforts, without being intrusive. He was pleased that Rose was not critical of her daughter's desire to paint, and that she tried to see the deeper aspects in her depictions; something she had never tried to do when her husband took up the brush at a critical time in their lives.

Ebenezer was pleased to see this new talent and looked forward to the day when Marie would bring him a painting she considered worth selling. He wished Leeds was still the home of the Steels so that he could display this latest protégée to them but they had moved back to London as the demand for Laurence's work had grown. Maybe one day Ebenezer would take a painting by Marie for them to see, but with his advancing years a journey to London did not present a pleasing prospect.

In 1880, the day after her twenty-first birthday in November, Marie visited Ebenezer's shop.

'Thank you for your magnificent present, Mr Hirst, and thank your wife too.'

He beamed at her gratitude. 'I hope that easel will support many wonderful paintings from the brush of my most beautiful client. Now, I have some news for you. I have sold your painting, *Along the River Aire*.'

Marie gasped. She stared at him, hardly able to believe what she had just heard. 'Mr Hirst, you're wonderful!' She rushed at him, planted a kiss on his cheek and hugged him.

'It's you who did the painting, not I.'

'But you sold it! Please excuse me? I must tell Mama.'

Ebenezer watched her race from the shop and wished he were young again.

Marie's steps were on air as she hurried home. She burst into the house but as she crossed the hall to the drawing-room she felt an uneasy atmosphere. The room was empty. Alarm gripped her though there was no real reason for it. She rushed to the kitchen and found a hush there too where generally all was a-buzz with action and chatter. She hardly needed to ask her question, it was visible on her face. 'Where are Mama and Papa?'

Their cook, a kindly motherly person, came over to her, solemn-faced. 'They were called urgently to your grandfather's.'

Marie did not wait to hear any more. She was out of the kitchen and the house in a flash. She hurried as fast as she could to her grandfather's. She had a special affection for him, even though she did not approve of his grumpiness towards her father when she learned the story behind it. Reaching the house, she found her mother and father in the old man's room. There was no response from Conan when she came to the bedside. Not a word was spoken. Her mother smiled weakly at her as she put an arm round her shoulders and Marie felt comfort when her father's hand took hers.

Tears welled in her eyes as she asked in a hushed voice, 'How bad?'

Her mother swallowed hard and shook her head, as she whispered, 'He had collapsed in this room. How long he lay before he was found...' The words choked in her throat.

Their vigil at the bedside lasted no more than an hour. Rose's father was buried at a quiet ceremony five days later.

There was little to tidy up. Conan had left a will, which bequeathed everything to his daughter except a small legacy to Marie. Arthur was not mentioned. Rose slid her hand into his as they left the reading of the will. 'I'm sorry, love,' she said sincerely.

He shrugged his shoulders. 'Not that I wanted his money, but it would have been something to have had a mention.'

'You were always kind and considerate to him in spite of his attitude, and I thank you for that.'

The house and furniture were sold quickly and, once that was settled, Rose paid a visit to the solicitors and altered her own will, dividing everything she owned equally between Arthur and Marie.

Christmas was a quiet time but, when they had completed their Christmas dinner, Arthur leaned forward on the table; a gesture that Rose and Marie knew was the prelude to some serious announcement. 'Rose, when your mother was ill you felt your duty was to be here and...'

'You made the unselfish suggestion we should move back,' Rose put in.

He dismissed this observation with a slight shake of his hand. 'Then we stayed on because of your father. But I believe your heart has always been in Scarborough. Whenever we managed to get a few days there you always relaxed and enjoyed it. How would you like to move back there?'

Rose did not reply immediately. She looked thoughtfully at her empty plate and slowly fingered her spoon.

Marie, who immediately liked the idea, kept quiet. After all it was up to her mother to decide, but Arthur was aware of the approval in his daughter's eyes.

Rose raised her head slowly. She was solemn-faced as she looked at her husband and daughter. Then her face broke into a beaming smile and her eyes lit up with excitement, and they knew she had teased them with her pretence of doubt. 'Oh, Arthur, it would be lovely! Wouldn't it, Marie?'

'Yes, Mama,' she cried with joyous enthusiasm.

'Then that is settled,' said Arthur with a finality that said everything would be taken care of. 'It will be wise to wait for the spring weather. It will soon be here.'

The Newton house was a hive of activity in early March as furniture was sold or moved to Scarborough along with family heirlooms and personal belongings.

They took no settling in and soon felt as if they had never been away, though Marie now saw the place with adult eyes and a mind that was newly aware of the town as a subject for paintings. Their friends, especially Oliver and Fanny Brooks, were pleased to see them back and soon the Newtons were involved in a new social life, different from that which they had had in Leeds but just as pleasant.

Life settled into a peaceful five years of routine with Arthur continuing to sell his paintings, keeping to his promise of many years ago that he would never leave Ebenezer. The dealer was faithful to Arthur also but wished his protégé would rediscover the accomplishment that had deserted him. Ebenezer drew some hope from the fact that Marie's talent was developing and that one day it might influence her father to resurrect his own lost spark. Marie was devoted to her painting and though she had many suitors and enjoyed a good social life, showed no inclination to marry yet.

Colette, sitting in the window of her sitting-room, which gave a striking view towards the east bank of the river, kept turning her attention to the gateway, seeking her first glimpse of Bernard on his return from Scarborough. She was filled with the happiness he'd brought her and hoped he would never suspect that there had always been a tiny space in her heart reserved for another man.

During the moments she allowed thoughts of Arthur to intrude she would wonder what life would have been like for her if she had not been betrayed. But those were only dreams; the reality was here as she waited for Bernard to return. It would be a joyous meeting, eager and loving.

People walked by, catching her eye, until one riveted her attention. A police constable had turned in at the gateway and was advancing with measured step towards the front door. Colette's heart missed a beat. Why was a policeman calling here? This was the hour when Bernard should be arriving home. Well, the constable would just have to wait for him. Even as she entertained that thought, she had a sense of foreboding. She rose from the window seat and hurried from the room. She was at the top of the stairs when she heard the maid open the door and the constable ask, 'Is Mrs Clayton at home?'

The seriousness of his tone chilled Colette to

the very marrow. Then panic seized her and she flew down the stairs, her feet scarcely touching the steps. The maid turned to announce the visitor. The words were never uttered. Colette's nod indicated that she would take charge.

'Mrs Clayton?'

She nodded again and indicated to the man to step inside.

'I'm afraid I have some bad news. There has been an accident in the town. A horse bolted at the Angel and trampled on Mr Clayton as he was leaving the coach.'

She sensed the answer but still had to voice the question. 'Is he...?'

The constable nodded. 'I'm afraid so, ma'am. He died instantly.'

'Oh, no!' The words were a cry of anguish. Colette slumped on to the chair that stood near the bottom of the stairs. Feeling flowed from her, leaving her numb with shock. The colour drained from her cheeks. She stared in disbelief without seeing anything.

'Ma'am, should I call one of the maids?' the constable asked with deep concern.

All Colette could do was nod and wave her hand in the direction of the drawing-room. 'My son.'

The constable understood her meaning and went to fetch him. A few moments later seventeen-year-old Edward appeared, his face drawn with shock.

'Mother!' He fell to his knees beside her and hugged her round the waist. Her arms circled his shoulders. Each sought comfort from the other as tears held them mute.

The constable hurried from the hall and in a few moments the shocked servants were there to help in any way they could.

'Is there anything more I can do for you, ma'am?' the constable asked.

'If you could call on my sister and our dear friend, I would be grateful.'

'Certainly, ma'am.'

She gave him their addresses and he left the house.

The shock did not ease until Colette watched the coffin lowered gently into the earth between the ancient church and ruined abbey on the wind-swept cliff overlooking the town. Bernard had come to love this place as much as his wife did. As she turned away, with Edward holding her arm, Colette felt numb but realised that as her initial shock had been overcome so would her present feeling. She knew that Bernard would want her to face the future with a brave face and the realisation that life had to go on.

So they remained in the house that held so many pleasant memories for her. Everything that Bernard possessed came to her except for a legacy he had left to Edward. After a month Colette decided that she did not want the responsibility of the hotel, and as Edward had no interest in it, she sold it. She turned more and more to her photography and encouraged Edward with his art. He was grateful for the opportunity that had come his way, for without the necessity to paint for a living, he could devote his time to developing and

536

improving his technique. His mother offered criticism when he asked for it, and he soon realised that she was a shrewd judge of painting particularly the composition of a picture. He wondered from where she had got this insight but readily put it down to her photography.

'Arthur, Fanny is going to Hull next week to a three-day exhibition connected with the jewellery trade. She wants me to go with her. What do you think?' Rose put the question tentatively.

Arthur laid down his newspaper and leaned back in his chair. He knew he would have to be careful with his answer. Rose had not been well these last six months. Her health had been up and down and the doctor had privately mentioned his concern to Arthur.

'I don't like the reoccurrence of this pain though there is no set pattern to it and there are times when it seems to disappear altogether. Has she had any particular worries lately?'

Arthur could think of nothing.

'She is taking the pills I prescribed?'

'Oh, yes, just as you told her.'

'Good. We'll keep a close eye on her. Let me know immediately if you have any suspicion of anything untoward. Meanwhile don't alarm her in any way. Let her lead as normal a life as possible but see that she does not overtax herself.'

These words were in Arthur's mind as he pondered Rose's question. After a few moments he replied, 'I don't see why not. The change could do you good as long as you don't overdo things.'

'Fanny's a very considerate person. I'm sure

she will see that doesn't happen.'

'Then why not?'

'You are sure you don't mind?'

'Of course not.'

'I wish Marie hadn't had to go to see Ebenezer and taken the opportunity to spend a few days with her friends in Leeds.'

'I'll be all right. You go, don't worry about me.'

So it was that Arthur and Oliver saw their wives embark for Hull on Tuesday of the following week. Alone that evening, a glass of whisky beside him, Arthur stared into the dancing flames of the fire. There really had been no need for one, the present settled weather was warm by day though the nights were just beginning to remind people that autumn was not far away. Out of consideration for that, one of the maids had lit the fire while he was having his evening meal.

Nicely satisfied, the whisky bringing a sense of well-being, Arthur sat mesmerised by the flames' movement. The newspaper slipped from his fingers. His thoughts drifted away from the present. He was not conscious of it happening but his days with Colette became vivid in his mind. This had not happened to him for a very long time. For one brief moment he was disturbed, a feeling of guilt touched him, but was gone equally quickly as he settled pleasurably into his thoughts. How long he stayed there he did not know, nor did he care, but when he became aware that he was still in his chair with an empty glass on the table beside him, he found his thoughts of Colette still did not leave him. As he picked up the newspaper the dark print of the date stood out: 7 September

1889. Tension gripped him. Tomorrow was the eighth and that was a special day! The day he had last seen Colette. The day he had made the drawng that still remained in his sketchbook.

He stood up and hurried from the room to his studio. He picked up his brush, stood back from the painting that was half finished, surveyed it and then attacked it, first with bold strokes and then with finer, more delicate touches. The painting took on a new aspect and when he put the final mark upon it and stepped back he saw he had brought to it a new life that had transformed it from merely mediocre to remarkable. His mind focused on his own achievement and he realised instantly that it was thanks to Colette's influence. Arthur cursed himself then. Why hadn't he allowed this to happen before? Instantly he knew the reason. With Rose so close he would have felt guilty entertaining such thoughts and so he had shut them out. Tonight she was in Hull and his mind felt free from any stain of guilt.

The following morning Arthur was out of bed as soon as he was awake. He completed his dressing quickly and had only the shortest of breakfasts before leaving the house to go to the station.

Chapter Twenty-five

As he walked there he felt he was on a pilgrimage, one of his own making. Even as he bought his ticket he felt doubtful about committing himself to the journey especially on this day, 8 September 1889, but the compulsion to return to Whitby and his past overwhelmed any uncertainty. Once he had settled in his seat he recalled the horse-drawn coach he had last used to do this journey twenty-three years ago in 1866, so different from his present mode of transport. Then recollections of yesterday took over; how thoughts of Colette had influenced his painting, and the considerations that had brought him on this journey.

His heart beat faster at the thought of setting foot in Whitby again where so much had happened in his life. But if aspects of his past were to be placed in proper perspective, and he was to allow the inspiration that had come to him yesterday to continue, there could be no turning back now.

The years fell away. He was back in Whitby at last.

On the pier he became so absorbed in his drawing, noting colours and tones alongside his picture, that he was oblivious to people glancing in his direction and did not notice the young man who came to stand behind him and watch, with deep interest, the skill that brought life to swift pencil marks on a sheet of paper.

It was only when he paused to view his drawing with a critical eye and stretch his cramped back that Arthur became aware of the young man.

Thinking that he had disturbed the artist, the onlooker apologised. 'I'm sorry, sir, if I disturbed you. I should not have intruded.'

Arthur gave a dismissive wave of his hand. 'You did nothing of the sort. I'm pleased if my humble drawing is of interest to you.'

The young man gave a gracious inclination of his head as he said, 'It is, sir. It is a wonderful interpretation of that view. Will you do a painting based on that? I see you have made some notes.'

'I hope to. Are you interested in art? Perhaps you are a practising artist yourself?'

'You flatter me, sir, by thinking that, though I love to draw and paint.'

'I am pleased to hear it. Have you any speciality?'

The young man smiled. 'I have attempted still life but my preferences are twofold, people and landscapes, though I must admit I do enjoy drawing the ever-changing scenes around the harbour here.'

'Then you have plenty of subjects to hand.'

'I have, but I don't believe I do them justice.'

'You will. Practise. Practise. Draw, and go on drawing, it is the only way to learn and develop.'

'Thank you for that advice, sir.' The young man hesitated as if he had more to say. 'Do you live in Whitby, sir?' The tentative way he put the question indicated to Arthur that there was more behind it.

He gave a shake of his head. 'No, I don't.' The disappointment that the young man showed prompted him to ask, 'Why?'

He looked embarrassed. 'If you did I was going to pluck up courage to ask if you would look at some of my work and tell me if I showed any promise.'

'Alas, I am only here for the day.'

'Will you be coming again, sir?'

'No. This was a special journey.'

The young man nodded. 'I understand. Well, it has been a pleasure to see you working and to talk to you.' He held out his hand. 'I wish you well, sir.'

Arthur felt a warm, friendly grip. He liked the bright enthusiastic light in this young man's eyes. As he started to turn away Arthur glanced at his drawing and then called, 'I've enough here from which to do my painting and I've time before my train leaves, so if you'd like me to see your paintings now...'

Excitement coloured the young man's face. 'You would do that, sir?'

'If you would like me to?'

'You don't need to ask me that twice, sir.' He held out his hand. 'Edward Clayton, sir.'

'Arthur Newton,' he replied.

Edward stared at him in amazement. 'We have one of your paintings of Whitby. I am privileged that you should be interested in my work.'

'I'm sure it will be my pleasure.'

The young man chattered about art and Whitby as he led the way through the streets. Arthur lost concentration when he saw they were nearing

New Buildings. He answered the young man automatically but his thoughts winged back in time. Colette had lived around here.

'Here we are, sir.' He pushed open a gate.

A chill ran through Arthur. The very house in which she had lived! He had only been inside once but had escorted her there on many occasions. Could she still live here? No! Too many years had passed. She must have left. In a daze Arthur followed the young man along the path to the front door. Edward went straight in and held the door for him. Once inside, he took Arthur's coat and hat and hung them on a stand with his own.

'This way,' he said. He opened a door on the right and, as he strode across the room, said brightly, 'Mother, I've brought a gentleman who is going to look at my paintings.'

The person he addressed was sitting in a chair with her back to the door. He leaned over her and kissed her on the cheek.

As Arthur stepped round the chair Edward said, 'Mother, this is Mr Newton.' He did not notice their reactions for, anxious to fetch his work, he was already moving away. If he had looked back he would have seen astonishment registered on both faces but he would not have been able to read the confusion of thoughts in two minds.

The door clicked shut.

'Arthur!'

'Colette!'

They both spoke at once, amazement in their voices. Then they lapsed into a moment of uneasy silence.

'How are you?' He broke the tension with a

polite question.

'Very well, thank you.' Colette's intonation too was polite. She did not want this unexpected visit to have any unsavoury repercussions for her son.

'You married. Happily, I hope.'

'I married a childhood sweetheart, a fine, generous and considerate man. He died two years ago.'

'I'm sorry. He gave you a personable son.'

Colette acknowledged his comment with an inclination of her head, and said as both warning and plea, 'Edward knows nothing of us.' She quickly added, 'And you?'

'I'm still in Scarborough.'

'Your wife?'

'Not well. She has her good days and her bad days.'

'I'm sorry.'

Arthur gave a shrug of resignation.

'Your painting is not what it was. What happened? You had such promise once.'

He gave a half-smile. 'You kept track of that? Bought one too, I see.' He indicated the painting.

She was not oblivious to the appreciation in his eyes and was pleased by it. 'Not one of your very best, but there was still evidence there of your enormous talent and my husband liked it. I watched your progress by looking in Mr Redgrave's window and whenever I took photographs to his shop. You have not achieved the heights I thought you would.'

He ignored the comment and said, 'I am pleased you kept to your photography.'

'It has helped since Bernard died. Will you be in Whitby again?'

544

Arthur's heart leaped. Was she issuing an invitation? Dare he assume that and say yes? Could he use the excuse that he could help her son with his painting?

An uneasy silence settled between them. Each felt they had so much to say but did not know how to begin. In those moments their eyes held each other's and they knew that the feelings they once had had never been completely extinguished. He had to be truthful with her this time.

'Circumstances enabled me to make a brief visit today,' he explained, 'but ordinarily it is hard for me to get away.'

Colette knew that Arthur had not visited Mr Redgrave's shop for a long time and had assumed that his wife had put an embargo on his coming to Whitby. Why had he done so today? Nostalgia? An attempt to rediscover the past, if only in memory? She found herself wanting answers to these questions and had a strong desire to tell him so much more. But any chance to do so disappeared when Edward returned.

'I'm sorry to have taken so long, but I have lined up some pictures in the hall. I hope I haven't delayed you, Mr Newton?'

'No, I have time. Your mother and I have had a pleasant chat.'

Edward smiled with pleasure. 'I'm so glad.' He edged towards the door and Arthur and Colette followed.

She stood back, close to the foot of the stairs. Arthur made a quick survey of the paintings and then looked at them one by one. He made no comment until he had satisfied himself then glanced at Edward and saw his look of eager anticipation.

'Young man, you have a talent that deserves to be nurtured.' He glanced at Colette. 'Mrs Clayton, encourage him. See that he paints and paints and goes on painting.'

She nodded and said quietly, 'I will.' She knew that Arthur was speaking with conviction, for she too had recognised her son's talent at an early age and had been glad that Bernard encouraged him to draw.

It seemed that Arthur had read her thoughts when he said to Edward, 'Did your father paint?'

'No, sir, but he had an eye for a picture and knew what he liked.'

'Shall we have a closer look?' Arthur suggested.

'If you have time, sir?'

He nodded and for the next half hour analysed some of the paintings, offered advice, and gave the young man numerous tips.

The clock in the hall struck the hour.

Edward started. 'Oh, my goodness, I didn't realise it had got to that time. Mr Newton, please excuse me. I have an engagement in half an hour and must change.'

'Of course.' When Edward had bounded up the stairs with all the exuberance of youth, Arthur turned to Colette with a smile. 'A young lady?'

She gave a little laugh. 'No. He has no one serious though he escorts several. This engagement is with some fishermen. He likes to go out with them.'

'Ah.' Arthur nodded knowingly. 'Hence some of those seascapes.'

'Yes.' A moment's silence fell between them to be broken by Colette. 'Will you take some refreshment?'

The temptation to do so was strong but he deemed it wisest to leave now. 'Thank you, I'm afraid I do not have time. I must be going. I should call on Mr Redgrave. It has been a long time.'

She nodded. 'I understand.'

He retrieved his hat and coat and she accompanied him to the door. She opened it and as they faced each other a charged moment hung between them.

'It has been a pleasure to see you again, Arthur.' The words caught in Colette's throat, and as much as she tried to control it she could not prevent the tears from coming to her eyes.

'The unexpected has turned this day into a truly memorable one for me. It will be a treasure I will long hold in my mind.' He took her hand and felt the warmth of love still there. He kissed her on the cheek, tempted to let his mouth linger.

'Take care of yourself.' She met the longing in his eyes with her own and both knew that their love for each other had never really died. Colette returned his kiss quickly.

He stepped over the threshold and started down the path. She swung the door to, then, with it almost shut, stopped and opened it again so that she could call out to him, 'My son has another name as well as Edward … it is Arthur.'

He stopped in his tracks and swung around but the door had closed.

He stared hard at it.

Edward Arthur? The words made their impact.

'Edward Arthur,' he whispered, then started back towards the house. He took three paces and stopped.

'My son?' Arthur's mind reeled. Was it possible? Was that what Colette had been telling him just before she'd closed the door? And was that action an indication that she wanted the matter closed, wanted him to do nothing about it?

He started forward again. His thoughts clamoured a warning then and brought him to a halt. Dare he reopen the wound that had injured Rose? She was no longer in good health and a shock such as this could be disastrous. And what of Marie? Any revelations made now could devastate her. There was also a risk of destroying Edward's love for his mother, who obviously meant so much to him. And could he betray Colette again by going against her wishes, made plain by the way she'd closed that door?

Arthur turned slowly back and walked away.

Chapter Twenty-six

'Arthur, take Rose to the south coast. I speak to you as a friend as well as a doctor. The climate there is warmer and she'll be away from the north-east winds that tend to hit Scarborough and can be biting in the winter.'

Arthur frowned. 'I don't know how she'll take it. She's a northern lass and loves this place.'

'It will be hard for you all to make the move, I know. Marie's connections in the art world are all in the North, after all.'

Arthur nodded. 'When you first hinted that it might be a solution I mentioned it to Marie. Although she would like us to remain in Scarborough, she was solicitous for her mother's health and agreed she would do all she could to persuade Rose to move. Besides, Marie has the talent to build up a new reputation in the South.'

'Good. She's a sensible young woman, a great credit to you both. Why not let me have a word with Rose first?'

'Would you?'

'It will break the ice, help prepare the ground for you.'

After a fortnight's persuasion from the doctor, Arthur and Marie, Rose finally agreed.

Arthur immediately left for the south coast where he found a house of modest size that would suit their needs and had a wonderful view across the sea. A week later they left Scarborough.

Arthur had written to both Ebenezer and William, telling them he was moving but would still supply them with paintings. They were delighted, thankful that his work had been restored to its former excellence during the last four years. The spark was back; and there was new life in his paintings which brimmed with detail and colour whenever the subject demanded it, but it was his night scenes that were once again regarded as his masterpieces. Commissions began to multiply and he was never at a loss when he stood before a blank canvas.

He knew the reason for his success though he kept it to himself. Colette was in his heart once more; she was there beside him while he stood in front of an easel. The knowledge that she had always retained some love for him, in spite of the bitterness of his betrayal, continued to inspire him.

The move to the south coast appeared to be benefiting Rose. The warmer climate helped her breathing and she found renewed energy. But just when life seemed to be treating her kindly had a relapse and this time nothing could save her. She died peacefully with Arthur and Marie beside her in the autumn of 1890.

Marie tried to persuade her father to return to Scarborough for she knew his heart had always been in the North. When she first made the suggestion he was tempted. He would be nearer Colette, freer to visit Whitby, and who knew what that might lead to?

He pondered the question and examined all the possible consequences. What would it do to Marie to find she had a brother for instance? But the question which dominated his thinking was what it might mean to Edward. They could truly be father and son. That almost decided Arthur but what of the other people involved? Another man had raised Edward, one he had always regarded as his father. Was it fair to intrude on those memories? But more than anything Arthur was afraid of what it might do to the relationship between mother and son. It could bring heartache to them both. How would Edward regard his mother, a person he dearly loved, when he found out she had deceived him, and worse than that even, in all probability deceived her husband too? The risk of hurting Colette again was too great. So Arthur cast the idea of resuming their relationship from his mind. He would stay where he was.

In the spring of the following year Arthur opened a sketch-book and stood looking at a rough drawing of the bridge and river at Whitby and notes he had dated 8 September 1889. His mind winged back to that day and the unexpected meeting with Colette. He took up his brush and began to paint.

'When are you going to bring your latest conquest to meet me?' asked Colette with a teasing twinkle in her eyes as she eyed her son across the table on which had been laid a tempting array of luncheon dishes.

'Now don't get the wrong idea,' he replied, 'Tessa's a very good friend and a pleasant companion.'

'It's time you were deciding on one of the girls you say that about. You're twenty-four. Don't get so wrapped up in your painting that you neglect the other things in life. A girl won't wait forever.'

Before Edward could reply there was a knock on the dining-room door and a maid appeared.

'Sorry to disturb you, ma'am! A carrier has just delivered a large package for you. I've had it taken to the drawing-room.'

Colette and Edward exchanged a surprised look which told each other that they were not expecting anything. 'Thank you. We'll be there in a few minutes, we've nearly finished here.'

'Yes, ma'am.' She started for the door then stopped and added, 'The carrier said he has had it a few days but had specific instructions that it should be delivered today.'

'Even more mysterious,' commented Edward as the maid left the room.

'Well, after that I can't wait,' said his mother rising from her chair.

He followed her. They found a well-wrapped package resting against a chair. 'The shape of a framed picture,' he commented. 'But who would send us one?'

Colette had taken a pair of scissors from the sewing basket she had left when she went for her meal. She attacked the wrapping and binding with speed. Edward eased the hessian away and then started on the paper.

'Careful,' he warned as his mother went on clipping, 'it's an oil.'

They proceeded with caution until all the protection was removed.

'It's a landscape,' he said, noting the orientation of the painting without identifying the subject until he had turned it so that they could view it properly.

'My goodness,' gasped Colette, her heart racing, for there was no mistaking whose work this was. She bit her lip, holding back a tear. Edward must not see how moved she was.

'I've seen that painting when it was only a sketch.' His voice was low, charged with curiosity and wonderment. Why had this particular painting been sent to them? No, something prompted him, not to us; the package had been addressed to his mother. 'Mr Newton drew this in his sketchbook that day I brought him to see my paintings two years ago. Look, it has *that* date on it: the eighth of September 1889.' He stared at his mother. 'Today is the eighth too and the carrier was particularly instructed to deliver it on that date. But why?'

His mother did not answer, but continued to stare at the painting offering thanks in her mind for the fact that Arthur was painting brilliantly again.

Edward spotted a packet on the table. He went to it and saw it was addressed in the same writing as that on the picture wrapping. 'Maisie must have forgotten to tell us about this one,' he said picking it up.

'Open it,' said his mother, hardly knowing what she was saying so absorbed was she in studying all the nuances of the painting, trying to read what Arthur was conveying through this picture of Whitby looking upstream from the West Pier towards the bridge. She saw in the exceptional use of light and shade that emphasised certain aspects of the buildings, the ships and their movement, the highs and lows of a man's life finally bursting into the full blossoming of his talent in this magnificent painting.

'But it's addressed to you,' said Edward.

'Oh, open it,' she replied tartly, not wanting her concentration to be broken.

Edward did so. He recognised the sketchbook even though he had last seen it two years ago. He flicked it open and the page revealed the pencil drawing of the painting they had just uncovered.

'It's Mr Newton's sketchbook,' he said quietly, surprised that it should have been sent along with the painting. He flicked through the pages quickly. They were blank. He started to close the book when he realised he had not opened it at the first page. An unearthly feeling crept through him as he stared down at it in amazement and awe. Thoughts that made no sense rushed through his mind. 'Mother, it's you.' His voice was scarcely above a whisper but it penetrated a mind that concentrated on one thing, a painting that revealed so much of the painter's love for her and her love for him.

Colette turned towards her son. He moved closer and held the book so that they both could see the drawing that riveted his attention.

'Yes, it is me,' she admitted quietly.

'The date.' He drew her attention to it. The eighth of September 1866. You knew him then?' he asked full of curiosity.

His mother nodded.

'Why didn't you tell me when I brought him here?'

'There were good reasons, and we were both shocked to see each other again.'

'This is a beautiful portrait of a beautiful young lady drawn by someone I would say was very much in love with his subject.' Edward looked thoughtful. 'The eighth of September ... the day he did that harbour study too. That is why he wanted the painting delivered on the same date. Though they are years apart it obviously holds a special meaning for you both. You were in love?'

She nodded, reached for the book and took it

gently from him. Her mind flew back to that day. Even though it had ended in shattered dreams, it had been a day dawning with great joy, the culmination of a time when she and Arthur had been so in love, a love that was expressed in every line of this drawing. She looked at the page and saw something that Edward had not read to her. Freshly written across one corner, so as not to distract from the picture, were the words, 'Always my love and inspiration, 8 September 1891'. Her eyes filled with tears. 'You said the packet was addressed to me, I don't suppose you were meant to see this.'

He hardly heard her. Something else had tugged at his mind. He looked at the signature on the painting. *Arthur Newton.* Arthur... An artist. Edward Arthur... A young man who was said to have an artistic gift ... inherited from whom? He turned towards his mother. 'He's my father, isn't he?'

She looked at him with tears in her eyes, begging forgiveness for harbouring this secret. He came to her and lovingly held her tight. He would ask no questions now; he would learn their story later. Now he knew there was only one thing they both wanted.

Colette sensed what he was about to say. 'No, Edward, you mustn't try to find him.'

'But I need to, and I know you still love him.'

With tears in her eyes, she pleaded, 'Too many lives would be blighted. Your father is married and has a daughter.'

'What? I have a sister?'

'A half-sister.'

'Then I have a double quest.'

'No, Edward, please.'

Her pleading eyes, fraught with tear-filled anguish, could not be denied. He held her tight. 'All right, Mother. But one day, when the time is right, we will find them, wherever they are.'

Author's Note

The artistic background to *Yesterday's Dreams* came from an interest in the work of John Atkinson Grimshaw (1836–93). Arthur's life bears no resemblance to that of the artist and is purely fictional. The decision to portray Colette as a photographer came from my interest in the work of Frank Meadow Sutcliffe, the Whitby photographer who vividly recorded Whitby life in the late nineteenth and early twentieth centuries.

To John Atkinson Grimshaw and Frank Meadow Sutcliffe I owe a debt of gratitude.

I found a number of books of help with these two backgrounds, in particular: *John Atkinson Grimshaw* by Alexander Robertson, published by Phaidon, *Frank Meadow Sutcliffe Photographs* compiled by Bill Eglon Shaw, published by The Sutcliffe Gallery, Whitby.

The publishers hope that this book has given you enjoyable reading. Large Print Books are especially designed to be as easy to see and hold as possible. If you wish a complete list of our books please ask at your local library or write directly to:

Magna Large Print Books
Magna House, Long Preston,
Skipton, North Yorkshire.
BD23 4ND

This Large Print Book for the partially sighted, who cannot read normal print, is published under the auspices of

THE ULVERSCROFT FOUNDATION

THE ULVERSCROFT FOUNDATION

... we hope that you have enjoyed this Large Print Book. Please think for a moment about those people who have worse eyesight problems than you ... and are unable to even read or enjoy Large Print, without great difficulty.

You can help them by sending a donation, large or small to:

**The Ulverscroft Foundation,
1, The Green, Bradgate Road,
Anstey, Leicestershire, LE7 7FU,
England.**
or request a copy of our brochure for more details.

The Foundation will use all your help to assist those people who are handicapped by various sight problems and need special attention.

Thank you very much for your help.